A BABY TO BIND HIS INNOCENT

MICHELLE SMART

HIRED BY THE IMPOSSIBLE GREEK

CLARE CONNELLY

MILLS & BOON

First Published in Great Britain 2020
by Mills & Boon, an imprint of HarperCollins*Publishers*
1 London Bridge Street, London, SE1 9GF

ISBN: 978-0-263-27823-1

MIX
Paper from
responsible sources
FSC C007454

This book is produced from independently certified FSC™ paper
to ensure responsible forest management.
For more information visit www.harpercollins.co.uk/green.

Printed and bound in Spain
by CPI, Barcelona

Michelle Smart's love affair with books started when she was a baby and would cuddle them in her cot. A voracious reader of all genres, she found her love of romance established when she stumbled across her first Mills & Boon book at the age of twelve. She's been reading them—and writing them—ever since. Michelle lives in Northamptonshire, England, with her husband and two young Smarties.

Clare Connelly was raised in small-town Australia among a family of avid readers. She spent much of her childhood up a tree, Mills & Boon book in hand. Clare is married to her own real-life hero, and they live in a bungalow near the sea with their two children. She is frequently found staring into space—a surefire sign that she's in the world of her characters. She has a penchant for French food and ice-cold champagne, and Mills & Boon novels continue to be her favourite ever books. Writing for Modern is a long-held dream. Clare can be contacted via clareconnelly.com or at her Facebook page.

Also by Michelle Smart

Her Sicilian Baby Revelation
Her Greek Wedding Night Debt

Cinderella Seductions miniseries

A Cinderella to Secure His Heir
The Greek's Pregnant Cinderella

Passion in Paradise collection

A Passionate Reunion in Fiji

The Sicilian Marriage Pact collection

A Baby to Bind His Innocent

And look out for
The Terms of the Sicilian's Marriage by Louise Fuller

Also by Clare Connelly

Redemption of the Untamed Italian
The Secret Kept from the King

Crazy Rich Greek Weddings miniseries

The Greek's Billion-Dollar Baby
Bride Behind the Billion-Dollar Veil

Discover more at millsandboon.co.uk.

A BABY TO BIND HIS INNOCENT

MICHELLE SMART

This book is for my partner in crime, Louise Fuller.
Thank you for making Ciro and Claudia's book
such a joy to write. xxx

PROLOGUE

'WE MUST FIX THIS.' Ciro Trapani drained his bourbon and fixed his eyes on his brother's shattered face.

The past four days had seen Vicenzu age by a decade. The ready smile had been lost, and the always amused eyes were now dank, murky pools of grief. And guilt.

They both shared the grief and guilt, but for Vicenzu the guilt was double.

After a long pause, in which Vicenzu drained his own drink, he finally met Ciro's stare. His features twisted and he gave a sharp nod.

'We have to get it back,' Ciro stated. 'All of it.'

Another nod.

Ciro leaned forward. He needed to be certain that whatever they agreed today, Vicenzu would stick to it.

The family business was gone. Stolen.

The family home was gone. Stolen.

Their father was dead.

Ciro had looked up to his brother his entire life and, while their personalities and temperaments differed, they'd always been close. The man sharing a table with him in this Palermo bar was a stranger. He knew Vicenzu thought they should wait for a decent mourning period to pass before they did anything to avenge their father but the fury in Ciro needed to put plans into action *now*. And Vicenzu needed to play his part. What had been stolen would be recovered by whatever means necessary. Their devastated mother needed her home back.

'Vicenzu?'

His brother slumped in his chair and closed his eyes. After another long pause, he finally spoke. 'Yes, I know what I have to do, and I'll do it. I will take the business back.'

Ciro pressed his lips together and narrowed his eyes. Cesare Buscetta, their father's childhood tormentor, the thief who'd legally stolen their parents' business and home, had gifted the business to his oldest daughter, the inappropriately named Immacolata. Right then, Ciro did not believe Vicenzu had the wits about him to take her on and win. Vicenzu had always been closer to their father than Ciro. His sudden death four days ago and the subsequent revelations of everything that had been stolen had all contributed to mute his brother's natural exuberance and turn him into this lost ghost-like person.

Vicenzu must have recognised the cynicism in his brother's expression for he straightened. 'I will get the business back, Ciro. This is my responsibility. Mine.'

'You are sure you can handle it?' A question he would never have needed to pose four days ago before their world had been ripped apart. Getting the family home back would be a much easier task. Cesare had gifted the house to his younger daughter. From what Ciro had gleaned about the reclusive Claudia Buscetta, she was a spoilt, pampered princess with a brain that compared unfavourably to a rocking horse.

His brother's nostrils flared, a glimmer of the old spark flashing from his eyes. 'Yes. You get the house back for Mamma and leave the business to me.'

Ciro contemplated him a little longer before inclining

his head. 'As you wish.' He caught a passing bartender's eye and indicated another round of drinks for them before addressing his brother again. 'You must stop blaming yourself. You weren't to know. Papà should have confided in us.' That he hadn't was something they would both have to live with.

'If I hadn't borrowed all that money from him he would never have been forced to sell.'

'If I'd made more visits home I would have been on hand to help,' Ciro countered grimly. This was the guilt that lay so heavily in him. He hadn't been home to Sicily since Christmas. The sabotage against his father had started in the new year. 'Papà should have told you—told both of us—how precarious the family finances were but what's done is done. The only person to blame is that bastard Cesare. And his daughters,' he added, his top lip curling with distaste.

Fresh drinks were placed before them. Ciro raised his glass aloft. 'To vengeance.'

'To vengeance,' Vicenzu echoed.

They clinked their glasses and knocked back the fiery liquid.

The plan was sealed.

CHAPTER ONE

One week later

CLAUDIA BUSCETTA WIPED the copper worktop clean, listening hard to the romantic story being narrated on her audio device, her heart so full she didn't know how to contain it.

She'd only lived under this roof for ten days but already it felt like home. This was no ostentatious show home like the sprawling villa she'd grown up in. This was a true home, with a wonderfully equipped kitchen in which she could bake to her heart's content, and a vegetable garden and orchard large enough for her to grow all the fruit and vegetables she could manage.

For the first time in her twenty-one years, Claudia was all alone…unless she counted the security guards her father had posted outside the grounds. He'd wanted to have them housed inside with her but mercifully her older sister, Immacolata, had made him see reason. After all, the business Imma had been gifted adjoined the farmhouse and its estate that their father had bestowed on Claudia. Imma would be on hand to help if Claudia got into any difficulty, just as she'd always been there to help throughout her life.

Of course, her father had made her promise never to leave her new home alone. She must always be accompanied by two bodyguards. As if she could go anywhere without them! She couldn't drive. The nearest village was a mile away on top of the hill filled with the olive groves that constituted the main part of Imma's new business but there were no shops there. If Claudia wanted to go shopping she needed to be driven.

A loud buzz rang out, startling her. Pausing the audiobook, she pressed the intercom her father had installed on the kitchen wall. 'Hello?'

One of the security guards spoke. 'There is a Ciro Trapani here to see you.'

'Who?'

'Ciro Trapani.'

The name meant nothing to her. 'What does he want?'

'He says it's a private matter.'

'My father has approved this?' She supposed he must have done if the security guards were prepared to give her the choice of letting this Ciro man into her new sanctuary. Claudia's approval was only required after her father had given his. That was the way of her world.

'Yes.'

'Okay. Let him in.'

Curious, she opened the front door and stood outside to wait. A sleek black car drove slowly towards her. She caught the tail-end of the electric gates closing in the distance.

The car came to a stop in front of the triple garage to the side of the farmhouse. Strange. Her visitors so far, which had consisted of her father, her sister and the family lawyer, had all parked at the front of the house.

Her curiosity evaporated when the driver unfolded himself out of the car and she found herself staring at the sexiest man to have ever graced her eyes. Impossibly tall, with thick dark hair in a quiff and oozing vitality, he could have walked off the cover of a men's health magazine.

He sauntered towards her with an easy laconic stroll and an even easier laconic smile on a face hidden beneath aviator shades.

Noting the hand-stitched dark grey suit he wore over an open-necked pale blue shirt and polished black brogues, Claudia surreptitiously dusted off the flour still clinging to her long black cotton top and silently kicked herself for not changing out of her jeans, which had grass stains at the knees from her early-morning bout of weeding.

When he reached her, he pulled the shades off and fixed her with a dimpled smile that would make a nun's knees go weak. Fitting, seeing as it made *her* knees go weak and she'd once seriously contemplated joining a convent.

'Miss Buscetta?' Green eyes sparkled. A large hand with a glimpse of fine dark hair at his wrist extended towards her.

That *voice*. Oh, it was rich and deep and it made her toes grind into her slippers.

A crease appeared in his handsome brow and, with horror, she realised she'd been too busy gawping at him to either reply or take his offered hand.

But was it any wonder? She'd never met a man like this before. The only men outside her family she was acquainted with were her father's employees.

Pulling herself together, she clasped the long, tapered fingers with her own and felt a surge of warmth flow through her veins. Unsettled, she quickly released them.

'I'm Ciro Trapani. Forgive me for turning up like this but I was in the neighbourhood. Would you mind very much if I were to say goodbye to this place?'

Now Claudia's brow was the one to crease. Say goodbye? What on earth was he talking about?

He flashed his dimpled grin at her again. 'This estate

belonged to my parents. I grew up in this house. They sold it to your father before I had a chance to say goodbye to it.'

'You lived here?' Claudia knew nothing about the previous owners other than their obvious love for their home.

'For the first eighteen years of my life, yes. I live in America now but this has always been home to me. My only regret is that I never came back to Sicily in time to say goodbye before the deeds were transferred.'

Oh, the poor man. How sad for him. Claudia would always make regular visits to the villa she'd been raised in so had had no need to say goodbye.

He must have taken her silence for a refusal for he raised his broad shoulders and shook his head ruefully. 'I'm sorry. I'm a stranger to you. I was being sentimental. I'll leave you to get on with your day.'

When he turned his back and took a step away, she realised he was going to leave. 'You can come in.'

He looked back at her, a quizzical expression on his handsome face. 'I don't want to impose.'

She laced her fingers together. 'You're not imposing.'

'You're sure?'

'Definitely.' She swept an arm towards the door. 'Please, come in.'

Ciro followed her inside, hiding his smirk of satisfaction at how easily he'd made it through the doors. A week of careful preparation and things were going exactly to plan.

'Can I make you a coffee?' she asked as she led him to the kitchen.

'That would be great, thank you. Something smells good.'

She blushed. 'I've been baking. Please, take a seat.'

While she busied herself with the coffee machine, Ciro sat himself at a kitchen table that should never have been placed there and took the opportunity to study her. He must not allow himself to take too much notice of all the new kitchen furnishings or the fury he had under tight control would explode from him and his thirst for revenge would be over before it began.

He'd been all for coming straight to the house after he'd made his pact with Vicenzu. Patience had never been one of his strengths but he'd had enough awareness to know he couldn't meet Claudia Buscetta until he had his emotions under a better degree of control.

She was much prettier than he'd envisaged. Chestnut hair with subtle gold highlights was tied in a loose plait that fell halfway down her back and framed a beguiling face with huge dark brown eyes, pretty rounded cheekbones, a snub nose and generous lips. Shorter than he'd envisaged too, she looked slender beneath the shapeless oversized top she wore. That she had a wholesome air of innocence he considered laughable but her attractiveness was welcome. It would make his seduction more palatable.

'Where in America do you live?' she asked as she opened a cupboard and removed two mugs from it. This particular cupboard had, until less than two weeks ago, contained an abundance of dried pasta. The shelf beside it that had housed his mother's recipe books now had colourful ornaments on it.

'New York.'

'Isn't New York dangerous?'

'No more dangerous than any other major city.'

Her perplexed eyes met his briefly. 'Oh. I thought…' She blinked, shook her head and opened the fridge. 'How do you take your coffee?'

'Black, no sugar.'

The oven's timer went off. It was such a familiar sound that Ciro clenched his hands into fists to stop fresh rage bursting out. His childhood had been punctuated with that timer beeping, always followed moments later by his mother's call for dinner.

Protecting her hands with oven gloves, Claudia removed the item, filling the kitchen with even more of that evocative pastry scent. By the time she'd finished, the coffee was ready. She brought the mugs to the table and sat across from him. When she met his eye he was intrigued to see a flush cover her cheeks before she darted her gaze away.

'How are you settling in?' he asked.

'Very well.' She jumped back to her feet. 'Biscuit?'

'Sure.'

She returned with a ceramic tub and removed the lid. 'I made these yesterday so they should still be fresh.'

He helped himself and took a bite. Immediately, his mouth filled with heaven. 'These are amazing.'

The same flush of pleasure as when he'd complimented the smell that had filled the kitchen covered her face again. 'Thank you… Would you like some of the apricot tart when it's cooled down? If you're still here…' More colour stained her face. 'I'm sure you have things to be getting on with.'

'Actually, I don't.' He took a sip of his coffee and eyed her openly. 'I'm on a short vacation.'

'Oh?'

'My father died recently. I'm trying to sort his affairs and help my mother.'

Her next, 'Oh,' had a very different inflection. 'I'm sorry. That's awful. I didn't know.'

Sure you didn't, he thought cynically. *He only died the day after your father legally stole this house for you.*

'He had a heart attack.'

She was an excellent actress for her large, soft brown eyes brimmed with sympathy. 'I'm sorry,' she repeated. 'I can't begin to imagine how you're feeling.'

'Like I've been shot in the heart. He was only sixty.'

'That's no age.'

'No age at all. We assumed he had decades left.' He gave a theatrical shake of his head. Claudia Buscetta might be an excellent actress but she had nothing on Ciro, who'd had a week to prepare for this moment and knew exactly how he was going to orchestrate things. 'It's the regrets that play on the mind. If I ever marry and have children—which I really hope to do if I ever fall in love—he won't meet them. My children will grow up not knowing their grandfather. If I'd known the stress he was under…' He gave another shake of his head.

'Is that what caused it? Stress?'

'We think so. My parents have had a lot to deal with recently.'

A very pretty hand fluttered to her mouth. 'It wasn't connected with them moving from the house, was it?'

Having the house stolen from them, I think you mean.

'It was an accumulation of things.'

'I can see how much your parents loved this house.' She cradled her mug with both hands. 'I know they felt it necessary to downsize but it must have been difficult for them.'

How she uttered that complete rubbish with a straight face beggared belief. But then, she was a Buscetta, a family which straddled the line between legal and illegal like a circus of tightrope walkers. Ciro's father, Alessandro, had gone to school with Cesare. Even as a child Cesare had been a thug who'd terrorised everyone, including the teachers. Ciro had only met Cesare for the first time that day but his name had been synonymous with thuggery and criminality in the Trapani house for as far back as Ciro could remember.

He supposed Claudia had adopted the downsizing line as a way to salve her conscience. It had to be easier to sleep at night than admit the truth that her father had bribed a senior member of Alessandro Trapani's staff to sabotage the business until he was on his knees financially and had no choice but to sell both the family home he'd planned to grow old in with his beloved wife and the business that had been in the Trapani family for generations.

Instead of unleashing the vitriol burning the back of his throat, Ciro kept his focus on the long-term objective and folded his arms on the table while he stared at her. 'It was difficult. What makes it worse is that I wasn't here for them. I should have been. That's what sons do. They take care of their parents and shoulder their burdens. It's something I'll always have to live with but, for now, I have to look after my *mamma*.'

'How is she coping?' she asked softly.

He grimaced. 'Not great. She's staying with her sister in Florence and taking things one day at a time but I'm hoping she'll be ready to move back to Sicily soon.' *Once I've taken this house back for her.* 'I'm sorry. I didn't mean to depress you.'

'Don't apologise.'

'I don't know why I just told you all that. I don't even know you.' He made sure the look in his eyes told her how much he would like to get to know her.

The pink staining her cheeks told him she understood the silent message. Not only that she understood it but that she was receptive to it. Ciro, while not being a playboy of his brother's standard, had never had a shortage of women willing to throw themselves at him. It was amazing what billionaire status coupled with looks the world considered handsome did for a man's sex appeal. As such, he was something of an expert at reading a woman's body language and the language he was reading from Miss Buscetta was one of interest.

He'd spent the past week learning as much as he could about her. He'd been disappointed to find there wasn't much to learn. Educated in a convent until she was sixteen, she had, until only ten days ago, lived the life of a recluse in her father's heavily guarded villa. He would bet his last cent that she was a virgin; a rosebud waiting for a man to set her into bloom. Only a man with immense wealth and a scandal-free history would be allowed to touch one of Cesare Buscetta's precious daughters. A man such as Ciro himself.

A man like Cesare Buscetta saw nothing wrong with the games he'd played to wrench the Trapani family home and business from them. To him, it was just business. Ciro knew this because he'd done more than just investigate Claudia's boring background. Before coming here he'd visited her father on the pretext of proposing a potential business deal. He'd held his nose and broken bread with his enemy because he'd needed to know how best to play the man's daughter. If Cesare had treated him with suspicion he would've engineered a meet with Claudia somewhere else. But Cesare, so arrogant in the justifications of his own actions, had welcomed Ciro like a long-lost son. He'd even had the nerve to mention the school days he'd shared with Alessandro. To hear Cesare speak of it, those days had been full of high japes and escapades. He'd failed to mention his penchant for flushing the heads of the kids who refused to pay protection money to him down the toilet, or the time he'd threatened Alessandro with a knife if he didn't complete a homework assignment for him.

When, at the end of their meeting, Ciro had casually mentioned he would like to pay a visit to his childhood home for one last sentimental goodbye, Cesare had immediately called the guards posted at the farmhouse to inform them that Ciro must be allowed entry if Claudia permitted it.

His lack of self-awareness was as breathtaking as his daughter's faux sympathy.

Ciro lifted his cheeks into a smile at the woman who was as much his enemy as her father. 'Ready to show me around?'

'You know the place better than I do. I don't mind if you want to say goodbye on your own.'

He shook his head slowly, making sure his eyes contained the right mix of interest in her and dolefulness at his situation. 'I can think of nothing I would like more than for you to accompany me…but only if you want to.'

She fingered the end of her plait, then gave a tiny nod.

Walking through his childhood home with Claudia Buscetta by his side, her body language telling him loud and clear that she was attracted to him, Ciro suppressed the laughter that wanted to break free.

This was going to be even easier than he'd thought. It was almost anticlimactic how perfectly it was all falling into his lap.

'You seem distracted, Princess.'

Claudia, who'd been daydreaming about a certain hunk of a man, looked at her father's bemused face and felt a blush burn her cheeks. They were sitting in the smaller of the villa's dining rooms at a table that could only seat twelve, her father at his customary place at the head, Claudia to his left. Dish upon dish of delicious delicacies had been brought out for them to share but she'd hardly noticed what she'd forked into her mouth. She felt as if she'd been floating ever since Ciro had left her home.

'I had a visitor today,' she confessed, knowing she wasn't telling him anything he didn't already know.

'Ciro Trapani?'

'Papà…' She tried not to cringe as she made her revelation. 'He's asked me on a date.'

Her father's beady eyes gleamed. 'And what did you say?'

'That I would think about it. But really, I wanted to ask you first.'

'Good girl.' He nodded his approval. 'And what answer do you want to give him?'

She closed her eyes then blurted it out. 'I want to say yes.'

'Then say yes.'

'Really?' She didn't dare expel a sigh of relief. Not yet. Her father took overprotectiveness to unimaginable heights. That Claudia was an adult had not changed this. Unlike her highly educated, clever sister who could, if she ever felt it necessary, break away from him and be self-sufficient, Claudia could not. She was dependent on him for everything. He'd gifted her a home but if she wanted the funds to maintain it and clothe herself, she needed to be as obedient as she'd always been, hence why she was at his dining table sharing a meal with him rather than eating dinner in her own home. He'd called not long after Ciro had left, inviting her over. Refusal had not been an option.

She loved her father…but she feared him too. Sometimes she hated him. The yearning for freedom and independence had been growing in intensity since adolescence, but she could never act upon it. She had never rebelled and never said no to him. She'd never dared. 'You don't mind?'

'He's a hardworking businessman from a good family—apart from his brother, that is—and with a good reputation. He's very rich, did you know that? Worth billions. And he's at the age when a man wants to settle down and find a wife.'

'Papà!' She felt her cheeks go crimson again.

Her father poured himself more wine. 'Why would he not consider you for a wife? You have impeccable pedigree. You're from a good, wealthy Sicilian family and you're as beautiful as your mother was.'

Claudia refused to show any of her distaste at this supposedly flattering assessment of her attributes, especially when her father so clearly admired Ciro enough that he had no objection to him taking his youngest daughter out.

'It's only a date,' she reminded him quietly. Her first ever date.

'My marriage to your mother started with a date. Her brothers came as chaperones.' He raised his glass to her. 'Go on your date but remember who you are and where you come from and the values I've instilled in you. They're values a man like Ciro Trapani will appreciate.' He downed his wine in one large swallow.

CHAPTER TWO

CLAUDIA SAT CONTENTEDLY at her childhood dressing table while her sister plaited her hair. It was something Imma had done for her hundreds of times throughout her life but never on a day like today. Claudia's wedding day. Their father had wanted to fly a famous hairdresser over from Milan to do her hair but on this, Claudia had got her own way. She wanted her big sister to do it.

'Any nerves?' Imma asked as she wound the thick plaits together, cleverly binding them with diamond pins that should—if all the practice they'd put into it worked—sparkle when the sun or any form of light fell upon them.

Claudia met her sister's stare in the mirror. 'Should I have?'

'I don't know.' Imma smiled. 'I've never been in love. I just wondered...you two have only known each other such a short time.'

'I've known him for two months.'

'Exactly!'

'What's the point in waiting when we both know what we feel is true?' Claudia said simply. 'I want to spend my life with him. Nothing will change that.'

She'd known by the end of their first date that she was half in love with Ciro. He made her feel giddy, as if she could dance on air. For the first time too, she'd sensed an escape route from her life. He'd proposed two weeks later, having already asked her father's permission. The speed of the proposal had taken her aback but she hadn't hesitated to say yes.

Until Ciro had come into her life, she'd been trapped. Her life had had no meaning and no means of getting any. What kind of employment could a woman unable to read or write and who struggled with numbers get? Claudia lived in luxury but it was a gilded cage without freedom. Only a year ago she'd come to the conclusion that she should hand herself to God and work for Him. The nuns who'd tried so hard to educate her at the convent school lived a simple, peaceful life. She loved them all and still spent plenty of time with them. Her father would have been delighted to have a nun for a daughter. After all, Claudia was named after a vestal virgin. In the end, Imma had talked her out of it. She would be joining for the wrong reasons. Claudia loved God but taking vows should be a vocation, not an escape. It would be wrong.

This marriage would be an escape too but her feelings for Ciro were so strong that it couldn't be wrong, could it?

Finally, she would have freedom from her father's all-seeing eyes. It was a shame that she'd spent little time with Ciro since his proposal but he'd been incredibly busy with his business, working hard to clear his diary for the wedding and their honeymoon.

Imma, keeping her hold on Claudia's hair steady, leaned forward to place a kiss on her cheek. 'I know you love him and I don't want to put doubts in your mind—I'm just being overprotective. I worry about you.'

'You always worry about me.'

'It's part of the job of being your big sister.'

Their eyes met again in the mirror and in that look Claudia knew they were both thinking of their mother. She'd died when Claudia was three. Imma, only eight years old herself at the time, had taken on the role of mother. It was Imma who had cuddled her when she cried, Imma who'd cleaned her childhood cuts and grazes and kissed them better, Imma who'd taught her the facts of life and prepared her for the physical changes adolescence would bring. There was no one in the world Claudia loved or trusted more than her sister.

Visibly shaking off the brief melancholy, Imma put the last pin in Claudia's hair. 'It's just as well you're sure about Ciro after all the money Papà's spent on the wedding.'

They both laughed. Their father's love of spending money was legendary but for Claudia's wedding he'd outdone himself. Insisting on footing the bill for it, in the space of five weeks he'd overseen what would undoubtedly go down as the Sicilian wedding of the century. Claudia had woken in her childhood bed that morning to the sound of a helicopter landing on her father's private helipad. She'd looked out of the window to see five Michelin-starred chefs hurrying behind the huge marquee in which the wedding celebrations would take place. Behind that marquee and out of her eyesight was another marquee that had been turned into a kitchen fit for an army of top chefs—another three helicopters dropped the rest of them off shortly after—to create the wedding banquet of which dreams were made and the evening buffet that would follow.

Claudia would have been content to have a simple wedding but had gone along with her father's plans to turn it into an extravaganza because it made him happy. Ciro hadn't minded either, content to go along with whatever she wanted, and so that had settled it.

As much as it made her all fluttery inside to know that for this one day she would be the princess her father had always proclaimed her to be, the greatest excitement came from knowing that in a few short hours she would be Ciro's wife.

She would be free…

Ciro walked through the villa's garden to the private chapel at the back with his brother.

'How much of his blood money has he spent on this?' Vicenzu muttered under his breath.

'Millions.'

They exchanged a secret smile.

Ciro still had trouble believing how easily his plan had knitted together. He'd assumed it would take months before he could propose with a good degree of certainty that Claudia would say yes but by the end of their first date she'd been like a puppy eating out of his hands. Cesare had been less than subtle about his wish for Ciro to marry her. He didn't know whether it had been father or daughter who'd been the keenest for them to marry. Cesare's insistence on paying for the entire thing had been too delicious for Ciro to put up more than a half-hearted effort to get him to change his mind.

Cesare's vast extravagance on this sham of a wedding meant Ciro did not have to fake his smiles. Every step taken through the villa's transformed garden felt lighter than the last. Vengeance took many forms, some more palatable than others.

Another helicopter delivering another batch of guests flew overhead when they reached the chapel. The sound of rotors had been a background noise for the past hour.

The chapel too had been spruced up for the occasion. The white exterior had been freshly painted while inside the long wooden pews had been re-varnished, the stained-glass windows scrubbed and every religious artefact polished. When they entered it, the opera singer flown in from New Zealand to sing while Claudia walked up the aisle was performing vocal exercises accompanied by a world-famous pianist.

Before long, the chapel was filled with people there to witness the happy union between Ciro and Claudia. He cast his eyes around, satisfaction filling him. These people were the people Cesare held most dear, the people he loved to throw his weight around with and the people he wanted to impress. Once Vicenzu had fulfilled his part of their vengeance, all these people would know Cesare had thrown his money on a sham. And if there was a nagging sense of guilt lining Ciro's guts at his pretence, one look at his mother overrode it.

She sat in the front row next to his aunt. They'd flown in earlier that morning from Florence, their arrangements the only aspect of the day Ciro hadn't let Cesare control. Grief had marked her previously youthful, happy face with lines that would be permanently etched into her skin. She'd been surprised at his sudden intention to marry but too heartsick to ask any questions. Even if his intentions towards Claudia had been genuine, he doubted his mother would have had the emotional energy to invest in the ceremony as anything more than a spectator. There had been mild surprise that Ciro was marrying the daughter of her husband's childhood nemesis but other than that, nothing. Their father's lawyer had been correct—their father had kept the sabotage he'd received at the hands of Cesare's hired thugs to himself. His mother had been unaware of the immense pressure her husband had been put under. Ciro and Vicenzu were of the opinion to never tell her.

When this was done, once Claudia signed the family estate over to him as she'd promised—God, how easy was this? The suggestion had even come from her!—he might consider nominating himself for an acting award.

She'd kept up the naïve, unspoilt, wide-eyed act beautifully too. No doubt she was waiting for his ring on her finger before showing her true nature. She'd been a little too thrilled at his marriage proposal, given after he'd asked her father's permission. Cesare had pretended to mull it over but Ciro had read the delighted dollar signs in his greedy little eyes. They had both agreed, at Ciro's suggestion, that a joint business venture should be put on the back burner until after the wedding.

It would be put on the back burner for ever. Only when Vicenzu got the business back for them too would their vengeance be complete. Only then would they confront Cesare and his daughters with the truth and watch the dawning realisation that they'd been played at their own game but that this time the Buscettas had lost.

A sudden buzz permeated the chapel's air. The bride had arrived.

Exactly on cue the double doors opened and the opera singer expelled the first note of her aria.

Such was his loathing towards Cesare that Ciro's attention was initially fixed on him, beaming like a fat peacock as he slowly walked his daughter down the aisle.

And then he looked at his bride.

Her face was veiled behind white Sicilian lace held in place by a diamond tiara. Her white dress was the dress of a princess, exactly as her father purported her to be. Heart shaped around the cleavage with small lace sleeves off the shoulder, it puffed out at the waist and formed a train held by her sister and five cute children he didn't recognise. Cesare had probably paid for them as he'd paid for everything else.

When Claudia reached him and Cesare melted away to take his seat, Ciro lifted the veil. What he found there…

In an instant his mouth ran dry. The pretty woman had

transformed into a ravishingly beautiful princess. Truly, breathtakingly beautiful. Those big brown eyes… It was like peering into a vat of melted chocolate. He wanted to dive into it.

Maybe it was because he'd lowered his guard as the plot he'd woven came to fruition but for the first time since he'd met her, the shackles he'd placed on his attraction to her broke free. Desire snaked through his loins and thickened his blood. And all he could do was stare…

Only the non-subtle cough from the priest brought him back to the present.

Their wedding Mass began.

Ciro hardly heard a word of it. He was too busy trying to shake off the strange, unwelcome feelings rippling through him.

This marriage was a sham, he reminded himself.

One day in the distant future, when his thirst to experience life and build an empire had been quenched, he would settle down and marry for real. His future wife would be someone trustworthy, a partner with whom he could raise a brood of babies and lavish the same love and security on that his parents had lavished on him. His future wife would be the antithesis of Claudia.

Claudia was the daughter of his enemy and an enemy of his in her own right. She'd been party to the dirty tricks that had caused his father's death. She was poison.

By the time they exchanged their vows, he'd got his body back under control and was able to look into the melted-chocolate eyes with only mild discomfort.

Superficial desire was the most he could allow himself. He needed his body to perform in consummating the marriage—he would not give Claudia any grounds to annul it—but genuine desire for a woman he despised? The thought was sickening.

* * *

The ceremony passed Claudia like the most wondrous dream. It *was* a dream. A dream come true. When they left the chapel to uproarious cheers, a pair of pure white love doves was released. Filled with happiness and wonder, she watched them fly away.

After the photos were done, the happy couple and their one hundred guests made their way to the marquee for the seven-course wedding banquet. Another hundred guests would join them for the evening party.

The marquee's interior only enhanced her feeling of being in a dream. Luxury carpet covered the base while fairy lights crisscrossed the canvas roof, the entire marquee supported by Roman pillars wound with artful posies of roses. There had to be thousands of the beautiful blooms. And there had to be thousands of balloons too, of silver and gold, pastel shades of blue, pink and green, the colours blending together beautifully and combining with the roses to evoke an atmosphere of romance at its most opulent. The round tables were lavished with white tablecloths embroidered with gold leaf, gold cutlery and crystal glasses. Each guest was to sit on an elegant white chair…with the exception of the bride and groom. They were to sit on golden thrones.

Dazed, she accepted a glass of champagne from one of the army of silver-service waiting staff and, standing beside her handsome new husband, dazzling in a navy-blue wedding suit, greeted each guest in turn.

Unused to being in the spotlight, she left all the talking to Ciro. She hoped that in time some of his natural confidence would rub off on her. Where did he get it from? Forming a multibillion-dollar business from scratch? Was it something that had grown over the years or something innate in him? Listening to him chat amiably to one of her father's business associates, she realised she knew very little about her new husband. Their dates had always been spent discussing the future. She'd avoided asking much about his past because she knew he still felt his father's recent death so keenly. Every time he was mentioned a shadow would form in Ciro's green eyes that never failed to make her heart ache.

A shiver laced her spine but she shook it off. This was her wedding day. She had the rest of her life to get to know her husband.

Ciro stood with his new wife and, hands clasped together, the flash of cameras showering them, they cut the exquisite wedding cake.

He'd enjoyed the day hugely and had played up his role of devoted groom. He'd made sure to cast long lingering stares at his new wife, to hold her hand at every available opportunity and even to spoon-feed her some of the berry *millefoglie* they'd been served for dessert. Pleasure had lit her eyes at this small intimacy, colour staining her cheeks when he'd followed it with a light kiss to her lips.

Ciro had decided it was better to keep his hands to himself until they were married, in part to prove to Claudia—and her father—that his feelings for her were honourable and true, and in part to keep his focus where it needed to be. Claudia's easy acceptance of his work commitments had helped him keep the amount of time they spent together to a minimum. All they'd shared were a few chaste goodbye kisses, which had only added to his loathing of her. He despised how his senses reacted to the scent of her perfume. He despised that his lips found hers to be so soft and sweet. He despised how he could stare into her eyes and feel flickers of awareness deep in his loins.

And he despised how, as the day had gone on, the shock

of desire he'd experienced in the chapel had snuck back on him and nothing he did could rid him of it.

The closer the time came to leave the celebrations, the closer the time came to consummate their marriage. The deeper the anticipation burned.

Claudia's ears rang with the applause and catcalls of their guests as Ciro's driver steered them out of her father's estate to the hotel where they were to spend their first night as newly-weds. Tomorrow evening they would fly on Ciro's jet to Antigua for their honeymoon. Her gorgeous new husband had made the honeymoon arrangements himself.

A warm hand closed over hers. 'Happy?' Ciro asked.

She met his eyes and smiled. 'I feel like I'm on top of the world.'

'It was a magical day.' Cheeks dimpling, he hooked an arm around her shoulders and pulled her to him. With her cheek resting against his chest, the strong thud of his heart beating against her skin, she inhaled his evocative woody scent then exhaled slowly.

Soon, very soon, there would be no clothes to act as barriers between their skin. It was a thought that had played in her mind constantly throughout the evening celebrations, unleashing butterflies in her stomach that had become more violent as the time for them to leave drew nearer. She didn't know if anticipation, excitement or fear had the greatest hold over her. Ciro knew she was a virgin. It hadn't been mentioned explicitly but then, it hadn't needed to be, no more than it had needed to be said that he'd had many lovers in his life. His experience meant he would know what he was doing and so making love should be as pain-free as it could be for her—at least, she hoped so—but his experience also meant her inexperience was likely to leave him disappointed. She wished she could have discussed it with Imma but, considering she was a virgin too, it would be akin to the blind leading the blind.

'Your father looked as if he enjoyed himself,' he said, cutting through her jittery thoughts.

She nodded into his chest and closed her eyes. Ciro's acceptance of her overprotective father was another of the many things she loved him for. She wasn't blind to her father's faults. He could be overpowering and intimidating but Ciro was comfortable enough in his own skin to let her father get his way without demeaning his own masculinity and Ciro had an easy charm that when he wanted things *his* way, he could put it across without it coming out as a challenge. She'd never imagined a man like Ciro existed.

She tilted her head and stretched her neck so she could plant a soft kiss on his lips. 'Today has been the best day of my life.'

He kissed her back. 'And mine.'

Soon they arrived at the clifftop hotel that would be their love-nest for the night. It was as opulent as everything else had been that day. Ciro tipped the porter who carried their overnight luggage up to the honeymoon suite, their other suitcases being held in the hotel's storage for their departure tomorrow evening and then, for the first time that day…for the first time ever…they were truly alone.

CHAPTER THREE

SHYNESS AND NERVES hit Claudia as starkly as the silence. 'This is nice,' she said, trying to inject brightness into her voice. Nice was definitely an understatement. Rose petals and tea lights in pretty glasses made a trail from the luxurious living area and through the opened double doors to the bedroom. There, an enormous four-poster bed draped with gold muslin curtains sat raised on a dais. More rose petals formed a giant love heart on the gold bedspread. On a glass coffee table by the sofas sat a bottle of champagne in a bucket of ice and two crystal flutes.

Ciro indicated the champagne. 'Shall we?'

'That would be nice.' She winced to hear herself use that insipid word again. Insipid—a word she'd learned only a month ago as part of her push to educate herself—was the opposite of how she felt inside. The butterflies in her belly now fluttered so hard they'd reached her throat and tied her tongue. Ciro popped the cork and poured them both a glass. When he passed Claudia's to her, some of the golden fluid sloshed over her shaking hand.

He raised his glass. 'To us.'

She chinked hers to it and spilled more over herself. 'To us.' Scared how croaky her voice sounded, she took too large a sip.

Green eyes held hers speculatively before he took the

glass from her and placed it with his on the coffee table. 'You seem frightened.'

She swallowed and forced herself to hold his gaze. 'A little.'

A hand palmed her neck. 'You have nothing to be frightened of. We don't have to do anything you don't want or anything you don't feel ready for. If you want us to wait, then...'

'I don't want to wait.' She took a long breath. Waiting would only make things worse, give her mind even more time to play on her fears. And really, what did she have to be scared about? Ciro would make it special... Wouldn't he?

He gazed into her eyes a little longer before his dimples flashed. 'Let's take our champagne onto the balcony for a while. How does that sound?'

She managed to muster a smile through her tight cheeks. 'That sounds good.'

Fingers laced together, they carried their drinks through the bedroom and stepped through the French doors onto a large balcony that overlooked the Tyrrhenian Sea. A heart-shaped love-seat with big squishy heart-shaped cushions sat beneath an overhang covered in tiny romantic lights.

Ciro, having read the fear in Claudia's eyes when they'd been left alone in the suite, found himself dealing with a God-awful feeling of guilt. He thought back to his first time. There had been too much excitement for fear to get a look-in. But first-time sex was different for women and, as much as he despised her, he knew he had to be gentle. If he had to wait to consummate the marriage then so be it. Better to wait than scare her off sex for life. He wanted revenge but that didn't mean destroying her completely.

He held the train of her dress so she could sit comfortably, then sat beside her. Her rigid pose spoke volumes.

For all that she said she didn't want to wait, she was clearly terrified.

He placed a finger on her neck. She stiffened further.

Hooking an arm around her waist, he moved her gently so her back rested against his chest. 'Listen to me,' he said. 'We will not do anything you don't want. We don't have to do anything at all. Any time you want to stop, you tell me and I will stop. Don't be afraid of hurting my feelings. Okay?'

She twisted to look at him and took a small sip of her champagne. 'Okay.' Then she sighed and turned her face away to look back out at the spectacular view.

Draining his champagne, Ciro put his glass on the side table then carefully ran a finger over the plaits of her hair. Her wedding hairdo had held up beautifully throughout the day. He guessed having pins in it, however sparkling they were, must be uncomfortable. If he was to make this good for her—if they got that far, which right then he seriously doubted—he wanted her to feel as comfortable and relaxed as she could be.

He removed the top pin. It slid out more easily than he'd expected. One by one, he pulled them all free until the plaits fell like coils of silken rope down her neck. Satisfied all the accessories keeping her hair in place had been removed, he worked on undoing the plaits. The looser they became, the more the trapped scent of her shampoo was released. It was a soft, delicate fragrance that delighted his senses in much the same way her perfume did. When all her hair was loose, he gently ran his fingers through the thick mane that was as silken to his touch as to his eyes then kneaded his fingers over her skull. More of the delicate scents danced through his airwaves. Burying his face in the soft tresses, he filled his lungs completely. 'I love your hair,' he murmured.

Claudia, who'd found her fears slowly melting at his tender ministrations, twisted to look at him. His was a tone she'd never heard from him before, somehow more heartfelt than his declarations of love for her…

'I love *you*,' she whispered.

Green eyes held hers. The firm mouth flattened then loosened before he slid an arm around her waist to secure her against him and press his lips to hers. If he'd lunged at her with one of those hard, demanding kisses she'd seen in movies she likely would have recoiled in fright, but his kiss was gentle and caressing. When his tongue slid between her lips and found hers, her senses filled with a brand-new taste tinged with champagne that evoked thoughts of dark chocolate and danger. This was Ciro's taste, she thought in wonder; as intensely, headily masculine as the man himself.

Gradually, the kiss deepened. Tiny flutters of excitement awoke in her belly, muting the flutters of fear that had been there before. Secure against him, pressed into the crook of his arm, she placed a hand on his shoulder then tentatively wound it around his neck. His skin was warm beneath her fingers, the bristles on his nape like velvet.

When he broke the kiss, he rubbed his nose against hers. 'Don't move,' he murmured, rising to his feet. There was no time to question him for he hooked an arm around her waist and slid the other under the train of her dress. In one fluid motion, he lifted her into his arms, making her stomach plunge and then rise with the motion.

He stared into her eyes before giving a lopsided smile that made her stomach swoon all over again. 'The groom is supposed to carry the bride over the threshold,' he said, then carried her effortlessly into the suite and sat her on the rose-petal-covered bed.

Her heart hammering so hard the echoes reverberated

in her ears, Claudia gazed at Ciro. This beautiful man was her husband. Her *husband*. It didn't feel real.

Palming her cheeks, he kissed her again. 'Remember,' he whispered, 'we don't have to do anything you don't want to do.'

Claudia wanted to thank him for his tenderness and understanding but found her words stuck in her throat. Instead, she took a deep breath and pressed her lips to his.

'Give me a moment,' he said, stepping away to close the French doors, draw the heavy curtains and switch the main lights off. The flickers of candlelight illuminated the room in a soft glow that eased her fears some more. They softened Ciro's hard features, making him appear more human than god-like.

Standing only a foot before her, his eyes swirling with intensity, he removed his dinner jacket, tie and cufflinks and then, button by button, undid his shirt. He shrugged it off and let it fall by his feet.

Her mouth dry, Claudia stared at a body that rivalled any of the great Roman statues. Broad-shouldered and narrow-hipped, toned but not overly muscular, his golden skin was unblemished by anything other than fine dark hair around flat brownish-red nipples and lower down on his abdomen… A sudden burst of moisture quelled the dryness and she found herself sitting straighter, unable to wrench her eyes away, the flutters in her belly intensifying. And there was something else inside her too, a faint heat building low in her pelvis…

Ciro divested himself of the rest of his clothing bar his briefs. He'd sensed Claudia's fears slowly seeping away but when she'd caught sight of the outline of his erection, her eyes had widened.

Slowly. He must take this slowly. But, *damn*.

He knew his desire for Claudia was a little too deep

for comfort but not for a moment had he thought he'd be here now experiencing a hunger he felt down to his marrow. Her kisses… As unpractised as they were, they *did* something to him.

He took her hands. Such pretty hands. The usually short nails had been extended by whatever women did to make their nails artificially long and painted a pale pink with tiny diamantes on the tips. A shudder ripped through him to imagine them scratching his back as he took her to the heights of pleasure.

Control it, he commanded himself. This, their first time together, was all for Claudia, not for him. Her pleasure was all he could allow himself to think about.

He tugged her to her feet and cupped her face to gaze into her beautiful large brown eyes. 'Are you ready for me to take your dress off? Or do you want me to stop?'

Her throat moved before a shy smile curved her pretty cheeks and she turned her back to him. Gathering her hair together, she piled it on top of her head and held it there.

Tiny clasps ran down the spine of the dress and it took him a few attempts to undo the first. The second came a little easier. By the fourth, he'd got the knack, but he took his time, pressing gentle kisses to the exposed flesh.

By the time he'd reached the clasps that ran over her bottom her breaths had become heavy and little trembles shook her slender frame. The dress now undone enough to remove, he pinched the sides of it and tugged it down to her feet. She stepped out of it and after a moment of stillness, turned around.

His heart caught in his throat. He closed his eyes, disconcerted at the strange feeling, but when he opened them and found Claudia's large beguiling eyes staring at him, the very foundations of his world seemed to shake.

Slender and softly curved, covered only in matching white lace underwear, she was ravishing.

He stroked her cheek. 'You take my breath away,' he whispered.

She swallowed and placed her fingertips to his chest.

His heart thudding so hard it felt as if it could thrash out of his ribcage, he gently laid her down and helped her wriggle over the rose petals until her head rested on a pillow. And then he kissed her. He kissed her mouth, rained kisses over her face and then slowly trailed his lips down her neck. The pulse at its base pounded hard.

Her skin was without doubt the softest and sweetest he had ever tasted with a scent that drove straight into his loins. In an effort to keep his ardour in check he tried to occupy his mind with things like financial reports, but the headiness of his responses to Claudia was too strong and all he could do was remind himself over and over to take his time and make this good for her.

When he reached her breasts she gave a sharp intake of breath and stiffened then almost immediately sighed and relaxed. Sliding a hand under her back, he found the clasp for the strapless bra and after a couple of fumbles undid it. Discarding it, he placed a kiss on one of the ripe nipples and heard her breath hitch and then a low, faint moan. Gently, gently, he kissed and caressed breasts that were much fuller than he'd expected and a hundred times softer.

The rest of her body was equally soft. Working languorously, he kissed, caressed and massaged her flat stomach, her gently rounded hips, discovered her inner thighs were a particularly sensitive zone for her, then moved all the way down to her feet. The only part of her body left unexplored was her most feminine part. She'd stiffened and automatically covered it with her hand when his mouth reached her abdomen and he'd known this would be a step too far for her. But he could smell her heat and it was as evocative and heady as everything else about her.

Claudia had had no idea pleasure could feel like this. Something deep inside her, something never before imagined or known, had come alive and it had spread into every part of her. Ciro's every touch heightened the sensations fizzing on and beneath her skin. There was a deep ache between her legs that burned and throbbed. For a moment she'd thought he was going to kiss her most private part and had had a brief flash of panic—surely people didn't do *that*?—but then he'd moved away and she relaxed into his tender attention and allowed herself to be enveloped by all the incredible feelings rushing and burning through her.

As his hands and mouth continued their assault of her senses, making their way back up her now boneless body, she hazily realised that her fear had disappeared. When his mouth found her breasts again, he trailed a hand gently over her pubis and touched a place that sent a bolt of sensation juddering through her, powerful enough to make her gasp and for her eyes to fly open.

What in goodness had caused *that*?

But then the wonderful weight of his body was on hers again and her mouth caught in a kiss filled with such hunger that all her thoughts became a cloud of Ciro. Something hard jutted against her inner thigh that made her insides clench then pulse even more strongly than before. She hadn't noticed him remove his final item of clothing…or hers. When he broke the kiss to stare deep into her eyes, she read the question in them. Her hand trembled as she palmed his cheek and lifted her head to kiss him.

His throat moved and he stroked her hair as he adjusted himself between her legs before sliding a hand under her bottom to raise it a little. The hardness that moments ago had pressed against her thigh was now right there…

With one hand holding hers protectively and their lips brushing together, he moved his buttocks. His hardness pushed inside her.

Claudia sucked in a breath and forgot to expel it.

He pushed a little further.

Dear *goodness…*

Her fingers reflexively tightened on his. She stared into his eyes. His jaw was clenched with concentration.

Bit by bit his thick hardness filled her. And, bit by bit, Claudia dissolved.

His gaze not leaving hers, he placed his elbows either side of her head and withdrew…only to slowly drive back in. And then he did it again. And again. And…

Dear goodness…this was incredible. Whatever had she been frightened of? This…this…

Sensations she'd never conceived of thrummed through her heightened nerve-endings, taking her higher and higher to a place she'd never known existed.

She melted into another of his kisses and wrapped her arms tightly around him. His chest brushed against her breasts as he continued to move inside her, a steady but increasing rhythm, every thrust taking her closer and closer to…

And then, just as she thought she'd found the pinnacle of pleasure, a flood of pulsations rippled through her, starting deep in her pelvis and spreading out through her veins; a riptide so intense that she found herself crying out Ciro's name and clinging to him, begging him not to stop, to never stop, never stop…

But even the most beautiful of experiences had to end and, just as she was floating back to earth, his thrusts became deeper, his groans longer and she realised he was about to reach his peak too. The moment that thought entered her dazed head, he gave an unintelligible shout and thrust into her one last beautiful time, holding onto his climax just as she had done, then, with a groan that sounded as if it ripped through his throat, collapsed on top of her.

For the longest time they lay there, his breath hot against her neck, her fingers stroking his hair, the only sound their ragged breaths and the beats of their hearts echoing together in her ear.

'I love you,' she whispered.

He lifted his head and stared at her. The expression in his eyes was unfathomable. But then he kissed her and rolled off, hooking his arms around her so she rolled with him and nestled into his chest.

Claudia drifted into sleep with more happiness in her heart than she had ever believed existed.

Ciro's eyes opened to darkness. Claudia lay beside him, an arm draped over his waist. Her deep, rhythmic breathing told him she was fast asleep.

He pinched the bridge of his nose and tried to get air into his tight lungs. He felt sick. He was especially sickened that he wanted nothing more than to roll her onto her back and make love to her again.

Damn it, it wasn't supposed to feel like this. He'd expected to feel like the king of the world. Not in his wildest dreams had he expected his plan to come together so quickly and so well.

Nor had he expected that making love to Claudia would leave him feeling as if something fundamental had shifted in him. He knew he'd made it good for her but all he felt was guilt. Her whispered words of love before they'd fallen asleep had contained such sincerity that he'd known he could never say them again to her because they weren't true.

He was going to break her heart.

Disgusted with himself, he carefully extracted himself from under her arm and climbed out of bed.

The champagne they'd shared still sat on the coffee table, the bottle two-thirds full. He lifted it to his lips. It had gone flat, but he didn't care and drank deeply.

Not feeling in the slightest bit better, he padded quietly back to the bedroom, bottle in hand, and pulled his phone from his jacket pocket. Checking that Claudia was still asleep, he carefully drew back the heavy curtain enough to open the French door and step onto the balcony. He didn't notice he failed to close the door properly. It swung back open a couple of inches.

Resting an arm on the balustrade, he called his brother. It went to voicemail. Not unexpected considering it was the middle of the night.

'Vicenzu, it's me,' he said. 'Look… I can't do this for much longer. I've fulfilled my part. She's going to sign the house over to me today. You need to get your side done, and quickly. Whatever it takes to get the business back, do it, because I don't know how much longer I can keep the pretence up.'

Disconnecting the call, he swigged the last of the champagne.

It was the shift in the air that woke Claudia. She groped her hand over the mattress and found it empty. Scents she'd never known before filled her senses. Hazily, she realised it was the scent of their lovemaking.

About to call out to Ciro, she noticed the curtains had been drawn back a little, the French door ajar. She got out of bed, intending to join him, but as she reached the door his deep rich voice cut through the clear night air and seeped through the gap.

She heard every word.

CHAPTER FOUR

'ARE YOU SURE you're feeling okay?'

After a day spent being pampered in the hotel's spa, they'd returned to their suite. Claudia had immediately put the television on and curled up on the sofa.

She barely lifted her eyes to look at him and give the same answer she'd given every other time he'd asked. 'I'm a little tired.'

'Shall I order you a coffee?'

She glanced at her watch and shook her head.

Ciro had imagined waking on the morning after their wedding to find Claudia pressed against him, soft words of love ready to spill from her lips. The reality had been he'd woken alone and found her in the suite's living area, fully dressed, watching television and drinking coffee. 'Oh, good, you're up,' she'd said with a smile that wasn't quite as wide as normal. 'I'm *starving*.'

He'd offered to order room service, but she'd been insistent that she wanted to eat breakfast in the hotel restaurant. When he'd leaned down to kiss her good morning her response had been a brief brush of her lips to his before she'd jumped to her feet with another smile and bounded to the bathroom. She'd locked the door behind her.

His imaginings that their day would be spent with Claudia holding onto his hand and planting kisses to his lips every other minute had been disabused too. She'd booked herself in for so many spa treatments that he'd seen hardly anything of her. To Ciro's disquiet, it had been *him* living in a near-constant state of arousal, him unable to tear his eyes away from her beautiful face in those times he actually saw her, him who ached to carry her back to their suite, lock the door and spend the hours before their flight making love. Claudia's body language told him clearly that she had no interest in doing that.

He kept telling himself that she was probably on a bit of a low after the high of the wedding and feeling overwhelmed by everything. She'd been a virgin. It could simply be that she was feeling a little sore.

He opened the minibar and found the bottle of bourbon he'd requested. 'Do you want one?'

She shook her head and pulled her knees up to rest under her chin.

'Claudia?'

'What?'

'There's something wrong. I know there is. Tell me.'

Dark brown eyes locked on his briefly before fixing back on the television. Was that *contempt* he'd seen flash at him? The disquiet that had been gnawing at him all day grew.

He downed a large measure of bourbon then crossed the room to kneel before her. Taking her hands in his, he stared at her, silently willing her to look at him.

'Talk to me,' he urged. 'Tell me what you're thinking. Did I hurt you last night? Are you worried about us not using contraception?' That had been a mistake he'd kicked himself for ever since. He'd been so concerned about making it good for her and so caught up in the moment that, for the first time in his adult life, contraception had been the last thing on his mind. He could only pray it wasn't a mistake that came back to haunt him. A child had no place in this sham of a marriage.

And yet, even though his marriage wasn't real, even though he despised her, he found her aloof, silent treatment unbearable.

When she continued to ignore him, he let go of her hands to grab the remote and turn the television off.

Her jaw clenched. She looked again at her watch, looked up at him, looked back at her watch, lowered her knees to straighten herself then looked him straight in the eye. 'Yes, you hurt me and yes, I'm worried that we didn't use contraception. No child deserves to be born into a lie.'

Claudia felt no satisfaction to see Ciro recoil or the horror-struck comprehension rise on his face. She'd waited thirteen hours to confront the lying creep. All day she'd had to listen to him repeat 'are you okay?' and watch him giving her all those fake concerned looks, all the while resisting the urge to scream in his face and pound her fists against his chest.

All the tenderness he'd shown her, all the loving caresses, all the passionate kisses…

None of it had been real.

She'd stood by the French doors for an age, brain frozen, limbs immobile, the shock of what she'd heard and the implications too much to process. Then the paralysis had abated and, her heart hurting, she'd crept back into bed, trying desperately to think coherently. Ciro's words had played like a reel in her head. Her stomach had plummeted too, to remember the sparks that had flown between Imma and Vicenzu at the wedding. She needed to warn her sister. Get her advice. Try and make sense of what her heart so longed to deny but which the rational part of her head would not.

Ciro didn't love her.

When he'd eventually come back to bed, champagne fumes wafting from his pores, she'd feigned sleep and waited for him to fall into slumber before slipping out of bed and taking her phone to the bathroom. To play safe and drown out the murmur of her voice, she'd switched the fan on.

She didn't know how Vicenzu planned to take the business from Imma but, if his brother was anything to go by, he would have no scruples in getting what he wanted. From the shock in Imma's voice, Vicenzu's plan had already been set in motion. Claudia had promised to wait until four p.m. before confronting Ciro. This would give Imma time to come up with her own plan of attack before Ciro could warn his brother that they knew.

The thirteen hours she'd spent waiting to confront him had been the longest she'd endured. The hands of her watch had turned with the speed of a snail on sleeping pills. At least that was one thing she could read, she thought bitterly. She couldn't read words or men but she could read a watch.

But those thirteen hours had given her time to think and prepare. As humiliating as it was to admit, Claudia had been a doormat all her life. She'd been too frightened of the darkness in her father to speak out or stand up for herself, no matter how loudly she'd screamed inside.

She'd thought marriage to Ciro would free her from tyranny but all she'd done was exchange one hell for another.

The longer the day had gone on, the more the cold shock of Ciro's despicable betrayal had turned into hot fury. It needed an outlet. She'd thought of her favourite heroine, Elizabeth Bennet, and asked herself what she would do in this situation. Elizabeth would steel her spine and confront it head-on. And so must she.

A favourite line from Elizabeth rang in her head.

My courage always rises at every attempt to intimidate me.

It was a line Claudia always thought of with longing, wishing she had such courage. From now on it would be her mantra.

Ciro got to his feet and walked nonchalantly back to the bottle of bourbon. 'I'm sorry if I hurt you last night,' he said, his voice as steady as the hand that poured himself another measure. 'I tried to be gentle.'

'I'm not talking about sex.' She managed a small laugh while inside her heart wept to remember how wonderful his lovemaking had been. What she'd thought of as the most beautiful experience of her life had been tainted for ever. 'Although remembering that hurts me too.' She swallowed. 'You should be ashamed of yourself.'

His throat moved before he downed the measure. 'I am ashamed. I should have remembered to use a—'

'Shut up.'

Ciro closed his eyes. Claudia hadn't raised her voice but those two words were delivered with a punch that landed right in his stomach. Every curse he knew flew through his head as the nagging worry that had played in his gut all day rose to the surface. She knew.

'I heard you. Last night. When you crept out on the balcony.'

'What do you think you heard?'

'Don't bother trying to gaslight me. I *know* what I heard.' Her eyes flashed as she casually mimicked, '*"Vicenzu, it's me. I can't do this for much longer. I've fulfilled my part. She's going to sign the house over to me today. You need to get your side done, and quickly. Whatever it takes to get the business back, do it, because I don't know how much longer I can keep the pretence up."*'

His mouth dropped open. Ciro couldn't remember the exact words he'd said in the message he'd left for his brother but was pretty sure she'd just recited them verbatim.

She leaned forward and rested her elbows on her thighs. 'Why?'

He stared at her, head spinning, wrong-footed and taken completely off guard.

'Let's not waste time with more lies,' she said into the dumbstruck silence. 'I've spent the day hiding my feelings and I don't think I can bear to breathe the same air as you a minute longer. You disgust me. But before I go, I want to know why you went to all this trouble. You married me to get your family home back, your brother is planning to get your family business back from my sister… Why? If you didn't want your father to sell them, why not buy them yourself? It's not as if you can't afford it.'

'Claudia…'

'Don't *Claudia* me.' Her voice was like ice. 'Either you tell me this minute why you've married me for a *house*, of all things, or I'm going to call my father and ask him.'

Ciro shook off the stupor that had caught him in its net and hardened himself. Claudia might have been a virgin in the bedroom but no child of Cesare Buscetta could be called an innocent. 'Cut the act, Princess, and stop pretending you don't know exactly what your father did.'

Her brow knotted.

'Let me refresh your memory.' He stepped casually towards her, his words slow and deliberate. 'Your father approached my father in January with an offer to buy the business and the family estate. Papà said no. He didn't want to sell. The business had been in the Trapani family for generations and he wanted it to stay that way, and he wanted to grow old with my *mamma* in the house where they'd raised their children. Your father wouldn't accept no for an answer and resorted to sabotage to get what he wanted.'

'Liar.' Her denial came out as a whisper.

He crouched down to look into the dark eyes ringing with an excellent attempt at confusion. 'Your father was the puppeteer in the background pulling the strings that entangled my father so tightly he couldn't escape. Papà was on the verge of losing everything, and then your father swooped back in like a black-hearted knight with his derisory, his *insulting*, new cash offer. It was barely enough for my father to pay off the debts your father's sabotage had heaped on him. Papà had no choice but to sell the business that had been in the family for generations and the home he'd spent his entire married life in just so you and your precious sister could have a property and a business that was legal.'

He laughed loudly, right in her face. 'Because, Princess, that's the kicker. The business and property sale were both legal. Your father made very sure not to get his hands dirty on this particular deal but only because he didn't want the stain to reach his precious princesses. He had no need to use guns or threats to get his way when good old-fashioned sabotage followed by a heroic rescue act worked so well. When I visited your father the day I met you, do you know what he said?' He moved his face close enough to see the flecks of gold in the darkness of her eyes. 'He said *nothing* about it. To him, it was insignificant. To your father it was just business. If ruining my parents' lives meant anything to him he would have refused me entry into his home and quadrupled the guards he posted on you and your sister. But it didn't mean anything to him. He wanted a nice clean home and a nice clean business for his precious princesses. He got what he wanted and moved on. But I can't move on.'

The colour on Claudia's golden skin had drained from her face. Her eyes were wide and dazed, her mouth opening and closing but no sound coming out.

Straightening, he cast her a look of pure disdain. 'Look at you, sitting there, pretending to be shocked at all this. *You* signed those deeds transferring the ownership of the house to you, *you* signed them, *you* saw the pathetically low sale figure that had been placed on it, *you* saw the state my father was in and still you signed it. A day later he was *dead*.'

He walked back to the bar but at the last moment resisted pouring himself another drink. He needed to keep his head clear while he considered the best way to handle this situation.

What the hell had he been thinking making that call to Vicenzu? All he'd had to do was keep up the happy and in-love act for a few more months at most. Idiot! Claudia hadn't signed the house over to him yet. His twilight call of guilt-laced desperation to his brother had ruined everything.

Leaning against the wall, he folded his arms across his chest as he faced her. He would not allow himself to soften at the shock that had seemingly enveloped her. He would not allow himself to feel guilt for the woman whose actions had contributed towards his father's death. 'Cat got your tongue, Princess? Must be hard for you, finding yourself on the receiving end of the fraudulent, immoral behaviour your family's so famous for.'

Long dark lashes shadowed her face as she blinked slowly. A solitary tear ran down her cheek but when she spoke, her voice was calm. 'I never met your father. I signed my part of the deeds with my father's lawyer. I knew nothing of…' She squeezed her eyes shut and inhaled deeply through her nose. 'What's the point? You won't believe me.' Her eyes snapped back open and fixed on him like lasers. 'Actually, I don't care if you believe me. What you have done to me is sick.'

She jumped to her feet and hurried to the bedroom where she grabbed her overnight case and threw it onto the bed.

'What are you doing?' If she thought she could leave and go running back to Daddy she had another think coming. Ciro had no idea how he could prevent it but he would try…

'You want the house so much, you can have it.' Her fingers struggled to co-operate but finally Claudia managed to unzip the case and remove the deeds that had been prepared for her by Ciro's lawyer.

The nausea crashing in her stomach was so strong she feared she might vomit right here and now.

Dear heaven, she believed him. All day her mind had whirled with questions. As Imma had pointed out, Ciro could have bought the house and the business with the daily interest he received. Why marry her for it? It had to be about more than bricks and mortar. In the back of her mind had been the terrible, disloyal thought that it was connected to her father.

He had no need to use guns or threats to get his way when good old-fashioned sabotage followed by a heroic rescue act worked so well…

Once, when Claudia had been very young, she'd run out of drawing paper. On a whim, she'd gone into her father's office looking for a fresh supply, a room she was expressly forbidden from entering. But her father had been away on business, the nanny busy doing something with Imma, the rest of the staff doing their chores, and Claudia had been too keen to get her little hands on more paper and draw more pretty pictures for a concept like consequences to deter her. She'd blithely rifled through the contents of his desk drawer but her short bout of rule-breaking had been brought to an abrupt halt when she'd touched something cold and metallic.

As young as Claudia had been, she knew a gun when she saw one. She remembered lifting it out of the drawer, remembered the heavy weight of it in her tiny hands and remembered the fear that had clutched her chest. The fear had been as cold and had tasted as metallic as the gun in her hand. She'd put it back where she'd found it and fled from the office, too frightened to tell anyone, even her sister, what she'd found. Did her father have a gun because he needed it for protection? If so, did that mean Claudia and Imma were in danger? Or did he have it because *he* was the bad guy? She didn't know and was too frightened to ask but the bubble she'd lived in up to that point had burst. She started paying attention. She listened. Hard. And she never disobeyed her father again.

Holding the envelope containing the deeds tightly to her chest, she stared at the hateful face of the man she'd stupidly believed herself in love with and plucked a figure from thin air. 'I want twenty thousand euros.'

'Claudia…'

'Twenty thousand euros and I'll sign the deeds.'

Disbelief shadowed his face. 'You're offering to give me the house? Still?'

She never wanted to set foot in it again. 'I want cash.'

'It's Sunday.'

'You think I'm so stupid I don't know what day it is?' she snarled. 'Get me the cash. You have half an hour.'

'Where are you going?'

She opened the door without looking back at him. 'To

get the signing of the deeds witnessed. Half an hour, Ciro. Get me the cash.'

Fuelled by so much rage and humiliation that the pain in her heart was nothing but a numb throb, Claudia took the stairs all the way down to the lobby. After telling one of the receptionists what she wanted, the duty manager was summoned and agreed to be the witness. 'Where do you want me to sign?' he asked.

Thankfully, Ciro's lawyer had placed sticky fluorescent arrows on the pages that needed signing.

'You need to sign first,' the duty manager said, handing a pen to her.

There were two blank boxes with the arrows pointed at them. She peered at them cautiously, recognised her own name in the space next to the top one and placed the pen by it before hesitating. Embarrassment flushed over her face. 'Do I sign here?'

'Yes.'

She signed it carefully, using the same signature she'd used only months before when the same property had been transferred into her name. It sickened her to know she'd swallowed her father's lies so readily. Because they had been lies. She knew it in her heart.

But now was not the time to think too hard about it all. She needed to hold herself together a little bit longer and stay strong.

'Do you have my money?' she asked when she stepped back into the suite.

Ciro, who'd been sending messages by all different media to his brother to warn him that Claudia knew, working on the presumption that if Claudia hadn't told Immacolata yet then she would soon, shoved his phone into his back pocket. 'It'll be here any minute.'

'Good.' Walking purposefully to the bedroom, she

zipped her case back together and carried it to the door, the deeds still tucked under her arm. Her eyes narrowed as she noticed him looking at it. 'You'll get this when I get my cash.'

He didn't like this hard side to her. It was the side he'd spent two months waiting to be revealed but now it was here in the open, all he could think was how little it suited her. 'What are you going to do?'

'You mean, am I going to tell my father.' Her face contorted. She opened her mouth to continue but a loud rap on the door cut her words off.

'That will be my man with the cash for you.'

She stepped aside to allow Ciro to open the door. He took the briefcase with a terse nod of thanks. Placing it on the table, he opened it, then stepped back so Claudia could look.

She stared at it for a long time. 'That looks like more than twenty thousand.'

'It's a hundred thousand.'

'Trying to buy my silence?' The look she cast him could have stripped paint. 'Count twenty thousand out for me. I don't want a cent more.'

'I'm not trying to buy your silence.'

'Just count the money.'

He complied, wrapping the crisp notes in a band. She snatched it from him and placed it in the handbag she had secured around her chest. When she next met his stare, the expression blazing at him could have dissolved the walls never mind stripped them. 'I have a cab waiting for me so I will make this quick,' she said. 'You are going to leave Sicily as we planned. Go to Antigua if you want, go to America, go to Mars, wherever you like, just keep away from Sicily. I don't want my father to know that you married me on a lie.'

'You want to protect *his* feelings?'

'No,' she spat. 'I'm not ready to face him yet with what he's done. I want to get away from all the lies and deceit because between the two of you, I don't know who I hate the most. If he knows I've left you, he'll want me to go back to him, so consider this a quid pro quo—you get the deeds...' she shoved them into his chest before sharply stepping back '...and I get the cash to disappear for a while. I will send him regular messages about how much I'm enjoying our honeymoon and the start of our married life so he doesn't worry that I've dropped off the face of the earth, so you need to keep your head down and keep away from Sicily. Got it?'

Ciro kneaded his temples. His head pounded. He was not a man used to being bested at anything but, in this, Claudia had turned the tables on him with meticulous precision. 'How can I trust you'll keep your word?'

Angry colour flared over her cheeks. 'How dare you? I'm the victim here. You told me you loved me, you married me, you made love to me and all along it was all a sick lie. If you'd told me from the start what my father had done, I would have signed the house straight back over to your mother.'

He gave a bitter laugh. 'You expect me to believe that, Princess?'

'Haven't I just signed it over to you? Look at the deeds—the house belongs to you now. Give it back to your *mamma*, do whatever the heck you want with it. I don't want it. It should never have been given to me in the first place.'

She picked up her travel case and opened the door. The speed with which she'd executed her plan was astounding. Ciro found himself in the rare position of being on the back foot of a game which he'd designed. 'Where are you going?'

'That's none of your business.' The door slammed shut behind her, only to fly back open again. 'If my father contacts you, you tell him we're delirious with happiness, got it? They're the kind of lies you're a pro at so I don't imagine it'll be a problem for you.'

'How long?'

'For as long as I decide necessary. I'll be in touch when I'm ready. Goodbye.'

CHAPTER FIVE

CIRO STOOD ON the balcony of his New York penthouse apartment and replied to his brother's vague message with an equally vague one of his own. The wind was picking up, bringing with it a chill. After the inhuman heatwave the city had lived through in recent weeks, the coming storm was a welcome respite. He doubted the storm in his stomach would receive any respite soon.

Five weeks ago, he'd been certain Claudia had told her sister about their plot but, with Vicenzu and Imma having since married too, he accepted he'd been wrong.

He'd relived their confrontation many times, remembering her facial expressions and body language, dissecting her words and actions. There was no getting around it: she'd been horrified to learn what her father had done to his. And she'd been horrified at what Ciro had done to her. The guilt he felt at this fought with the bitter knowledge that, innocent as she might have been of her father's evil games, she was still a Buscetta. She'd spent twenty-one years living with and learning from the monster. It would be impossible for his malevolence not to have seeped into her.

He'd had his lawyer check over the deeds. That had been no game or gimmick. She really had signed the house over to him. In theory, Ciro had achieved everything he'd set out to achieve. Vicenzu was also inching closer to getting the family business back—*why* hadn't Claudia told her sister? That was another thing he was no nearer to making sense of—but there was no satisfaction to be felt and no wish to celebrate. Not when Claudia had vanished off the face of the earth.

He couldn't stop thinking about her. Before their wedding his thoughts had been consumed with her father and his own planned vengeance. Now his thoughts were consumed only with her.

Where was she?

He felt as if he'd fallen into limbo, waiting for Claudia to surface so he could resume his life. He'd done as she'd ordered and kept his head down, quietly getting on with the running of his business. She'd stuck to her part too. If Cesare had any clue as to what had happened between them, Ciro would know about it. He would already have a bounty on his head.

He'd tried to call her but it hadn't connected. She'd blocked him.

After a fortnight the waiting had become intolerable and he'd set a crack team of private detectives onto finding her. They'd come up with precisely nothing. She could be anywhere.

Claudia sat in companionable silence with Sister Bernadette on the old stone bench. Around them, the nuns and volunteers who worked the convent gardens were picking fruit.

'I have to leave soon,' Claudia said. 'Tomorrow. I think.' As much as she would like to stay in this serene sanctuary, real life needed to be dealt with. Her time here, though, had not been wasted. She had learned much about herself and about her father. Questions she had never thought or dared ask before had been asked, and truthful answers given.

Those truths had broken her heart all over again.

Sister Bernadette gave a smile that perfectly conveyed her sympathy and understanding. 'We will miss you.'

'I will miss you too.' She covered the elderly nun's hand with her own. 'I cannot thank you enough for taking me in.'

'You are always welcome here, child.' Sister Bernadette gently squeezed Claudia's hand and got to her feet. 'I must prepare for vespers.'

Claudia watched her walk away feeling she could choke on the emotion filling her heart.

How she wished she could stay but it was impossible. Three weeks into her sanctuary she'd taken the test that had changed the course of her life.

She was pregnant.

Placing a hand on her still-flat belly, she closed her eyes and breathed in slowly. Now that the shock and pain of Ciro's betrayal had dimmed to a dull ache, her path was clear and real unfettered freedom beckoned.

After two weeks spent thinking and planning and channelling her literary heroines, she knew what she had to do.

She had to leave Sicily. Whatever happened, she would not raise her child here. Her father's reach was too great. She would be at his mercy—and so would her child.

She would never be at his mercy again.

And nor would she go running to Imma, not unless the worst came to the worst and it became absolutely necessary. She prayed for her child's sake that it didn't come to that. She prayed that she could build a cordiality with her enemy.

Claudia had thought a lot about her childhood these last two weeks and how desperately she had longed for her *mamma*. She would never willingly put her child through that.

But from now on, she would be at the mercy of only her own decisions and choices. She would not be answerable to anyone. She would be like Elizabeth Bennet and take control of her own life.

As terrifying as it was, she had to go to New York and start a new life in the city her child's father called home. He had as great a responsibility to their child as she had and she would do her best to make sure he lived up to it.

Much as she wanted to take that freedom immediately, she knew she wasn't ready to live in a city as scary as New York on her own just yet.

Just reaching for her phone set her heart off at a canter. She spoke into it. 'Unblock Ciro.' Like magic, her phone unblocked him. She spoke into it again. 'Call Ciro.'

She only had to wait two rings before it was answered. 'Claudia?'

Her skin tingled and her throat closed to hear his rich voice. For a moment, she couldn't make herself speak.

'Claudia?' he repeated. 'Is that you? Are you okay?'

It was his fake concern that cleared her vocal cords. 'Hello, Ciro.' As she spoke his name, a fat bee landed on the lavender beside her bench. For some unfathomable reason, the sight of it made her smile. 'Are you in New York?'

'Yes. Where are you?'

'Sicily.'

'Really?'

'Yes. I want you to sort a flight to New York for me. We need to talk.'

'Has something happened?'

'You could say that.'

'I'll send my jet over.'

'A scheduled flight will be fine. I don't care where I sit.'

'I'll have you on the next flight out.'

'Make it for tomorrow. There's something I have to do first.' She disconnected the call before he could respond and breathed deeply to quell her racing heart.

Ciro paced the arrivals area of the airport surrounded by assorted people holding makeshift signs with random names. There was a family to the left of him, a father and two small children. From the excitement evident on the children's faces and their manic energy, they were waiting for their mother's arrival.

There was a manic energy in his veins too. It had been there since Claudia had broken her silence and called him.

As the wait lengthened—the storms currently hitting the east coast had turned flight schedules on their head—he found his attention lingering on that family. The life Ciro lived meant children were rarely on his radar. He'd always assumed he'd marry and have kids one day when he was ready to slow down, but that one day had always been far enough away for him not to bother thinking about. His gut told him he needed to start thinking about it right now.

If, as his gut was telling him, Claudia was pregnant, how could he reconcile being father to the grandchild of the man directly responsible for the death of his own father?

Agitated, he bought himself a coffee and had taken his first sip when a tranche of travellers emerged. Amid the crowd, dressed in slim-fitting jeans, a long blousy cream top and an artfully placed blue silk scarf, her long dark hair tied in a high ponytail, was Claudia.

Ciro's heart thudded against his ribs. His mouth ran dry.

Their eyes met.

Claudia ordered her suddenly jellified legs to keep going and tightened her hold on her overnight case and the strap of her handbag. It had never occurred to her that one look at Ciro would still have the power to make her heart flip over and her lungs shrink.

And then she was standing before him, gazing into the green eyes she'd once stared at wishing she could swim in them, wondering how it was possible she'd forgotten how deeply attractive she found him.

She hadn't forgotten. She'd buried it away, ashamed of an attraction that had been built on such heinous lies.

He gave a slow incline of his head then leaned down to pick up the case she didn't remember placing on the floor. The movement set off a waft of his woody cologne and for a moment the world spun as memories of their wedding night flooded her. They were memories she'd buried away along with her attraction for him.

'How was your flight?' he asked with overt politeness as they walked to the exit. 'Was there much turbulence?'

'Some. It could have been worse.' She'd been too busy worrying about seeing Ciro again to worry about the frequent bouts of turbulence they'd flown through.

'Have you got a coat? The weather's atrocious.'

She shook her head, not looking at him. She hadn't thought to check the weather conditions, had assumed New York would be basking in similar glorious heat to Sicily.

He put her case back on the floor and, keeping hold of his coffee cup, handed her the long black thing he'd been holding. 'Here. Wear this.'

It was a long waterproof overcoat. Everything in her recoiled at the thought of wearing something that belonged to him and she shook her head violently and thrust it back at him. 'No, thank you.'

His chiselled jaw clenched, the firm mouth forming a tight line. Then he picked her case back up and strolled out of the exit without waiting to see if she followed.

Hurrying after him, Claudia took one step outside and

found herself instantly soaked by the deluge falling from the dark grey sky and almost knocked off her feet by an accompanying gust of wind. Only a strong arm wrapping around her waist kept her upright.

There was no recoiling this time, only a surge of warmth, which she had no time to analyse for Ciro had swept her forwards to a waiting oversized four-by-four, his huge frame shielding her against the worst of the elements. Moments later she'd been bundled into the massive vehicle. The door closed, muting the noise of the elements lashing down on them. Ciro, his dark hair flattened by the rain, his expensive suit drenched, tapped on the raised partition between them and the driver set off.

The car was warm and in no time at all the chill from the downpour that had soaked her lifted.

'How long will it take to get to your apartment?' she asked, looking out of the window. Conditions were so bad she could see nothing but wet grey.

'With the weather and traffic as it is, hopefully no more than a couple of hours. I would have used the helicopter but in these conditions…?' His shoulders rose in a 'what can you do?' shrug.

A few, long minutes of excruciatingly uncomfortable silence followed until Ciro broke it. 'Where have you been?'

'In a convent.'

His burst of incredulous laughter sliced through her, laughter that stopped as quickly as it had begun. 'Seriously? You were hiding in a convent?'

'I needed a place where I could think and cleanse myself from your lies and my father's behaviour.' Twisting to look at him, she found her heart twisting too and exhaled slowly, placing her hand on her stomach, reminding herself of the need to remain strong and calm.

His breathing heavy, he took a while to respond. 'I apologise for what I did to you.'

'You mean marrying me on a lie?'

His head jerked a nod. 'I thought you were part of your father's plot against mine.'

She thought about that for a moment. 'We had an English nanny when we were growing up and she taught us that two wrongs don't ever make a right. Did no one teach you that?'

Ciro turned his head and found himself trapped in the dark depths of Claudia's stare. Every inhalation taken since getting into the car had found him breathing in her scent. It was the same perfume that had coated her skin on their wedding night and it coiled inside him, unleashing memories that had haunted his dreams ever since she'd gone into hiding.

He clenched his jaw and willed away the surging heat in his veins. 'What would you have done if our roles had been reversed? Wouldn't you want vengeance on the man responsible for the death of *your* father? Wouldn't you want to take back what had been stolen from you?'

Her chest rose, eyes narrowing slightly before she gave a slow shake of her head. 'I would never set out to humiliate or destroy anyone. I wouldn't involve anyone else. I could never live with myself if I hurt someone.'

'Then you're a better person than me, Princess. If someone hurts me or those I love, I strike back twice as hard. Steal from me and I will take it back with extras. Your father did both.'

'And how's your vengeance working out for you? Do you feel better in yourself now you have your family home back?'

'I feel great.' To accentuate his point, he spread his arms out and hooked an ankle on his thigh.

The weight of her stare penetrated him for the longest time before a smile crept slowly over her face.

'Do you know, you are a terrible liar?' She actually laughed. '*"There are none so blind as those that will not see."* I was so desperate to believe you loved me and so desperate for some real freedom from my father that I blinded myself. And deafened myself too.' Another short burst of laughter. 'If I had opened my eyes I would have seen the lies. If I had opened my ears I would have heard them. Your voice and body language tell the truth whatever comes out of your mouth.'

The proverb she'd quoted hit him. He'd been as guilty of it as she. The woman he'd believed to be stupid had, he realised, an insightfulness that saw right through him.

'What do you want to talk about?' he said roughly. 'We're not going anywhere so let's talk about it now.' The car hadn't travelled more than a mile since they'd left the airport. At the rate they were going they'd be lucky to make it to his apartment before nightfall.

'Haven't you guessed?'

His chest tightened into a ball. 'You're pregnant?'

She nodded. 'I took the test two weeks ago.'

'You've waited *two weeks* to tell me?'

'I needed time to think.'

'You should have told me immediately.'

She raised her shoulders and pulled a rueful smile. 'And you should have used contraception.'

He blew out a long puff of air and dragged his fingers through his hair. There was a painful roiling in his stomach similar to the feeling he'd had when he'd left his loving family in Sicily for a new life in America, but far stronger. There was no excitement amid the trepidation this time. Only dread.

He was going to be a father. He was going to be father to a child with Buscetta blood.

'You're okay with this?' He met her stare again. Claudia's calmness was as disconcerting as the news she really was carrying his child.

'That we're having a baby? Yes. I've always wanted to be a *mamma*.'

'You *wanted* this?'

Her face scrunched with thought. 'When our child was made I thought we loved each other so at that point, yes, I wanted a baby.'

'And now? After everything that's happened?'

'That doesn't change anything.'

'You still want it?'

'Of course. Don't you?'

He muttered a curse under his breath. 'How do I know what I want? You've had two weeks to think about this.'

'You've known since our wedding night we could have made a baby.'

'Having suspicions is very different from having facts.'

'Agreed. But you *have* thought about it.' She squeezed her eyes shut momentarily before fixing them back on him. 'I need to know if you can love a child that's the blood of your enemy.'

Her astuteness caught him off guard. Again.

'And please don't lie to me,' she added before he could formulate a response. 'Whatever happens in the future I will not accept anything less than complete honesty from you.' Her scrutinising eyes did not leave his face. If he was to lie, she would know…

'I don't know,' he finally answered. 'I never meant to bring a child into this.'

She pondered this for a few moments. 'Thank you for being honest.'

'How can you be so calm?' he asked, his incredulity finally reaching breaking point. 'I've lied to you, I've got you pregnant, I tell you that I don't know if I can love our child and you sit there as if we're discussing a new car.'

There was the faintest flicker in her eyes. 'Would you prefer me to rant and rage at you?'

'You're the one demanding honesty. That would be a more honest reaction than this serenity you're displaying.' Anger he could deal with. Anger meant he could shout back and displace some of the guilt that lay so heavily on his shoulders.

She pulled out the hairband holding her ponytail together. 'I've worked through my anger.' Her chestnut hair tumbled down. He remembered the scent of it. Remembered how it had driven deep into his bloodstream. 'You're the father of my child and I can't change that.' She massed the long, silken locks together and gathered them on her shoulder. Still staring at him, she continued, 'I can't undo the lies you told. I can't change *anything*. But I can influence the future and do my best to make sure our child has the best possible start in life that it can.'

His throat had caught. He had to cough to clear it. But, damn, she was plaiting her hair...and he was remembering all the heady feelings that had rushed through him when he'd unplaited it.

Damn it, he didn't want to remember. He wanted to agree a plan on how to proceed from this point, drop her off at his apartment then go out and get rip-roaring drunk. Alone.

'You're right,' he said, straightening. 'I *have* thought about what should happen if you're pregnant. As you're insisting on honesty, I tell you now that I don't want our child to be raised in Sicily with your father's influence.'

'I don't want that either.'

'You don't?' This from the daddy's girl who'd refused a date with him until she'd got her father's approval first.

He waited for her to elaborate but she continued plaiting her hair.

'I'll set you up in an apartment,' he said. 'If we live in the same city it will make it easier to—'

'For now, I will live with you.'

'What?'

She wound the band at the end of the long plait and jutted her chin. 'Only until the baby's born. I'll need support through the pregnancy and you're the only person I know here. I've never been to America before. I don't know the city. Living with you will give me time to adjust and it will give us the time we need to build some form of relationship that's not built on hatred. We don't know each other. All we know are the fronts we showed each other during our courtship—I'm willing to admit that I put on a front too.'

The air in the car seemed to have thinned.

'And how can you develop feelings for our baby if you're not there to share the pregnancy?' she continued, clearly unloading all the thoughts she'd spent weeks developing while he was stuck playing catch-up. 'You're always travelling. If we lived apart I'd need to schedule time with you like we did before.'

'I don't want to live with you,' he said bluntly.

She didn't even flinch. 'I don't want to live with you either. Believe me, I feel nothing but contempt for you but my feelings don't count any more and neither do yours. I grew up without my mother and I've always felt there was a huge piece of my life missing. I don't want that for our child and I don't want it to be born with warring parents. You were prepared to live with me to get a house—are you seriously telling me you won't live with me for a short while for your child's sake?'

Ciro didn't answer. How could he live with this intoxicating woman even with an end date in sight? Every time he looked at her desire ripped through him but that desire was tinged with revulsion. He accepted that she'd been innocent of her father's criminally underhand activities but she was still Cesare Buscetta's daughter. How could he reconcile the two competing parts, the desire and the loathing, without losing his mind?

'I've spent two weeks thinking about this,' she said into the silence, 'and I think we both owe it to our child to try and find a way to get along in friendship rather than hatred. I don't expect it to be easy but let's give it until the baby's born.'

He breathed deeply. That was still, what, seven, eight months away? 'Live together until the baby's born?'

'Yes. We can look for an apartment for me and the baby in the new year and get it ready so I can move straight into it when the time's right, but for now we'll need to keep up a front that we're happily married. The last thing I want is for my father to think there's anything wrong with us until I'm ready to tell him. I've enough to deal with.' Her gaze penetrated him, burned him. 'But, Ciro…' She faltered before continuing. 'If at any time your heart tells you that you won't be able to love our baby, you must tell me. Our child is innocent of everything and I won't have it raised in hate. Better an absent father than a hateful one. If you tell me that I will leave and you will never have to see me or the baby again.'

CHAPTER SIX

THE RAIN STILL lashed Manhattan when the driver arrived at Ciro's apartment. Mercifully, a doorman with a giant umbrella appeared and held it over Claudia's head while she got out of the car. She could hardly see more than a foot in front of her but her other senses were working fine and when they hurried through the door she was ambushed by a really strong scent of perfume.

They strode through a small lobby to an elevator. Ciro placed his thumb on a wall scanner and the elevator doors opened. Not speaking or looking at each other, they stepped into it. Ciro pressed a button and they ascended, so smoothly Claudia hardly felt any motion. When it stopped and the doors slid open, she found herself stepping into another small lobby. Behind a horseshoe desk sat a wafer-thin middle-aged woman with a severe black bob and the most amazing, eccentric spectacles Claudia had ever seen, with rainbow stripes and small studded diamonds.

Ciro introduced them. 'Marcy, this is Claudia. Claudia, this is Marcy, my PA.' He made the introduction in English and then repeated it in Sicilian Italian.

He made his PA work in a lobby?

Marcy stood and shook Claudia's hand.

'I love your glasses,' Claudia blurted out in English.

Marcy beamed. 'So do I!'

Ciro put his thumb to another scanner beside a steel door then put his eye to a higher one. When both scans were complete, there was a noise like a puff and a green light appeared on the door itself. Ciro pushed the door open and held it so Claudia could enter.

It was like entering Wonderland.

'I didn't know you spoke English,' he said when the door closed behind them.

'Imma and I were raised by English nannies so we could be bilingual.' The foyer they stepped into had shiny black granite flooring, a Roman statue on a plinth, and stairs that wound upwards. 'You have two floors?'

'Three.'

'I thought apartments were one level?'

He grunted and led her through the open double doorway to the left that had the most magnificently decorated high plaster ceiling. 'Living room.' Back through the foyer and through the open door on the other side. 'Dining room.' He pointed to a door at the end. 'Pantry, kitchen and staff room.'

There was no time for Claudia to marvel at the grandeur of what she was being shown for Ciro had set off up the stairs laid with a beautiful hardwood that continued on through the long hallway. He opened various doors and barked out their usage. 'Gym. Library. Games room. Guest room. Your room.'

'My room?' She stepped into a beautifully appointed bedroom that was as high, bright and airy as the rest of the apartment. She'd expected Ciro's apartment to be dark and no-nonsense masculine but, while hardly feminine, it was tasteful and elegant, blending contemporary styles with Italian renaissance, not a single detail missed, right down to the hand-carved doors and the beautifully crafted window frames.

So this was how a billionaire lived, she thought in wonder. Claudia had grown up in a magnificent villa with extensive grounds but this was something else. Ciro's wealth made her father seem a pauper.

'The luggage you had couriered has been placed in the dressing room for you,' Ciro said. 'I didn't know what you wanted me to do with it. I'll get one of the staff to unpack for you when they come in the morning.'

She opened the door he'd indicated and saw her suitcases laid neatly on the floor. They must have been there since the wedding, shipped over in anticipation of her moving continents for the love of her life. Her heart clenched to remember the excitement that had filled her when she'd been packing for her new life…and then her heart stopped to see her wedding dress hanging on the open rail. She hadn't given the dress a second thought since leaving Sicily. Seeing it there, hidden away with the rest of her stuff, made her want to weep.

'Do your staff know we're married?' she asked quietly.

'I assume so. Enough pictures were leaked to the press of our wedding day.' Ciro looked out of the south-facing window at the bleak grey view. It matched his mood perfectly.

'Then we should share a bedroom.'

Every cell in his body stiffened.

She sighed. 'Ciro, like it or not, I am your wife. Married couples share a bed. What does it tell your staff if you put your new wife straight into a guest room?'

'Who cares what they think? They've all signed non-disclosure agreements.'

'*I* care.'

'We have enough issues without throwing sex into the mix.'

Her cheeks flared with colour but she held her ground. 'I never said anything about us…' she swallowed and managed to look both disgusted and dignified '…having sex.

I don't want us to share a bed for *that*, not ever again, but we've been married for five weeks and not spent a night together since the wedding. For me to move in now and go straight into a guest room will look strange. I know pride is a sin but I can't help how I feel and I know that if I was to look your staff in the eye knowing that they know we're in separate rooms, I'd feel humiliated.'

A sharp ache pierced his chest at the confirmation he'd killed any feelings she'd had for him. He didn't *want* her to have feelings for him and wished he could kill the tumultuous emotions she evoked in him as easily.

'We don't have to share for long,' she added into the silence. 'A few weeks. Just for appearances' sake.'

'I didn't realise appearances meant that much to you,' he said stiffly, furious that she was neatly backing him into yet another corner.

'No one likes to be humiliated and I've been humiliated enough.' Her eyes narrowed. 'How were you going to play things if I hadn't overheard you? Where would I have slept? How would you have handled things?'

Knowing she would see straight through any lie, he shrugged sardonically and plumped for honesty. 'I was going to install you in my bedroom then spend our marriage travelling without you until you gave me the house and Vicenzu got the business—'

'Install me?' she interrupted. 'What, like I was a bathtub or something? Isn't that the kind of thing that's usually installed?'

How could he answer that without sounding even more like a douchebag?

She folded her arms and pursed her lips. 'You don't even think of me as human, do you?'

'Of course I do,' he answered shortly. If he didn't have such a deeply human response to her they wouldn't be in this mess. If he didn't have such vivid memories of their one night of lovemaking he wouldn't be so reluctant to share a bed with her again, even if only for a few weeks. He was a man, not a machine, and Claudia was as hot a feminine temptation as he could bear.

Claudia stared out of the bedroom window, one of four in the master suite. The apartment's insulation and glazing were of such good quality she could hear nothing of the raging storm outside. With the dark night sky enveloping them, she could see hardly anything of it either.

Rubbing her arms for warmth against the sudden shiver that snaked through her, she drew the curtains. The silence was stark.

Ciro had gone out. Immediately after they'd shared a takeaway dinner he'd announced he had business to attend to.

Business at nine o'clock in the evening?

She hadn't bothered disputing this obvious lie. In truth, she was glad of some space away from him. She'd got her way about the sleeping arrangements. Ciro had carried her cases to the master suite himself. Her wedding dress remained in the guest room. She'd had a strong feeling he didn't want to touch it any more than she did.

His bedroom was surprisingly beautiful. The walls were painted a soft grey, the ceiling the same white decorative plaster as she'd seen in the living room, the curtains and thick carpet a soft shade of cream. The maroon duvet on the emperor-sized bed brought colour to the room, as did the tasteful colourful paintings of semi-nude women, which had not an ounce of sleaze in them. The overall feeling was one of peace. And she'd just bulldozed her way into Ciro's tranquillity.

Despite everything, she was proud of herself for holding her ground and not caving in.

The Claudia she'd been before the wedding would have rolled over and let him have his way.

Did he really think she wanted to be here? That she got any pleasure from forcing him to take her in? That she got pleasure from insisting they share a bed when the thought of sleeping beside him made her all twisted up inside?

She despised him for what he'd done to her but he was the father of her child. She could only pray that Ciro could bring himself to love it. She didn't expect him to forgive her father: forgiveness was something she was struggling to find herself. But she did expect him to forgive their innocent child for the accident of its birth. If he couldn't do that then he was not worth the effort of her trying and she'd leave without a second of remorse. If she could put aside her hurt and humiliation over what Ciro had done to her, then he could try too.

Too restless to sleep, she decided to explore the apartment properly. She remembered Ciro telling her during their courtship that he'd had his New York apartment remodelled a year ago to his specific tastes. What, she wondered, did his specific tastes say about him? She wasn't educated enough to say with any certainty but her exploration gave the impression of a man comfortable in his masculinity and his sexuality—there were lots of tasteful paintings and statues of nudes of both sexes—and a man who was tactile. All his furniture, hard and soft, had a touchable quality to it, materials chosen that were both aesthetically pleasing and pleasurable to the touch. It was an apartment that was a feast for the senses.

Back on the second floor and about to climb the stairs to the top, she felt drawn back to the library. Libraries were not Claudia's natural home and she tended to avoid them, but this one had the same feel to it as Ciro's bedroom. It surprised her that a man of Ciro's drive and restlessness had the patience to read.

She turned the soft lighting on and ran her fingers along the floor-to-ceiling bookshelves. Had Ciro read all these books? There must be thousands of them. She wondered if he had any Austen or Brontë on these shelves and figured it unlikely. She would give the clothes on her back to read their magical words with her own eyes rather than have to listen to them.

She pulled one of the books out and peered closely at the cover, trying hard to decipher its title. The effort made her brain hurt.

'That's a good book. You should read it.'

So shocked was she to hear Ciro's voice that the book slipped from her fingers. She hadn't heard him return.

Flustered, she quickly picked it up and slid it back where she'd got it from.

'Sorry,' she muttered, then felt her face flame again when she looked at him. He was propped against the doorway. The sleeves of his shirt were rolled up, the top three buttons undone. The butterflies that had unleashed in her stomach on their wedding night awoke and Claudia became suddenly aware that she was dressed in her pyjamas. That they covered her from neck to foot didn't matter. Beneath them she was naked.

He stepped into the room. His thick dark hair was damp from the rain. 'Don't be. Books deserve to be read. I thought you'd be asleep by now.'

'Don't you mean you *hoped* I'd be asleep by now?'

She caught a faint glimpse of his dimples. 'That too.'

'Sorry to disappoint you.'

Being greeted by Claudia in a pair of silk pyjamas, her

hair tied in two long plaits, could in no way be described as disappointing, Ciro thought.

Hoping to find some oblivion in the trusted method of alcohol, he'd met up with an old friend at a favourite bar two blocks away. He'd intended to get as rip-roaring drunk as he'd done in his university days and return home only when he was guaranteed to pass out. Four strong drinks in and the alcohol hadn't made a dent in his system. Six drinks in and he'd noticed a woman alone at the bar making eyes at him. She'd been extremely attractive with an abundance of cleavage on show. Three months ago he would have had no hesitation in introducing himself, buying her a drink and seeing where the evening led.

But that had been then. When he'd looked at the woman, all he could see was Claudia and suddenly it had hit him—in his desperation for oblivion and space from her, he'd left her alone in his apartment on her first night in Manhattan. Alone and newly pregnant.

Something sharp had speared his guts, bitterness had filled his taste buds and before he knew what he was doing he was throwing cash on the table for his share of the bill and bidding his friend goodnight.

What kind of a cold, selfish, heartless bastard was he turning into? That was the question he'd asked himself as he'd hurried through the storm back to his apartment. Part of him had hoped she'd be asleep, but as he'd climbed the stairs the sensation building in his loins and the fizzing in his veins told a different story. And that was the entire crux of his problem, he acknowledged grimly. His attraction for Claudia was at war with his loathing of who she was.

He shook his head. 'I'm the one who's sorry. I shouldn't have left you, not on your first night.'

'You probably did us both a favour,' she murmured. 'I think we both needed some space to breathe.'

He gazed at her, taking in afresh her slender beauty. Was he imagining that her breasts, jutting beneath the silken pyjama top, had grown since their night together? Did pregnancy work that fast?

Aware that his loins had tightened, he wrenched his gaze from her. 'How are you feeling in yourself? Healthwise?'

'I'm well. A little sleepier than normal.'

'Have you seen a doctor yet?'

'No.' She pulled a rueful face. 'My doctor back home is friends with my father. I didn't want to risk him telling Papà about the baby until I was ready.'

His stomach cramped at the mention of her father and it took all his effort to keep his voice even. 'When do you think that will be?'

'I told him this morning before I got my flight here.'

The cramping tightened. 'You told him before you told me?'

'I told Imma too, the day I took the test,' she said without an ounce of contrition. 'With my father… I needed to get it done.' Claudia squeezed her eyes shut. 'I didn't tell him I knew about the sabotage of your father's company or the other things I've learned about him since our wedding. Not explicitly. Imma can deal with that when she's ready. But I needed to prove to myself that I could face him down.'

'What do you mean?'

Her throat moved before she answered. 'I knew that when I told Papà about the baby he would want me—you and me—to raise it in Sicily. I needed to look him in the eye and hold my ground and tell him our child would be raised in New York.'

'How did he take it?'

Her nose wrinkled. 'I don't know. I think I shocked him. I've never said no to him before. I laid it out to him then left before he could argue about it.'

About to delve into this further, it suddenly came to him what she'd said about her sister. 'What else have you told your sister? I was under the impression you hadn't discussed what you overheard me say to Vicenzu with anyone.'

Now something sparkled in her eyes and she covered her mouth briefly before saying, 'Ciro, I told Imma that morning after you'd crept back into our bed. I only waited all those hours to confront you so she had time to counteract whatever plot your brother had dreamed up.'

'But they're married now,' he pointed out. Immacolata was considered to be the clever Buscetta sister. If people underestimated Claudia's intelligence so greatly then how much were they underestimating Immacolata's? A woman like that wouldn't tie herself to a man she knew hated her.

'Their marriage…' She shook her head. 'All I will say is whatever you think about it is probably wrong.'

'Immacolata married him even though she knew the truth?'

'Yes.'

Ciro thought about all the vague messages exchanged between him and his brother since his wedding night. Ciro had deliberately kept his non-committal, his pride not wanting his brother to know that while he had succeeded in getting the family home back, on every other level he'd failed spectacularly. 'Does Vicenzu know that she knows?'

She sucked her cheeks in and covered her mouth again. Was she smothering a laugh…? 'You and your brother really need to start working on your communication skills.'

He couldn't argue with that.

Whatever she'd been smothering turned into a wide yawn. Her eyes widened. 'Excuse me.'

'Tired?'

She yawned again, even more widely.

'Not surprising.' He looked at his watch. 'It's five in the morning in Sicily. You should get some sleep.'

She suddenly grabbed hold of the nearest bookcase and blinked a number of times. 'I was fine a minute ago.'

'You've probably been running on adrenaline.'

She nodded absently, still blinking, still holding on to the bookcase.

'Are you okay?'

She seemed to shrink. With a start, Ciro realised her legs were giving way beneath her. In three long strides he reached her and lifted her into his arms.

Her eyes widened, this time with shock. 'What are you doing?' Her voice had become a mumble.

'Carrying you to bed. Don't argue. You look like you're about to pass out.' As he spoke he carried her to the hallway then navigated the stairs.

Rather than argue, she rested a hand on his shoulder and pressed her cheek against his chest. Her hair tickled his throat, its sweet fragrance dancing into his senses. She fitted into his arms as if she'd been made especially for them…

She was asleep before he reached the bedroom.

Keeping a tight hold of her, he pulled the duvet back then carefully laid her down before covering her. She turned on her side and burrowed her head into the pillow, tucking her fingers beneath her chin.

Ciro couldn't tear his gaze from her. The longer he stared, the tighter his chest became and the more his fingers itched to touch her. His willpower broke before he even realised he was tracing a finger lightly over her cheekbone and then gently stroking the silk of her hair.

Then he closed his eyes and inhaled deeply before turning on his heel and leaving her to sleep. Alone.

CHAPTER SEVEN

CLAUDIA HAD NEVER been as disorientated as when she woke the first morning in Ciro's apartment. The room was dusky but light peered through the crack in the curtains…

She sat bolt upright, flames burning her veins as her last memory of the previous evening suddenly flashed through her. Exhaustion had swallowed her and Ciro had carried her to bed.

She noticed his side of the bed looked untouched. She clutched her flaming cheeks, bitterness filling her mouth as she realised he'd taken advantage of her exhaustion to sleep elsewhere. No chance of a comatose woman arguing with him about appearances.

Her mood lightened when she drew back the first set of curtains. The storm that had coloured her arrival in America a dismal grey had gone, in its place cloudless blue skies and dazzling sunshine. With wonder building inside her, she stepped out onto a terrace she hadn't noticed before. That wonder had nothing on the joy that lifted her at the view. Since when did New York have greenery? She'd thought it a sprawling concrete jungle but right in front of her lay a vast canopy of trees that must have stretched for miles… Was that a *lake* she saw in the midst of it? Yes, the greenery was edged by skyscrapers but to see nature blooming in the place she'd thought had eradicated everything that wasn't modern soothed her.

She walked the length of the terrace lined with brick flower beds filled with hardy manicured plants feeling that she was walking in a whole new world. It traversed most of the perimeter of the top floor and, even in the parts overlooked by other skyscrapers, remained entirely private. So taken was she with all the magnificence of everything that it took a beat for her to notice on her way back to the bedroom that Ciro had come out too.

Their eyes clashed. Her heart crashed. It took another beat before either of them spoke.

He looked up at the sky. The lines around his eyes crinkled. 'The weather more to your liking?'

'Very much. I'm sorry for oversleeping—I don't think I've ever stayed in bed so late.'

She caught a faint glimpse of his dimples. 'You needed it. Ready for something to eat?'

'Have I missed breakfast?'

'If you want breakfast, have breakfast.'

'Lunch will be fine. Is it okay for me to have a shower first?'

His brow furrowed, his eyes speculative. 'You're an adult, Princess. You don't have to ask.'

'I know…' She shrugged sheepishly. 'It's going to take a while for me to stop feeling like a guest here.'

'Sure.'

He didn't say anything about her *not* being a guest, she noted. 'Can you do me a favour?'

'That depends what it is.'

'Can you stop calling me Princess? It sounds like you're mocking me.'

He bowed his head. 'Sure. Take a shower and then we'll get some lunch.'

He didn't deny that it sounded like a mockery, she noted, glaring at his retreating back.

She followed him back into the bedroom. It didn't surprise her that he'd made himself scarce from it.

Ciro was on a call to his Madrid store manager when Claudia entered the living room.

Gone was the vulnerable waif dressed in pyjamas he'd had a short conversation with on his terrace. In her place stood a woman dressed in a loose cream V-necked top that skimmed her cleavage, smart figure-hugging trousers that rested above her ankles and a bold blue slim-fitting jacket with oversized sleeves. Her dark chestnut hair hung loose and gleamed in the natural light that poured in from the windows. Large hooped gold earrings hung from her pretty ears. Around her shoulders she carried an oversize handbag. She looked dazzling.

He sucked in a breath and immediately found his lungs assailed by her perfume and his loins tightening.

Damn but his attraction to her was accelerating.

He'd slept on the sofa in his library, thinking it a good compromise to sharing his bed. There would be no disarranged guest bed for his staff to notice and he could sleep without being disturbed too. It hadn't worked. His head had been too full of Claudia, imagining her asleep in his bed, remembering the softness of her skin, the swell of her breasts, the firmness of her thighs, all the things he should have banished from his mind, for sleep to come. It had been bad enough during those five weeks she'd dropped off the map but now she was here in the flesh, disturbing him on more levels than he could count. She hadn't been in his home for a day yet and already everything felt different.

Was it the allure of forbidden fruit causing it, his vow never to touch her again perversely making his desire grow? He'd assumed that making love to her once would be enough to sate that desire but the opposite had happened. The way he felt, he didn't dare even touch her.

'Ready to go?' he asked.

She nodded. 'Where are we eating?'

'I thought we could go to my restaurant for lunch.'

'You have a restaurant?'

'In the store.'

He led the way to the elevator, passing Marcy, who was on a call and lifted a hand to acknowledge them.

The elevator stopped two floors down and the doors opened. Ciro stepped out and waited for Claudia to follow.

She didn't move. Her eyes were wide as she took in the vast expanse before her. If he hadn't stuck his foot in, the doors would have closed with her still in it.

'*This* is your department store?' she asked, finally leaving the elevator.

'This is my flagship store,' he confirmed. 'The biggest of the Trapani department stores and the hub of my business.'

'It's *huge*.' Claudia had never been in a place like it. They didn't make department stores like this in Sicily. It wasn't just the size that stole her breath but the richness of the décor…the *beauty* of it all. 'That explains the perfume.'

'What perfume?'

'When we entered the building yesterday I smelt perfume. I wondered where it came from.' They were on what was obviously the homeware floor but the scent of perfume was still strong. 'I didn't know you lived above one of your stores.'

'I have apartments above all of them. It makes life easier for me.'

She remembered him saying he owned twenty-one department stores across Europe, North America and the

Middle East and that he planned to open many more. 'But this is your main home, isn't it?'

He nodded.

They walked through the finely dressed shoppers bustling around them. Claudia's eye caught a display of quirky and beautiful vases. She leaned closer to look at a jade-green one shaped like a swan and concentrated on its price tag. The numbers were a blur so she counted them… Five figures before the decimal point! She stepped back sharply before she could accidentally knock it over.

Her eye was next caught by a display of top-of-the-range electronic food mixers with more attachments than she'd known existed.

'I thought you were hungry,' Ciro said, his voice bemused.

'I am but these are amazing. Look at this—it chops, whisks, blends, kneads and…' Her voice tailed off as embarrassment at getting as excited over a food mixer as a child got over a bag of sweets suddenly curdled in her.

'Tell me the colour you want and I'll have one sent up to the apartment for you.'

She shook her head and started walking again, following her sense of smell in the direction of warm food now wafting in the air around them. 'You don't have to humour me.'

'I'm not humouring you.'

'I can't afford it.' Her heart wrenched to remember all the baking equipment she'd left behind in Sicily, left when she'd thought she would return to them and use them every summer as a cherished wife.

A warm hand caught hold of her wrist and stopped her walking.

She twisted round and almost slammed into him.

Shocked at the blast of heat his proximity sent through

her, she stepped back, only to barge into a passing shopper. Embarrassed anew, she apologised profusely. When she turned back to Ciro, she caught him wiping the hand he'd caught hold of her with on his trousers and her embarrassment tripled.

'I'm not humouring you,' he repeated, acting as if there were nothing wrong with erasing the feel of her from his skin. 'You can have whatever you like from the store. It all belongs to me. Take whatever you like from any floor whenever you like. I'll let the staff know.'

Further embarrassed to be made to feel like a charity case from an unwilling benefactor, she nodded, knowing she would never take anything from these shelves. She would let Ciro feed her and give her a roof to live under, but she would never take anything else from him, not when the mere touch of her skin repelled him.

She kept pace with him as they walked past a queue of beautifully dressed people snaking out of the restaurant door and into a room so plush and elegant that she gasped. The store's restaurant had to be a destination in itself.

They were led to a window table by a fawning waiter. Leather-bound menus were placed in front of them.

'Shall we eat off the lunch menu or do you want something more substantial?' Ciro asked.

'The lunch menu's fine.' When she looked up, he'd opened his menu and was peering through it. She pretended to study hers too.

'What do you fancy?'

'I don't know.' How could she tell him she couldn't read their own language, never mind a foreign one? He thought her stupid enough as it was without her confirming it for him. She'd been lucky with the few restaurants he'd taken her to during their courtship as the waiting staff had always recited the specials of the day and she'd always pounced on one of them as her choice. 'What do you recommend?'

He raised a shoulder but didn't look at her. 'It's all good.'

She closed her menu and pushed it to one side. 'Why don't you order for me?'

He lifted his head, a furrow in his brow. 'Has the fact it's the twenty-first century passed you by? Or are you too used to doing Daddy's bidding to think for yourself?'

Angry, humiliated heat seared her skin. 'That's offensive.'

He didn't look in the slightest bit chastened. 'You admitted last night that you've never said no to your father before. That implies you always do his bidding. You ask permission to have a shower and now you're asking me to choose the food you eat? That's the behaviour of a child. You're an adult. It's time you started acting like one.'

'I'd say putting our baby above my own feelings and being here with you means I'm already doing that,' she snapped back, 'So keep your character assassination to yourself.'

If she'd had any thought of confessing her inability to read or write, he'd just killed it. To tell him the truth would be tantamount to giving him a loaded gun to use against her.

Luckily, the waiter returned to their table to take their order. Ciro indicated for her to order first.

Managing a small smile for the waiter, she said, 'I'm in the mood for something light but filling. What do you recommend?'

Ciro smothered his annoyance. Claudia, he was learning, had a strong-headed stubborn streak in her, traits she must have inherited from her father, and as he thought this his mood soured further.

He kept telling himself that she'd had nothing to do

with her father's plot against his, but while that was true she should have opened her eyes. Wilful ignorance was no excuse.

He drank some lemon-infused water and looked at her. She was staring out of the window, ignoring him.

A change of subject was needed. 'What do you intend to do to occupy your time before the baby's born?'

She turned her head slowly to face him. Long, dark lashes swept downwards before she answered. 'I have no idea.'

'Are there things you've always wanted to try or do but have never been able to before?'

'Not anything in particular.'

'New York is a big, diverse city. I doubt there is anything you can dream of doing that you can't do here. You can finish your education. Take classes. Learn new skills. Anything you want.'

'I don't drive. Getting around will be hard for me.'

'There you go—you can have driving lessons.'

Her fingers tightened around her glass. 'I've had lessons. Driving is not for me.'

Ciro found his own fingers tightening too. For all her stubbornness, Claudia was a sheep. A follower. Someone who hung back, having no dreams, no plans or hopes for the future. He didn't understand how anyone could be that way. As his mother had said many times, Ciro had been born with fire in his belly. He'd been restless to leave Sicily and get out into the big wide world. He'd wanted to experience everything the world had to offer and make a name for himself. He'd succeeded beyond his wildest dreams. Claudia's apathy was alien to him.

'Most New Yorkers use public transport,' he informed her.

Her eyes widened. He detected alarm. He supposed public transport was beneath this pampered princess. 'Don't worry, I wouldn't expect you to mix with the general public. I'll have a driver put on standby for you.'

If he hadn't been watching so closely he'd have missed the almost imperceptible shudder she gave at the suggestion.

His irritation grew. 'Happy to spend the next seven, eight months just hanging around the apartment, are you?'

A flash of anger reflected back at him from the doe-like eyes. 'I've only just got here and already you're looking at ways of getting me out from under your feet?'

'It's not my feet you'll be under, Princess. I don't spend much time in the apartment—I've taken today off to help you settle in but tomorrow I'm off to Los Angeles for a couple of days.'

'I've asked you not to call me that. And do I assume that your trip means you're intending to deal with me the way you'd intended to before? Install me in your apartment and then run away so you don't have to deal with me to my face?'

'I'll be back by the weekend. We can spend all the time together you want then.'

'If you're just going to keep picking on me and criticising me then I'd rather not bother.'

'I'm not picking on you.'

'Aren't you? It seems that you're determined to find fault with me. You assumed I wouldn't want to use public transport because I have a dislike of the general public. How dare you assume that? I don't think I'm better than anyone else—I *know* I'm not.'

'I didn't mean it like that.'

'I've asked you not to lie to me. That's exactly what you meant. How can you get to know the real me if you keep making assumptions to suit your own prejudices?

Do you have any idea how sheltered my upbringing was? I've never used public transport in my life! The thought of using it here in a city as dangerous as this—the thought of going *anywhere* in this city alone—is terrifying for me.' She looked back out of the window. Her jaw was tight, her throat moved, and she was blinking a lot…

With a muttered curse, Ciro realised she was on the verge of tears. Before he could even think of addressing it, the waiter brought their lunch to their table.

When they were alone again, she picked up her fork and stabbed a chunk of avocado.

Thankful she'd held the tears at bay—he was *useless* at dealing with crying women, even if their tears were of the crocodile variety—he attempted to moderate his tone. 'Where did you get the impression New York's such a dangerous place?'

She didn't look at him. 'From my father.'

'He told you that?'

A short nod and then the avocado disappeared into her mouth.

'I don't know where he got that impression from but it isn't true. It hasn't been true in decades. Sure, there are areas it's best to avoid but all cities have those areas.'

'He told me about it when I left school. I wanted to visit America and see all the landmarks from the movies I loved but he explained how dangerous America and the rest of the world really is.'

Blood pulsed in his temples to imagine her as a child watching the same movies as he'd watched and formulating similar dreams. The difference was Claudia had been all too easily dissuaded from following hers. Nothing on earth could have dissuaded Ciro from following his dreams.

'And you believed him?' he asked.

'Why wouldn't I?'

'You didn't think to do your own research?'

She gave a sharp shake of her head. Her face, he noted, had turned the same colour as the cherry tomato she'd just popped into her mouth.

'Do you just take whatever anyone tells you as gospel?' he pushed, his disdain towards her growing. 'Five minutes researching crime statistics would have given you the truth.'

After a long beat she put her fork on her plate, her elbow on the table and rested her forehead in her hand. 'Ciro… Please, stop this.' After another long beat she raised her eyes to meet his. Sadness and defeat shone at him. 'I couldn't do my own research because I can't read.'

Ciro stared at her, wondering what on earth she was talking about. 'Can't read what? Off an electronic screen?'

'Letters. Words. I can't read anything.'

'What the…?' He cut himself off. He shook his head. He blinked. He shook his head again. 'What kind of joke is that? Of course you can read. I've seen you.'

'No, you haven't.'

'I have. In my library last night.'

'I was holding the book, not reading it. I would give *anything* to be able to read it.'

'But I've seen you read through menus…' And then his skin chilled as he thought back thirty minutes to when she'd asked him to order for her and then stubbornly got the waiter to recommend a dish when he'd refused.

And then he remembered how during their months of courting she'd always chosen from the specials board after it had been recited by whoever was serving them.

He shook his head again to clear the white noise filling it. 'But you're obviously well read. You can tell by the language people use. And you've mentioned books you've read.'

'Books I've *enjoyed*,' she contradicted softly. 'Imma introduced me to audio books when I was fourteen. I love listening to them.'

'But...' He swallowed. He'd known Claudia for over three months now. He'd married her. She carried his child. How could he not know something so fundamental about her? 'How the hell can anyone reach the age of twenty-one without learning to read?'

'I've recently discovered that I'm dyslexic. Severely dyslexic.' She bit into her bottom lip. 'I never knew it. I thought the same as everyone else that I'm just stupid.'

'You're not stupid.' That was one thing he could say with certainty.

She smiled wanly then picked her fork up and stabbed a prawn. 'I don't see letters as other people do. To me they're just squiggles. The written word means absolutely nothing to my brain. It never has.'

His appetite gone, Ciro pushed his plate to one side. 'Why didn't you tell me this before?'

She inhaled through her nose and stared back out of the window. She spoke so softly he had to strain to hear the words. 'I was ashamed.'

'Of what?'

And then she turned her face back to him. Her eyes glistened. 'Of being illiterate. Men like you...'

'Men like me?'

'You could have married anyone you wanted. You were my only choice and I was desperate to marry you.' Her voice barely rose above a whisper. 'I had all these crazy feelings for you and I wanted the freedom you represented so badly. I was terrified that if you knew the truth you'd have second thoughts and call the wedding off.'

Ciro expelled a long breath slowly. 'What made you think that?'

'Because you're so successful and have such *confidence*. You're not scared of anything and anything you set your mind to do, you do it. Look at all this…' There was a spark of animation in her eyes as she made a circular motion with her hand. 'I can't begin to imagine how hard you've worked and the drive you needed to create it all. I'm only telling you about my dyslexia now because it's *horrible* knowing you think of me as pampered and lazy for not being career-minded. It's not because I don't want to be but because I *can't*, just as I couldn't dispute what my father told me about the world—I had no way to check even if I'd wanted to. Imma was at university so she wasn't part of the conversation and none of Papà's staff were going to contradict him. Technology has made my life easier recently and I have a voice-activated phone that can read messages and the pages of websites aloud to me but back then, I had *nothing*. I believed Papà because I had no reason to think he'd lie to me.'

Ciro's head spun, thought upon thought running through his head, guilt roiling his stomach. How had he not picked up on this before? Now that she'd told him, he could see all the signs he'd missed. Normally, he didn't miss anything but with Claudia…

With Claudia he'd ignored the signs because, as she'd rightly pointed out, he'd had preconceived prejudices against her and had used them to suit his preconceived assumptions.

'I'm hopeful that now I know the cause of my illiteracy I might be able to get some help for it,' she said after a long period of silence passed between them while Ciro tried to put some order to his thoughts. 'But please, let me adjust to my new life here first. This is all very overwhelming for me.'

He rubbed his temples and blew out more air. 'You

should have told me before. You're the one who keeps going on about honesty.'

'I know,' she whispered. 'I was scared. I'm sorry.'

Somcthing squeezed around his heart to see the despondency in her eyes and he found himself saying, 'I'll be in LA until Friday. How about we spend the weekend exploring the city and our neighbourhood together? It'll do you good to become familiar with everything and then you'll be able to judge for yourself if New York's as scary as you think it is.'

She considered this for a moment before nodding. 'That would be nice.'

'It's settled, then. And, Claudia… I'm sorry if I upset you. That was never my intention.'

Her eyes held his before she gave a sad smile. 'Wasn't it?'

CHAPTER EIGHT

CLAUDIA LAY ON the library's reading sofa listening to her favourite book being narrated through her headphones. Outside the closed door she heard distant voices and movement but as Ciro's apartment was currently filled with his cleaning staff, she didn't think much of it. In the four days she'd been here, she'd become as accustomed to their presence as she'd been when living at home. The one good thing was that Ciro's staff didn't live in. They came in daily to clean and sort the laundry and then left.

She'd spent the two evenings Ciro had been in LA alone. The first night had been strange and a little frightening. She'd never been alone before. Even the three months in the farmhouse had been spent with her father's security detail on hand if she needed them, her privacy an illusion she'd gone along with because it had been more privacy than she'd ever enjoyed in her life. She'd still been at the mercy of her father's bidding.

Being alone here felt very different. Ciro had left her the number of his concierge, who provided her with anything she required, but there was no feeling of being spied on, no one reporting on her movements…yes, it felt very different. But good.

The only downside had been her stupid mind's refusal to stop thinking about Ciro. After she'd told him about her dyslexia, nothing more had been said about it but she'd sensed a change of mood in him. Whether he thought less of her for it—if it was even possible for him to think less of her than he already did—only time would tell.

She hadn't told him for sympathy but because she'd realised that, without the truth, he'd continue seeing her as spoilt and lazy. It had been the hardest thing she'd ever had to say but she'd rather him think her stupid than think that.

Pushing thoughts of Ciro away for the fiftieth time since she'd laid down, she squeezed her eyes even tighter and tried to concentrate on Elizabeth's verbal sparring with Mr Darcy.

It took a beat for her brain to register the library door open then a further beat for her senses to register the woody cologne diving into her airstream.

Yanking the headphones off, she sat up straight and swung her legs around. 'You're back,' she said, then winced at the stupidity of her observation. Of course he was back. He was standing right in front of her, all tall, dark, brooding machismo.

The butterflies in her stomach awoke with as great a start as she'd done and set about on a violent rampage that in turn set her heart off on a canter.

How was it that every time they parted she forgot how devastating he was? And how was it that every time she saw him after a period apart the intensity of her reaction to him increased?

Aiming for nonchalance, she added, 'Sorry, I didn't think you were due back for a few more hours.'

Her heart jolted from its canter to see his dimples flash then accelerated at a frightening rate.

'I finished sooner than I thought.'

'Did you have a good trip?' She had no idea how she

managed to ask that with the eruption taking place inside her.

Ciro shrugged. LA was his least favourite city and not a place he ever felt enthused about going to. Unless you were a social butterfly, there was nothing to do there. When he travelled for business he always liked to do something new outside business hours, something invigorating. 'It was productive. How have you been?'

He'd been disconcerted to find he'd been the one to call and check that everything was okay. Only the one call, after yesterday's final meeting when he'd been unable to take the silence any more. After the tension during their lunch together and Claudia's shocking dyslexia admission, they'd spent the rest of the day in different parts of the apartment. He'd spent another night in the library. The tension had still been tangible between them when he'd said goodbye the next morning.

She nodded, perhaps a little too vigorously. 'I've been fine, thank you.'

'Good. I need to take a shower—I thought we could go out to eat. Have a think about what you fancy and... What's wrong?' Her eyes had swept away from him to stare at the floor.

Her shoulders rose. 'I thought you'd be tired after all the travelling and meetings so I made Chicken Cacciatore.' Then, more brightly, she continued, 'It doesn't matter, it'll freeze. I'll have it next time you're away.'

He could hardly believe she'd thought to cook for him, especially after the way things had been between them. And now he was thinking about it, he remembered catching the scent of cooking when he'd first walked into the apartment but the kitchen was far enough away from the foyer and the aroma of furniture polish had been strong so it hadn't really registered with him.

'When will it be ready?' he asked.

'It's ready now—it's keeping warm in the oven. I just need to cook the pasta I've made to go with it.'

'Great. I'll have a shower and then we'll eat together.' It took a lot of effort to keep the stiffness from his voice. From the moment he'd stepped into the library everything inside him had tightened, his body automatically waging war on itself. 'I can't remember the last time I ate in the dining room.'

A smile lifted her cheeks. It was a smile that could stop traffic. It certainly stopped his heart from beating effectively. 'You eat like a native New Yorker.'

'How do you know what a native New Yorker eats?'

'I've been getting tips from Marcy.'

His laughter came as automatically as his body's raging war. 'Now, she *is* a native New Yorker.'

Ciro swallowed his first mouthful of Chicken Cacciatore and stared at the woman who'd made it.

Her fork, halfway to her delectable mouth, hovered midair. 'Is it okay?'

'Claudia, this is fantastic.'

Her cheeks stained pink, her pleasure at his compliment obvious.

'I know you like to cook but this is something else—this is restaurant standard.'

Now the staining on her cheeks was of embarrassment. 'Don't be silly.'

'I'm serious. And I say it as someone who's dined in many Michelin-starred restaurants.'

Her furrowed brow showed her continued scepticism but instead of arguing, she popped a forkful of chicken into her mouth.

He had a sip of the wine she'd opened and found it complemented the dish perfectly. 'Who recommended the wine?'

The furrow on her brow deepened. 'It's the wine I always serve with this dish.'

'Are you a secret sommelier?'

'What's a sommelier?'

'A professional wine steward. They're trained to pair food with wine.'

'People are *paid* to do that?' She pulled a musing face. 'As our English nanny used to say, you learn something new every day. Whenever I used to make a new dish I would raid Papà's wine cellar until I found the perfect wine to go with it.'

Ciro fought not to let the clenching of his guts at the mention of her father show on his face. Claudia was making a huge sacrifice to allow him to be father to their child. She must hate him for what he'd done to her but she was putting their baby's needs above her own and he needed to do the same. Somehow he must learn to separate her from her father. If he couldn't, then how could he separate his child from its grandfather?

He'd come to think her insistence on living with him until the birth was the right call.

'Trial and error?' he asked.

She nodded, then gave a sudden giggle. It was so rare and unexpected that it sounded like music to his ears. 'Once, when I was trying out a new Tuscan recipe, I sampled eight bottles of red. He wasn't very happy with me—one of them was a ten-thousand-euro Barolo.'

'Did it pair with the recipe?'

Her initial giggle turned into a peal of laughter. 'No!'

'You clearly have a good nose.'

Shoulders shaking with mirth, she twitched said nose. It was such a ridiculous gesture that Ciro found himself laughing too. He drank some more of the superb wine then looked at Claudia's glass of water. His good humour wilted.

She was drinking water rather than wine, he guessed, because she'd sworn off alcohol for the pregnancy. She'd never struck him as much of a drinker, but, like the majority of their compatriots, was partial to a glass of wine with her evening meal.

Claudia must have sensed a dimming in his mood. 'What's wrong?'

He met the dark brown stare that seemed to read him so easily. 'I'm just thinking how easy men have pregnancy.'

She leaned across the table to pat his hand, her eyes mock-rueful. 'You wait until I'm the size of a whale and craving toothpaste on toast. You won't find it so easy then, having to run around after me.'

It took a moment for her jocular words to penetrate because at the first touch of her skin on his, a jolt of sensation dived through his bloodstream. Claudia must have made her tactile display without thinking for her cheeks suddenly coloured and she quickly removed it, leaving an imprint on the top of his hand so warm it should glow red.

The pads of Claudia's fingers tingled madly, the nerves begging her to reach out and touch him again. She gripped her glass of water tightly and tried to pretend nothing had happened, pretend to be calm but, really, what had she been *thinking*?

She hadn't been thinking. She'd been enjoying the moment and the lowering of their respective barriers and, for a few seconds, had forgotten herself and slipped into an intimacy neither of them wanted.

But…

The butterflies had started off again. In truth, they hadn't shut up since he'd walked into the library. Everything inside her just felt so much more alive when Ciro was around, her senses heightened so much she could feel the drumbeats of her heart and hear the blood whooshing in her veins.

When she dared look at him again, his jawline was as tight as his smile. 'I know very little about pregnancy,' he said, clearly going down the *let's-pretend-that-never-happened* route. 'I'm aware of the physical changes it brings but the rest of it…' He shrugged. 'I know you're going to need my support but you'll have to tell me when you need it because I'm clueless.'

'I don't know much more than you,' she admitted. 'Once we've seen a doctor everything should be clearer.'

'You want me to come with you?'

'You're the father. You should be there.'

'I don't have to travel anywhere next week so I'll get an appointment made for a day then. Does that work for you?'

'My diary's a little full but I'm sure I can rearrange things to fit it in.'

Their eyes held. Her heart skipped to see amusement spark in his stare. And something else. Something that took hold of her skipping heart and squeezed it tightly before releasing it to send blood exploding through her.

Claudia stood in front of the mirror in her dressing room and brushed her hair. She'd had a shower, brushed her teeth and changed into her pyjamas, her usual bedtime routine, but there was nothing usual about how she was feeling. Her stomach churned with such strength she wished she could put it down to pregnancy nausea. But she couldn't. She'd fooled herself before about her feelings, insisting to herself and her sister that she did love Ciro when all along it had been deep attraction mingled with a plaintive need for the freedom he represented. She wouldn't lie to herself again.

But her attraction to Ciro hadn't died. It still burned inside her. There had been a moment towards the end of their meal when their eyes had locked again and she'd suddenly been consumed with memories of the feelings and sensations that had erupted in her when they'd made love. She felt them on her skin now. And inside her too. Ripples of heat low in her pelvis, a hungry ache…

Gritting her teeth, she began plaiting her hair as she always did before bed.

How could she still feel such physical hunger for him? Ciro had played her for a fool in a sick game of revenge. She'd swallowed his lies about love and while she accepted her words of love had been a lie too, she'd never meant to be deceitful. He *had* meant to be deceitful. If she hadn't overheard him, she would still be ignorant of the game he'd been playing. Imma was convinced the Trapani brothers' ultimate aim had been the entire Buscetta family's destruction.

Claudia wanted them to build a supportive relationship for their baby's sake but she would never trust him again.

'We need to get you a dressing table.'

She gave a small scream. So lost had she been in her thoughts she hadn't heard Ciro enter the bedroom. 'You startled me!'

When their meal had finished the semi-easy atmosphere between them had suddenly changed. Conversation had become stilted. Eye contact had ceased. And the charge in her veins…

She'd got up from the table abruptly, frightened of all the feelings rampaging through her. 'I'm going to bed now.'

He'd still had half a glass of wine to drink. He'd looked at her briefly before swirling the dark liquid and giving a short nod. 'Sleep well.'

She hadn't asked if he'd be joining her in the bed. She hadn't known which answer she most wanted to hear.

This was the first time he'd entered the bedroom with her in it since her first morning.

She met his eyes in the reflection of the mirror. A faint smile tugged on his cheeks. 'I'll call out next time.'

Breaking the eye contact, she continued working on the French plait and pretended not to notice Ciro watching her from the dressing room's threshold. She couldn't pretend the butterflies weren't flapping and dancing in her belly or that her usually steady hands didn't have a tremor in them.

Ciro knew he needed to move. The longer he stood watching Claudia plait her beautiful hair, the stronger his yearning to stand behind her and unplait it as he'd done on their wedding night and run his fingers through those silky strands. The stronger his arousal.

When she'd finished the plait, she used a band she'd had wrapped around her wrist to secure it. Her eyes found his again.

He inhaled deeply through his nose. 'I'm going to brush my teeth.'

She answered with a nod but didn't move.

Forcing his body to co-operate with his brain, he performed an abrupt turn and walked to the en suite. Before he stepped in his senses were assailed with the scent of Claudia's shower gel and the mintiness of her toothpaste. His chest closed so tightly he could hardly breathe. He opened the bathroom cabinet, saw her toothpaste and toothbrush in a glass together on the top shelf, and almost smiled to remember her quip about craving toothpaste on toast.

Ciro had personally designed his bathroom. Not once in the planning had he imagined he would one day walk into it and see a woman's toiletries neatly arranged in his cabinet and feel that his heart could pound out of his chest. The cabinet had four shelves. Claudia hadn't moved any of his stuff, her own carefully placed so as not to intrude.

Placing his hands knuckles-down on the sink, he took some more deep breaths. He *must* get a handle on this. He'd decided on the flight back to New York that he couldn't sleep on the library sofa again. He'd torn a muscle in his back a few years ago, one of those injuries that could easily recur without warning. Two nights on a sofa followed by two nights on his firm LA bed had reminded him of the importance of sleeping on a decent mattress.

Claudia was going to live with him for the foreseeable future. He'd agreed they would share a room for a few weeks and it was time to bite the bullet and do it. He had no doubt he was in for some nights of torture but it wasn't for ever, only a few weeks, and then she'd move into a guest room far away from him.

Face washed and teeth brushed, he stripped down to his boxer shorts. No more sleeping nude for him. He'd always assumed he'd have retired before he started thinking about wearing pyjamas. Maybe it was time to bring those pyjama-related retirement plans forward.

Claudia had drawn the curtains and was curled up in bed when he left the en suite. Not until he climbed in beside her did she speak. 'You're sleeping with me?'

'Yes.' He turned the light out.

Plunged into darkness, they lay backs turned, the bed large enough for them both to stretch out without encroaching on the other's space.

The distance wasn't enough. There was not a single cell in his body not alert to Claudia's presence beside him. The thudding of his heart was deafening.

Claudia was afraid to breathe…no, she *couldn't* breathe. From the moment the mattress had made the slight dip to accommodate Ciro's hulking form, her lungs had closed. She was afraid to move. One small movement might find her brushing against him. She squeezed her eyes tightly shut, trying to block out the tingling warmth growing low in her pelvis. She still couldn't breathe. She couldn't hear Ciro breathe either. They both lay with the rigid stillness of one of his statues. They could *be* a couple of statues, lying there as a form of modern art.

Her left arm, tucked at an awkward angle under her pillow, started to ache. But she didn't dare move.

She felt her temperature rise, heating from the inside, the waves flowing to her skin. The four nights she'd already spent in this bed had been without any issue whatsoever. Ciro kept his apartment at a Goldilocks temperature, which she'd found, until this moment, to be just right. The mattress was firm and comfortable, the duvet soft yet heavy, the two cocooning her to sleep as if they'd been designed with her needs in mind. She'd slept better in this bed than she'd ever slept before. But that was then.

Ciro kept as firmly to his side of the bed as she kept to hers. There had to be a foot of empty space between them but her whole body was as hot as if he'd draped himself over her. Her heart thrummed as madly as when he'd kissed her.

Eventually, she could bear it no longer and slowly poked her foot out from under the duvet. It brought a welcome coolness to her foot but the rest of her still burned and her awkwardly placed arm was now killing her. With a burst of impetus, she shoved the duvet off and rolled onto her back. She didn't know which was the greatest relief: the chilly air on her skin or the blood flowing through her left arm and shoulder.

Ciro shifted beside her.

She held her breath. She was quite certain he was still awake.

Awake or not, he didn't make any further movements, not in all the time it took for her to eventually drift into sleep.

CHAPTER NINE

CIRO SLIPPED OUT of bed, slung a pair of shorts on and headed straight to his gym. He needed to work these awful, conflicting, heady feelings out of his system.

He'd woken with an erection to rival the Empire State Building and had been on the verge of waking Claudia with a kiss to the nape of her neck before sanity had washed through the last of his sleepiness.

He'd never known torture like that existed. To lie beside Claudia and not touch her had been as close to hell as he'd ever experienced.

He wished he had the power to accelerate time to the birth of their child. He'd buy her an apartment close enough that he could have easy contact with the baby but far enough away that he wouldn't run the risk of bumping into Claudia.

That day couldn't come soon enough. She hadn't even been here a week and already he could feel himself unravelling at the seams.

Claudia didn't think she'd had a worse night's sleep in her life. The only mercy came when she woke to find Ciro already up and gone. She showered and dressed quickly then wandered to the kitchen to make herself a hot chocolate. She was sipping it on the terrace when he finally appeared, dressed in a black T-shirt and faded jeans and carrying a mug of coffee. She had no idea where in the apartment he'd been hiding.

She tightened her hold on the mug and hoped his eyesight wasn't good enough to see the sudden clatter of her heartbeat.

His eyesight could have been the best in the world and he wouldn't have noticed. He took the seat furthest from her, nodded a tight-lipped greeting without meeting her eye, and swiped his phone on.

'Have you got laryngitis?' she asked after a few minutes of being ignored.

He raised narrowed eyes. 'Why do you ask that?'

'Because you haven't said a word since you joined me. I thought things went pretty well between us over dinner last night but here we are now and you're sitting there ignoring me again. You blow hot and cold…it's hard,' she finished with a shrug.

He put his phone down. So many differing emotions flared in the green of his eyes that, for once, it was difficult to judge what he was thinking. A pulse throbbed on his temple. When he spoke his rich voice was curt. 'I don't know how to be around you.'

'Just be yourself. Isn't that the whole point of this? For us to be honest about who we are? For us to try and forge something that will allow us to be parents together?'

The pulse on his temple seemed to go haywire. 'I'm trying but it's harder than I thought it would be. Much harder. I look at you and see this beautiful, innocent woman who I've treated appallingly and then I remember you're the daughter of the man who killed my father. My heart tells me you were ignorant of his criminal ways, but my head can't see how you lived with someone your entire life and remained blind to his true nature. Forget your dyslexia, you're a smart woman and you're observant. You notice *everything*. So tell me how I'm supposed to believe you were ignorant to who your father really was.'

No one had ever called her smart before but she couldn't savour this unexpected compliment because too many other emotions were swelling inside her.

'There was no one there to contradict him.' Agitated, she put her mug on the table and gathered her hair together. 'I wish I could make you see what it was like for us growing up. I was three when Mamma died. I don't remember anything before that and I don't know if her death made Papà more protective than he would have been.' As she plaited her hair, Claudia wished with all her heart that her sister could be there with her. She missed her badly. Imma would know the right words to say. 'I never had any freedom. Whenever we left the villa it was always with armed guards protecting us, even at school—and our school was probably the smallest and safest in the whole of Sicily. I was never allowed to go to friends' homes like the other girls were. I never mixed with boys. The only people we mixed with were paid by my father. They weren't going to tell us the truth, were they?'

'But you must have known there was something crooked about him. You believed me when I told you what he'd done to my father. If someone had told me something like that about my father I would have laughed in their face because he was a good, honest man with scruples. You believed it without question.'

'It was…' She thought frantically for the right way to explain it. 'I wasn't completely blind. I always knew there was a darkness to Papà and it's something that's scared me since I was a little girl. It's partly what made me so obedient. When you told me what he'd done…something clicked into place. Things I'd been too afraid to talk about, feelings I'd had, things I'd seen and heard that made no sense, the fear that's always lived in me… Like a giant jigsaw puzzle with all the pieces suddenly slotting together. I knew in my heart you were telling the truth. One of the reasons I went to the convent when I left you was because those nuns educated me. They've known me since I was six. Many of them educated my mother. I learned things from them that made other things click into place too.'

'What things?'

'Like my dyslexia. Like the whole of Sicily being frightened of him. That it's not just your family he terrorised. That the home I grew up in comes from money that's been paid for by other people's blood. For you to think I'd be complicit in any of that…' She blinked back hot tears. 'Whatever happens between you and me, I will never go back to him. I'd rather live on the streets.'

Her plait done, she went to pull the band off her wrist to tie it together but her wrist was bare.

For the longest time the only sound was the heaviness of Ciro's breaths. His frame was stiff, his features rigid, his green eyes intent on her face.

And then, slowly, his shoulders loosened and the expression in his eyes softened.

'I'm sorry.' He gave a laugh that sounded rueful rather than humorous. 'I keep having to apologise, don't I?'

She thought of what her father had done to his family and a fresh burn of tears set off behind her eyes. She swallowed them away and croaked, 'This isn't easy for either of us.'

His Adam's apple moved. 'I'm making it harder than it should be. I'll try harder. I promise.'

Their gazes lingered before he drained his coffee. 'I promised to show you around the city. Is there anywhere in particular you'd like to go?'

Relief blew through her veins at the change of subject. Much more of it and she wouldn't have been able to hold the tears back any longer. She didn't want to cry in front of Ciro. She pointed at the sprawling canopy of trees and cleared her throat. 'I'd like to go there.'

'Central Park?'

'*That's* Central Park?' Old childhood movies flashed in her mind. 'Don't they do horse and carriage rides there?'

'They do. Would you like to go on one?'

A sliver of excitement unfurled in her. 'I'd love to.'

'Anything else?'

'I keep thinking I see a castle…'

'That's Belvedere Castle.'

'Can we go there too?'

'We can go anywhere you like.'

Ciro left the elevator and expelled the air he'd been holding the whole way down. Every time he inhaled Claudia's scent his senses ran riot and his fingers itched to touch her. He was grimly determined that however their weekend panned out, he would be cordial and engaging. He hadn't meant to be cruel and ignore her earlier but when he'd walked onto the terrace, the urge to haul her into his arms had been so potent that he'd needed to drag his focus away from her until he'd regained control of himself.

None of this was Claudia's fault. She hadn't asked to be played in his game of vengeance. It wasn't her fault that she intoxicated him.

He had to accept that he'd got her wrong. Everything about her. All wrong.

And now he owed it to her and their baby to try. To really try. And that started now.

His vow almost shattered a moment later when they

went to step outside the building to begin their sightseeing tour and Claudia suddenly grabbed hold of his hand.

The jolt of electricity that rushed through his veins was more powerful than when she'd patted his hand over dinner, but her hold was too tight to shake off.

'Look at all the *people*,' she breathed, eyes wide.

Feeling the fear vibrate through her, and seeing the golden colour of her skin turn ashen, he felt a wave of something like compassion join the electrical rush. And anger.

Cesare had done this to her with his horror stories.

He'd never believed his loathing of the man could increase but in that moment it did.

Relaxing his clenched jaw, he forced a smile to his lips. 'You have nothing to be frightened of. These people are just going about their business, the same as we are.'

'What if I lose you?'

'I'll stick to you like glue.'

She kept her eyes on his for the longest time before taking a deep breath. Dropping his hand, Claudia lifted her chin and stepped onto the bustling street. There was a bravery to her movements that made his heart twist unbearably.

Ciro stepped into the apartment at the same moment Claudia reached the bottom of the stairs. She was still in her pyjamas. Judging by the puffiness of her eyes, she'd only recently woken.

'Good timing,' he said, holding up the paper bag in his hand. 'Breakfast. Shall we eat on the terrace?'

She gave a wide yawn and blinked vigorously, then followed it with a smile.

He walked behind her up the two flights of stairs to the bedroom and through the French doors. Her bottom was only inches from his eyeline…

Claudia, he suddenly realised, had the peachiest bottom in the world. As she normally wore long, loose-fitting tops over slim jeans or trousers, her bottom was usually hidden, but the silk of her pyjamas accentuated its peachiness. It took real effort not to let his gaze lock on it.

'What have we got?' she asked as she sat on the wrought-iron chair with its soft cushion to pad her bottom.

Damn, he was thinking about her bottom. Again.

But how had he not noticed its divine peachiness before?

'Bagels.' He opened the bag and removed the contents. 'This one is egg, cheese and bacon.' He pulled the second bagel out. 'This is avocado, bacon and cream cheese. Take your pick.'

She smiled, enthusiasm and gratitude flashing in her eyes. 'These smell delicious. I've never had a bagel before.'

He popped the lip of his coffee lid then remembered the carton in his pocket. 'I got you peach juice.' The one real pregnancy symptom Claudia was suffering was her stomach recoiling from coffee.

'*Peach* juice? Is that a thing?'

'Orange juice,' he corrected, silently cursing himself for his slip of the tongue. 'I meant orange juice. Please, take your pick of the bagels.'

'Which one do you want?'

'Stop being polite and take one.' She went for the avocado. Her lips parted and she took a generous bite. As she chewed, her eyes met his, beaming her pleasure at him.

Arousal, which he'd been fighting since following her up the stairs, broke free and shot through him like a heated blade.

Damn, damn, damn.

Mercifully, the table hid the discomfort he was experiencing in his trousers. Thank God he'd be leaving for the office soon and could put some distance between them.

He needed it. Three nights spent trying to sleep beside Claudia coupled with two days showing her around their immediate neighbourhood and some of the sights New York had to offer had done nothing to dent his awareness. Familiarity had not lessened his attraction to her one iota. The opposite had occurred. Saturday night had been worse than Friday, the image of her delighted face when they'd taken the horse and carriage ride a continual flash behind his retinas.

Yesterday, Sunday, he'd been determined to exhaust himself enough that he crashed out the moment his head hit the pillow. They'd walked for miles, followed by a long evening watching a Broadway show. He'd still hit his pillow with energy to burn. He'd still lain on his bed with heat raging through his loins and every one of his senses attuned to the woman sleeping with her back to him.

He watched her fold her wrapper into a neat square before placing it back in the paper bag.

He wanted to reach out and pull her to him. He wanted that peachy bottom on his lap and grinding into his arousal…

He finished his bagel with one large bite and pushed his chair back. 'I should get to work.'

Claudia could hardly comprehend the wrench she felt at this.

The weekend they'd shared had gone much better than she'd hoped. Clearing the air of her bottled-up feelings had definitely helped and she vowed never to hold back from speaking her mind again.

They'd walked for miles and talked for hours. Who would have thought they'd share a love for old Hollywood movies? Who'd have believed their top ten movies shared seven in common?

But what had really touched her was the way Ciro had

accommodated her dyslexia without being asked and without it even being mentioned. At the American Museum of Natural History, he'd read the exhibit descriptors to her just as he now read menus to her and all without making it obvious and heaping embarrassment on her. He simply took it in his stride and not once did he patronise her.

And now he was going to work and the weekend they'd shared would be officially over.

It scared her how badly she wished he would stay.

She shouldn't feel like this. One nice weekend with this man didn't change what he'd done to her or alter the fact that she couldn't trust him. She was only here for their baby. He only let her be here for the baby.

But still she wished he would stay.

'Of course,' she said steadily. 'And I should shower. I hope your day goes well.'

The violence in her stomach was as frightening as her wayward thoughts and, terrified she really would ask him to stay, she got hurriedly to her feet but, in her haste, her thigh bashed against the table. Before she had time to register what was happening, Ciro's barely touched coffee toppled over. The lid flipped off and hot black liquid gushed over the table and spilled onto his lap.

Horror spilled through her as quickly as the coffee had spilled. 'Oh, God, Ciro, I'm *sorry*,' she cried, hurrying over to him. 'Are you hurt?'

He looked more disbelieving than pained. His gaze drifted to his lap. The coffee had spilt over his left thigh and soaked through the fabric of his charcoal trousers. There were splatters of black coffee on his white shirt too.

Guilt and panic set in. 'You need to take those off.'

He held a hand up to her, an unspoken warning to keep back. 'I'm not hurt.'

Getting to his feet, he strolled into the bedroom and disappeared into the en suite, closing the door behind him.

Claudia hovered outside the door, wringing her hands together. When she couldn't stand the wait any longer, she knocked on it. 'Ciro? Are you okay? Is there anything I can do?'

More long minutes passed before the door opened. Ciro had stripped his clothes off down to his snug black boxer shorts. She looked down to his thighs and was horrified to see the left one marked a bright, angry red.

Covering her mouth, she burst into tears. She'd never done anything to harm anyone before, not ever, and to see the damage she'd inflicted on his thigh was more than she could bear. 'I'm…so…sorry,' she gulped between sobbing breaths.

Now a pained look did cover his face. Through the muffling of her ears, she heard him curse and then found herself pulled against his chest, his strong arms wrapping around her and holding her tightly to him.

'Don't cry. It was an accident,' he murmured into her hair.

Trying desperately to control her tears, Claudia tried even harder not to sink into him. Being held like this, Ciro's warm breath brushing through her hair, her cheek pressed against his smooth chest, his heartbeat strong against her ear, breathing in his woody scent…it all just felt so *right*.

But, much as she wanted to stay right where she was, Ciro was injured and she reluctantly pulled out of his hold and gazed up at him. 'We need to get you to hospital.'

He smoothed her hair from her face. There was a tenderness to the gesture that made her want to cry harder. 'I messaged my doctor a few minutes ago. He'll be here shortly. I'm supposed to run cold water over the injury while I wait for him.'

'Then what are you doing comforting me?' Snatching hold of his hand, she led him back into the bathroom. 'Get in the bath.'

A wry smile played on his lips as he obeyed her bossy command, a smile that turned into a wince when he lifted his left leg in.

'How can you say it doesn't hurt?' Her heart hurt even more to see his obvious pain. She took the shower head off its attachment and turned the cold tap on.

'It didn't…' His eyes widened as she aimed the shower head on his injury. 'That's *cold*.'

She wiped the last of her tears away with the back of her free hand and attempted a smile. 'It's supposed to be.'

Ciro gritted his teeth against the pain, rested his head back and closed his eyes. He knew from experience that concentrating on the pain only made it worse. 'Talk to me.'

'About what?'

'Anything.' From feeling no pain, his thigh now felt as if someone had taken a blowtorch to it. 'Distract me. What did you dream of being when you were a little girl?'

'Working in a pastry shop.'

He opened one eye, about to query this unexpected answer. His attention was immediately taken by sight of her pyjama top. The spray from the showerhead had soaked into it. The white pyjama top had become translucent. Claudia's cherry-red nipples jutted out in all their erotic glory mere inches from his face.

Oblivious, she elaborated. 'Our nanny used to take us to a pastry shop every Saturday for a treat. We were allowed to choose one item and it could be whatever we wanted. I could never make my mind up because I wanted everything.'

He managed a pained laugh and dragged his gaze from her breasts to her eyes. Her eyes were every bit as beautiful as her breasts.

Still holding the spray on his thigh, she smiled, showing her small, pretty white teeth. 'What did *you* want to be?'

'A world-famous wrestler.'

Her peal of laughter cut through his pain like balm. 'And when did you decide that conquering the business world was better than being a wrestler?'

'When Papà told me it was all choreographed.' He shook his head in mock-sadness. 'He destroyed my dreams.'

'Liar.' She lifted the showerhead and aimed it at his chest, making him shudder at the unexpected blast of wet cold. Her grin widened at his reaction before she aimed it back on his injury.

'You have an evil streak in you.'

'So I'm learning.'

Their eyes locked together and, without any warning, Ciro found himself trapped in the molten depths of Claudia's beguiling eyes. Her smile dropped in a mirror image of his own disintegrating smile as a powerful charge surged between them. It happened so quickly he was powerless to stop it, powerless to stop the wave of unfiltered desire that crashed through him.

He wanted this woman more than he'd wanted anyone or anything in his life. Torture did not begin to describe how it felt to lie beside her night after night and not be able to touch her.

Why couldn't he touch her? In that moment, all his reasoning had flown out of the window. Every cell in his body vibrated in awareness of this ravishing woman. And, for the first time since their wedding night, he felt her body's vibrations of awareness of him too. It was there in the sudden shallowness of her breaths, in the heated swirling in her eyes, in the way she leaned closer to him…just as he leaned closer to her. The charge bound them both. He ached to touch her. To kiss her. To devour her. To mark her as his for ever…

Their faces had drawn so close together that he was inches from claiming those generous lips for his own when the intercom buzzed.

Claudia's eyes widened and she reared back. The showerhead slipped from her fingers and the cold water sprayed over his groin. The erection he hadn't noticed form—there had been too many other heightened sensations coursing through him to be aware of something as trivial as an erection—immediately deflated in protest at the frigid spray.

'That will be the doctor,' he managed to say as he grabbed the showerhead and saved his groin from frostbite. His words sounded faint inside the drumming of his head. 'If you press the top intercom button it will open the door for him.'

She blinked and nodded with equal rapidity, no longer looking at him. Her cheeks had turned the colour of tomatoes. 'I'll show him the way up.'

She was halfway out of the door moving at a speed that would have made a short-distance runner proud when he called after her. 'Claudia?'

She waited a beat before turning back to face him.

'You might want to change before you greet the doctor.'

She followed his gaze down to her chest. Immediately, she slapped an arm over her breasts. He didn't think there was a colour on the spectrum that could describe the colour cloaking her embarrassment.

CHAPTER TEN

'CAN I GET you anything else before I go to bed?'

Ciro's chest expanded at the melodious sound of Claudia's voice. He looked up from his book to see her enter the living room carrying two mugs of steaming hot chocolate, and found it expanding even more. 'I'm good, thank you.'

'You're sure?'

'I'm sure.'

Since the doctor left, Claudia had fussed around him like a mother hen. Her guilt at his burn—only minor, the damage only on the surface of the skin—was obvious but he had a strong feeling she would have looked after him even if she didn't feel responsible for it. As much as he'd always believed anyone with Buscetta blood's heart was stone, this day had proven as nothing else could that Claudia's heart was as soft as her skin.

Ciro's need for space away from her had been thwarted and they'd spent a whole day and evening together alone, trapped in the apartment. The torture of his nights had spilled over to his day and there had been no relief.

Whether Claudia had been whipping up delights in the kitchen or keeping him company in the living room watching an old movie they'd both loved as kids, he'd never been so aware of another human's presence. The gentle sway of her walk, the sound of her footsteps, the way she used her hands as an additional expression of speech, the way she pulled her knees to her chest and crossed her ankles when resting on the sofa… Every movement she made, every word she spoke, every breath she took, all soaked through his senses.

For once she wore something other than jeans or pyjamas, having matched one of her preferred loose tops with a short black skirt. Not only did she have the peachiest bottom in the world, but the shapeliest legs to match it.

With a shy smile, she put one of the mugs on the small table beside the reclining leather armchair he'd stretched out on, then drifted past him to stand at one of the living-room windows, cradling her own drink.

There was a long pause of silence while she gazed down at the bustling street storeys below. 'What made you move to New York?'

'New York's an old obsession of mine from when I was a kid. Vicenzu came to university here, I visited, fell in love with it for real and followed in his footsteps.'

'But it's so big and so *busy*.' She sighed. 'Every time I step outside I think I'm going to get swallowed up. How do you get used to it?'

He put his book down and reached for his drink. 'I remember the moment I got out of the cab on my first visit here. I felt like a kid seeing Santa. I never had to get used to it because right from that moment, I knew I was exactly where I wanted to be.'

'Do you ever miss home?'

Home, he knew, meant Sicily.

He stretched his neck. 'Sometimes. When I hear a song my *mamma* likes or catch a movie I watched with my father.'

She looked at him and bit into her bottom lip. 'How is your *mamma* doing?'

He gave a heavy shrug and cleared his throat. 'She takes things a day at a time.'

Her eyes closed as if she were saying a silent prayer. 'Has it helped her, being back in her own home?'

Ciro didn't know how to explain things without hurting her. But with Claudia, only the truth would do. 'She doesn't want to live in it without my father.'

Her eyes widened and immediately filled with tears.

'Their marriage…it was solid, you know?'

She shook her head and he remembered she'd grown up without a mother.

'They loved us, me and Vicenzu, but they adored each other. When I was a teenager I would work with Papà in the school holidays…he always hoped one of us would take the business on…and I remember going into his office. I must have been fifteen, and he was chatting with his lawyer explaining why he didn't want to merge with an American conglomerate. He'd already turned down their offer of a buy-out. I think he'd accepted by then neither Vicenzu or I would take the business on but he hoped grandkids would come along and one of them would want it. But he turned down the big bucks for the buy-out and then he turned down the offer of a merger even though it would have given him financial stability. The olive industry can be precarious because you're at the mercy of the weather. One bad summer and the crop's ruined. He turned the merger down because it would have meant frequent travelling to America. He had a picture of Mamma on his lap and I *knew* he was turning it down because he couldn't bear to be parted from her. Mamma hates travelling. She'll fly to Florence to visit her sister and that's enough for her.'

'Are you close to her?'

'Not as close as I should be,' he admitted. 'And it's entirely my fault. I couldn't wait to get out of Sicily. It was nothing against my parents, I just had this drive to get out into the world and make my mark. It was always in me. I remember thinking when I overheard that conversation between Papà and his lawyer that he was a fool. How could he turn all that money down? It would have set him up for life. But that was teenage arrogance on my part. I'm happy travelling the world and building an empire. My parents were happy living a simple life. Don't get me wrong, we had money. We never went without. But it wasn't a great fortune.' And certainly hadn't been enough to protect the business against Cesare's sabotage. 'All they wanted was to be together and for their boys to be happy. That was enough for them.'

There was a sharp stabbing in his guts as he thought, for the first time, about what his father would say if he knew his son had married a woman in vengeance. His father's heart had been big and generous.

He would be ashamed of him.

For the first time, Ciro could admit that he was ashamed of himself.

His parents had raised him well. He'd had love. A lot of love. He'd had their time. He'd had security. He'd had everything a child could ask.

They had raised him to be better than this.

'Do you have any memories of your mother?' he asked, suddenly keen to turn the subject away from himself. Claudia's mother, he'd learned, had died of bacterial meningitis, a swift and deadly disease if not treated early.

She tilted her head, her face screwing with concentration. 'Her shoes. I remember she had a pair of bright red heels. I remember trying to walk in them. I was so little they swallowed my feet.'

He swore his heart tore a shred. 'That's all you remember?'

'I think I remember her perfume. Sometimes I'll smell someone's perfume and it makes me think of her.'

Ciro knew exactly what she meant. In the five weeks Claudia had hidden away in the convent he'd imagined he'd smelt her perfume numerous times.

'I went in a perfume shop a few years ago trying to find it,' she said. 'I spent hours in there, spraying them all. I wanted to find it so badly but none of them was quite right. None of them was The One.'

Another shred tore from his heart. 'Didn't you ask your father?'

'He said Mamma wore lots of different perfumes. Imma doesn't remember the name of it either.'

'She was eight when your mother died, wasn't she?'

She nodded. 'Sometimes I envy all the memories she has of her. Imma's five years older than me so had five extra years with her. She remembers everything about her, right down to the softness of her skin and the texture of her hair. All I have is a vague sense of her perfume and a clear memory of one pair of shoes.'

'No wonder you envy your sister.'

'No, I envy her memories. She has the memories but she also has the pain. I was too young for Mamma's death to affect me much, but Imma…' Her chest rose. 'She never got over it. Her childhood ended that day.'

And, he suspected, Claudia's childhood had changed dramatically from the one she would have had if her mother hadn't died. There had been no one to counter her father's dominance and remove the clips he'd put on his daughters' wings.

The ideas Ciro had had about her growing up as a pampered princess were nothing but his own preconceived prejudices, just as everything else about Claudia had turned out to be.

As if she'd followed the train of his thoughts, she said, 'What my father did to your parents…' Her voice broke. 'Ciro, I wish I could take it all back. I wish I'd never told Papà I wanted my own house. Every time I think of calling him, I remember what he did to your father and God alone knows who else and I feel *sick*. How can a man who does the things he does call himself a child of God? How can he sleep at night? I don't understand it. I don't think I want to understand it.'

'Listen to me.' He straightened in his seat and stared at her, making sure he had her full attention. 'You are not responsible for what your father did.'

'If I hadn't mentioned my wish for a home of my own…'

'Don't think like that. None of this was your fault.' And it made him queasier than the most violent of hangovers to remember how he'd held her equally culpable.

One solitary teardrop fell. 'You believe me?'

'Yes.' Claudia would never be party to anything that hurt another person. If he hadn't been full of such rage and carried such a thirst for vengeance, he would have recognised that the first time he met her.

He just wished he'd realised the truth before destroying her life. How he would live with the guilt, he did not know.

Throat moving hard, chin wobbling, she rubbed her eyes with the palms of her hands then blew out a long puff of air. 'You don't know what that means to me.'

He could see what it meant.

Their eyes locked. Familiar, dangerous emotion fisted inside him. Trapped with only Claudia, he'd found himself staring at her too many times with a thudding heart and arousal coiling in his loins…and caught her staring back at him too many times to deny any longer that something was happening between them.

Under the soft lighting, he saw the flush cover her

face before she looked away and murmured, 'I should get to bed.'

The dangerous feelings raging through him grew as she walked softly to him. She leaned down to pick up his empty mug. The fabric from her top brushed against his arm. Her scent swirled in his senses and that was the moment his hand took control and decided this was not something he could fight any longer.

He caught her loose plait and gently closed his fingers around it.

Time became suspended in the moment it took for her to turn her face towards him. Her chest rose and fell in short, ragged bursts and when those beautiful doe-like eyes locked onto his…

He lost the ability to breathe.

Claudia found herself caught. Trapped. Not in Ciro's light hold of her plait but in the weight of emotions pulsing from his eyes.

Her chest tightened and squeezed the air from her lungs. He slowly dragged his fingers to the base of the plait then released it to brush his fingers up her spine to her shoulder. Thrills raced through her. Every nerve ending in her body tingled in heightened anticipation of what he would do next.

He cupped the nape of her neck and gently pulled her to him.

Her heart thumped too hard for any other sound to penetrate. The ache she carried for him became a pulse of need that throbbed and swelled deep inside her. Ciro's breath swirled lightly over her lips and she closed her eyes to savour the sensation and its chocolatey warmth.

Her concentration had been shot since that moment in the bathroom when she'd been certain he was going to kiss her. She'd cooked and baked manically but her mind kept drifting back to their wedding night, her body reawakening to the memories with a vengeance that kept her short of breath. Everything she'd done and said since their almost-kiss had been with a heated weight in her pelvis and a fizz in her veins. Every time their eyes locked she'd felt such need rip through her that she'd had to hold onto something to stop her weakened legs swaying.

The hand not cupping her neck flattened against her cheek. His ragged breaths grew hotter and hotter against her tingling mouth until the firmness of his lips pressed against hers and every cell in her body melted.

His kiss was slow. Incredibly slow. Sensuous. An exploration. An erotic fusion that sent dizzying thrills soaring through her. One hand massaged her neck, the other caressed her cheek before gliding down her arm and winding across her back.

He pulled back to gaze into her eyes. There was pain in the green depths but it was a pain she understood, a pain she shared. It was the pain of a desire grown so big it could no longer be contained. A groan vibrated through his powerful chest and with one effortless tug, he pulled her onto his lap and sealed their bodies together. And then he devoured her mouth with the hunger of a starving man.

Oh, but this kiss was *everything.*

Claudia had been raised to believe only men craved sex and that women endured it. Her attraction to Ciro had been instant, there right from the start, but she'd been too frightened of the act itself to imagine it with anything but a broad brush. She'd hungered for Ciro but not for sex… Not until she'd spent the most magical night of her life with him. Everything she'd discovered only hours later had shattered her innocence more than the deed itself, but the memories of that time with him had refused to die.

Ciro had ignited a fire in her belly. Attempts to dampen

it had come to nothing. The long nights sharing a bed with him, aching for his touch, longing for the magic that had made her one and only time with him so incredible had made her hunger for him turn into its own life force. She craved him. She ached for his touch, yearned to experience the wonder of it again without fear and simply enjoy the incredible sensations he roused in her and the closeness they'd shared.

Chests fused together, their mouths moved at a ferocious tempo. Ciro's hands roved everywhere, sweeping over her back and down her sides, over her thighs, cupping her bottom and then moving back up to tug her hairband off and throw it to one side. His fingers worked quickly to undo the plait and then ran through her hair until it fell like a sheet over them both and he turned his face to inhale its scent.

Holding her securely, he lay back on the recliner, taking her with him until she was straddling him and their lips locked together again. Claudia kissed him with all the passion contained in her soul and then she kissed his neck, marvelling at the strength of it, the woody scent and smoothness of his skin, before finding his mouth again and melting into more of their erotic lip-play. While their mouths and tongues danced their seductive duel, Ciro lifted her top up. Somehow she managed to free her arms without having to move her mouth from his but to get it over her head meant breaking the lock. She shifted her position so her weight wasn't on his burn…and immediately felt the hardness of his erection right there between her legs. The pulse that tore through her was so powerful that she had no control of the moan that flew from her mouth.

Dazed, she reared back to stare into his eyes again, needing to see as well as feel that these dizzying feelings weren't hers alone. It felt as if her heart could beat right out of her chest.

He reached an arm up to rub the backs of his fingers down her cheek, his voice hoarse as he said, 'What are you doing to me?'

She had no idea what he was talking about.

He must have understood her ignorance. He cupped her cheeks and pulled her down so the tips of their noses touched. 'I have never wanted anyone the way I want you.'

The potency of his words was thrillingly immediate. She kissed him. 'I've never wanted anyone. Only you.'

Ciro's heart swelled with the same force as the swelling in his loins. Never had he wanted to possess someone the way he wanted to possess Claudia. He didn't want to have sex with her. He didn't even want to make love to her. He wanted to be as one with her, something he didn't even pretend to try and understand, just knew in that moment that that was how he felt.

'Take your top off,' he said thickly, then found the rest of him thickening too when she whipped it over her head and threw it onto the floor.

Her plain white bra tugged at his heart. They'd made love once before but in many ways Claudia was still an innocent with no clue as to the power she held in her sensual body.

She had power over him. That much he knew for certain. If someone told him right then that to take possession of Claudia meant he lost everything else, he would lose it all gladly.

He unclasped the bra and her beautiful, generous breasts spilled free. Lifting his head, he took one nipple into his mouth and was gratified to hear her moan of pleasure. She ground onto him but there was no relief, only further torture. Never in his whole life had he needed to be inside someone the way he needed to be inside Claudia.

The same urgency was in her too. He could feel it in her every touch and kiss and in the way she scratched at his T-shirt. Arching his back, he helped her remove it and then tugged his shorts down to free his erection from its constraints. Her arms wound around his neck, their chests fused back together, and she ground down on him with even more urgency. 'Ciro, please. I want…' Her words died on her lips as another moan fell in their place.

He rubbed his hands over her back and down to her bottom. Slipping his hand under her skirt, he groaned as he clasped the peachiness.

Her face, flushed with passion, hovered over his, her breaths short gasps. 'Ciro. *Please.*'

The only barrier between them now was her knickers. With her pleas for possession ringing in his ears and the feeling that he could spontaneously combust at any moment he wound them as tightly as he could and then ripped them apart.

He didn't know if he thrust up or if Claudia ground down or if it was a combination of both but the second that last barrier between them was gone, he was inside her tight, wet confines and fighting harder than he had ever done before to stop an instant climax.

Gritting his teeth, he wrapped an arm around her waist and clasped her bottom with the other hand, then held on for dear life as she began to move in earnest. That she was moving on instinct only made it more potent.

Her moans grew loader as she rode him, mouth on his cheek, her breasts crushed against his chest. Ciro did everything he could to hold on but this was too much, the sensations ripping through him were just too much, he was clinging by his fingertips… But then the tone of her moans became a breathy pitch and he felt her thicken around his raging arousal. Wrapping his arms even more tightly around her, he thrust up one last time and, with a loud shout that roared from deep in his chest, let go.

Claudia, dazed and utterly spent, finally loosened her hold around Ciro's neck and nuzzled into the crook. His woody scent had a new musky hue to it and she sniffed it with a sigh and rested her hand on his shoulder, closing her eyes to the gentle but no less potent sensations penetrating her skin as he stroked her back. Their chests were bonded so tightly together she could feel his heart beating in tandem with her own.

'Is your thigh okay?' she murmured.

He pressed his mouth to the top of her head and strengthened his hold around her.

Slowly, she drifted to sleep, waking only when he shifted beneath her. She lifted her head and found him staring at her with a look that made her heart soar.

'Ready to go to bed now?' he asked, his voice husky, before he pulled her down for a long, lingering kiss.

That kiss, more even than the earth-shattering pleasure of his lovemaking, made her feel that her world had changed for ever.

CHAPTER ELEVEN

CLAUDIA CREPT THROUGH the darkness to her dressing room and donned the first items of clothing that came to hand before slipping out of the bedroom and calling her sister. She had a good excuse to call but what she really wanted—needed—was to hear Imma's voice.

A night of making love to Ciro had left her as confused and out-of-sorts as she'd ever been.

It had been wonderful. Magical. Heavenly.

And yet all she wanted was to curl herself into a ball and bawl her eyes out.

She was not supposed to sleep with him. That had never been part of their agreement.

But, sweet Lord, it had felt so right. At least it had until Ciro had fallen asleep and her chest had started to tighten around her thudding heart. The spacious walls of the apartment felt as if they were closing in on her.

Her feelings for him were veering dangerously out of control. Somehow she had to find a way to lock them away because they could never have a future together as anything other than co-parents.

So she did the only thing she could when her feelings felt as if they might explode inside her. She baked.

Even before Ciro heard Claudia's voice, he knew she'd slipped out of bed. Only the faintest light filtered through the curtains. He squinted at his watch. Five a.m. He couldn't have been asleep for more than an hour. Yawning widely, he debated getting up, tracking her down and carrying her back to bed for another bout of lovemaking.

He'd never known a night like it.

But his exhaustion was such that when Ciro next opened his eyes he found he'd slept for another two hours. The bed was still empty.

He climbed out and got straight into the shower.

He lathered shampoo into his hair, the full weight of what he'd done to her sitting heavily in him. He'd stolen her innocence. He'd lied to her. Used her. Got her pregnant. And now they'd made love again.

Never had he had sex with a woman and felt as if the fabric holding him together were fraying at the seams. And now it had happened twice. Both times with the same woman. And this time the fraying was a hundred times worse.

He'd just shared the best night of his life with the woman whose father's actions had directly caused his own father's great heart to collapse. He *knew* that was nothing to do with her; that she was as big a victim as anyone—maybe the biggest victim of all—but that didn't change the self-loathing that he could share such heady joy with his enemy's daughter.

He just could not reconcile the warring parts inside him.

Shower done, he had a quick shave, then threw a shirt and some trousers on.

As he walked down the second flight of stairs he was greeted with the unmistakable aroma of baking. His steps faltered as childhood memories of waking to similar scents hit him. His mother had often made fresh pastries to feed her growing boys and devoted husband.

How he wished he'd appreciated all they'd done for him more, wished he hadn't treated them as a twice-yearly obligation to be filled, always busy building his empire and experiencing life and assuming they would always be there.

He found Claudia washing her hands at the sink, wearing a knee-length emerald shirt dress, hair plaited, her legs and feet bare. She did not look like a woman who'd gone a whole night without sleep.

Her smile contained a touch of wariness, as did her murmured, 'Good morning.'

Desire pulsed through him, strong and relentless, pounding through his veins in that one meeting of their eyes, his thoughts immediately flying to the image of her naked in his arms.

Wrenching his stare from her guarded gaze, he ran his fingers through his hair to stop them reaching for her. 'I need to get to work.'

Her teeth razed her bottom lip, her next smile warier than the first. 'When will you be back?'

'I don't know. I've got three meetings scheduled and a conference call with Paris.'

'Would you like a bagel before you go?' She nodded at a tray of bagels lined up on a cooling rack on the worktop he'd failed to notice when he'd walked into the kitchen because his attention had been so thoroughly caught by her. That explained the evocative aroma.

'I'd better make it quick. My first meeting's in half an hour.'

'Smoked salmon and cream cheese?'

'Sounds great.'

While she pulled two plates out of the cupboard and got busy preparing breakfast for them, he remembered hearing her voice when he'd first woken briefly. 'Who were you talking to earlier?'

'Imma.'

'Is something wrong?'

She spread cream cheese over one half of each opened bagel. 'The voice activation app on my phone's stopped working. I needed a bagel recipe and I didn't want to wake you.'

'Did she read the recipe out to you?'

She nodded, layering the salmon above the cheese and then reaching for the black pepper grinder.

'How does that work if you can't write it down?'

'I remembered it. I can't read or write but I've taught myself to pay attention and retain information. Tell me a recipe once and I will remember it for ever. Read me a news article and I will remember it word for word.' She picked up one of the plates and handed it to him.

No wonder she'd been able to recall the words Ciro had said to his brother that fateful morning verbatim, he thought.

'Can you read *anything*?' he asked after he'd taken his first bite of what was easily the most delicious bagel he'd had in his life.

'My name, Imma's name, Papà and our surname. I struggle with Cesare but given enough time I can make it out.' A blush that went all the way to the roots of her hair covered her face. 'I can read your name too.'

That should *not* make his heart thump.

'How come you were only recently diagnosed? Surely a condition as severe as yours should have been picked up years ago?'

'I've not had a formal diagnosis,' she explained. 'I talked to Sister Maria when I stayed at the convent recently. She was my first teacher. She told me they—the nuns—suspected I was dyslexic when I was six. They told my father but he hit the roof at the suggestion his princess might have something wrong with her. They did their best to help me but were too scared of him to fight my corner.'

'But surely your father must have realised you needed help? He must have read your school reports. Hell, all he had to do was compare your work to your sister's.'

The first hint of bitterness flashed over her face. 'I've been thinking about this a lot and I think having a stupid daughter suited him. He never got the son he wanted so he made Imma his business heir—she got all the brains—and decided I was more suited for being a decorative pet around the house. It's not like I was going to go off and forge a career, was it? I mean, come on, Ciro, who's going to employ someone who can't read or write and struggles with numbers?'

'You have a problem with numbers too?'

'I can see them individually, although I get my twos and fives muddled up, but put two numbers together and I can't see them. When I was little I wanted to work in my favourite pastry shop but when I asked them once—I couldn't have been more than ten—they said it involved more than just baking. I would have to do things like work the tills and stocktakes and write orders down. All the things I can't do.'

The thump in his heart now echoed violently in his guts as he remembered accusing her of wilfully signing her section of the transferred deed into her name. What had he said? Something about how she should have noticed the pathetically low sale price of it? Claudia would remember the exact words he'd used.

How badly wrong could one person be about another?

Ciro looked into the dark brown eyes of the woman in whose belly his developing child lived and felt as wretched as he'd ever done. A pampered princess? She should have been so lucky. This was the woman whose mother had died when she was three, leaving her at the mercy of a narcissistic father who'd exploited her severe learning difficulties for his own advantage so she would be dependent on him for ever…or until she married a man her father deemed worthy enough to look after her.

And in that moment, Ciro realised Cesare Buscetta *did* love his daughter. Because with hindsight came perspective. It hadn't been only Ciro's billionaire status that had attracted him as a prospective son-in-law but the strong family ties he'd grown up with. Cesare had assumed that Ciro would be as protective over his wife as his father had been over his and would shower his wife with the same amount of love. Assumptions Ciro had fed.

Whether it had been narcissism that had stopped him getting help for her or not, Cesare's protectiveness was undeniable. He'd seen Claudia's need for independence but had judged her—wrongly in Ciro's opinion—as not being ready for it so had sought the perfect property for her, one in which she could have that elusive freedom while still being under his care and protection. The Trapani family home.

He was about to say this to her when his phone buzzed, breaking the moment.

It was Marcy, reminding him of the meeting he was supposed to be at. He swore under his breath.

'You need to go?' Claudia guessed.

He nodded. 'I'm sorry.' He didn't even know what he was sorry for. And he didn't know why the sadness in her eyes felt so unbearable.

'Don't be.' She mustered a small smile. 'Are your offices far from here?'

'I thought I'd told you.' But obviously he hadn't because she would have remembered. 'My main office is on the other side of the floor.' At her blank expression he elaborated. 'You know where Marcy's stationed? Do you remember seeing the other door?' Thinking of Marcy, he took one of the freshly baked bagels for her.

'To the left of her desk?' Claudia asked.

'That's my private entrance into the offices. All my admin staff work from it.'

'I didn't know that.'

'It makes things easier to oversee, everything being under one roof.'

'Why doesn't Marcy work in there with them?'

'She does sometimes but she has a noise sensitivity. Call me if you need anything, okay?'

She nodded.

Bowing his head, he walked swiftly out of the kitchen, suddenly desperate to get away from this beguiling woman who had finally made him understand his enemy.

He understood Cesare's protectiveness towards Claudia. Because he felt it too.

Three days later, Claudia stepped out of the elevator and walked purposefully to the exit.

She could do this. She *would* do this.

The doorman smiled politely and opened the door for her.

Immediately, her senses were engulfed. Waves of people bustled past in all directions; tourists and dog-walkers heading to and from Central Park, shoppers, workers hurrying to appointments… People going about their business. That was what Ciro had said.

For the third night in a row, they'd made love long into the night.

They were still to talk about this change to their relationship and for that she was glad. Her feelings were so confused that she wouldn't know what to say. All she knew was that when it came to Ciro, she was helpless to resist. He'd woken something in her that overruled her rational thoughts.

Alone in the day, she would try to harden herself and remind herself that living with him was only a temporary thing until the baby was born. Then he would come home and she would look at him and find herself melting before he'd even touched her.

He'd left for work before she'd woken that morning but she had a vague memory of a brush of lips against hers and a gentle caress of a hand over her hair. She'd climbed out of bed, her chest tight and the need to get out and feel the sun on her face running strongly inside her.

Their being lovers did not change her ultimate goal. Real, unfettered freedom. How could she find it if she was too scared to leave the apartment on her own? Would Elizabeth Bennet hide in the shadows and wait for a man to take her hand to cross the road? No, she would not.

But it wasn't Elizabeth Bennet she brought to mind when she took the deepest breath of her life and joined the throng. It was Ciro.

Ciro closed his eyes before entering his apartment. It was the same every time he returned from work. He had to brace himself.

'Claudia?' he called.

'I'm in the kitchen.'

He should have guessed. His kitchen had had more use since Claudia moved in than in all the years he'd lived here. Ciro did not cook. With take-out, restaurants and cafés in New York being plentiful and catering to all tastes, he saw no need to hire a chef. Whatever he fancied at whatever particular time could be provided with one swipe of his phone. His kitchen had been remodelled with the rest of the apartment only because it would have been out of keeping if he'd left it. It was a space he would have converted into something else if it wouldn't have devalued the apartment.

His guts knotting, he followed the growing scent of fresh baking and found her loading the dishwasher. It didn't matter how many times he told her he employed staff to clean everything, she still insisted on cleaning up after herself. On the kitchen's island stood one of the biggest cakes he'd seen outside a wedding and decorated so beautifully it could be considered a work of art.

But the cake was only a peripheral observation for his gaze locked straight onto Claudia. Her jeans and T-shirt were covered in flour. Some had found its way into her hair and a great splodge of pink icing sugar sat on her left cheek. His chest squeezed around his heart so tightly that for a moment he couldn't speak.

Tearing his gaze from her, he looked again at the cake. 'That is amazing. Did you make it?'

She smiled and nodded. 'It's for Marcy's daughter. It's her birthday. They're having a party for her.'

'Marcy asked you to make it?'

'We got talking the other day. She told me she loved the bagels I'd made—I didn't realise you'd given one of them to her—and when I told her how bored I was here and how I used to bake for the convent she asked if I'd like to make the cake.'

'You baked for the convent?'

'Cakes and pastries mostly. They'd sell them and put the money raised towards their good causes.'

'You've never mentioned that before.'

'It wasn't a regular thing. Just something I would do once or twice a week.'

'You don't consider that regular?' Ciro rubbed his fingers into his skull, wondering how the investigators he'd sent to dig into her background had missed this fact about her. But then, he had to acknowledge, they'd failed to infiltrate Cesare's home. Give the man his due, he surrounded himself with flunkies who were loyal.

'I wanted to do it every day but I kept getting under Papà's chefs' feet. They rationed my use of the villa's kitchen.'

He stared some more at the cake. 'I know people who would pay a fortune for a cake like that.'

'I wish I knew how to turn it into a career. The only things I'm good at are cooking and gardening.'

'You want a career?'

'All I've ever wanted is to be independent. I know you're going to buy me an apartment when the baby's born and pay maintenance for it but I don't want you keeping *me*.'

This was the first time Claudia had mentioned moving out since they'd become lovers. Hearing it from her mouth like that and the nonchalance with which she said it…

It made every sinew of his body tighten.

'You're my wife and the mother of my child,' he said, somehow managing to keep his tone even. 'You're my responsibility. Both of you.'

She looked him square in the eye. From the tone of her voice when she answered, she was struggling to keep her voice even too. 'I'm not your responsibility. I don't want to be your responsibility. I've had enough of being answerable to men. I will never deny our child anything but when I leave here I want to earn my own money. It might sound silly to you but I want to pay for my own clothes and all the things that are mine alone.'

'That doesn't sound silly,' he said, speaking through the lump that had formed in his throat. 'And knowing your strengths is a good place to start. Would you like me to look for a tutor who specialises in adult dyslexics? Someone who can help you in that respect?'

'That's very kind but your days are busy enough.'

'I will make the time. It's good that you're looking to the future. You're too young to spend the rest of your life with nothing to occupy you but while you're living here, let me provide for you. You're carrying my child and I feel enough guilt without having more added to it. If there's anything I can do to help you career-wise or in any other way, tell me. I *want* to help.'

He *did* want to help.

But he could not fathom why the thought of her leaving, a thought that only weeks before he'd believed couldn't come soon enough, now felt crippling. By rights, the time had nearly come for Claudia to move into a guest room. That thought was even harder to contemplate.

Breathing deeply to counteract the strange weight of emotion filling him, he looked away from the beautiful brown eyes and found his gaze locking on a huge bouquet of flowers displayed on the window sill. 'Where did they come from?'

Her face went so red that for a moment he was convinced she had an admirer. Then a worse thought occurred to him and he stared at them as if they'd grown poisonous tentacles. 'Are they from your father?'

She must have caught the tone of his voice for her eyes narrowed. 'Would it be a problem if they were?'

'This is my home.' His guts had filled with nauseous violence. 'I don't want to share my private space with anything that comes from that man.'

Her eyes narrowed further still. 'Half of my DNA comes from him.'

And didn't he wish he could forget that half? 'The better half must come from your mother.'

Claudia squeezed her eyes tightly shut, hating that in Ciro's eyes she would always be tainted. What did this say for his future relationship with their innocent baby, who he rarely spoke of, not even an idle question about potential names? He'd gone with her to see the doctor but even there he'd shown barely a glimmer of interest.

His cruel comment about her DNA felt like a knife in her heart.

When she was certain she'd held the burn of tears at bay, she put the dishwasher tablet in the slot then turned around to face him. 'I bought the flowers. I thought the apartment needed cheering up.'

'You ordered them?'

She shook her head. 'I walked to the florist and bought them there.'

'You left the apartment on your own?'

'Yes.'

'That's wonderful.' He remembered how tightly she had clung to his hand when they'd first stepped outside and the way she'd stuck so closely to him wherever they had gone. This had been a massive thing for her and she had done it. Just how incredible was she? 'I'm proud of you.'

'Proud that it means I'm less of a burden to you?' she challenged, jutting her chin in the air. 'Don't worry—I'll be gone before you know it, and you can stop worrying about my father tainting your precious space.'

'Claudia… I never meant it like that.'

'Don't *lie* to me. Now please excuse me, I need to shower.'

With what could only be called dignity, she left the kitchen, leaving Ciro staring at her retreating figure. It took all of a minute before guilt snaked into him.

CHAPTER TWELVE

CLAUDIA WAS ALREADY in the shower when Ciro entered the bedroom. She'd locked the bathroom door so he had to wait impatiently for her to finish. When she came out, a large towel wrapped around her damp body, she took one look at him, scowled, and folded her arms across her chest.

With a muttered curse, he scooped her into his arms and, before she had time to protest, laid her flat on the bed.

His face hovering above hers, he gazed into the dark brown eyes still burning loathing at him…and blazing with the same fire that lived inside him. 'You are not a burden to me,' he bit out. 'Do you have any idea how incredible you are? I'm proud of you for everything, *bedda*, from the way you fight your fears to the way you've trained your brain to compensate for your dyslexia…that, to me, is incredible. And sexy.' And then he sealed his words with the kiss he'd ached to plant on her beautiful generous lips from the moment he'd walked into the kitchen. The fusion of their mouths together acted as balm to his soul.

'I hate your father, yes, and I hate every reminder of him,' he murmured in a gentler tone, brushing his mouth over her cheeks and finding his way to her neck. 'I despise him for what he did to my father but I despise him too for what he did to *you*. You're his daughter but you are entirely your own woman.' He pulled her towel apart and let his eyes feast on the body that grew in beauty by the hour. 'And I want you more than I have ever wanted anyone.'

She didn't say anything but her breaths had become shallow. When he looked back into her eyes, something reflected at him from the molten depths that made his heart expand to match his arousal.

'I will be the first to admit that I've made mistakes—huge mistakes—where you're concerned,' he continued, tracing his hands over her body, thrilling at the little jolts and quivers she gave in response. 'I'm not perfect. I'm human.' He took one of her hands and guided it to his arousal. 'Everything I feel for you is more than I have felt before.'

Her eyes widened. Her fingers squeezed around it.

'See?' he said roughly as he dipped his head to capture a perfect nipple in his mouth. She moaned and writhed beneath him. 'This is what you do to me. You drive me crazy. You are all I think about, day and night. I imagine us in bed…' He captured the other nipple and ran his tongue around it. 'I imagine making love to you all the time.' Making his way down her belly, he continued his sensual verbal assault. 'I want to touch every inch of your flesh.' He reached the top of her pubis. He could smell her hot excitement and filled his lungs with it. 'I want to open you up like a flower and taste your hidden secrets.'

Her moan seemed to come from her very core.

Claudia knew where he was going and knew too that all she had to do was close her legs or say no and he would stop. Since they'd become lovers, she'd waited with breathless anticipation for him to try and kiss her there again, never knowing if it was relief or disappointment she felt when he didn't. Because, since that moment of horror on their wedding night when he'd first tried to kiss her there—the classic books she enjoyed certainly didn't contain love scenes with an intimacy like *that*—she'd often found her thoughts drifting to it, heat bubbling inside her, wondering…

How would it feel? Would there be pleasure in it for her as there was when he touched her there? Would Ciro take pleasure from it?

And then she melted like chocolate fondue to realise he'd been waiting for her to be comfortable with him as a lover, had understood that sex and intimacy for a recent virgin was a big deal. He'd been taking things slowly with her because he *did* understand her. He'd been taking things slowly because he cared for her.

And, as all these thoughts ran through her head, his tongue pressed against the centre of her pleasure that sent a shock of electricity jolting through her.

His tongue? She'd expected a brief brush of his lips…

'Relax,' he murmured as he shifted into a more comfortable position and gently parted her thighs. He looked up to meet her stare. She caught a flash of dimples before he buried his face between her legs.

His tongue pressed gently but firmly against her swollen bud, doing something to her that felt… Oh, it felt wonderful. One hand glided over her belly and she caught hold of it and squeezed it tightly, then closed her eyes and submitted to the most delicious pleasure imaginable.

She didn't want it to end.

How could she have thought something that felt so *incredible* was dirty or sinful? How naïve she had been. Ciro had opened her body to him and he'd opened her mind with it.

Whatever happened in the future, she would never regret their becoming lovers. If this was all they had then she would treasure these feelings for ever.

Then, just as she thought she'd reached the peak of sensual intensity, everything exploded inside her. She cried out his name, rippling sensations crashing through her and sending her soaring higher than she'd ever been before.

There was no time to catch her breath for the moment the waves began to subside, Ciro moved and kissed his way quickly up her belly and her breasts to her mouth—it took a beat for her to realise the strange new taste on his tongue belonged to her—and as he kissed her he drove deep inside her with a strength that had her crying his name out again and again, until she didn't know where she ended and he began.

It was only when it was all over and she lay dazed in his arms that she realised she had no idea when he'd removed his clothes.

Ciro tried to hold onto the dream. Beside him, Claudia shifted and snuggled closer, her warm hand groping in the dark for his.

He'd dreamed of their child. A beautiful baby girl who looked exactly as he imagined Claudia had looked as a baby.

In his dream he'd been lying on the sofa with his daughter bouncing on his lap. The love that had filled his heart during the dream…

He tried to breathe but his heart had expanded so much it had squashed his lungs.

Over a month later and, to Claudia's delight, Ciro announced they were going to a gala at a trendy art gallery. With firm instructions to get herself a cocktail dress, she explored the women's section of his department store with a fawning personal shopper hanging on her arm telling her everything she tried on looked perfect.

Knowing perfectly well the shopper was ingratiating herself with the boss's wife, Claudia hid her amusement and enjoyed the experience. She'd never shopped for clothes before without having to think about how her father would react to seeing her in them.

Ciro, she knew, wouldn't care what she wore. All the same, she wanted to make him proud.

Things between them had changed immeasurably. She was in no doubt of the sincerity of both his guilt and his desire for her. He'd even cut short a five-day trip to Paris to three days. Heat engulfed her every time she remembered how he'd walked into the apartment, locked eyes with her and, without uttering a word, scooped her up and carried her to the bedroom.

Neither of them had mentioned the original agreement that she share his bed for only a few weeks. It hadn't needed mentioning.

She didn't know if it was the intimacy of the act he'd performed on her that made her feel they'd reached a whole new level of closeness but she felt as if they were properly together, a team, a couple, partners. For the first time since the wedding, she looked to the future with hope in her heart.

Their baby was due in less than six months. It wouldn't be long before her body began properly changing. So far, her belly had developed a slight roundness but she'd been assured that would suddenly accelerate and she'd turn into a beached whale. If that made the passion between them dwindle to nothing then she'd cross that bridge when she came to it. She was confident that they'd forged a good enough friendship that when she moved into her own apartment, they could co-parent their baby as friends. If the passion between them still existed…they'd find a way to make it work, even while living under separate roofs.

She hoped they could make it work but refused to take it

for granted. She'd gone into their marriage blind. Now she refused to close her eyes. Ciro had broken her heart before. She would not give him the ammunition to break it again.

She was coming to learn, though, that at heart he was a decent, thoughtful man. Sometimes she overheard him on the phone to his *mamma*. His patience and kindness with her made Claudia's heart ache. The ache would grow to know it was her father who'd destroyed Ciro's *mamma*'s life.

Three weeks ago, he'd given her the numbers of three tutors who specialised in dyslexic adults. He'd inputted the details into her phone and then dropped the subject. No pressure.

The tutor who'd sounded the friendliest was coming to the apartment on Monday.

Ideas for a career were formulating in her mind too, a career she could do in her future home with the baby at her side.

She took an age getting ready for the gala and when she was done and paraded herself in front of Ciro, his eyes widened and he wolf-whistled. She practically preened! If she'd ever mastered whistling herself, she would have whistled him because he *oozed* masculinity, his black dinner jacket emphasising his divine physique.

The look they exchanged in that moment was red hot. If they'd been within hand's reach of each other, their glamorous outfits would have been ripped off in seconds.

So it was with joy in her heart that she arrived at the gala with her hand wrapped tightly in Ciro's.

The art gallery itself was nothing as Claudia had imagined. She remembered a trip to Florence as a child of twelve to the Uffizi. Huge frescoed ceilings, exquisite sculptures and vast oil canvases rang large in her memories. It had felt like stepping back in time to a distant age.

This gallery rivalled the Uffizi for size but there the similarities ended. Everything here was white, the floors, the walls, the ceilings, everything apart from the art itself, which was as different from the Uffizi's exhibits as night was from day. These pieces were *modern*, Ciro informed her. All guests were expected to enjoy them before the gala proper started.

The problem, she quickly found, was that these creations needed explaining.

Not being able to read hadn't marred her enjoyment at the Uffizi because the art spoke for itself. Caravaggio's *Sacrifice of Isaac* and Gentileschi's *Judith Beheading Holofernes*—Imma had read the titles to her—had horrified Claudia with their violence but she'd known immediately what they meant and what they were portraying.

Here, she didn't have the faintest idea what the huge cube that was taller than Ciro was supposed to mean. Or the dangling six-foot sculpture of a wooden chair. Or what one of the rare canvases to occasionally line the walls was supposed to represent; all she saw were splatters of random colour.

But, judging by the earnest talk around her as their fellow guests consulted their guide books, these were *'works of art, darling'*.

'Do you actually like this stuff?' she whispered to Ciro when she was certain no one was listening. His apartment was filled with the type of artwork she adored and which, when she had a place of her own and if she had the money, she would buy for herself.

He grinned and dipped his mouth to her ear. 'Awful, aren't they?'

Claudia gave a bark of laughter, absurdly pleased that they were of the same mind on yet another thing, then found her laughter muffled by Ciro's lips crushing hers for a very short but *very* hungry kiss.

The anticipation of what would happen when they got back home later thrummed through her veins. Judging by the lusty stares she kept getting from Ciro and the possessive way he kept hold of her hand, he was counting down the minutes too.

An extremely eccentric-looking couple joined them, clutching guide books to their chests.

'Have you been in the Angelino room yet?' the man asked. He wore a bright purple and yellow checked crushed velvet suit and a neon green bow tie. Claudia was so taken with his outfit that she failed to hear his question.

'Yes, we've been in there,' Ciro said, gently squeezing Claudia's hand. If her eyes got any wider they would pop out.

'What did you think of the Gatsby piece?'

That would be the floating hat, Ciro remembered. An ordinary, cream, Panama hat suspended between the wall and ceiling by seemingly invisible means. He thought quickly and remembered an old quote he'd read in a book one time. 'Fantastic,' he said with a beam, 'is not the word.'

'Quite,' the man said with an approving nod before turning to Claudia. 'And what do you think, young lady, of the Shadow piece?'

'Is that the mannequin one?' she asked, her hold on Ciro's hand tightening reflexively. He'd read the titles of all the pieces to her.

'Well, hardly a mannequin, but yes, that's the gist of it.'

How he would love to turn to the man and say, 'It's a mannequin with its head chopped off. I use that exact model to display the clothes in the women's section of my department stores.' But this was a networking night. He hadn't paid forty thousand dollars for his and Claudia's tickets to get into an argument with a man who might one day be useful to him. You didn't get to the top of your game by being rude and alienating people. New York was a big city, but paths crossed in unexpected places and by unexpected means. Besides, the man didn't mean any harm. Chances were he was scouting for opinions on the pieces so he could form his own opinions off the basis of them.

'Please excuse us,' Ciro said with a smile, 'but we still need to visit the Rodrigo room before the meal starts.' Whisking Claudia away, he said under his breath, 'Shall we go upstairs?'

'Definitely. I think I might die if I have to listen to any more.' Their eyes met again, amusement dancing between them, locking them together as co-conspirators. They were still laughing when they reached the second floor, which had been cleared of all 'art' to create a huge restaurant and dance floor. A rock band, famous for its hedonistic excesses, was tuning up on the stage, the drummer swigging from a bottle of vodka. As the evening went on, Ciro noticed the singer giving Claudia the eye. Lots of men were. He didn't blame them. Dressed in a long sparkling gold dress with spaghetti straps and which dipped in a V to skim over her growing cleavage, her glorious hair worn loose and falling like waves, she looked spellbindingly beautiful.

But it was more than her beauty that made him feel like the cat who'd got the cream. The shy woman who'd clung to his hand throughout their wedding celebrations and hung back to let him do all the talking had grown in confidence enough to instigate conversations and not just be carried along by them. A number of people at the gala had attended their wedding and, though he knew it shouldn't surprise him, he was still surprised when she remembered their names without having to be prompted. What a memory she had. What a woman she was.

Later, as he held her tightly on the dance floor, it suddenly came to him that he no longer saw her father whenever he looked at her. All he saw was Claudia, his beautiful, brave wife…

His heart made a sudden lunge as his head sped forwards six months. To when she would leave.

CHAPTER THIRTEEN

As Ciro had a week-long trip to Japan starting the next day, he insisted on taking Claudia out for dinner on Sunday evening. The restaurant he chose was a small, exclusive place famed, according to Ciro, for its excellent cuisine. It was only a short walk from the apartment, and they strolled the busy streets to it with their hands clasped together. For the first time since her arrival in New York, Claudia felt comfortable walking through it. She doubted she would ever think herself a native New Yorker but it was good not to feel like a complete alien in her new home city. She was certain that when the time came to move into her own apartment, she'd be able to embrace the freedom without fear.

'I've had an idea for a career,' she said when they'd finished the first of their nine-course tasting menu.

His eyes sparked with lively interest. 'Tell me.'

'I thought I could open a cake business.'

He grinned. 'Excellent idea. Marcy keeps raving about the cake you made for her daughter.'

'She's asked me to make her a Christmas cake and her sister's asked me to make a cake for her wedding anniversary,' she told him, unable to contain her pride. 'Her cousin's getting married next year and wants me to make the cake for that too. And they want to pay me for them!'

'So they should. Do you want to open a shop?'

'Gosh, no!' She shuddered. Then she thought again. 'Maybe one day,' she pondered, thinking aloud. 'When the baby's older and not dependent on me as much. But for the time being I thought I'd go with word of mouth. I thought I could ask for testimonials from them and take lots of pictures to build up a portfolio, then when I'm ready and our baby's older and I'm hopefully…' she held up crossed fingers '…able to read more, I can get a professional website done. When it gets to that stage, could I speak to someone from your marketing team for advice?'

'Of course. I said I'd give you whatever help you need. I meant it.'

'Thank you.' She sighed.

'What's wrong?'

She shrugged. 'It's just so frustrating that even now, when I have the chance to make something of myself, I still need help. It's frustrating to know I'll always need help.'

'There's nothing wrong with asking for help when you need it. I would never have created my own business if I hadn't asked.'

'Did you?'

He nodded. 'My first store was a derelict building six blocks from here. I saw its potential but I didn't have the cash to buy it or do any of the things needed to remodel it or buy stock in or anything.'

The waiter arrived back at the table with their second course, which to Claudia's eyes looked like a giant langoustine artfully draped with skinny brown sticks in a white broth with a bit of lettuce on the side, and which took longer to describe than it must have taken the chef to cook.

When she took her first bite though, her taste buds exploded and she made a mental note to beg the chef for the recipe.

'How did you get the money?' Claudia asked when they'd finished the dish, keen to hear more. 'Did you go to the bank?'

'Three banks turned me down. Then I remembered my friend Ollie's father was a private investor so I asked him for the loan.'

'And he gave it to you?'

'Yes. I sold the store two years later—I came to dislike the location—and paid the whole loan back plus interest, and I had enough left over to get a mortgage on the building that became my flagship store. The rest is history. If I hadn't asked for that loan you and I wouldn't be sitting here.'

'What would you have done?'

'I don't know. I knew I wanted to see the world and make a fortune. I knew I had a good business brain and an analytical mind. I had the potential and knew I would recognise the opportunity when it came along. And now I have lots of business interests.'

'Other than the department stores?'

'I invest in graduates like myself. If they have a business idea I can see working, then I invest in them. If you decide you want to open your own shop, I expect you to give me first refusal as backer for it.'

'Only if it was a proper loan,' she said. 'I wouldn't want to be a charity case.'

'You're the mother of my child. You'll never be a charity case to me.'

Their third course was brought to the table. Claudia hadn't noticed them take the dishes from the second.

Once she'd swallowed the first delicious bite, she said, 'Can we look for an apartment for me after Christmas?'

Green eyes found hers and held the stare before he had a drink of his wine. 'That soon?'

'We did say we'd look in the new year,' she pointed out. 'New York doesn't frighten me any more. I'm learning my way around and becoming comfortable with it. I feel ready to make the move now. I'm not bothered about the location, although somewhere close to you would be great, and I'm not bothered about the size. All I'll need are two bedrooms but if I'm going to make a success of the cake business, I'll need a decent-sized kitchen.' She pulled a rueful face. 'I struggled for space when I made the birthday cake.'

'Don't you like my kitchen?' he teased, although there was something in his eyes that bothered her.

She tried to be diplomatic. 'It's pretty basic.'

'Basic?' He arched a brow.

She smiled. 'In proportion to the rest of the apartment it's tiny. And its layout's impractical if you're trying to make more than one thing at a time.'

'I thought you liked my apartment?'

'I love it. I just hate the kitchen.' Remembering that he'd remodelled the entire apartment to his specific tastes, she felt herself blush. 'Sorry.'

It had been many weeks since Ciro had seen such a dark stain of colour cover her cheeks.

'Don't be sorry. The kitchen was an afterthought to everything else I had done. It was rarely used before you moved in.'

'You surprise me,' she said drily.

He grinned. 'But if you hate it so much, I can get an architect friend of mine to look at reconfiguring things. The staffroom's never used. We can knock into it and create a space that's twice what we currently have for you.'

Confusion flittered in her eyes. 'Why would you do that?'

He leaned across the table to take hold of her hand. He'd

spent the day waiting for the right moment to broach this. That time was now. 'Because, *bedda*, I want you to stay.

Her eyes flickered.

'I want you to stay. When the baby comes. Stay with me. Be a family.'

Now her eyes drifted down to their clasped hands. Slowly, she extracted hers and rested them both on her lap. 'This is rather sudden.'

'I've been thinking about it for weeks.' Since the dream he'd had of their baby and the knowledge that he could love it—that a part of him already did love it—Ciro had thought of little else. The strong feelings he'd experienced at the gala had only cemented what he already knew. 'I don't see the point in you moving into your own place any more, not now that things have changed so much between us. You and me…we're great together. Our child will have two parents under one roof and you won't have to navigate the world alone. I'll be there to support you in everything you do.'

It felt as if an age passed while he waited for her to respond. 'I had no idea you were thinking along those lines.'

'You must see it makes perfect sense.'

She shook her head and reached for her water.

'I understand your caution,' he admitted.

Her expression was wary. 'Do you?'

He drained his wine and stared at her intently. 'I've treated you terribly. I blamed you for your father's actions. I've been cruel. Horrible. My only excuse is that I've been grieving for my father.' He closed his eyes and sucked in a breath to counter the torturous throb thinking of his father always produced. 'His death is the single biggest pain I've felt in my life. I felt such guilt. I *feel* such guilt. I should have visited more. I should have picked up the phone more. I should have made myself more available. I made the fatal assumption of thinking he would always be there for me. Do you remember how you told me you can't change the past? Well, that's what I've been struggling with, because I want to change it. I want to turn back time and be there for him and shoulder that burden. I want to be there for my *mamma* too.'

Claudia's head remained bowed but he knew she was listening to every word.

He leaned forward. 'I need to slow down. I've been so busy setting the world on fire over the last decade that I never stopped long enough to meet someone I could share my life with. Marriage was always something for the future. Now I have you and a baby on the way, I feel differently. I'm ready to be a father. The times we've spent living together, getting to know each other… I don't deny that I got you wrong. Badly wrong. But I swear that's all in the past. We can look to the future, starting now. We can remodel the kitchen to make it more practical for you—hell, we can buy a house with a garden if that's what you want. Just tell me what you need and I will make it happen.'

It seemed to take for ever for her eyes to meet his. Sadness shone from them. 'I'm sorry, Ciro, but this isn't what I want. Maybe it will be one day, but not yet. And I don't think you want it either.'

'Haven't I just told you that it *is* what I want? And I *know* you want it too.' Heat pulsed through him to think of how she came apart in his arms and the intensity of what they shared. The future he'd spent the day imagining for them blazed in bright, sunny colours.

A sudden spark of anger blew the sadness away from her eyes. 'Stop making assumptions,' she said tightly. 'You always do that. You assumed I was like my father and now that you've decided I'm nothing like him you assume, because it's nice and convenient for you, that what I really want is to give up the freedom I've spent my entire life waiting for to continue a marriage that was only ever a lie.'

His belief that she'd be enthusiastic about his plans for their future dissolved. Coldness crept into his bloodstream. 'I've apologised for that numerous times.'

'I know, and I do believe you're sincere, but what you did forced me to think properly about my life and the kind of future I want. We both knew when I moved in with you that it would only be temporary. Us becoming lovers has changed things but it hasn't changed my plans and I haven't said *anything* to make you believe differently.'

'What happens to us, then?' he challenged. 'I buy you an apartment, you leave and that's it, we're over?'

Her brows drew together. 'Why would it be over? We can still be together. I don't have to move far. We can still be a family, just not in the traditional sense. Maybe it will happen one day but not yet. I'm not ready for that.'

The coldness in his blood rose to form an icy pounding in his head. 'Not ready for it? It's the life we're already living.'

'But it was only ever temporary.' Closing her eyes, she put her elbow on the table and rested her forehead in her hand. 'I want my freedom. That's all I've ever wanted, the freedom to get out of bed knowing I'm not answerable to anyone, the freedom to make my own choices…the freedom to just be *me*.'

His guts coiling and knotting, Ciro waved to a passing waiter for a fresh drink. Then he fixed his attention back on Claudia and drummed his fingers on the table. 'You know, *bedda*, in all the time we've been together, I've not said anything about the fact you used me or asked you to apologise for it.'

She visibly recoiled. 'I have *never* used you.'

'I was your escape plan from your father.'

'That's not all you were. I was crazy about you.'

Her use of the past tense only made the tempest in his guts rage more violently. While he'd been basking in the headiness of their lovemaking and thinking of a future as a family for them, she'd been marking down the days until she could leave him.

'I was your escape plan and now I'm just your convenient bolt-hole and soon I'll be the convenient bank account to buy you a home of your own.'

Now her brows shot upwards. 'Don't make it sound like I'm demanding you buy me an apartment. If you'd had your way, you'd have installed me in one the minute I arrived in New York! And it's not for *my* convenience. It's so our baby can grow up with both its parents in the same city.'

'Sure you don't want me to have custody?' he retorted scathingly. 'I'd have thought having a baby will cramp your style when you finally get the freedom you want so badly.'

Her face drained of colour. 'That's unfair,' she whispered. 'I love our baby, you know that, and I will do whatever it takes to give it the best start in life. He or she's the reason I'm here and you know that too. Whatever freedoms I have to give up for it will be no sacrifice at all.'

'But it would be a sacrifice to give up those so-called freedoms for me?'

'That's completely different and you know it. You don't want me to give up my future because you're in love with me but because you've decided that as I'm here and not as bad as you thought, then I'll do.'

The waiter arrived with another bottle of wine. He poured Ciro a glass. Ciro downed it in one then, his face a grimacing mask, got to his feet and pulled his wallet out of his back pocket.

'What are you doing?' Claudia asked, trying to make

sense of how a conversation that had started with support and laughter had descended into such poison and so quickly.

Live with Ciro permanently? He hadn't given even a hint he'd been thinking about it. And now that *she* was thinking it, all she felt was a familiar fear.

'Going home. I've lost my appetite.' He pulled out a wedge of bills without counting them and threw them on the table. 'Are you coming? Or shall I call a cab for you?'

'I'll come with you.' But she'd barely finished speaking when he strode to the exit.

Shrugging her jacket on, she hurried to catch up to him and was relieved to find him waiting on the street for her, his face the same mask.

They didn't exchange a single word on the walk back to the apartment. Ciro kept his hands rammed in his jacket pocket and his chin jutted out. But he kept his strides to a length that made it manageable for her to keep pace, a gesture that made both her heart ache and anger froth.

Why did he have to spring this on her like that? They'd discussed her future plans many times. He'd given her every encouragement in them, and now he was acting as if she were the unreasonable one for not falling into line just because he'd changed his mind.

He wasn't even asking her to stay for her!

When they stepped into the apartment, he didn't pause to remove his shoes, heading straight up the stairs, climbing them two at a time.

She found him in the bedroom, his suit already stripped from his magnificent body.

The look of contempt he threw her as he strode into the bathroom made her veins freeze.

She shook her head, trying to clear the white noise filling it. 'This is ridiculous.'

He opened the bathroom cabinet. 'Wanting to be a proper family with my wife and child is ridiculous, is it?'

'No, but getting angry with me because I don't want to live with you is. I rushed into marriage with you before without opening my eyes and I won't commit my future and throw away my freedom to you again until I'm certain we can make it work, and I won't have you bullying me into making a snap decision on something I might live to regret again on a whim.'

'*Bullying* you?' he snarled, slamming the cabinet door shut without having removed anything from it. 'You sleep with me every night. You act as if you care for me…'

'I *do* care for you. Very much.'

'But not enough to give up your precious freedom.'

'Not when my freedom's come at such a high price.' Her whole body trembled. 'My entire life has been built on lies. The father I love is a monster. My childhood was one massive lie. The man I thought I loved lied in God's house when we made our wedding vows. I've been lied to over and over again, and all to keep me under the thumb and in the power of men. Can you blame me for wanting my freedom? Can you blame me for being cautious?'

The pulse on his temple throbbed madly. 'You're comparing me with your father?'

'You've just done that all by yourself.'

Cold green eyes bore into hers for endless seconds before a flame of anger shot through them and he left the bathroom and strode into his dressing room.

He left the door open and swiftly pulled a pair of jeans on. 'I'm going to check into a hotel.'

She gritted her teeth. 'Why?'

Stretching a T-shirt over his head, he tugged it over his broad chest then strolled back into the room and over to Claudia's favourite nude painting and pulled it off the wall. To her disbelief, she saw that it hid a safe. If she didn't feel as if she'd just had a truck slam into her stomach she would laugh at the cliché.

Moments later a green light flashed and the safe door swung open. From it Ciro pulled out a battered briefcase, which he opened with a stony-faced flourish. It contained money. A lot of money.

'Here's five million dollars,' he said in the same monotone. 'Take it. It's yours. Marcy will be at her desk early. Give her your bank account details and I'll transfer another five million. That along with this apartment should be sufficient payment for a marriage that's only lasted three months.'

'You're *ending* things?' Her brain felt numb but her heart and everything else inside her contracted and throbbed violently.

'How can I end something that was only temporary?' he shot back.

It was only as he walked towards the bedroom door that she realised he really did mean to leave.

A shot of furious adrenaline pulsed through her veins and she darted past him to block his exit. 'What is wrong with you?'

'I'll tell you what's wrong, *Princess*. Thinking we could have a future together. Thinking we could be a family. I've done everything in my power to make up for the wrongs I did to you, but it isn't enough. You won't trust me. You won't even consider making things permanent between us because you've got it in your head that the minute you agree I'm going to lock a ball and chain on you and stamp my thumbprint on your forehead—*just like your father*. That you can think such things of me...' His nostrils flared with disdain. 'You want your freedom? Well, guess what,

Princess? Your freedom starts now. I'll sign the apartment over to you. *Fitting*, don't you think?'

'I don't want your apartment,' she cried. Feeling herself on the verge of swearing, something she never did, she sucked in a breath.

'It's the safest place for my child,' he responded coldly. His arms wrapped around his chest, the muscles in his biceps bulging. 'It has security and people on hand if you need them.' A burst of emotion flared in his voice. 'Don't think for a second that I will abdicate my responsibility for her. I love our baby and I *will* be a father to her. Try and keep her from me and I will fight you. Now move or I will move you.'

He would do it. Everything on his face and in his body language told her he would scoop her up and set her aside if she didn't let him pass.

Folding her arms tightly across her chest, Claudia raised herself onto her toes so her face was as close to his as it could be without having to touch him. She was barely aware of the tears falling down her cheeks until she opened her mouth and tasted their saltiness. 'You wonder why I can't trust you when you treat me like this? When you throw me to one side because I won't roll over and abide by your wishes? I've had a lifetime of being a doormat. If I'm going to have a real marriage then I want one that's got love at its core and which is built on mutual respect. If you'd shown a little more patience maybe I would have found that with you but you don't *have* any patience; everything has to be immediate. You didn't give yourself time to grieve for your father because you were too consumed with your vengeance and now you're eaten with guilt and think a ready-made family will ease it.'

'Don't you *dare* bring my father into this.' His eyes had become blocks of emerald ice.

'He's the reason we're here!' Claudia's chin trembled so hard and her throat was so constricted that getting the words out hurt. 'I forgave you a long time ago for your despicable lies because I understood you were acting out of grief for him. I *made* myself forgive you for our baby's sake. I hope for our baby's sake that one day you can forgive yourself too.'

His expression didn't change. She might as well have been talking to a brick wall.

His expression didn't alter either when he clamped his hands on her sides, lifted her off her feet and moved her two steps away from the door.

He didn't look back as he walked down the stairs and out of the apartment and out of her life.

CHAPTER FOURTEEN

THE BUSTLE, BRIGHT colours and noise of Tokyo were something Ciro normally enjoyed. He'd only been to the city a couple of times before and found it an energising and fascinating place to be. Like when he worked in the Middle East, the business practices and customs were different from what he was used to, something he usually relished. On this trip he couldn't find any enthusiasm for anything, not even the huge building he was in the process of buying.

When he'd thought his future involved a family he'd considered making this the last purchase of his business empire.

As he gazed out of his hotel window, far too wired to sleep even though it was two a.m. Tokyo time, a message came through from his lawyer. The cash offer he'd made for an apartment three blocks from his department store had been accepted. Once the cash was transferred, it would be his. He fired a message back telling him to get the deal finalised immediately, then messaged Marcy with instructions to get the new apartment furnished. Ciro disliked staying in hotels. Even the most opulent of them were bland and generic to his eyes. If he could return to Manhattan and have the new apartment ready for him to move into, that would be one less aggravation.

No sooner had he pressed send on the message than his phone vibrated in his hand.

A cold sweat broke out on his forehead when he saw the name of the caller. It was Claudia.

He hadn't seen or spoken to her since he'd walked out four days ago. He'd tried hard not to think about her too. It had proved impossible.

Suddenly wishing he had a strong drink in hand, he took a deep breath and answered it. 'Yes?'

The gentle sound of her clearing her throat echoed into his ear. 'Ciro?'

'Yes. Is everything okay?'

'I've just had a call from the clinic.'

His heart rate, already erratic from the sound of her voice, clattered violently. 'Is something wrong with the baby?'

'No, no, please don't worry. They called to tell me I'd missed the scan appointment. I'm really sorry. They sent me a letter but they addressed it to Mrs Trapani and I didn't recognise the words so I didn't open it. I assumed it was for you and you'd open it when you got back from Japan. I've got a pile of letters waiting for you.'

'Give them to Marcy. What's happening with the scan? Are they rearranging the appointment?'

'They can fit me in this afternoon. I said I'd speak to you—'

'You should go.'

'Are you sure? I don't want you to miss it.' Her anxiety at this made his clattering heart give a sudden wrench. 'We can rearrange it for when you get back.'

'No. Go ahead. Scans are important. We can book another one further down the line that I'll come along to. Take Marcy with you—she can deal with the paperwork.'

'I feel terrible. I'm so sorry.'

'Don't be. It isn't your fault.' The only person at fault was, as always, her bastard father. If he'd given her the help she'd needed all those years ago, Claudia wouldn't be so reliant on other people to do her reading for her. 'Let me know how it goes. And send me a video or a picture, okay?'

'Of course I will.'

'And, Claudia…?'

'Yes?'

'Thanks for letting me know.'

Her, 'You're welcome,' was a whisper that barely brushed his ears before the line went dead.

She'd hung up on him.

Claudia sat on the bed gazing at the framed scan of her baby daughter with a heart so full of love it choked her. She'd got Marcy to email Ciro the same picture and the video the clinic had made of it too. It warmed her cold bones to know he would be looking at it with the same love.

Her phone rang. Her heart caught and she held her breath as she pulled it out of her pocket. Would it be Ciro responding to the emails? Marcy had warned her he had back-to-back meetings that day. All the same, her stomach plummeted when she recognised her sister's name on the screen.

Looking at her reflection in the bedroom mirror, Claudia forced a smile to her face before answering the call. She'd seen a heroine do the same thing on a television show once, the smile supposedly inflecting in the voice. She had no idea why she felt the need to do it too or why she felt so flat, so…bereft.

She guessed that particular heroine didn't have a sister who could read voices. Imma listened to her greeting and her concern was immediate.

'I'm fine, I promise,' Claudia assured her. Imma already knew that she and Ciro had gone their separate ways. For once, Claudia hadn't confided everything, simply said they'd brought their day of parting forward. Too many bitter, hateful words had been exchanged for her to want to relive them.

'You've never been alone before,' Imma pointed out.

'I was alone whenever Ciro travelled on business. This is the same. Just longer.' Just permanent.

'Come back to Sicily,' Imma begged. 'Please. I'll look after you and the baby.'

'I don't need looking after,' she told her honestly. 'New York's my home now. I'm getting to know my way around, and Ciro's here if I need him.'

Imma snorted.

'He's my baby's father and he loves her,' Claudia said quietly. Ciro's vehemence in stating he would fight her if she tried to keep their baby from him had been heartfelt. She supposed such a threat should frighten her, but it didn't. She'd been terrified from the moment she'd taken the pregnancy test that he wouldn't be able to love their baby and now that she knew he did, she could sleep easier. Not that she'd been able to sleep much since they'd parted. It didn't matter how much she tried adjusting the air conditioning, her bones always felt too cold to sleep.

Maybe she just needed to get used to sleeping in the guest room. She hadn't been able to bring herself to sleep in the bed they'd shared.

They chatted a little longer, Imma filling her in on everything going on back home in Sicily. At some point Claudia was going to have to return and visit her father. She spoke to him occasionally and though it broke her heart to avoid him, it was nothing less than he deserved. But he was still her father and she still loved him.

For what he'd done to Ciro's family and all the other families he'd hurt, though, she would never forgive him.

Ciro threw half the bagel he'd bought for his breakfast in the bin. He didn't know why but he found them bland now. He wondered if he'd damaged his taste buds because in recent weeks all food seemed bland to him.

As this was his first day off in a fortnight he set out to do what he'd promised himself he would do weeks ago and headed to the guest room that adjoined his new master suite. It would make an excellent nursery for the baby. That was if he stayed here long enough before the birth without selling up and buying somewhere else. As with his marriage, purchasing an apartment chosen and paid for in haste while on a trip to Japan meant he could repent at his leisure. When it came to this apartment, he had plenty of repenting to do. He hated the place.

When it came to his marriage…

He shoved the thought from his mind, just as he always did when the image of Claudia floated in his head.

They spoke. They communicated, sometimes directly, sometimes through Marcy. But never in person. She had an obstetrician appointment next week that she'd invited him to attend. It would be the first time they'd seen each other since their parting.

How much easier it would be to hold onto his fury if she weren't so damn considerate. Typical Claudia, putting their baby first.

The only person she wouldn't put first, he thought grimly, was him.

Trying again to shove thoughts of Claudia aside, Ciro rubbed his hand over his mouth and contemplated the room's dimensions, pondering where best to place the nursery furniture, and then pondering what nursery furniture even entailed. There was a lot he had to learn before his daughter's birth.

His brain moving on to colour schemes, he opened the dressing-room door to double check it would be large enough for all the baby clothing he intended to buy. A couple of large cardboard boxes were neatly stacked in it.

He groaned. He'd got his staff to pack all his personal possessions for him at the old apartment—now Claudia's apartment—then unpack everything for him here at the new one.

Tempting though it was to leave the boxes and get his staff to sort them tomorrow, now he knew they were there, he figured he might as well just deal with them himself.

Crouching down before them, he picked at the packing tape of the top one then ripped it off.

Tissue paper covered the contents and he roughly pulled it out.

And then his heart stopped when he recognised the white Sicilian lace the tissue paper had been hiding.

Claudia's wedding dress.

Seeing that dress was like looking at a ghost.

He stared at it with blood rushing through his ears. The room began to spin.

Groping as if in a dream, he pulled the dress from the box and, getting to his feet, removed the clear plastic protector. Memories flooded him before he could stop them, filling him until every cell in his body throbbed. How beautiful she'd looked in this dress. How sincere her vows had been. How the last time he'd seen this dress had been when she'd point-blank refused to have the guest room and insisted on sharing his room with him.

He'd bought himself a new apartment but it was as if she'd come with him in spirit. She was everywhere he went. He couldn't go into the kitchen without seeing her there baking. He couldn't go into his new library without seeing her stretched out on his old reading sofa. He couldn't even use the bathroom without remembering the cute way she brushed her teeth.

And now this dress lay in his arms like a physical manifestation of her absence and the *pain* that tore through him…

The room spun harder and without any warning his legs gave way beneath him and he slumped to the floor.

Crumpling the dress to his chest, he held it tightly and tried to breathe. There was a stabbing burn behind his eyes that made the room become a blur. But he could still see her face. It was right there in his retinas. Her dazzling smile. Her sweetness. Her *goodness.* All radiating there in front of him, blazing with her fieriness. Her protectiveness. Her strength. Her bravery. This was a woman who'd grown up with only a pair of red shoes and an elusive scent to remember her mother by whereas he…

He'd had over thirty years with both his parents. His father was gone but he still had his mother. Claudia hadn't lost her father in a literal sense but in a figurative sense he was gone. The man she'd believed him to be didn't exist.

Ciro had grieved for his father and looked at the world through vengeful eyes, needing to strike back and *do* something to balm the pain in his heart. Claudia refused to be a victim. She did what she believed to be right in her heart and used her conscience to guide her. It would never occur to her to use their child as a weapon against him and she would be horrified if anyone suggested it.

And he'd walked away from her. And for what? Because she wasn't stupid enough to trust a man who'd betrayed her so badly with promises of for ever? Because the woman who'd been hidden away and suffocated all her life wanted to strike out and learn to breathe on her own?

He'd spouted about wanting to slow down but had expected Claudia to speed up and when she'd refused to move to his timescale, he'd dropped her like a hot stone, the insinuation he was like her father the last straw. She hadn't even said that—in his hurt and rage, he'd interpreted it like that because, as they said, the truth hurt. He *had* tried to browbeat her into falling in line with his plans. All he'd heard from her lips was rejection. His pride couldn't take it. As always with him, it had been all or nothing. No patience.

He'd never had any patience. Never had the ability to sit still for anything longer than a movie. Even the books he liked to read were fast-paced, the food he ate ordered for speed as much as taste.

Without him even noticing, Claudia had taught him to slow down and enjoy the simple pleasures life had to offer.

She'd given up everything for their baby so Ciro could be a father to it. She'd fought tooth and nail for them to forge a relationship. And, as always, he'd wanted more. He always wanted more. He'd never been satisfied with his lot, always pushing, always striving for better, for greater.

Nothing in his life was or ever had been better or greater than Claudia.

Two days later and Ciro left the boardroom and headed to his office. The working day was almost done. As he passed his administration team, he noticed a group of them huddled around a desk. When they saw him, they parted like the Red Sea and scattered back to their desks.

He grimaced, not that they'd been talking together but that they were clearly wary of his mood. He'd be the first to admit he hadn't been the easiest person to work for in recent weeks.

And then he noticed what they'd all been huddled

around. A box with the lid open revealed a two-tier cake decorated with an artistry and craftsmanship any *patissier* would be proud of. Instinct told him who this particular *patissier* was. Claudia's name, printed with a flourish on the side of the box, confirmed it. Marcy, with Ciro's permission, had ordered the cake boxes for her.

'Is there a celebration I should know about?' he asked Rachel, the woman whose desk the cake was on.

She managed a quick, wary smile. 'It's my cousin's twenty-first birthday.'

He had no idea if his staff knew he'd left Claudia. Marcy was utterly discreet but his staff had eyes. He did not employ stupid people. He cleared his throat. 'I hope your cousin likes it. You're having a party?'

She nodded.

Reaching into his back pocket, he pulled his wallet out and removed two hundred dollars. He handed the cash to Rachel. 'Wish her a happy birthday and get the first drinks in on me.'

Her surprised words of thanks were distant echoes as he left her and continued to his office.

He locked the door and slumped into his chair, cradling his head as the latest wave of pain he'd been fighting since seeing that cake finally unleashed inside him.

Everything inside him hurt.

He couldn't describe even to himself how much pain he was in. But he welcomed it too. This was what he deserved: every ounce of pain as penance for what he'd done to the purest-hearted woman to walk the earth.

When the wave had subsided, he stared at the wall of his office that partitioned the lobby. On the other side of the lobby was the apartment. Claudia was in there. What was she doing? Baking another cake? Cooking something else? Listening to a book? Watching a movie?

He hadn't set eyes on her in three weeks.

They had been the most painful three weeks of his life. He had no idea how he was going to react when he saw her in a few days at the obstetrician appointment.

He had no idea if he could wait that long to see her again. He missed her more than he'd known it was humanly possible to miss someone.

Claudia turned the dishwasher on and, with a sigh, filled the sink for the items she didn't trust the dishwasher with. She picked up one of her new knives. The knife set was the first thing she'd bought with the money she'd been paid for a cake she'd made. It was the first money she'd ever earned and it had felt even more amazing than she'd dreamed.

But the joy of the moment had been tainted when she'd picked up her phone to share her joy with Ciro and had put it down without calling him. He wouldn't want to hear it.

She'd called Imma instead but it hadn't been the same. It was Ciro she'd wanted to share the moment with. It was Ciro she'd longed to show the cake boxes with her name emblazoned on them.

Because it was Ciro who'd never let her illiteracy define her or allowed *her* to let it define her.

Closing her eyes, she sent a prayer for the pain in her heart to ease some time soon. *And, please, God, let me stop missing him. It hurts too much.*

Only three more days and she would see him again. The pregnancy was accelerating. Soon she would be overwhelmed with appointments for baby checks. Through the messages they'd exchanged, she knew Ciro would want to attend all of them.

Putting the sharp knife into the hot, soapy water, she knew she had to get a handle on her emotions, and soon. She had to stay strong like Elizabeth Bennet. Even when

Elizabeth realised Mr Darcy wasn't the unpleasant, arrogant man she'd believed him to be and her feelings developed into a love she didn't think could be realised, she remained strong…

Love?

There was a lurch in Claudia's stomach so strong that she reflexively tightened her fingers around the sharp blade of the knife.

The water in the sink quickly turned red. She gazed at it in horror and lifted her shaking hand out, feeling as if she'd slipped into a nightmare. All four fingers of her left hand had a slice mark where they joined her hand. All four slices were dripping blood. Red splatters hit the floor.

She couldn't get her brain to unfreeze enough to tend to the wounds. Horror thrashed through her veins and into her heart. Her breaths became shallow. She couldn't take in air. The room began to move, not in a full-powered spin but in stomach-churning slow motion.

She loved Ciro.

Her stomach tightened. She blinked and put her good hand to it and felt it tighten again. That was her baby.

She could feel her baby!

Finally getting air into her lungs, she took a clean tea towel out of the drawer and absently wound it over her wounded fingers, all the while her brain racing at a hundred miles an hour. She needed to share this moment with Ciro. He would want to know.

He should be here sharing it with her…

The wail rose up her throat and escaped from her mouth before she even knew it had formed.

The slow-motion spinning accelerated and she grabbed hold of the worktop to stop herself falling. She could do nothing to stop the tears falling. She could do nothing to stop the sobs ripping out of her.

It took for ever before she had herself under any semblance of control but the feeling of being in a dream/nightmare didn't lessen and it was with her feet working of their own accord that she headed for the front door, wiping fresh tears from her eyes every other step.

She needed to find Ciro. He needed to know she'd felt their baby move. He was still in the building. She knew it in her heart. All she had to do was find him.

She opened the front door and for a split second thought she really had fallen into a dream.

Standing on the other side of it, his finger poised to ring the intercom, stood Ciro.

CHAPTER FIFTEEN

ALL THE AIR was punched out of Ciro at the first sight of her. He could barely remember walking from his office to the apartment. Once minute he'd been at his desk, the next his legs had been moving, the only thing with any solidity the image of Claudia that had become stuck on his vision.

And there she stood, right before him, her face blotchy, half of her plaited hair undone, eyes red…

'What's wrong?' he asked, snapping from stupor to alert in an instant. And then he noticed the tea towel wrapped around her hand and the blood soaking through it. 'My God, you're hurt.'

She shook her head but the tears spilling down her face told him a very different story.

'We need to get you to hospital.'

But her head shook again and her throat moved a number of times before she croaked, 'It looks worse than it is.'

Working on automatic pilot, he put an arm around her waist and gently led her back inside. He had to fight through the loud pulse in his ears to think coherently. There was a first-aid kit in the kitchen. He would look at her injury there. If he judged it to be serious he would take her straight to hospital, whether she wanted him to or not.

She let him guide her, as meek as a newborn lamb.

The sight he found in the kitchen only increased his

horror. It was as if a massacre had taken place. There was blood on the hardwood floor, on the kitchen counter, in the sink…

Sitting her on the window seat, he hurried to the cupboard with the kit in it and grabbed it, then was back at her side in a flash.

Not a word was exchanged as she let him carefully unpeel the tea towel.

He winced to see the damage and quickly pressed the tea towel back into place, ordering her to hold it tight. She complied.

'This needs medical attention,' he said as he ripped through the wrapping of a fresh, sterile bandage. 'We need to get you to hospital. No arguing. I'll call my driver. He'll get the car ready for us.'

'No! It isn't that bad. Really.'

'For my own peace of mind, will you please let me take you there?'

'It'll be a waste of time and money.'

'*Bedda*, it looks like a slaughterhouse in here.'

She winced. 'It only looks that bad because I had a mad few moments and didn't do anything to stop the bleeding.'

'Why wouldn't you tend to something like this immediately?' he asked, bewildered at this kind of irrationality from someone usually so level-headed.

'I…' She swallowed and clamped her lips back together.

'Look, I'm going to call my doctor out, okay? I won't be able to rest until you've had a professional look at the wounds.' Not waiting for her to answer, he made the call.

When he ended the call, he found her looking at him, her dark brown eyes glistening.

'I felt the baby move.'

'Did you?' His heart thumped. 'What did it feel like?'

'Magical.' A tear fell down her cheek. 'I'm sorry you

weren't there to share it. That's where I was going. To find you. So I could tell you.'

'You put off doing anything about your hand because you wanted to tell me the baby moved?'

'It didn't hurt much,' she mumbled, looking away. But then her gaze shot back to him and something like focus came into her eyes. 'What were you doing at the door? Were you coming to see me?'

He took a deep inhalation and nodded.

'Why?'

The heavy weight compressing his chest spread to smother his throat. It took a moment for him to clear it.

Tentatively, he took her uninjured hand in his. The weight loosened a fraction when she didn't immediately tug it away. The beautiful brown eyes that rarely missed anything kept a steadfast gaze on him.

'I just…' he cleared his throat again '…needed to see you. *Bedda*... I've missed you.'

She drew a sharp breath.

He brought her hand to his lips and pressed a kiss to it. 'I'm sorry, *bedda*. For how I reacted. For running away. For being an arrogant, impatient bastard.'

Her throat moved as she breathed deeply through her pretty, snub nose.

His heart ached to look at her. Everything in him ached.

He'd hurt her so much and in so many ways. How could she bear to share the same air as him?

'I've always been impatient,' he said. 'I had so many dreams as a little boy and I couldn't wait to get out into the world and live them. I was always pushing, always striving for the next fix, always restless. I neglected my parents. Not deliberately but I took them for granted. I fitted them into *my* schedule, never considering how they would drop everything for one of my visits. I knew they were proud of me and that felt great. Because it was all about *me*. When my father died…' He breathed into her hand. The softness of her skin soothed his raging heartbeats. The gentleness of her stare felt as if his soul were being bathed in honey.

'You know how much his death devastated me,' he said quietly. 'You were right about so many things. I *didn't* give myself time to grieve. And I did blame myself as much as I blamed your father. I don't know if Papà thought of confiding his troubles in me. I don't know because I wasn't there. When I left Sicily at eighteen, I left body and soul and my parents knew it. That is something else I must live with—my neglect of the two people who gave me more love than a child could wish for. But you were wrong about one thing.'

Her eyes flickered.

'I don't want a ready-made family with you to ease my guilt or because it's convenient.'

He let go of her hand and dragged his fingers down his face. The sigh he gave contained such hopelessness that Claudia's heart wrenched to hear it.

'You made me feel things right from the start. Real feelings. And then I found myself trapped in a hell of my own making, locked in a marriage with my enemy's daughter and I couldn't handle it. Even when I asked you to stay and be a family, I was fighting the truth.'

'Which is?' she whispered.

'That I love you. These weeks without you have been the worst of my life. I am broken without you. You, Claudia Buscetta—and you must always wear your name with pride because your goodness counteracts every one of your father's evil deeds—are the most loving, beautiful human being in the world. You deserve so much more than life has given you and I will regret my treatment of you to my dying day. I am here to ask—beg—you to give me one more chance. Please. I can't breathe without you. I'll accept whatever terms you make but, please, I beg you, let me share your life as well as our baby's life.'

As Claudia listened to this most prideful of men bear his soul, the last of the coldness that had enveloped her since he'd left melted away and sunshine heated her skin.

Leaning closer to him, she palmed his cheek. Now that she dared look at him properly, she saw the weight of the grief lining his handsome features. His eyes were heavy with sleep deprivation. He needed a shave.

'You never asked how I injured myself,' she said quietly.

His pain-filled eyes flashed with curiosity.

She rubbed her nose to his. Her senses exploded with joy as his woody scent hit her. 'I accidentally cut myself because I suddenly realised I love you. A moment later our baby moved. Ciro, it felt like she was kicking sense into me.'

He stared at her, brow furrowed with confusion.

'You're not the only one who's been fighting their feelings.' She stroked his cheekbone. 'I was too frightened to trust you again and *terrified* of trusting my feelings for you. I kept going over the past rather than thinking of all the wonderful things you've done for me in the present. You refused to let me make excuses for myself. You forced me to stand tall and be counted. *That's* what you've given me, Ciro, my self-respect. If having the freedom to live without you means being cold to my bones for the rest of my life then it's a freedom I don't want. The only freedom I want is the freedom to love you and wake beside you every day and the freedom to know you will love and support me in everything I do, just as I will love and support you in everything you do.'

Ciro's heart thudded. He hardly dared believe what

Claudia's mouth and loving eyes were saying. He swallowed. 'You love me?'

'Yes. I love you,' she repeated softly against his lips. 'And I want to spend the rest of my life with you. Together. Under the same roof. You, me and our daughter. You're my world, Ciro.'

Something cracked deep inside him, a fissure that ripped open, expelling the last of the darkness that had made itself at home in him since his father's death. Into its place poured dazzling sunlight. Wrapping his arms around her, he crushed his mouth to hers and kissed her with all the love flowing in his heart.

'Oh, my beautiful love,' he whispered. 'I swear I will always love and cherish you. Always.'

'Always,' she echoed.

And he did love and cherish her. Always.

EPILOGUE

Ciro drove through the security gates that protected this exclusive New York suburb, nodded at the two guards on duty, and continued to the end of the long drive where he drove through another electric gate, this one exclusively protecting his estate. As happened every day of his working life, his heart lifted to see his huge white home gleaming under the sun and he had to resist putting his foot down to get there quicker. With three children, there was always the risk one of them might come flying out from behind one of the trees in the orchard to spray his car with rubber bullets.

He got out, threw his keys at his head groundsman to park for him and hurried into the house.

To his disappointment, Claudia wasn't in. The huge kitchen, with its three hobs and three ovens designed by her own beautiful hands, was filled with jars of jam she'd made from the fruit she grew in their huge plot. They would go into the Christmas hampers she made every year for his Manhattan store, a natural follow-on from the cake-shop concession she'd opened in it and which had proved to be a massive hit with his clientele.

There were no labels on the jars. That would be done by the assistant Ciro employed for her. Suddenly hungry, he wondered if she'd notice if he opened one of them to spread over the crumpets she'd made the day before.

About to pilfer one of the jars, he suddenly noticed the letter left on the kitchen island, which by itself was as large as the kitchen of his old apartment.

Written in large, unsteady, childish writing, the note said:

Dear Ciro
Taken Alessandro and Roberto swimming.
Rosa at playdate.
I love you.
Claudia xxxxx

Seeing Claudia's penmanship never failed to choke him. He knew she would have perspired with the strain of writing this simple letter.

His beautiful, brave wife would never be able to read fluently—their youngest child, three-year-old Roberto, had an older reading age—but every letter written and every letter read was a feat of endurance that filled him with more pride than he could contain.

He was about to swallow his first bite of crumpet when the front door flew open and his two youngest children hurled themselves at him like ballistic missiles. Their mother followed, took one look at what was in his hand and the opened jam jar on the counter, and her eyes narrowed.

Using their children as a human shield failed to save him from her. She wrapped her arms around his neck and licked the jam from the corner of his mouth. 'You, Ciro Trapani, are in so much trouble.'

'Are you going to punish me?' he murmured, squeezing her peachy bottom.

'Oh, yes,' she breathed.

'I can't wait.'

That night, baby number four was conceived.

* * * * *

HIRED BY THE IMPOSSIBLE GREEK

CLARE CONNELLY

PROLOGUE

IT WAS THE fourth time he'd been called upon to act in this capacity at one of these events, but undoubtedly not the last. For each of the previous four weddings, Santos Anastakos had been required to stand dutifully at his father Nico's side—best man, oldest son, quietly watchful—as his father had promised yet another woman to love her for as long as they both should live.

Santos's expression as he surveyed the guests was unknowingly cynical. Despite the alleged joy of the occasion, Santos couldn't summon much more than a vague degree of tolerance for his father's proclivities. Proclivities that had seen him marry eight—nine, counting today—women over the span of his lifetime.

It's different this time, Santos. This time, she's 'the one'.

Santos had long since given up arguing with his father about the foolishness of his marriage addiction. Similarly he'd abandoned firm suggestions that Nico get counselling for what had become an embarrassing and ridiculous tendency to fall in love faster than most people changed jobs.

All Santos could do was watch from the side lines and quarantine the Anastakos fortune from any fallout from the inevitable divorce. It was ungenerous to entertain such thoughts whilst standing at the front of a crowded, ancient church, listening to Nico and his latest bride proclaim their 'love' for one another.

How could that concept fail to earn his derision when he'd seen, over and over and over again, how quickly and completely love turned to hate and hurt? His own mother had been overthrown for the next Mrs Anastakos when Santos had been only three years old, and Santos had been shuttled between father and mother for the next few years before—at his father's insistence—being sent off to boarding school.

As the chaplain joyously proclaimed the happy—for now, at least—couple man and wife, Santos grimaced. He had made himself a promise after his father's third marriage had dissolved in a particularly bitter and public fashion: he would never be foolish enough to get married, nor to fall 'in love', whatever the hell that meant—and nothing in his thirty-four years had tempted Santos to question that resolve. Marriage was for fools and hopeless romantics—of which, he was proud to say, he was neither.

CHAPTER ONE

Three months later

'YES?' THE SINGLE word was infused with derision, impatience and a Greek accent that, while she'd known to expect it, still caught Amelia a little off-guard. She stared at the man—Santos Anastakos—for several seconds, the purpose for coming to this grand estate in the English countryside momentarily forgotten as she computed several things at lightning speed.

There was something so vibrant and charismatic about the man—so larger than life, so glowering and intimidating—that she could only stare at him, blinking for several seconds, as she scrambled her brain back into working order. He was dressed in a tuxedo, styled for an evening somewhere considerably grander than even this beautiful, ancient country home.

'Mr Anastakos?' she confirmed, though of course it was him—she'd seen his photograph in the papers around the time of Cameron's mother's death, when news had broken that the billionaire magnate had fathered a love child over six years earlier.

'Yes?' The word was again impatient. A light breeze rustled past, giving a hint of relief on this summer's evening, and her long, dark hair shifted a little, an errant clutch pushing across her face so she had to lift a hand to contain it, instinctively brushing it away and tucking it behind her ear.

'Darling, we're going to have to get a move on if we're to make it on time.' A woman's voice came from within the house, echoing across the marbled tiles which glittered and shone beneath Santos's hand-crafted shoes.

'I don't have all night,' he expelled, his lips flattening into a frown. 'Are you lost? Did your car break down?' His eyes were wide-set and almond-shaped and lined by thick, dark lashes. Where his complexion was swarthy and dark, his eyes were the most magnificent blue, almost silver, with flecks of black close to the iris. They shifted beyond her now, as if searching for a car or some other physical clue as to why she was here.

'Not at all. I came here to speak with you.'

His eyes narrowed, returning to her face, and she wished quite illogically that they'd turn away once more. There was something in the strength of his gaze that caused her usually unflappable pulse to flutter in a way that was incredibly unsettling. It increased when his gaze travelled downward, over the plain pink blouse she wore, towards the cream trousers that were shaped over her slender hips and legs. It was little more than a cursory inspection, as though her outfit might give away some hint of who she was and what she was doing on his doorstep.

'Have we met before?' There was a hint of wariness in his question, an emotion she couldn't fathom.

'No, sir. Not at all.'

Relief. She frowned, wondering how many people he must meet to think he'd forgotten her. 'Then what can I do for you?'

'I'm Amelia Ashford…'

'Ashford.' She could see the moment comprehension dawned. 'The famous Miss Ashford?'

'I don't know about that.' She smiled even when the idea of fame had her wanting to curl up in a ball and hide. Fame was the reason she'd opted to use her grandmother's surname when taking up this teaching position—a desire to be known only for her teaching work and nothing else.

'You are Cameron's teacher?'

'Yes.' She smiled at him, a crisp smile that flashed on

her face like lightning then disappeared again. 'I wanted to speak to you about your son.'

His shoulders squared at that, as though he resented her description of their relationship. But that wasn't Amelia's concern, whatever the rumours said—and there were plenty, about this man's parental neglect of Cameron, his refusal to support Cameron's mother… It wasn't for Amelia to speculate. Her only care was the little boy of whom she'd always been fond and whom she now considered to be quite dear to her. Perhaps her estrangement from her own parents made her feel more invested in Cameron than she otherwise would have been…but, no. The little boy was special and the grief he was suffering through demanded advocacy and support.

'Is something the matter?'

She compressed her lips, trying not to express any overt hostility. So far as she knew, this man had very little experience with children in general and his son in particular. Perhaps he didn't realise how unusual an occurrence it was for a primary schoolteacher to arrive at a parent's doorstep at eight o'clock in the evening.

It was unusual, but Amelia had timed it thus on purpose in the hope of avoiding Cameron. She hadn't wanted her little pupil to overhear them, nor to know more than he needed to at this point.

'This conversation would be better had inside. May I come in?'

His brows drew together, thick and full, giving his expression a forbidding and darkly handsome look. She thought then how intimidating he might be to some people, those who had to work with him or relied on his good opinion in order to advance professionally. Fortunately for Amelia, neither of those things applied to her. She was able to be professional and confident, her motives for coming to him motivated purely by concern for her young pupil.

'Do you make a habit of turning up uninvited at the homes of your students?'

'Not at all, sir, which should give you some clue as to how important I consider this matter to be.'

'What exactly do you consider to be important?'

'Your son.'

Again, there was something in his features, a look of annoyance or frustration, but it was gone again almost immediately. 'The nanny has put Cameron to bed already. If you wanted to see him…'

Her heart squeezed at that, and she swept her eyes shut for a moment, forcefully pushing emotions to the side. But, oh, it was almost impossible when she remembered Cynthia McDowell, who had adored and doted on her son, who had made up for all the lack of money in the world with an abundance of love and interest. To think of the dear little boy losing his mother, inheriting this man as a father and being shunted into a nanny's care all in the space of less than two months!

It only galvanised her, making her feel even more strongly about her reasons for coming to Renway Hall so late on a Friday evening. 'It's you I'd like to speak to, Mr Anastakos.'

'And it can't wait until Monday?'

She considered that a moment. 'Would Monday suit you better?'

'Not necessarily.' He shifted his shoulders. 'I'm not sure if any time would be convenient, given that I have no idea what you've come to discuss.'

'You'll just have to take it on trust, then, that I wouldn't be here if it weren't important.'

'I don't take anyone on trust,' he asserted silkily, nonetheless taking a step backward and gesturing into the hall. 'But I am intrigued.' He cast a glance at his wristwatch. 'I have five minutes.'

She bristled at that and—barely—resisted an inclination to point out that discussing his son's emotional health and welfare was something for which he should prioritise a little more time, particularly in the wake of recent events, but she didn't. It was important to keep her mind on what she wanted, and arguing unnecessarily with this man would do nothing to achieve her goal.

'Come with me.' He turned, walking down the corridor. She had a brief impression of an endless expanse of tiles and walls lined with ancient art—one in particular caught her eye, so she stopped walking for a moment to look at it properly.

'This is a Camareli.'

She felt him stop and turn without even looking in his direction. There was something about his presence that seemed to puncture the air around her—it wasn't necessary to look at him to know how he moved. He was dynamic, as though his absolute magnitude was so bright it was almost overpowering.

The painting depicted a Madonna scene. Bright colours had been used, but it was the nature of the brush strokes that had revealed the artist's hand before Amelia had seen the small signature in the bottom-right-hand corner of the painting.

'Yes.' And then, after a moment's silence, 'But we're not here to discuss art, are we, Miss Ashford?'

She jerked her gaze to his face, wondering at the rapid hammering of her pulse, the flipping of her heart inside her chest. Her features were cool, her eyes giving away nothing of her internal responses. 'No, Mr Anastakos. We're not.'

He began to move once more, turning through two wide doors into a room that had leather furniture and a grand piano. The art on the walls in here was world-class too—more famous, by artists of greater renown than Camareli.

Then again, she'd always had a thing for the lesser known Renaissance painters, and Camareli was just that.

'Maria, Cameron's teacher is here. I'll be a few minutes.'

A stunning blonde woman dressed in a slinky red gown moved with all the grace of a ballerina, standing from the white leather lounge she'd occupied a moment earlier and subjecting Amelia to the same slow inspection Santos had performed earlier. But, where Santos's eyes had seemed to trail heat over Amelia's body, the other woman's left only ice in their wake.

'But, darling, we'll be late,' Maria pouted.

Santos expelled a breath so his nostrils flared and his features showed disdain. 'Apparently it can't wait. Call Leo—he'll make you a cocktail.'

'Oh, fine, but if I'd known this would involve baby sitting and being abandoned all night I would never have come,' Maria complained, turning her slender body away from Santos and Amelia.

Amelia, for her part, could only look at Maria with a sense of wonder—she'd never seen a woman in the flesh who was so like some kind of Hollywood celebrity. Everything about her was a study in perfection, from her figure to her sheening hair; from her flawless make-up and sky-high heels to manicured nails.

'She's very beautiful,' Amelia remarked conversationally as they left the room, returning to the long marbled corridor.

'Yes,' Santos returned in almost the same tone, pausing at another doorway. This time, it led to an office, all modern furniture and computers. There was more artwork here, and a large mirror that showed a reflection of the stables.

He closed the door behind them and Amelia—for no reason she could think of—jumped a little.

'So, Miss Ashford? You have my full attention; what would you like to speak to me about?'

He gestured to one of the seats opposite his desk. She took it, crossing her legs and placing her hands in her lap, her eyes following him across the room, where he paused at a bar and opened a crystal Scotch decanter. He poured two generous measures then handed a glass to her, their fingertips brushing as he placed the Scotch in the palm of her hand.

'Thank you.' She cradled the Scotch without taking a sip. She'd bypassed the usual phases of wild abandon and teenage letting down of hair and had never really developed a tolerance for or interest in alcohol. Every now and again she enjoyed a few sips of a nice wine with a special dinner, or champagne on Christmas Eve, but it certainly wasn't something she imbibed on a daily basis.

Unlike Santos, she gathered, as he threw half of his own Scotch back in one go before resting his bottom on the edge of his desk, rather than taking up the seat opposite, so he was much closer to her than she'd anticipated. His long legs were just to her right, so she could reach out and touch them if she wanted.

The thought threw her completely off-balance in a way she'd never experienced in her life. She'd been on a few dates, but they had been academic exercises more than anything, something she'd been encouraged to try at Brent's urging and never really found comfortable or fun.

You have to give it time, Millie. Get to know a guy, see his good side. Just go with the flow!

But those dates had all ended the same way—with Amelia feeling bored out of her brain and wanting nothing more than never to see the man again. One particular date had left her so bored she'd almost fallen asleep at the table. It was very rare for her to factor her intellect into her thoughts but, at times like that, it was impossible not to realise that being a child genius, being exposed to some of the world's greatest minds from a very young age, had left her with absolutely zero tolerance for small talk. And particularly not with men who were quite clearly preoccupied with the more physical aspects of the evening.

A shudder shifted through her at the whole failed debacle of dating, but that didn't explain why now, so close to Santos Anastakos, she felt heat building inside her blood, warming her from the inside out.

The sooner she could get this over and done with, the better. She had to plead Cameron's case and then leave—she never had to see Santos again after that.

She geared herself up to start speaking, to say what she'd come to say, but Santos spoke first, his eyes roaming her face quite freely, his gaze curious now, speculative in a way that did nothing to help her overheating blood.

'How old are you?'

'I beg your pardon?'

His expression shifted; for a moment she saw scepticism there, perhaps even disapproval. 'You look too young to be a teacher.'

She ran her finger around the edge of the Scotch glass, feeling the indents in its shape. 'I've been at Elesmore for a little over three years.'

She brushed aside his disbelief. It wasn't necessary to tell him that she'd graduated with her first degree—physics—at the age of eleven, completed her second degree by thirteen and a postgraduate doctorate by fifteen, before doing an about-turn and deciding she wanted to become a teacher. He didn't need to know that she'd graduated from her education degree at sixteen and had spent a few years travelling and consulting for various space agencies before finally accepting a position in a small local comprehensive on the basis they wouldn't advertise who she was.

Anonymity and a lack of pressure had been her goal—normality after a lifetime of being pushed through one hoop to another.

'Which makes you…?' he prompted, taking another sip of his Scotch. His throat shifted as he swallowed and she found her gaze focussed on his skin there, covered by a hint of stubble, dark and thick. It would feel bristly if she reached up and ran her fingers across it.

She startled at the thought and wrenched her eyes to the view of the stables just visible in the mirror.

'My age isn't relevant,' she murmured, her fingers tightly gripping the Scotch glass. She was nervous! Amelia hadn't expected that but sitting in this man's office now, surrounded by proof of his business acumen and success, it was impossible not to recognise how dynamic and powerful he was—imposingly so. That was why she felt as though a kaleidoscope of butterflies had been let loose in her belly.

'Fine, then, let's discuss what is relevant,' he responded with a hint of something in his voice—something cold and unwelcoming, as though she were wasting his time and he wanted her gone.

'Mr Larcombe told me you're planning to pull Cameron out of Elesmore. That not only are you looking to remove him from the school he's been at since he was three years old, you're also intending to move him to Greece once the term ends.'

Silence fell, a silence that was thick and unpleasant, but Amelia resolutely didn't interrupt it, and several beats passed, each heavy with the words she'd flung at him; each filled with nothing but the sound of her thudding heart.

'And…?' The word was drawled by his lips, lips that were wide and chiselled, harsh and compelling; lips that drew her attention far more than she was comfortable with.

'And? Is it true?'

'Do you imagine the school headmaster lied to you?' His question was teasing, gently sarcastic in nature. It wasn't intended to be rude, she thought, but that didn't stop it from having an immediate effect on her.

Heat began to bloom in her cheeks. She wasn't used to being treated like an imbecile. She glared at him forcefully, her expression clearly showing how unimpressed she was, but she forced a brittle smile into place, remembering the old adage that you caught more bees with honey. 'I hoped he'd made a mistake somehow.'

'He didn't.' Santos shifted a little, inadvertently brushing her knee with his. It was like being jolted with a thousand volts of electricity. She stared at him in surprise, a reaction she was nowhere near experienced enough to conceal, and saw speculation move over his features. She blinked her eyes closed, before turning them towards the view once more, but it wasn't quite enough. He'd seen her reaction and was now wondering at the reason for it.

Great.

She was literally the opposite of the sophisticated beauty in the room down the hallway. Where Maria was stunning and expensive-looking, Amelia felt dowdy, dull and quite utterly out of her depth even having a conversation with a man like this. For goodness' sake, his *knee* had touched her knee and she was permitting that to turn her stomach into a tangle of knots! Preposterous.

'When the school year finishes, Cameron will move to Agrios Nisi with me.' He spoke as though he hadn't even realised they'd touched—his bloodstream wasn't running with the force of a thousand wild stallions.

'Why?'

'Because it's where I live. And I am apparently his father.'

She ignored the last remark. 'But what is there for him on Agrios Nisi?' The words were delivered with uncharacteristic fire, but Amelia couldn't help it. Ever since the headmaster had relayed the plans to Amelia, her head had been swimming with disapproval, and her heart with a sense of panic and pain. It wasn't right to drag Cameron away from everything and everyone he knew. The little boy deserved better than that, especially now. She knew, better than anyone, what it was like to be sent from pillar to post—and by your parents!

'Apart from miles of pristine coastline and a chance to have the kind of childhood any boy would kill for?'

A small noise of ridicule escaped her lips before she could stop it. 'What he needs, Mr Anastakos, is to be *here*—especially now.' She drew in a breath, trying to calm her racing heart and pounding pulse without much success. 'He's lost so much already this year. To take him away from the friends who adore him—and the faculty who also adore him,' she finished ineptly, her throat thick with the pain of how much Cameron had come to mean to her, 'Will be to inflict further trauma on a little boy who's already suffered considerably. I understand things weren't necessarily amicable between you and Cynthia but that hardly seems like a reason to punish Cameron. He deserves you to act in his best interests and keeping him here, in England, at Elesmore, is the very least you can do.'

'My relationship with Cameron's mother is none of your business.'

Amelia's eyes narrowed. 'No, but how you treat Cameron is, very much so.'

'As for Cynthia,' he continued, as though she hadn't spoken, 'It was neither amicable or otherwise. The truth of the mater is, we barely knew each other.'

Amelia blinked at this sterile description of the woman with whom he'd made a child and shook her head. 'Be that as it may, you clearly knew each other well enough to become parents, and now you're all Cameron has left. He deserves more than this.'

The silence that fell now was punctuated only by the sound of her own breathing. Santos stared at her from eyes that were almost oceanic in colour, his tanned skin slightly flushed along the hard ridges of his cheekbones. It was a face prone to sternness anyway, all symmetrical and sharp, as though a sculptor had been obliged to turn granite into humanity with only a blade as a tool, leaving no room for nuance and undulation, only harsh edges and finality. But now, like this? There was such obvious anger and rejection on his face that Amelia almost regretted coming here.

Almost, but not quite.

Cameron deserved to have someone fight on his behalf. At six, he was too young to realise how the adults in his life had failed him, but Amelia recognised the behaviours and, while she wouldn't ordinarily think of interfering, this was different. Cameron was different.

She refused to fail him.

CHAPTER TWO

'YOU THINK I'M wrong to take him away?' Santos straightened, drawing himself to his full six-and-a-half feet, looking down on the slight schoolteacher with a sense of rumbling fury. It wasn't entirely her fault. He'd carried this anger for weeks now—since learning that a woman he'd spent two nights with seven years ago had borne him a child and failed to mention even a hint of the boy's existence. He'd been denied any chance to know his own son, any chance to prepare for this, until Cynthia had died and both Cameron and Santos had been thrust well and truly into the deep end.

'Yes.' Her eyes didn't quite meet his. It was a frustrating habit she'd shown ever since he'd drawn the door inward to reveal her on the doorstep. One minute she was the personification of timidity and the next she was burning with passion and wild accusations, practically threatening to call child welfare, or whomever looked after inadequate parents in this country.

At least she wasn't attempting to obfuscate now. 'And you think you have any right coming here to lecture me about the choices I make for my son?'

Her eyes glanced in his direction, landing briefly on his squared jaw before skittering back to the window. His fingers tingled with an urge to reach for her chin and pull it towards him, to draw her stubborn, runaway gaze to his even when she refused to hold it.

'When they're so obviously contrary to his best interests? Yes, sir, I do.'

A muscle ticked at the base of his jaw; he felt it tapping

against his flesh and sought to control his emotions before he spoke. 'He is *my* son. I can do whatever the hell I'd like.'

'Even if that's going to hurt him?' She responded with fierceness now and something leaped inside his chest, interest and curiosity combined in one arrow of emotion.

'His mother's death hurt him,' Santos inserted quietly, the words devoid of emotion. 'His mother's choice to keep him a secret from me hurt him—and me—in untold ways. I am only doing what I would have insisted on six years ago, if Cynthia had bothered to inform me of her pregnancy.'

'I'm not interested in that,' the teacher responded, compressing her lips with a primness he found strangely tantalising. If it was true, she was unlike just about anyone in his life had been since Cameron's existence had been revealed. Everyone wanted to know about his secret child. 'However,' she conceded after a moment, 'I appreciate his pain isn't of your causing.'

'That's generous of you.' He took another sip of his Scotch and placed the cup on the edge of his desk, crossing his arms over his chest and staring down at her distractedly. 'Yet.'

She was the definition of dull. So very English, just like Cynthia had been, with that clipped accent and cool disposition. But, where Cynthia had been strikingly attractive and flirtatious, Amelia Ashford looked as though she'd rather be dragged over hot coals than spend another minute in his office. Except…

Yes, except for when their knees had brushed. She'd startled and made a soft noise, almost a moan, her lips parting and her eyes showing surprise. Was it possible that this woman was far less icy than her surface demeanour might suggest?

'If things had been different, perhaps you would have raised him in Greece, but there's no sense losing ourselves in the hypothetical. Cameron is English. He's lived here all his life, never even travelling abroad. His whole world has changed so much since the accident. He was very close to Cynthia; she adored him and every day without her is a struggle for him.' Emotion coloured thc last sentence, the threat of tears obvious in her softly voiced observation. 'Perhaps in time, when the shock has lessened and he knows you better, uprooting him wouldn't be such a monumental ask. But right now? I honestly think you'll worsen his grief tenfold. It's not fair, Mr Anastakos.'

'Fair?' He couldn't help himself. Despite the fact he could see the logic in what she was saying, disbelief fired through him, making him want to contradict her. 'You think having a small child dropped on my lap—a child I had no earthly idea existed six weeks ago—and expecting to know what is right or wrong for him is fair?'

'No,' she conceded quietly. 'Nothing about this situation is fair but you're the only one who can make a difference for Cameron. Right now, he needs all of us to pull together and help him. You can't take him away from everything he knows—everyone who knows him. He deserves better than that.'

'My son is an Anastakos. We have lived and died on Agrios Nisi for generations and he will be no different.'

Fire shifted through her eyes once more. Wide and brown, they landed on him with a strength that surprised him. 'Perhaps, but all I'm asking is that you give him time. What harm could come from leaving things as they are for another year? Let him take some solace from the school friends he's known since nursery, from the parents of his friends who know and adore him, from the teachers who—'

'Yes, care for him,' Santos interrupted, wondering why her impassioned plea was so irritating to him. 'You said that.' He didn't move his body by a degree, staying exactly as he was, his gaze heavy on her face. 'You care for my son?'

A hint of colour shifted beneath her olive complexion. 'I care for all my pupils.'

'And so you do this often, then? Go into their houses and accuse their parents of being selfish and wrong?'

Her cheeks darkened in colour as she stood, her throat moving as she swallowed convulsively. 'I'm sorry if I've offended you in some way.' The words were haughty. 'I would never forgive myself if I didn't ask you to reconsider. Cameron deserves that of me.'

She stood directly opposite him, toe to toe, though she was at least a foot shorter, so her head had to tilt in order for her eyes to meet his. 'He deserves more than this.'

Her words rang with accusation, making a mockery of her earlier apology, and something snaked through him, something born of masculine pride and ancient, primaeval impulses.

Her judgement was tightening around his chest and he felt a desire to unsettle her easy blame, to rail at her accusation and make her understand that this last month and a half had been a type of hell on earth for Santos as well. Having a child? It was something he'd always, always sworn he wouldn't do—a mistake he had never intended to replicate. He had a half-brother who could carry on the family name. Santos was free to remain single and alone, just the way he liked it. Having Cameron foisted upon him out of the blue—the product of a two-night affair with a woman he'd long since almost forgotten about—was like a stick of dynamite exploding in his face.

'Tell me, Amelia Ashford.' He couldn't help the mockery that curled through her name. 'What makes you an authority on this? Do you have children?'

Her cheeks were now the colour of the sky beyond the window, a vibrant peach, her eyes darker than the sun-ripened olives that grew wild over the southern side of Agrios Nisi.

'No.' She opened her mouth, no doubt to add further clarity to this, but Santos wasn't interested. He pressed a finger to her lips, intending only to silence her, but the moment his flesh connected with her mouth something tightened deep in his abdomen, hardening in his groin, insisting on being acknowledged.

Her eyes were saucer-wide, her lips parting on what he presumed to be an involuntary sigh. Her breath was warm as it wrapped around his finger, making it a temptation that was almost impossible to ignore. He wanted to sink his fingertip into her mouth, to see her full, pink lips wrap around it while those huge eyes of hers bored into his.

Christos, what was happening? She was hardly his type and, more than that, she'd arrived in his home purely with the intention of berating and insulting him. Perhaps that was it—the challenge in her words made him want to answer in a completely different way, to pull her body to his and drop his mouth, claiming hers, dominating her and answering her questions and accusations all at once...

'No?' He moved his finger, but didn't drop it away completely. Instead, he drew it sideways, along her cheek, before padding his thumb over her lower lip, cupping the side of her face in his palm and holding her beneath him, forcing her eyes to meet his after all.

She swallowed hard; he felt the movement of her jaw. 'I don't have children. But I do know Cameron.'

The words were husky and thick, desire making them more stilted than her previous verbal lashings.

His lips twisted in silent acknowledgement of that; he was no longer interested in discussing his surprise love child with this woman. He moved his body forward almost imperceptibly, closing the small distance between them just sufficiently to feel the softness of her surprisingly generous breasts against his chest.

'I—'

'Yes, Amelia?' What the hell was he doing? Playing with fire, that was what. She was his son's teacher and she'd come to him with perfectly legitimate concerns. While Santos Anastakos might have earned himself the moniker of billionaire playboy in the tabloids and on gossip blogs, he always knew where to draw the line. He'd never once become involved with a member of his staff, nor had he become involved in affairs—he didn't do messy, complicated, emotional. This woman didn't exactly work for him but nor was this straightforward. She'd come to him with concerns about his son and he was turning that into a sensual game of cat and mouse, enjoying the way she was sparring with him even when he resented the hell out of her accusations. This wasn't a date; it wasn't just a random encounter in a hotel bar. She was his child's schoolteacher, so why was he suddenly overcome with an urge to make love to her, right here and now?

Hell, he had Maria waiting for him in the other room, and there was very little doubt in Santos's mind as to how she wanted their evening together to end. If he wanted sex, then it was there at his disposal, but this wasn't about the slaking of a physical need. There was something about this particular woman that was drawing him in, making him want her with an urgency he hadn't felt in a very long time, if ever.

Amelia furrowed her brow as though she were confused, lost, and he knew he should step backward to give her some space and—politely—say to her, thank you for coming but don't tell me how to raise my own damned kid. Except he didn't want her to go. Suddenly the idea of Maria's practised flirtation sat like a noose around his neck and all he could think about was this woman's fire and spirit, her borderline hostility that was in and of itself so unusual for Santos to encounter these days—or ever.

If she'd had such an obvious reaction to the brushing of their knees, how would she feel if he kissed her? He dropped his head a little, as if weighing up the consequences of that. She smelled like honey and raspberry blossom, reminding him of the hedge along the side of this country estate, all sun-warmed and sweet.

Her eyes widened and perhaps she anticipated his intention. She lifted a hand to the front of his shirt, her fingers splayed wide over his chest, her eyes locked to his. He braced, wondering if she was about to push him away. She didn't. Her fingers buried themselves in the fabric, holding him right where he was, another breathy exhalation bursting against his jaw, then another, and another, her breathing as frantic as if she'd run a marathon. His body was hypercharged and attuned to every single shift of hers—he felt her breath, smelled her sweet fragrance, and the tightening of her nipples into buds against his chest made him swallow a guttural groan all of his own.

This was getting out of hand.

He'd never been one for delayed gratification. What was he waiting for? A damned starter's pistol? That had been fired the second he'd opened the door and seen her standing there.

'I'm not interested in discussing my son with you, Amelia.'

Again he felt her swallowing motion. 'Why not?'

He could barely think straight. His mind was filled with the idea of kissing her, of running his tongue over the outline of her lips before plunging it deep into her warm, wet mouth. Of tangling his fingers into the back of her hair, angling her head towards his so he had unfettered access to her mouth, throat, décolletage…

Why not? It was a fair question. One he didn't want to answer.

Because all I can think of right now is you.

How ridiculous!

Her breath was warm, each little pant of air fanning against his throat. She smelled sweet.

'I care about Cameron.' Her voice was shaking as badly as her body. 'I came here because I think that he's a little boy who's had the parameters of his world shattered beyond recognition, and if you take him away from school, from his friends and me, from England, you'll make it almost impossible for him to recover.'

Her speech was fine but it barely penetrated the fog of his brain. Her eyes were pinned to his, and a silent but volatile arc of electricity buzzed from her to him.

'We cannot stay here.' He said the words for his own benefit as much as hers.

'Not for ever.' Her hand on his chest shifted, as though she didn't realise she was still touching him. She dropped it to her side but stayed where she was, their bodies hemmed together by some powerful and invisible force. 'Just until he's over this terrible grief.'

His gut rolled at that, his belly filling with pain. Terrible grief. Yes, his son was grieving and, damn it, Santos was the last person on earth who knew how to help him. Hell, Santos had no idea how to be a father, let alone the kind of father who could assist his son in navigating this kind of emotional trauma.

'I will do what I think best for my son.' It was another pledge he made more for his own benefit than for hers. In the back of his mind, he wondered why he didn't move away, why he didn't step backward, but even as he knew he ought to his body was pressing forward, his head dropping lower, as though her lips were magnetic, drawing him closer.

'Then you'll stay in England?' They were strong words but she swallowed quickly, as though her mouth was dry, her breath thick. Her lips were the palest pink, with the perfect Cupid's bow shape. He wanted to crush his own to them, to feel their softness beneath his mouth.

Her breath was forced. He had no doubt she was thinking of kissing him, just as he was her. The air seemed to spark around them, humming with an electrical current.

'And would *you* like me to stay, Miss Ashford?'

Her eyes flickered closed, long lashes fanning her cheeks for a moment, and a tiny noise escaped from her lips. Then she blinked quickly before lifting her eyes to his once more, something like panic in their depths. Her reactions were fascinating. She was like a little butterfly, flittering and moving, so fine and nimble, so difficult to pin down.

'It's not about what I want, nor what I think *you* should do.'

'Liar.' His laugh was deep and throaty, husky, as the sound brushed her hair, lifting it slightly.

It seemed to shake her, waking her from some kind of dream. Her face tightened and her features became unreadable. Her voice, when she spoke, was authoritative. Impatient, almost. 'Fine, then. *I* would like *you* to put your son before yourself. There is no doubt in my mind that leaving England suits you very nicely. It will be much easier for you to continue your life with minimal inconvenience if you return to Greece. But Cameron's interests are served by remaining right here.' And then, to underscore her feelings, she sidestepped him, moving away a little, putting vital distance between them. Something he should have done moments earlier.

Only the flush of her cheeks betrayed that she was still feeling a rush of awareness—or that she'd ever felt anything for him whatsoever. In fact, in every other way she was suddenly ice-cold.

Fascinating.

He watched her from where he was, his eyes shuttered, taking her lead and suppressing the desire that had been rampant in his system a moment ago. He wasn't sure what had come over him but it had been stupid and inappropriate. He had Maria waiting in the room next door. This woman was his son's teacher! And absolutely not his type.

Beyond that, she'd come to his home to try to organise his life—something Santos had never particularly relished.

Her small sigh drew his gaze back to her face. 'All I ask is that you think about what you would want if you were in his shoes—your whole world changing with a sadness beyond words carried inside your heart. Ask yourself what you would need and please do only that, Mr Anastakos.'

She used his surname like a shield, pressing it between them to remind him that they were two strangers, nothing more.

And she was right—he had no idea why he'd let the strength of his impulses override every piece of common sense he possessed, but he had, and it had been wrong.

'I intend on doing the right thing by him.' His admission was gravelly, his eyes reverberating with the intensity of that pledge.

'I hope so.' She stared at him for several moments and he stood perfectly still, wondering if she was going to move closer, if she was thinking about him, if she was wishing he'd given into his impulses and kissed her. But then she blinked and shook her head, forcing a tight smile to her lips.

'Enjoy your date.'

He dipped his head in what appeared to be a nod but was actually a way to disguise his thoughts.

Santos might have been called 'the billionaire playboy' for years but he lived by a strict code of conduct, a black and white morality, and that always guided how he treated women. If his father had taught him anything—and indeed he'd learned many lessons from his father's choices, most vitally how he *didn't* want to act—it was that women deserved respect. He never slept with a woman who didn't want exactly what he did and he never slept with one woman while another was waiting in a different room of the same damned house. Shame coloured his own feelings for a moment.

'Then you've said what you came to say?'

'And I hope you'll listen to it.' Her tone was ice-cold, but there was worry in it too, as though she hoped he would heed her advice but severely doubted that he would.

He held her gaze for a long time, neither of them inclined to look away, but this time he found the power to break that connection.

'Then goodnight, Miss Ashford.'

His dismissal was every bit as cold as her own words but he didn't get any satisfaction from that. Her features showed hurt and he winced inwardly, watching as she reached the door. When her hand pressed to the handle, he spoke once more, his voice gravelly. 'Thank you.' The words were stilted. She angled her face just a little, enough for him to see the proud tilt of her chin. 'For caring about Cameron, I mean.'

A cursory nod and she was gone, pulling the door behind her with a near-silent click. He stared at it for several seconds before sitting down heavily in the chair behind his desk.

Maria would keep a moment or two. Santos didn't particularly want to see her when his cock was straining against his pants, desire for another woman making him almost desperate with needs. He sat down and tried to make sense of how a slight, prim schoolteacher had driven him to the edge of sanity with little more than the sharpness of her tongue.

Amelia stared at her ceiling, completely unable to sleep. Ever since she'd walked out of Renway Hall hours earlier, she'd been unsettled and filled with a gnawing sense of frustration that made almost everything impossible.

Her body felt different. Alive on a different cosmic plane, existing in a hyper-aware state so everything looked and felt brighter and sharper. She'd gone through the motions of a normal evening. A light dinner, fifteen minutes of meditation and then an hour on the Hayashi Analysis. Usually, that consumed her, the detailed analysis of star radius and formation stretching her brain in just the way she needed, followed by a quick back and forth messenger chat with Brent, usually about his work or hers, before dropping into bed exhausted and satisfied.

But not tonight.

Tonight Amelia had eaten only half her dinner, unable to fit anything else in a tummy that was already full of knots and butterflies. Each equation she'd performed on the Hayashi Analysis had taken twice the usual time, and she'd even found an error on one when she'd re-read her work. She'd cut short her conversation with Brent, pleading a headache.

But she didn't have a headache. Amelia had a body ache, deep in the pit of her abdomen, extending through every cell of her being. She was shaking with a need she'd never before experienced. When she closed her eyes, she saw him. When she breathed in, she smelled him. She lay in her bed and remembered the touch of his finger against her lips, the feeling of his body brushing hers. Her fingertips were still trembling as she lifted them to her lips now, feeling the skin there.

He'd been going to kiss her; she was sure of it. She had no experience in such matters but only a fool would have been unable to read the signs. His head had been lowering, his eyes rich with emotion, desire, want, need; he'd looked at her as though he'd been dying of thirst and she the only water for miles.

Something rolled through her, the ache intensifying, her need growing, so that all she wanted was to push out of bed and return to his home, time travel be damned.

And what would he say if she turned up at his front doorstep, dressed like this?

She cast a rueful glance at her pyjamas—bearing the familiar space agency logo on the right breast, they were a size too big, and the dullest shade of grey possible. They were, she decided from her very limited contemplation on the subject, the least seductive things imaginable.

She flopped back against her pillows and continued to stare at the ceiling. She had no doubt he was supremely experienced with women. Had he sensed her inexperience? Had he realised she'd never been kissed, beyond a chaste peck on the cheek? Would he still have looked at her like that if he'd known she was a virgin?

Of course not.

The woman who'd been waiting for him had been the kind of woman he was used to—beautiful, and undoubtedly worldly and experienced. For whatever reason, perhaps he'd assumed Amelia was of that ilk.

But she wasn't. She was worlds away from that. She needed to put Santos Anastakos out of her mind, once and for all. They were oil and water—they'd never mix.

CHAPTER THREE

THE IDEA HAD come to him in the early hours of Saturday morning. After a short and frustrating evening with Maria—he was far from the perfect companion given his preoccupation with a certain schoolteacher—he'd lain awake brooding over his predicament. He deeply resented *anyone* trying to run his life—he'd been doing a damned fine job of that since he was sixteen years old—but at the same time her opinion hadn't been completely unwarranted. On the face of it, he could even admit she had a good point. But staying in England was out of the question—Santos needed to believe there was another way he could live his life and still help Cameron settle into the reality of life without his mother.

And, some time before sunrise, it had struck him: the perfect solution.

A less than ideal weekend with Cameron had cemented the plan in his mind. What had he expected—that he could turn up in Cameron's life and be instantly accepted? That they would gel immediately? Santos wasn't close to his own father—he had no real model for parental behaviour—and Cameron was a grieving, troubled boy who seemed determined to keep Santos at arm's length.

He needed help and Amelia could provide that…all he had to do was convince her of the sense of his proposal.

Santos Anastakos had been born into a fortune but before his sixteenth birthday it had almost all gone—his father's lifestyle, poor business acumen and belief that each marriage would be 'everlasting' had meant he'd failed to sign pre-nups, meaning the fortune had been divided and re-divided enough times to diminish it significantly.

Santos had restored it, piece by piece, investment by investment, so that by his twenty-fifth birthday Anastakos Inc had been the fastest growing brand in the world and his personal fortune was one of the largest. It took skill and determination, and several habits had always guided Santos. He read people and committed their traits to memory but, more importantly, he looked for their weaknesses, things he could exploit to his advantage.

Amelia had shown him her weakness and he had no doubts as to how to exploit it to get exactly what he wanted. The ends justified the means, though—they had to. He was sinking, with no idea what to say or how to behave with his own damned son. For a man who commanded any room he entered, the complete lack of power made him feel impotent. He hated it.

He'd never wanted children; he'd been very careful to avoid having children—or so he'd believed. Nonetheless, Cameron was in existence, a six-year-old boy who was the spitting image of Santos at around the same age. His eyes were unmistakable—it was like looking in a miniature mirror. The DNA test he'd flown to England prepared to organise had been rendered unnecessary from the first meeting. Cameron was his son.

All that was left to do was work out *how* to be a father. People talked about parenting instincts but Santos had none. He didn't really like children—they were illogical and emotional, demanding. And yet there *was* something else, something he hadn't expected: a kind of soul-deep connection. He looked at Cameron and felt a link to his past, as though a part of himself had been severed from his body and become independent. He also felt an overwhelming fear: fear of ruining Cameron's life; of hurting him; of making him miserable; and, yes, of compounding the grief he was feeling now; fear that he wouldn't be the father Cameron needed—that he wasn't capable of being any kind of father.

He was terrified that his son would come to hate him.

He ruminated on this as he waited in his car, watching the entrance to the school. It was a nice enough school, he conceded, though far from what he might have chosen had he known he was a father. Cynthia had enrolled him in the local comprehensive—because anything else had been beyond her budget. The area was good, though, the buildings quaint in that English style and the street he was parked in lined with leafy trees.

Something shifted in the periphery of his vision and he responded immediately, training his gaze on the movement: Amelia. He pressed his hand to the door handle, preparing to step out.

But, for just a moment, he watched her. It was another warm day and today she was wearing a dress. Pale grey with an intricate pattern—perhaps flowers—it wrapped around her chest and tied at the waist, drawing attention to her gentle curves, the roundness of her breasts and neatness of her waist, so the same torpedo of attraction was spiralling through him, unwelcome and completely unwanted.

He wasn't here to notice her damned figure, no matter how tempting he found it. More important considerations were at stake. Cameron had barely spoken to Santos since coming to stay with him, but when he had it had all been about Miss Ashford.

'Miss Ashford this...'

'Miss Ashford that...'

'Miss Ashford makes me feel happy...'

'Miss Ashford understands me...'

'Miss Ashford says...'

And on and on and on.

It had been a little irritating before but, now that he'd met Miss Ashford for himself, it was downright distracting. He didn't need any help putting that woman front and centre of his mind. All weekend he'd found his thoughts straying to her, remembering the husky little breath she'd made up close, the way her lips had parted when he'd moved close, as though silently inviting him to kiss her. To the way her eyes had rolled back at the simple touch of his fingertip to her lips, almost as though she'd been on the brink of an orgasm from the light, meaningless flirtation.

And he'd wondered about what would have happened if he'd acted more swiftly, kissing her as soon as he'd wanted to rather than trying to fight his desire. She'd been doing the same exercise, he was certain of it, and she'd triumphed in a way he hadn't. She'd put an end to the preamble—for surely it had been? Another minute and his mouth would have claimed hers, his lips dominating hers…and then?

Yes, that was where he came unstuck, because 'and then' was a slippery slope to the kind of fantasies that made it hard for him to watch Miss Ashford even at this distance without feeling a stirring in his groin.

Pushing out of the car with a determined tilt of his head, Santos strode across the street, arriving at her side before she'd even registered his presence. She glanced up at him and, at the moment of realisation, made a husky noise of acknowledgement that almost skittled the carefully thought out proposal he was about to make, given how much it reminded him of Friday night.

'Miss Ashford.' He couldn't help it. The words were drawled with a hint of sensuality, so her pupils darkened and her cheeks filled with that ready blush once more.

'Mr Anastakos.' She took a step back, her eyes failing to meet his. Didn't she realise how crazy that made him?

'I need to speak with you.'

'Oh?' Her brows drew together and her hands fidgeted with her car keys. 'You do? About what?'

It was an artless response and inwardly he smiled. If she

thought he'd come to talk about their obvious chemistry then it proved she was at least as aware of it as he. It was a short-lived triumph. Desire for this woman would only complicate what he needed, and he was quite certain now that she was essential to his plan.

'Cameron.' Her expression shifted speculatively at the mention of the young boy. She hadn't been expecting that. 'Do you have a moment?'

'I…' Her teeth dragged on her lower lip and her body swayed a little, tiny gestures of temptation that didn't escape his notice. 'If it's a parent-teacher interview then I suggest you make an appointment through the headmaster's office.'

His smile was laced with scepticism. She'd already shown him how deeply she cared for Cameron. Her objection was weak at best, born of a desire not to act on the crazy, sensual impulses that were fogging them both. 'It's important.'

He could feel her prevaricating and then, finally, she sighed. 'Fine. What is it?'

He gestured towards a bench, a little way down the path in the shade of a considerable elm tree.

'That's okay. I don't have long right now so I suggest you cut right to it.' She cast a glance at her wristwatch, a small frown pulling at her features. The statement pushed under his skin, making him wonder where she was going, making him wonder a great many things: what was her life like, what did she do outside of school?

'I've thought about your objections to my plans.'

Her eyes clearly showed surprise.

'You weren't expecting that?'

'Frankly? No.'

'Why not?'

'Honestly?'

'Always.' It was a husky encouragement.

She bit down on her lower lip as she thought about that. 'You don't strike me as the kind of man who would change his mind.'

'No?'

She shook her head. 'You seem too arrogant for that.'

His brows shifted upwards and she clamped a hand over her mouth, her eyes sweetly apologetic. Sweetly? What the hell…?

'Oh, I still believe taking Cameron to Agrios Nisi is the correct decision.' He spoke firmly, allaying any relief she might have felt.

Her features shifted, sparking with the defiance that was instantly familiar.

'Then you haven't changed your mind?'

'No.'

'Oh.' Her disappointment was obvious, her full lips instinctively dropping into a small frown, and he repressed an impulse to wipe his thumb across her lower lip once more to remind himself of how soft and sweet they felt beneath his touch. As if she could read his mind, she lifted her own fingers to her lower lip, tracing the outline there. It was almost painful to watch her reciprocate, so he jabbed his hands in his pockets, focussing on his reasons for being here.

'I do not want to make Cameron's life harder than it needs to be. I am, naturally, mindful of what he's been through, and for how that's affecting him. I concede that these changes must be overwhelming to the boy and, like you, I want to protect him.'

'You do?' Her brow furrowed, her lip dropping further. His body tightened in an immediate and unwelcome response.

'Of course. Do you think I'm some kind of monster? That I'd revel in my own son's pain?'

'I didn't mean that.' Her cheeks bloomed into a pink the colour of plum blossoms.

'Didn't you?'

He scanned her face—not dowdy, not even remotely. 'Considered' would be a better word. Measured. Everything about her was carefully audited, even her reaction in his office. Desire had been swamping them both but she'd pulled herself back, wrapping herself in a veneer of ice, pushing him away before things could get out of hand. Her control was impressive. Or perhaps he was just surprised to meet a woman who wasn't vying to be taken to bed by him. It had been many years since he'd been turned down—if ever. It was little wonder the experience had dominated his thoughts since. It was the novelty factor.

'No!' Her denial was emphatic. 'But moving him to Greece is, in my opinion, going to be very difficult for him.'

'And you don't want that.'

'No.' Her voice softened, the hint of a smile curving her lips. 'I—I told you the other night…' She stumbled awkwardly over the words. 'I care for Cameron very deeply. I understand the position is awkward for both of you but *you're* the adult. It's your job to protect him.'

'And I intend to.' His eyes sparked with hers, narrowing speculatively. 'Which brings me to why I'm here.'

She waited, silent, her eyes boring into his now, her lips parted ever so slightly. He wished she wouldn't do that.

'I have a proposition for you.'

Her eyes grew more round, her lips parting further as she whooshed out a deep breath. 'Go on,' she prompted, though it sounded as if she'd rather do just about anything than hear whatever was coming next.

'Come with us.'

She blinked, shaking her head a little. 'What do you mean?'

'At the end of the school year, I will take Cameron to my island to live. Come with him and help him to adjust to his new life. Help him adjust to me.' The final request surprised him; he hadn't planned to admit how hard he was finding it to bond with his son, nor to forgive Cynthia for keeping their child a secret. Whenever he looked at Cameron he could see only what he'd missed out on, not what he'd gained.

'You're asking me to go to Agrios Nisi with you?'

'I'm offering you a job,' he clarified. 'Six weeks as Cameron's companion.'

Amelia frowned, again shaking her head a little. 'He has a nanny.'

'He's had three nannies since his mother died but, yes, right now he has a nanny and she seems competent. I think he probably likes her better than the other two. However, she is a career nanny. While she takes excellent care of him, I don't feel that she has much of a personal connection with Cameron. You apparently do.'

Amelia looked sideways a moment, lifting a hand and brushing her hair from her face. She wore on her middle finger a gold ring with a flat face, the kind of ring one might get at a college graduation ceremony. He didn't recognise the engraving; and she moved her hand again, much too quickly for him to commit the design to memory.

'I think Cameron is a very unique little boy and what he's been through…' Her voice tapered off a little, her eyes suspiciously moist. But when she turned back to face him there was a strength in her eyes, a look of determination. 'I care for all my students, Mr Anastakos.'

'But particularly for Cameron.'

She bit down on her lower lip, anguish in her eyes. He could feel her prevarication, her torment. She wanted to accept his offer but she was scared. Of what—him? Of what happened between them the other night?

'This would be a formal offer of employment,' he said smoothly. 'My lawyer would arrange a contract, you'd be paid a salary—given set hours and weekends—just like a regular job.' And then, after a pause, 'I would expect nothing of you personally.'

He saw his words affecting her, drawing her out, and she made a noise of consideration.

'I don't know. On the one hand, I'd do anything for Cameron, but…'

'But?' He challenged, though he knew the answer. Their chemistry frightened her. For whatever reason, the strength of desire that had arced between them wasn't something she wanted to indulge—ever.

Desperation drove him to tighten the screws regardless. 'Let's be clear: my plans will not change. One way or another, in two weeks I will take Cameron with me, away from here. If you care about him, and want to help ease him through the transition period, then accept my offer.'

She sucked in a sharp breath. 'You know, this runs pretty darned close to emotional blackmail.'

His expression didn't shift but he was left wondering in what way this didn't constitute full-blown emotional blackmail.

She flicked a glance at her wristwatch. 'I have to go.'

Something uncomfortably like panic had him reaching for her wrist, his fingers curving around her fine bones, his thumb padding over her skin before he could stop himself. 'Wait.' The word emerged as a deep, husky command. 'You haven't given me an answer.'

'Do I get to think about it?'

'Do you need to think about it?'

She pulled her hand away, rubbing her wrist; her eyes holding his were awash with doubts. 'I would have conditions.'

'Go on.' He dropped her hand, stepping backward, crossing his arms over his chest. He forced himself to give her the entirety of his concentration.

'I have work commitments outside of the school. I'd need an office for my use.'

That sparked his curiosity—hell, it ignited it into a full-blown fireball—but he knew better than to probe her further at this point. Once she was on the island, he could ask her all sorts of questions, if he found she still held his interest. Not now, while her acceptance was in the balance.

'That is not a problem.'

'Okay.' She chewed on her lip in a way that drove him utterly crazy.

'Okay? You'll do it?'

She stopped nodding and frowned. 'Okay, I'll think about it. Send me a contract and I'll advise your lawyers as to my response.'

CHAPTER FOUR

SHE HAD TO be crazy. For two weeks she'd back-flipped on this, wondering at her acceptance of this summer job—which was how she'd taken to thinking of it, the only way she could deal with what she'd accepted without going into a full-blown panic.

It was just work. A temporary assignment. And, more than that, it was an opportunity to help Cameron get through another trauma in his life. She knew what change was like for children—how many times had she been forced to move, to meet new people, to accept new teachers, homes, experiences? Her childhood had been marked by extreme loneliness, a state of utter sadness and displacement almost all the time, all set against a backdrop that making her parents proud was the only way she could make them love her.

People didn't seem to realise that having a very high IQ didn't obviate the normal developmental milestones. Amelia had been plagued by nightmares as a child, one in particular—being consumed by a void, an impenetrable darkness that filled her lungs with bleakness and a weight of despair from which she could never escape. Whenever she'd experienced that terror she'd woken and cried for her mother—but she'd never been there. Often, there had been no one who could comfort her.

Loneliness was familiar to Amelia and she hated that Cameron was going through that now. She wanted to comfort him and *that* was why she'd agreed to this. It wasn't the exorbitant amount Santos was paying her—her consulting work paid well; she didn't need the money. And it certainly wasn't for any other personal consideration. Santos was no draw-card whatsoever. If anything, he was a disincentive, a reason to refuse his offer.

But Cameron overrode every single one of those concerns. So here she was, holding thc little boy's hand as the helicopter circled lower over an island that was beyond anything she could have imagined. Lush greenery grew quite wild over most of it, with a small village in the north and pristine, white sand all around. The water that lapped at the island's edges was aquamarine.

As the helicopter came down lower, Amelia picked out an enormous house right on the water's edge, rendered in white with miles of tinted glass, making it impossible to see into it. The house was a testament to modern architecture, all clean lines and simple aesthetic. There was a swimming pool, several tennis courts, a fruit grove, a golf course and, as she looked towards the water, she saw a jetty at which were moored a yacht and several smaller crafts—speedboats and jet skis lined up side by side.

A curl of derision escaped onto her lips before she could contain it—of course a playboy like Santos had all the toys to go with the title.

She told herself that thc butterflies in her tummy had to do with the rapid descent towards the island and nothing whatsoever to do with the fact that soon she would see him again. Santos. She knew from Cameron that Santos had travelled to the island a few days ago, leaving the little boy in the care of his nanny, Talia. Amelia had suppressed her disapproval. Now that she was here, she could see some stability for Cameron's life.

The helicopter came in even lower, and beside her Cameron was very still and watchful. She angled her face, something clutching in the region of her heart. The first time she'd seen the little boy, he'd looked a bit like this. Far less well-dressed; his uniform had been stained—second-hand, Amelia had gathered—and quite ill-fitting. His face, though, had held a familiar sense of awe, and she'd understood it. He'd been starting nursery and she'd been doing her first teacher's assistant rotation—she'd told him she was nervous too, and that perhaps they'd feel better if they sat side by side.

He'd moved into different classes over the last few years but she'd always kept an eye out for him and had welcomed him to her class this year with absolute delight. Seeing his grief at the shocking death of his mother had hit Amelia right in the chest—she'd cried with him, for him, and on that first night had wished she could bundle him into her arms and take him home. The instinct had surprised her.

Amelia wasn't maternal. Her childhood had been as far removed from 'normal' as was possible. She had no idea how to be someone's parent, and no desire to be either. But there was something about Cameron with his soulful blue-grey eyes that had buried itself deep into her heart. Not loving him wasn't an option. It wasn't permitted to have favourite students, and she'd taken great care not to show a preference, but that hadn't meant she didn't feel it.

The same nervousness and anxiety she'd sensed in him as a slender little three-year-old was in his face now. She put a hand on his knee reassuringly and squeezed. 'The island looks beautiful.'

He turned to face her, those eyes that she'd fallen in love with haunting her now, because it was impossible not to see his father in their depths. They were identical—the same shape and colour, each set rimmed with thick, curling lashes. But this wasn't about Santos Anastakos. That wasn't why she'd accepted this job. It was all for Cameron.

'It looks hot.'

'You don't like the heat?'

He lifted his shoulders and turned away from her, his fragility palpable despite his above-average height. 'No. Not really.'

Amelia smiled but it was forced onto her face. She didn't particularly like the heat either but they'd both have to tolerate it for this summer. The helicopter touched down on the roof of the house and a moment later a man appeared, followed by a woman. Both were dressed in immaculate steel-grey suits.

'Miss Ashford,' the man greeted her, shouting to be heard over the whir of the spinning helicopter blades. She dipped her head forward as the helicopter pilot had instructed her to do, clutching Cameron's hand in her own, guiding him down the steps and away from the aircraft. The heat hit her like a wave in the face, sultry and thick, the air so warm it burst flame into her lungs.

'Yes?' she said when they were at a safe distance. Talia, the nanny, followed behind.

'I'm Leo.' He smiled, a kindly smile that matched his bearing. He wasn't much taller than her, though there was a tautness to him, a strength she could feel emanating from his muscular frame. 'I run security on the island and for Mr Anastakos generally. I'll be coordinating things for Cameron.'

'Things?' Amelia prompted impatiently.

'Security for any day trips, routines, that sort of thing.' He spoke with a Greek accent, though it was different from Santos's.

Amelia compressed her lips, ignoring the shift of disapproval. Given what Santos was worth, it wasn't entirely unreasonable that there should be some kind of security measure for Cameron yet it was just another adjustment for the young boy to make.

'I presume that here on the island he won't need too much?'

'No,' he agreed. 'This place is a fortress.'

She arched a brow. 'A fortress you can reach by air or

sea?' She gestured to the expansive ocean surrounding the island.

'Under surveillance,' he amended with a grin.

'I'm Chloe.' The woman behind him reached around to shake Amelia's hand. 'I run the house.'

Amelia nodded, wondering at the grandness of that—having a housekeeper and a security manager. It didn't surprise her, and yet she couldn't imagine living in such a fashion.

That feeling only increased as she was shown through the house. It was undeniably beautiful, and built right on the edge of the beach, so an infinity pool and terrace gave way to white sand and then pristine ocean. All of the rooms were on a large scale, with high ceilings, more impressive artwork adorning the crisp, white walls.

Cameron's room—or suite of rooms—made her heart clutch. No expense had been spared, but it was more than that. Whoever had overseen the decorating had done so with care. The books were perfectly chosen for a child his age, the toys likewise. There wasn't a cacophony of plastic. Instead, it was wooden blocks and construction toys, a selection of board games and paints. She inwardly approved of the selection, though she couldn't help but feel the stark contrast with the way Cameron had been living previously. She knew from brief conversations with Cynthia that their home had been a small flat above the high street where the smell of the fish and chip shop below had infiltrated each of the rooms with its greasy pungency. There was only one bedroom—Cameron's. Cynthia had slept on a fold-out sofa in the lounge.

It was hard not to judge Santos for that—for leaving the mother of his child to suffer in such abject poverty. Was it really possible he hadn't known about Cameron?

Compressing her lips on that thought, and attempting to blot Santos from her mind, she completed the tour with

Talia and Cameron. When Talia suggested taking Cameron to the kitchen for a snack, Amelia was secretly pleased. She felt overwhelmed with what she'd done; the enormity of stranding herself on this island with a man like Santos Anastakos had her wanting to beg the helicopter pilot to fly her right back to the mainland airport.

But she didn't.

Cameron's face swam before her eyes and all her doubts left her. She was right to be here. He needed this of her.

As it turned out, her anxiety was somewhat misplaced. After Cameron had a snack, she watched Talia and him swim, then joined them in a game of Snakes and Ladders before finishing a few chapters of a book in her room. She read Cameron his bedtime story and sat with him as he fell asleep—he hadn't asked her to but she'd sensed his sadness, understood that essential loneliness and wanted to comfort him as best she could.

She ate alone—the housekeeper Chloe had prepared some chicken and salad. Afterwards, Amelia took a cup of tea onto the terrace along with her book and curled her knees beneath her chin as she watched the sun set, the sky filling with a sensational mix of colours—purple, gold, orange, the beginning of berry-black. Despite all that she knew about the formation of the universe, and the metaphysics behind the sunset, she could never fail to be awed by the repetitive cosmic phenomenon, and particularly not when it took place over a seemingly limitless ocean.

It was dark by the time she'd finished her tea. She stood and moved into the kitchen, washed the cup and placed it on the side of the sink before filling a water glass to take to her bedroom. Carrying it and her book—a heavy hardback—she walked from the kitchen, her eyes flicking towards the night sky beyond on autopilot. The stars shone so brightly here, it made Amelia long for her telescope.

She wasn't looking where she was going, and apparently neither was he, because a second later Amelia connected not with a wall or a door but with a solid shape that knocked her backward. Her water spilled all over Santos's chest, covering his shirt in a spreading pool of liquid.

'Oh!' Her eyes dropped to his chest and couldn't look away. The water made every sculpted delineation visible. His torso was ridged with abdominal muscles, just like the statues of Greek gods she'd studied as a girl.

'I'm so sorry!' The words stumbled from her mouth and she briefly risked a glance at his face, then wished she hadn't. Fire seemed to arc from his eyes to hers, his perfectly shaped lips flattening into a line that could have represented disapproval, impatience or irritation. Far better to believe that than anything else.

She swallowed hard, trying to bring moisture back to her dry mouth.

'Let me...' She pressed her hand against his shirt, intending only to wipe away the water, but the same flames spiralled through her at the slight contact. 'Get you a towel,' she finished, spinning away from him quickly so she could retrieve something from the kitchen. Only she bumped into the edge of the kitchen door in her haste and embarrassment, and squawked awkwardly at the pain that flooded her.

Amelia closed her eyes on a wave of mortification.

Great. Just great.

'Is there anything else you'd like to walk into?' he asked and, heaven help her, Amelia had somehow managed to forget the deep huskiness of his voice, the sultry heat of his accent. It wrapped around her now, making thought and words impossible.

Amelia had begun speaking in full sentences at six months of age—apparently one of the first markers for an unusually high IQ—but in that moment she struggled to wrap her brain around a single word whatsoever.

She made do with firing him a terse smile then continued her trajectory—more carefully this time—into the kitchen, rifling through drawers until she found a tea towel. Spinning round to take it to Santos, she realised he'd followed her into the kitchen and was in the process of unbuttoning his shirt.

Good Lord. Her mouth was drier than the desert.

'Oh.' She stared at him. 'You're getting undressed.'

His grin was rich with amusement. 'I'm removing a wet shirt. It's not quite the same thing.'

'Isn't it?' It sure *felt* the same. 'I was just…going to bed.' Oh, no! That sounded like an invitation! She furrowed her brow, shaking her head a little. What the heck was happening to her? 'To read.'

'Do you have everything you need?'

She lifted her book. 'Yes.'

His smile was slow to spread but her reaction was instant. Her skin prickled all over with tiny darts of heat. 'I meant in the house. Did Chloe show you where everything is?'

Amelia nodded. 'Yes. She did.' And then, with a small shake of her head, 'Though not an office I can use.'

'Would you like to see it now?'

Her chest tightened. She did—she wanted to start her work routine the next day, and knowing exactly where she could work from would be vital to that, but the naked chest of Santos Anastakos was almost too much to bear. 'Would you like to get…erm…dressed first?'

'Would *you* like me to get dressed first?' He put the question back on her and somehow managed to make her feel like a child. Naïve and gauche. She shook her head and tried to look cool, as though she frequently spent time with half-naked, bronzed living replicas of sculpted Greek gods.

'That's fine.' She shrugged with an assumed and not entirely credible air of nonchalance. 'Which way?'

'Did you want to refill your water glass first?'

Heat stained her cheeks. She shook her head—she could come back later. He took a step backward, allowing her space to precede him from the kitchen, and she skirted past him, ever so careful not to so much as brush his skin. If he noticed, he didn't say anything, though she was sure she caught the tail end of a smile on his face when she glanced up at him.

'How was your flight?'

'Fine.' She lifted her shoulders. 'It was my first time in a private jet.'

'I thought it would be easier with Cameron.'

'He travelled well.' She fell into step beside him, feeling a little calmer as they moved onto safer conversational ground. 'He was excited by the helicopter.'

Santos's expression was distracted. 'I thought he might be.'

'Where do you work?'

'I have an office here.'

'On the island?'

'Yes.' He dipped his head forward. 'Though I travel to Athens most days. We have headquarters there and I usually have meetings that require my personal attention.'

Amelia's brow furrowed as she digested this. 'So you won't be here much?'

He fixed her with an enquiring gaze.

'I mean long-term. With Cameron.'

Santos's pace slowed to a stop. 'You're asking if I intend to neglect my son?'

Heat flowed in her cheeks. 'I—'

'You have a habit of seeing the worst in me, when it comes to him.'

'Do I?'

'You think I've moved him here and plan never to see him?'

'If today is any indication.'

'I work long hours.' He expelled a breath so his nostrils flared. 'Up until three months ago I had no idea I was a father. I am *intending* to make whatever changes are necessary to fit Cameron into my life but it will take time. Forgive me, Miss Ashford, for not having all the answers just yet.'

She felt a small shift of sympathy for him, but an even greater one for Cameron; after her own childhood she knew the facts Santos was failing to see. 'So long as you love him, above anything and anyone else, you'll work it out.'

The words seemed to lash Santos. He shifted a little, a physical reaction—a rejection?—and then began to walk once more, his stride longer this time, his face glowering.

'This area is generally off-limits to my domestic staff.' He didn't look at her. 'It will also be off-limits to Cameron and Talia. I work on sensitive projects. I require privacy and peace.'

Amelia's stomach squeezed. He was changing the subject, but she didn't want him to do that. She reached for his arm, ignoring the tingling wave that crashed through her at the small touch. 'Santos?'

He stopped walking, turning to face her without meeting her eyes, his nostrils flaring as he expelled a deep breath.

'You don't agree with me?'

Now his eyes dragged to hers, slowly, something dark in their depths. 'About…?'

But he understood. He was evading her question on purpose. 'You don't need to overthink things with Cameron. In time, and with an abundance of love, he'll find his way to you.'

A muscle jerked low in his jaw. 'And if I cannot give him those things?'

'What do you mean?' She lifted a brow, impatient for him to explain.

'You think it's so easy? You simply say "love the child" and it is done? A matter of months ago, I didn't even know about him.'

Defence of Cameron raised her hackles. 'So? That's not his fault. You're his father.'

'Whatever that means.' He spun round, walking once more, his stride long, not stopping until he reached an office door beside the one he'd indicated as his. 'From time to time my assistant flies to the island to work with me—she uses this space. In her absence, consider it yours.' It was a swift conversation change but she allowed it, seeing the futility in pushing him further at this point.

Amelia looked around the room—yet again, on a rather grand scale—and nodded. Two computer screens sat side by side on a large desk. Another desk, free of any clutter or technology, was set at a right angle to it, forming an L shape in which a comfortable looking black leather chair was anchored. A leather armchair sat across the room and the walls were lined with bookshelves.

'I presume this will suffice?'

'Yes,' she agreed, noting the things it had and those it did not, while her mind analysed his throwaway comment 'whatever that means'.

'But it's lacking something?'

Was she so transparent? 'No, it will be fine.'

'You're easier to read than a book. What do you need?'

She bit down on her lower lip but promptly stopped when his gaze was drawn to the gesture, overheating her already frantic blood. 'A whiteboard.'

He nodded crisply. 'Of course. I suppose as a teacher you're used to writing vertically.'

It took her a moment to connect her vocation with this work. 'Right.' She cleared her throat.

'I'll have Leo arrange one for you in the morning.'

'I don't want to put him to any trouble.'

'It's not a problem.'

'Well, not for you,' she pointed out, surprising them both with the joke. His smile was instinctive, but it died almost instantly. He stared at her for several moments and she felt as though he was choosing his words carefully.

'What if I can't love him?'

Amelia's eyebrows shot up. 'You're serious?'

His features were like stone as he nodded once. *'Nai.'*

'Oh, Santos.' She was so swept up in his worry that it didn't occur to her to use his surname. 'You *will*. Not just because he's your son, but because he's an amazing little boy. Open yourself up to the possibility of loving him and it will happen without you realising it.'

'Your confidence is naïve.'

She blinked, trying to remember the last time anyone had said anything even remotely approaching an aspersion cast on her intelligence.

'I can only assume your own childhood was a picture of rosy parental doting, but that's not the norm for many people. I am not close to my father. Nor is my brother. In my family, "love" is very far from how we do it. So how can you expect me to open myself to the possibility of loving him? How can I ever replace the mother he lost? I'm simply not built that way. *Christos*, I chose to not have children for this very reason, Amelia.'

She flinched a little, wanting to refute his assumption about her and his words about himself. Her childhood had been far from what he believed. But his own summation of his life and choices filled her with such sadness. His uncertainty was so unexpected that she was lost for words.

He spoke before she could, anyway.

'Regardless, he is my son, and I will care for him to the best of my ability. I will raise him so that he wants for nothing it is within my power to provide. But do not expect miracles while you are here. Your concern is my son's happiness, not his relationship with me.'

CHAPTER FIVE

AMELIA SLEPT FITFULLY and woke early. Santos had filled her dreams. He'd overtaken every single one of them, his words filling her with a strange heaviness.

She wasn't sure why his confession had caught her off-guard. Because he seemed so confident, so ruthlessly capable of anything he set his mind to? Or because he'd echoed one of her own deeply held fears? Her parents had hardly given her a shining example of what family life should be like, yet deep down, despite that, she knew that the love between a child and parent was generally inviolable.

Santos would see that. He *had* to.

Throwing back the lightweight cover, she pushed out of bed and padded across the room to the enormous windows that overlooked the ocean. Waves tumbled towards the shore in the cool dawn light. There was no heat accompanying the sun—yet—though she knew it would come.

But for the moment, the view beyond the window was so tantalising she didn't think twice. Pausing only to pull on a simple cotton dress and some sandals, she slipped out of her room, quietly moving through the enormous house that, at this early hour, seemed to be almost completely asleep. Which suited her perfectly.

She opened the glass doors just enough to slide between them, then almost ran towards the water. How long had it been since she'd swum in the sea? Years. Not since she was last in Cape Canaveral.

A smile lifted her lips as the tiled deck gave way to the cool sand, crunchy underfoot, and she could smell the tang of salt in the air. At the water's edge she slowed but kept moving forward. The water was warmer than she'd expected and she walked up to her knees; then, chancing a look over her shoulder towards the house to reassure herself that she was completely alone, she tucked her dress into the elastic hips of her underpants and went deeper still. It was the most sublime feeling—she wished she'd taken a little longer to change into bathers. Tomorrow, she'd know better. The idea of floating on her back as the waves rolled beneath her was almost too tempting.

With a small sigh, she began to walk parallel to the coastline, staying mid-thigh-depth, so each step required her to push through the water. The exercise felt good, the weight of the water a pleasant obstacle.

The coastline on the island was flat here, but only ten minutes or so later the sand gave way to small dunes that morphed into hills and finally cliff-faces, white with tufts of green sprouting through them. She eyed them with curiosity, wondering at the stones in their formation. Cliffs on islands like this tended to boast caves and naturally occurring dens. She wondered if there were any here. If she followed the water round, would she find a disused pirate sanctuary? The idea had her curiosity piqued and she walked on, further than she'd intended, until the wall of the cliff jutted out far enough to make further exploration impossible. She looked upward, the sheer size of the rock wall causing her to hold her breath a moment.

It would be impossible to explore without a swimming costume—and possibly without a boat. Putting it on the 'another time' list, she turned and began the walk back to the house, this time wading through water that was a little shallower, up to her calves.

The sun was just fully bursting into the sky by the time she reached a place in the water that was parallel with house. She stood for a moment with her back to the ocean, simply staring at the beautiful property. Had he built it? Or had his father? It was modern in style but it could still have been built anywhere from the fifties and refurbished over the years. While it was beautiful, it was isolated, and she wondered about that too. Did he feel lonely here? Or did he like that?

And why did she care? With a small groan, she began to move back towards the house, deciding coffee was in order. She scooped down to pick up her sandals from where she'd slipped out of them and carried them the rest of the way. On the terrace, she moved her feet back and forth, trying to get the sand off, before looking around for a tap.

'It's over there.' His voice ran down her spine, seductive and warm, but despite that she shivered, an involuntary tremble that made her legs a little unsteady. She looked at Santos as he gestured towards a tap, only his eyes remained on her, tracing the outline of her legs that must have been visible beneath the flimsy fabric of her dress.

'Thank you.' Her heart was rabbiting hard against her ribcage but she kept walking until she reached the tap, then switched it on, slowly cleaning her feet of all sand and sucking in air before she lifted to standing and spun to face him once more. He'd been angry the night before, rude and hostile.

Remember that, she cautioned herself, even as her body was already responding to his.

'I didn't know anyone else was up,' she explained a little caustically. 'I didn't mean to disturb you.'

He turned to face her, pinning her with the full force of his crystal-clear ice blue eyes. 'Didn't you?'

She pressed her teeth into her lower lip. 'Of course not.'

His response was a small shift of his mouth—she might have called it a sneer, except it lacked acerbity—and then lifted a coffee cup. 'Join me. The pot is still warm.' In truth, she was desperate for a coffee, but with Santos?

Perhaps her uncertainty expressed itself because he made a small sound of impatience. 'It's just coffee.'

Her eyes flared wide, clashing with his, and her stomach rolled in response. 'Fine. Thank you.' Her smile was strained. 'I can't function without the stuff.'

He nodded in agreement, moved inside for a moment to retrieve another cup then returned, filling it and handing it to her. She was careful not to allow even a hint of contact between their fingers when she took it from him, and at close proximity didn't quite meet his eyes.

She took a drink and then pulled a face, looking at him to see mirth in his eyes.

'It's very strong,' she said unnecessarily.

'It's Greek.'

'And all Greek things are strong?' She'd intended it to come out as a joke, but the close proximity to Santos had robbed her of the ability to sound anything but breathy. What was happening to her? Amelia had lectured at Ivy League schools when she'd been fifteen years old. Why did the presence of this man turn her into someone who could barely speak?

'And irresistible.' His words were teasing but there was an undercurrent to them that pulled at her belly, making it impossible to smile in response. She took another sip of the coffee, grateful for having something to do with her hands, anything that might make it look as though she wasn't affected by being this close to him; as though she didn't wish she'd stayed in his office that night rather than high-tailing it out of there as quickly as she could.

For goodness' sake! They hadn't even kissed that night! He'd moved close to her and he'd looked at her as though he'd *wanted* to. But for Santos Anastakos, famed playboy bachelor, that was probably just how he was wired. The kind of encounter that happened to him often. It was highly likely he'd put her from his mind as soon as she'd left his office—why in the world would she expect otherwise? Just because he'd become a constant figment of her thoughts and fantasies ever since was no indication of how he'd been affected by…by what? Standing close to one another in his office? She felt completely juvenile to have invested such a simple thing with so much importance.

He'd had a beautiful woman waiting for him—Amelia had had to scurry past her to vacate his home. Had she spent the night with him? The thought eroded the lining of Amelia's stomach, filling it with a hint of acid, and now her eyes did lift to his, staying there for several seconds. Of course she had! This was Santos Anastakos. The man was rumoured to live and breathe affairs.

'Who was that woman?'

Had he moved closer? She felt as though he was pressing to her, but he wasn't. It was just an atmospheric compression—not physically possible, given their matter states, but she could have sworn it was happening. 'Which woman?'

'Maria,' she supplied, conjuring a mental image of the stunning creature, all long legs and glossy hair.

A small frown pulled at his lips. 'A friend.'

Something a lot like relief burst through Amelia. It spelled trouble and disaster and a thousand other portents of ill that she knew she should pay attention to. Standing here with him like this was madness—nothing good could come from indulging a desire to be close to him. She was fighting with fire, but found she couldn't step away.

'Just a friend?' she asked, wondering what he must think of her, seeking reassurance over something like this.

Another small frown brushed over his features. 'Yes.'

She bit down on her lip, wishing that revelation didn't affect her.

'We were seeing each other for a time. We catch up occasionally, when it suits us both.'

Amelia had barely any experience with men, and precisely zero with men like Santos, but she gathered 'seeing each other' and 'catch up' were euphemistic terms hinting at a physical relationship.

Amelia's face was unknowingly expressive, her features contorting to show her discomfort. Only someone completely lacking in intuitive skills would have failed to understand the direction of her thoughts.

'I had my driver take her back to London after dinner,' he said quietly, and now she knew she wasn't imagining it. He moved closer, his legs brushing hers, the small cup filled with thick Greek coffee the only barrier between them. 'And dinner was somewhat rushed.' A smile that was hard to analyse. Self-deprecating? Annoyed?

She shook her head, needing to put an end to this. It had taken all her strength in his office; if she wasn't careful, she'd lose herself completely to this sense of madness. 'It's none of my business. I shouldn't have asked.'

'But you did.'

She nodded, searching for an excuse.

'Because that night in my office, if you hadn't moved away from me, I would have kissed you.'

She was drowning all over again, trying to draw in air and failing. She had no idea how to respond to that.

'And I don't think we would have stopped at a kiss, Miss Ashford.' Her name was a slow, sensual seduction on his lips. It shimmied through her, threatening to mould her into something new and unrecognisable. Her skin was covered in goose bumps, her blood rushing in anticipation and hope—she needed him to touch her. She needed him to kiss her, just as he'd said he'd wanted to. God help her, she was losing herself to him, to the ocean, the endless sea, of possibilities.

She angled her face to his, her lips parted in an unspoken invitation, her eyes wide. 'What would have happened, Santos?' She liked using his name. It was a leveller of sorts, making her feel like his equal instead of a woefully inexperienced child.

Something flared in his gaze, a heat that pooled lava in the pit of her abdomen. His hands curled around her coffee cup, lifting it to her lips so she could take a sip, then placing it on the table behind them without moving away from her at all. 'I would have made love to you.'

So simple, so erotic.

Her eyes swept shut on the imagery it conveyed, on the very idea of that! Where she should have been glad she'd broken the strange tension that had imprisoned them both, she felt only remorse now. What would it have been like to experience that?

'I would have stripped your clothes from your body until you were naked and trembling.' His fingers brushed her thighs, just beneath the hem of her dress. 'And I would have kissed you everywhere, tasting you, driving you to the brink of insanity before making you mine in every way.' He dropped his head and his lips brushed hers so briefly she thought she'd imagined it; but, no, there was an explosive feeling against her flesh that showed it had been real. A pulse ran the length of her spine.

He moved his mouth towards her ear, speaking low and soft. 'The first time would have been fast. I needed you too much to take it slowly. But afterwards, I would have carried you upstairs to my room, laid you naked in my bed and spent the night devouring you, not letting you sleep, not letting you breathe except to scream my name.'

'Santos.' The word was a hopeless surrender, thready and soft. She wasn't sure if she was imploring him to stop speaking that way or to speak less and *do* more but she whispered his name beseechingly.

She needed to regain her sanity, to keep hold of what she knew to be the facts. 'And then what?' The words were still soft, her voice box bowled over by sensual needs, but there was strength in the words too, courage and willingness.

'And then what?' he repeated, the hands on her thighs moving the fabric a little, so his fingertips brushed the flesh at the top of her legs. She trembled in response, a thousand waves rocking through her.

Thought became a distant possibility, an island far out at sea. But she had to cling to it—every instinct she possessed was telling her she'd drown if she didn't. This was Santos Anastakos—a playboy! Way out of her league in every way and used to women falling at his feet. Did she really want to become just another notch on his bedpost? 'And then you'd have made me coffee the next morning, sent me away?' She couldn't quite summon a smile. 'And forgotten my name?'

His head snapped up, his eyes narrowing. Looking at him properly, she could see the rough hewing in and out of his chest as he dragged in breaths—he was as affected by this as she was, as completely at risk of drowning, despite his considerable experience.

'Why do you say that?'

'You think I didn't look you up on the internet?' She was trembling all over. Her body had never been at war with her mind before and now they were poles apart. She was having a visceral reaction to the idea of stepping backward, but mentally she was already distancing herself from him and the tension that pulled at her belly when they were near each other.

His eyes became guarded, his features an impenetrable mask. 'And what did the Internet have to say about me?'

Heat flushed her entire body. 'That you make love to a lot of women.' She dropped her gaze. 'That you have a habit of breaking hearts.'

'Breaking hearts?' He repeated the words with an emotional resonance that wasn't exactly amusement; if anything, it was more like shock. 'Amelia, believe me, I don't break anyone's heart. No one's *heart*—' he said the word with disdain '—is involved. The women I'm with know exactly what I want from them before anything happens.' His eyes scrutinised her face. 'Do you think I would have broken *your* heart?'

'No, of course not,' she denied immediately. 'But I'm nothing like you think. I'm nothing like Maria.'

'I know that,' he conceded swiftly, a frown furrowing his brow.

'I'm not someone who just sleeps with men.' She wished the words didn't sound so prudish! So disapproving! She wasn't. If anything, she was jealous of all the normal sexual exploration teens engaged in, the comfortable getting to know one's body—and other people's bodies—all the while learning what incites pleasure and enjoyment. She wished she'd had that experience, but nothing about her life had been normal. Her academic abillity had been endlessly isolating, then her parents cutting her from their life had further isolated her—she was, and had been for a long time, all alone.

'And you've had your heart broken before,' he guessed bitterly.

She had, but not in a romantic sense. No, it had been her parents, again and again; it had been the realisation as a teenager that their love for her was intrinsically tied to her academic achievements, her rare brilliance the only quality of hers they cared for, and particularly how it benefited them. She would never forget how they'd reacted on the day she'd told them she was leaving the International Agency of Space Exploration to become a teacher.

She pushed those thoughts aside. Even in that moment the things her parents had said to her, their threats and anger, had the power to hurt. It had been a valuable lesson, one Amelia would always remember: even people who claimed to love you could turn on a dime. No one was safe—love was fickle.

Santos was looking at her as though waiting for an answer. She considered his question and finally shook her head. He was asking about romantic pain, and with that she was a stranger.

'Never.' Awkwardness made her want to run from this but something ancient and almost magical stirred between them, pulling a semblance of truth from her. 'I don't have enough experience with men to have been hurt by them.' Her smile was a little haunted by the direction of her thoughts.

She felt him grow still, his eyes roaming her face, but he didn't say anything. Silence stretched between them, speculative and analytical. 'Let me guess: you're a romantic.' He said the words like an accusation, as though being romantically inclined was the worst thing in the world.

'I'm careful where I invest my energy,' she corrected. 'I can't be bothered to spend time with men who don't interest me. I don't like pretence. And I don't particularly like the risks that come from indiscriminate sex.'

'Risks?' The word was said with rich disbelief.

'Risks.' She nodded. 'Like getting pregnant and being left to raise a child completely on one's own. Like Cynthia,' she added, though it wasn't necessary. It was obvious from his features that her words had hit their mark. 'Is that what you meant by saying you've never broken anyone's heart? Because I think Cameron is an exception to that.'

Amelia wished she hadn't said the words as soon as they'd left her mouth. They were totally harsh and unreasonable, words that had come from a place of fear and uncertainty, words her brain had issued to put her body on notice. She closed her eyes, pain lancing her, regret making her face crumple.

'I didn't know about Cameron,' he said, but the words

showed his own pain, his own hurt, and that made everything worse. 'If I had…'

'You didn't stay in touch with her?' Amelia prompted more gently, but nothing could remove the sting from the question.

'No. It wasn't like that.' When he swallowed, his Adam's apple moved and her eyes were drawn to that motion. 'We spent a few nights together. We used protection. Neither of us wanted…ramifications. We discussed it enough to know that.'

'It's none of my business,' Amelia said stiffly, wishing she hadn't opened this can of worms. She forced her legs to obey her mental commands now, taking a small step backward, just as she had in his office. 'I only meant…' The words tapered off into nothing, but he nodded brusquely.

'I understood your meaning.' He spoke as though they were in the midst of negotiating a business deal. 'You think I go around screwing whoever I want and that secret love children are a likely result of my irresponsible life choices? You think there are a dozen Cynthias out there, a dozen Camerons, and that I'm wilfully ignoring my parental responsibilities in pursuit of the next night of hot sex?' He moved his face a little closer to hers so she saw the specks of silver in his ocean-grey eyes. 'You think I wouldn't have given everything I owned ten times over to know I had fathered a son? You think there's any version of reality in which I wouldn't have chosen to be a part of Cameron's life?'

Hot tears stung Amelia's eyes. 'I didn't mean…'

He lifted a finger to her lips, silencing her. 'Yes, you did. You're wrong about me, but it's what you think. Have the courage of your convictions, Amelia.'

'I don't… I just…' She was babbling. She shook her head and now she did what she'd wanted to do earlier, lifting a hand to his chest, pressing her fingers there urgently.

'You think if we'd had sex you might have ended up pregnant and that I would have abandoned you? You think that's what happened to Cynthia? I am shocked that she didn't even try to tell me I was a father. At no point—that I know of—did she so much as pick up her phone to tell me about our son. Not when she learned of her pregnancy, not when she had the boy, never. He'd never even heard of me.'

'Perhaps she thought you were already onto your next conquest?'

'And so what if I was?' The words were said softly but there was a deathly darkness to them. 'We weren't romantically involved. We had sex. If I was with someone else after her, that does nothing to alter the fact that I'd fathered a child. I would have supported her, supported him.' The words swirled around them, laced with regret. 'And if she hadn't died, Amelia? Do you think I would ever have learned the truth about him?'

Amelia's heart splintered at that question, because he was right—while Cynthia had done the responsible thing and put Santos's name in her will, it was clear that she'd had no intention of involving Cameron's father in their lives for as long as she lived.

'I have no idea how she conceived Cameron. It never occurred to me that she might have. I was younger, stupid in some ways, arrogant—but even then I always took measures to prevent unplanned consequences. She knew who I was and how to contact me. She should have told me about him.'

'Yes,' Amelia whispered. On that, they were in total agreement.

'I don't take risks. I don't get women pregnant and go into hiding.' He drew himself to his full height, stepping back from her, and his eyes glittered with such a cold ruthlessness that she shivered. 'And I would never have taken that risk with you.'

She swept her eyes shut because his words were completely unnecessary. She felt the truth in his soul. For a scientist, it was the least scientific thought she'd ever had. Then again, her education hadn't been limited to physics. She'd studied the Classics too, ancient Greek philosophers, Shakespeare and Jonson; she'd studied words that had helped her make sense of feelings and right now that education was pushing to the fore.

Desire was sweeping through her, refusing to be silenced. She'd fought it from the moment she'd met him, but now she wondered *why* she was bothering. She hadn't chosen to keep hold of her virginity. It wasn't as if she attached any special significance to it. She'd just never met a man who inspired her interest—until now. So what was she hesitating for? It wasn't as though Santos was offering any kind of complicated affair. He'd made it abundantly clear he wasn't into relationships. This was almost too good to be true—a chance to sleep with someone sophisticated and experienced who wouldn't want anything more from her. It was just the kind of no-strings arrangement that would rid her of her virginity, and introduce her to the world of sex without the necessity of emotional expectations.

'I was surprised by how much I wanted you,' she said simply, lifting a finger and tracing his lip in wonderment, the touch so simple but also so utterly sensual. 'The truth is, another minute and I'd have been begging you to kiss me to…make love…to me.' She stumbled a little over the words she'd never spoken before in reference to herself. 'Regardless of who was in the next room and in spite of the fact we'd just met. That's why I left so abruptly—because, honestly, that scared me.'

He inclined his head a little, his eyes beaming through her. 'And now?' The words were gravelled and heavily accented. Her heart rabbited inside her chest.

'And now,' she repeated, lost in thought. His eyes hooked

to hers and he lifted his hands slowly, pushing the dress higher so he could slide his hands into the waistband of her underwear. She fluttered her eyes shut, breathing in deeply.

'Are you scared now?'

'Terrified,' she admitted with a tremor.

'Of me?' His thumb padded over the flesh of her lower back. She looked up at him then, meeting his gaze.

'That this will turn out to be just another dream.'

CHAPTER SIX

HE KISSED HER before he could second-guess his intentions, before she could even realise what he was doing. He crashed his mouth to hers, lacing their fingers together behind her back, dragging her towards him, his tongue sliding into her mouth at first in a slow exploration and then a cataclysmically urgent conquest. He groaned against her mouth, deepening the kiss, ignoring the persistent voice in the back of his head telling him there were a thousand reasons he should have the common sense to resist her.

'God, Santos.' She tore her fingers through his hair, her kiss laced with hunger, and he responded in kind, pushing her underpants aside so he could brush his fingers over her sex, teasing her there as he kissed her so hard her head pressed to the wall. She whimpered in his mouth, whispered his name, the words disjointed by passion; and, right as he felt her tremors build up to an almighty crash, he pushed a finger inside her, relishing the sensation of her muscles, their tight spasms almost bringing him to his own deafening crescendo. *Christos.* He felt like a schoolboy again, incapable of even a shred of control.

Despite what he'd just told her, he didn't actually make a habit of carrying condoms around his home. 'We need to take this to my bedroom.'

Her eyes widened. 'Through the house?'

He understood her hesitation. It was still early, but Chloe was probably awake. Leo too. 'You're right. Bad idea.' He looked over his shoulder towards the pool house. Carrying Amelia wrapped around his waist, striding quickly, he shouldered open the door, placing her on the day bed in the middle of the room.

She looked so completely bemused and sexy, lying there with her dress hitched around her waist, that he despised the necessity of leaving her even for a minutes.

'Stay here.' The words were unintentionally curt. He softened them with a smile, though he suspected it too came out terse. 'I'll be right back.'

He moved through the house quickly, retrieving protection from his bedside table and stalking back through the lounge area onto the terrace. He had escaped being seen and he'd never been more glad of anything in his life.

He wanted to have sex with Amelia more than he'd ever wanted another woman. It made no sense, but a part of him wondered if his fascination with her would dull once they slept together.

She was sitting up when he returned, and when he strode in her eyes were awash with feeling. *Christos*, she'd changed her mind. He braced for it, staring at her, waiting for her to tell him to stop.

She stood up and walked towards him; he held his breath. 'Well?'

Relief had him expelling all his breath in a rush, then grinning. His response was to kiss her, and at the same time to lift her dress from her body, pulling their lips apart for the shortest possible time, just long enough to drive it over her head... And then he was back, kissing her, running his hands over her soft skin, swiftly unclasping her bra, letting it drop to the floor so he could fully palm her beautiful breasts in his hands, no cotton in the way. She was slender, but her breasts were rounded, the perfect size for his hands. He felt their weight, delighted in the puckering of her nipples, the goose bumps that teased her skin. He lifted her again, feeling her legs around his waist, almost the most pleasurable thing he'd ever known.

He fell to the bed with her, his weight on top of hers, his kisses trailing down her body now, his mouth driven to taste every square inch of her. When he took each of her nipples into his mouth, she cried out frantically, throwing her head from side to side, her voice high-pitched, her cries reverberating around the pool house.

Her need for him was obvious and he was surprised by the strength of his own desires; they were tearing through him, demanding response. On the one hand he wanted to savour this, to delight in the feeling of teasing her, but on the other he just wanted to bury himself inside her. Just like the first time they'd kissed when despite the imperfection of that moment—the timing, the location—he had been desperate for her in a way that had driven all sense from his head. It was a miracle he remembered to draw the condom over his erection, his hardness aching at the touch, so desperate was he to fill her around him.

'Christos.' He buried his face in the space above her shoulder, his lips against the curtain of her dark hair, his breathing spasmodic. On autopilot he pushed his clothes from his body, impatience making his fingers catch in his zipper so that he cursed and then laughed unevenly. She was steadfastly watching him, her expression incomprehensible, her eyes fevered, her lips parted in a husky, silent invitation he couldn't ignore. He kissed her, the weight of his desperation pressing her head back to the mattress and into its softness, his hands roaming her body, parting her legs so he could wedge himself between her. The tip of his arousal brushed her womanhood and he groaned, the anticipation of what this would feel like making his blood zip and hum.

'Please!' She arched her back, rolling her hips in an ancient, primitive invitation that he had no intention of ignoring. Another time, he might have drawn this out, teased her desire to an even greater fever pitch, but his own needs were there, making that impossible.

'Yes,' he agreed, the word simple, his arousal pushing

between her legs. He had wanted her almost the first moment he saw her and that desire had only increased with every day that had since passed, so now that he was on top of her, poised to take her, he had no patience for a gentle coming together. He drove himself into her, releasing a guttural cry as impossibly tight muscles almost tormented him, almost rejected him. Beneath him her body stiffened and the tightness inside her gave way, the feeling unfamiliar to him at first, so he pushed up on his elbows to stare at her, a frown on his face. She was looking at him, her skin pale, her eyes not meeting his.

It couldn't be… 'Amelia?' he demanded, knowing he should pull out of her but unable to make his body obey his brain's commands just yet.

Her eyes, frustratingly, were shielded from his. He pressed a finger beneath her chin, wondering at the different emotional responses that were pounding him from the inside—a sense of betrayal chief amongst them, but even that wasn't enough to dwarf the still-present longing for her.

'Amelia?'

But colour was returning to her cheeks and she was moving her hips now, arching her back, his erection buried inside her, her own needs obvious. He watched her for a second and then groaned because, whether she'd been a virgin or not, she definitely wasn't now, and desire was still threatening to engulf them.

He shifted his weight, pulling out of her a little so she lifted up higher, her eyes finding his at last. 'Don't stop.'

He was rarely surprised by anyone or anything but he was surprised now—and furious at himself for being so unable to read her. Looking back, there were myriad signs of her innocence, but he'd been too swept up in his own physical attraction to her. No; it wasn't just that. She was a woman in her twenties—a schoolteacher, for Christ's sake—why in the world would he assume she was a virgin?

How was that even possible?

'We need to talk about this.' The words were grunted from between snatched breaths—all that his raging blood made possible.

'Later,' she insisted, still moving her hips, so he made a noise of acquiescence and dropped his mouth to hers, kissing her once more, pulling out of her slowly and easing himself back into her depths; trying with all his might to be gentle and to avoid hurting her when he wanted to take her with all his strength. It commanded every shred of willpower he possessed, but he held himself back, making love to her in a way that was only a fraction of his usual intensity; needing her to enjoy her first time, constantly needing to remind himself that she wasn't like him at all—this was all new to her.

Her muscles began to spasm around him, squeezing him hard, releasing then squeezing again, and her voice grew higher in pitch until she was saying his name over and over, the richness of his name in her plum British accent something he could listen to for ever. Later he would make her scream his name, when he took her just as he wanted, but for now…

The thought hit him from left field. *Later? For now?* There could be no 'later'. She was a virgin. This was her first time having sex. Hell, for all he knew she was imagining this to be the beginning of something longer term, and he didn't *do* longer term. But she knew that, didn't she? So why the hell was she having sex with him now?

Frustration gnawed at his belly. Santos hated not having all the answers almost as much as he hated surprises and today she'd made him feel both. She'd also made him feel as though he were floating through heaven on a cloud but that didn't matter. She'd lied to him. Not directly, but by omission; he wanted an explanation, and he swore to himself he'd get one.

* * *

'Well,' she said quietly when their breathing was more like normal. His weight on top of her was unexpectedly blissful, the roughness of his chest, his hairs there, pressing to her soft contours a new level of eroticism. Everything about this had been unexpected. She hadn't spent much time thinking about sex. It wasn't as though she'd had a reason to give it much consideration, having never really desired a man before. She understood the science behind it, and she'd obviously read books and seen films that featured sexual relationships, but nothing had prepared her for this.

Nothing.

Her body felt as though it had been pulled apart piece by piece and then reshaped gently, lovingly, into a whole new being. She sighed softly, stretched a little then stopped when the very movement threatened to dislodge him from her—she didn't want that.

When he lifted his head above hers, though, his expression was like ice. His cheeks were still slashed with dark colour, the way they had been when passion had filled his veins, but his features were now trained into a mask of cool inquisition. 'You were a virgin.'

It wasn't a question so much as a statement. An accusation. She swallowed hard, a small frown forming a divot between her brows.

'Yes.' There was no sense in lying.

He nodded stiffly then shifted, pulling away from her so she was tempted to reach for him and draw him back. Only, when he stood, his spine, was ramrod-straight, tension emanating from him with every step he took. She watched as he strode across the room, disappearing for a few seconds before returning with a towel slung low around his hips, his eyes boring into her from across the room.

Feeling at a distinct disadvantage, she sat up and reached for the closest thing she could find, a blanket that was loose at the foot of the bed. She wrapped it around her shoulders and somehow managed to speak calmly when she next addressed him. 'And you're annoyed about that?'

Perturbation expressed itself in the flattening of his lips. 'I don't give a damn about your sexual history except for one point, Amelia. I don't sleep with virgins.'

'That feels like a form of sexual discrimination.' She attempted a joke, but it fell flat. His mood was positively arctic and a shiver ran down her spine. Something like a stitch was gripping her heart, but a thousand times more painful than any she'd ever known.

'I don't want to date you.' The words were like a whip on her spine. 'I'm not interested in a relationship—with you or anyone. I'm the last man in the world you should have given your virginity to.'

The antiquated turn of phrase had her feminist hackles rising. 'I didn't "give" you anything,' she snapped, then made an effort to grab hold of her temper. 'We had sex—and you might not have known I was a virgin but I did.'

'Exactly,' he retorted decisively. 'You knew and I should have known. You should have let me decide if I wanted to be your first lover.'

'You make it sound like some great chore.'

'It is a responsibility and it can bring with it expectations. *Christos*, Amelia, what were you thinking?'

The truth was, she hadn't been thinking. It hadn't really occurred to her that he might notice, let alone mind. 'I just…'

But he was furious and it showed. 'Do not make the mistake of thinking this means anything.' He slashed his hand through the air. 'Nothing about this changes what I wanted from you when we came in here.'

His words were cutting—deliberately so, she suspected—as though he was looking to hurt her as a way of demonstrating how ill-suited he was to be her first lover. How disinclined to offer any kind of tenderness.

And his assumption had her temper bursting through her, its ferocity a relief from the throbbing ache that was spreading in her blood—not a physical pain so much as one born of rejection and hurt. She'd known both those feelings often enough to recognise them now, and she knew that refuge lay in her temper, so she armed herself with it gladly, fixing him with a glare she hoped would pass for impatience.

'You wanted to make love to me,' she said darkly.

'I wanted to have sex with you,' he corrected.

She almost rolled her eyes. 'And now that we've had sex you think I'm going to fall in love with you? Are you actually standing over there all terrified that I'm waiting for a proposal or something? Geez, Santos, I don't have much experience with men but I'm twenty-four years old—I have a fair idea of how the world works.'

And now she gave into temptation and rolled her eyes, pushing off the bed while carefully keeping her blanket tucked around her shoulders. Her dress and underwear were in opposite directions. She prioritised her dress, scooping it off the floor then turning her back on him while she dragged it over her head, dropping the blanket as the dress fell into place before whirling around to find him staring at her with a small frown on his face.

He opened his mouth, about to say something, but she cut him off. 'I wanted what you wanted. To have sex. And now I want nothing to do with you.' Her glare was only slightly reduced in effect by the suspiciously moist layer over her eyes.

She held his gaze for two long seconds and then began to stride towards the door; she'd come back to find her underwear later. But when she was almost at the door he was galvanised into action, his fingers curling around her wrist, spinning her round and holding her still.

'Damn it, Amelia, that's not—'

'What?' A single tear slid down her cheek and she ground her teeth.

Hold it together.

'I was anything but gentle with you. If I had known it was your first time—'

'Then you'd have never slept with me,' she snapped.

His eyes narrowed, his chest pushing out with the force of his breath. 'So you chose not to tell me?'

'I—no. I wasn't thinking clearly.'

'Damn straight. Did it occur to you that I wouldn't want this—to be your first lover? Did it occur to you that I prefer to sleep with women who know what sex is all about?'

Hurt and mortification contorted her features. She angled her face away and when she answered him it was in a voice that was rich with hurt. 'It didn't occur to me that you'd notice. Or mind.'

His laugh lacked humour. 'I've been with enough women to know the difference.' She doubted he meant the words to hurt but they did. Her insides were still trembling with the force of his possession, pleasure still receding, and he was reminding her of how many conquests he'd had?

'Yes, well, I was a virgin. I'm sorry you were disappointed, or whatever, but that wasn't my intention.' She yanked her wrist out of his grip, covering the slightly pink flesh with her fingertips, but not before his eyes had dropped to her wrist and observed the small marks there.

'Before I came here you told me I'd barely see you,' she said stiffly, moving to the door of the pool house. 'I hope you honour that promise.' Tilting her chin away from him, she turned her back and walked past the pool—even when she felt like running—and into the house. The sun had risen over Agrios Nisi but it breathed no light into Amelia.

* * *

He wasn't conscious of how long he stayed in the pool house. He dressed slowly, his mind ticking over what had just happened. Something caught his eye; he reached down and lifted her underwear off the floor, stuffing it in his pocket. Knowing it was there sent something spiralling through him—an urgent wave of need that hadn't been alleviated by their coming together.

How had she thought her virginity wouldn't matter to him? Why hadn't she realised it was something a man would want to know before having sex with a woman?

He stood at the foot of the bed, staring at it before sweeping his eyes closed and seeing Amelia—seeing her as she'd been in the throes of passion, and then in anguish afterwards, as he'd separated from her and hurled accusations at her until her eyes had gleamed and tears had moistened her beautiful, expressive eyes.

Christos.

The idea of being in a relationship with a woman was anathema to him and always had been. Not once had he questioned that. His father was blithely unaware of the true cost of his constant pursuit of 'love', but Santos wasn't. Santos had seen the emotional consequences first hand—initially with his mother, who'd had to be hospitalised for severe depression after the divorce, and then in Nico's subsequent wives. Each of them had suffered at the hands of his father and Santos had promised he would never be like him.

He enjoyed the company of women, and he loved sex, but sex was easy to control—it was an exchange, no different from the kind of commercially motivated deals he made every day. True, there was no exchange of money, just satisfaction, but the parameters were as inviolable as if a contract had been formed. Santos offered a good time in bed. Full stop. The end. There were no gifts, no promises, no damned romance that went beyond a drink in a bar, and only then as a precursor to a night of passion.

He didn't swap life stories with these women but on some level, he was always careful. Finely honed business skills served him well in his private life; it was impossible to switch those traits off. He never slept with a woman who didn't fit the mould he sought—a woman who was sophisticated and experienced, who understood what he wanted and was happy to oblige. He was, ordinarily, painfully careful to not take any woman to bed who didn't share his view on relationships.

A virgin? *Christos.* Even with what Amelia had said, the derisive way she'd scoffed at the very idea of waiting for a marriage proposal, it didn't change the fact that someone's virginity should *mean* something. Her first time should have involved more than a quick lay in the pool house, for God's sake. Surely she could see that? So why the hell had she come here with him? Why hadn't she told him, so he could at least have been gentle with her?

He ground his teeth together, all the 'what ifs' in the world not changing the facts.

He'd slept with her; he was her first lover. And he'd hurt her. Not physically, necessarily—though, hell, he'd taken no effort to ease her into it; he'd simply driven into her, removing the barrier of her innocence and making her completely his.

More than that, he'd hurt her with his behaviour afterwards. He'd been angry and, though he'd had every right to feel that, he should have exercised more control, keeping a grip on his feelings in deference to hers.

He hadn't. He'd said everything he'd thought and witnessed the ramifications of that. The way she'd looked away from him when he'd told her he was used to lovers who knew what sex was about! Talk about offensive and insensitive.

He closed his eyes and inhaled deeply; the room smelled like her.

Thialo. He'd *hurt* her. Amelia had been wrong not to tell him the truth, but she was still Amelia. Kind, generous Amelia who'd come to his house to beg him to be a better father to Cameron. And she deserved better than this—his mistreatment and now his disdain. With a dip of his head he moved out of the cabana, cutting across the terrace and moving through the house, taking the steps two at a time.

He knocked on her bedroom door; there was no answer. He hesitated only a moment, figuring he'd already crossed a line with her, before pushing into her room. It was empty. A second later he heard the shower running and something punched at his gut: it was as if she couldn't wait to wash him off her.

That stoked his masculine pride. If he'd been less in control of his impulses he might have pulled the shower door open and joined her, whispering against her flesh that he wanted to show her what her first time should have been like.

He didn't.

Instead, he sat on the edge of the bed and he waited. He hated that he'd hurt her, but not because Amelia meant anything to him. This was his own code of honour, one he'd sworn to uphold, and for the first time in his adult life he'd done something that didn't sit well within the bounds of that. He'd fix it, and then move on.

Easy.

CHAPTER SEVEN

'OH, MY GOD, Santos!' She stared at him, her heart pounding in her throat, her eyes huge as she regarded him across the room. He was dressed as he had been that morning, but it was impossible to see him without seeing *all* of him now. She refused to think about him naked, refused to think about how he'd felt on top of her, inside her. 'You scared me half to death!' She was pleased when the exclamation emerged with a degree of irritation.

'We weren't finished talking.' The words were quiet, carefully blanked of emotion, which was reassuring. Dressed in only a fluffy robe, she felt at a disadvantage, but she had no intention of showing him that. She moved towards the window—a safe distance away from where he sat on the edge of the bed—and planted her bottom on the window's ledge.

'I'm not sure there's anything else to talk about,' she muttered, lifting her shoulders as she dropped her gaze to the thick carpet.

'I was angry.' The words were simple and unexpected.

'No kidding.'

'I should have realised the difference in our experience but, the truth is, the intensity of my own needs for you deafened me to anything else.' His grimace was wry, and then he stood, moving towards her so she had only a few seconds in which to brace, to fortify herself against her body's instinctive reaction.

'I hurt you.'

She blinked, her heart turning over in her chest. Had she been so easy to read?

'I wasn't gentle, and I would have been if I'd known. I

would have made it so much better for you.' He expelled a breath, his eyes heavy on her face. 'Your first time shouldn't be rushed like that. It should have been special, different.'

She didn't admit that it had felt damned special to her—until his anger and disappointment had become evident.

'It was fine,' she said simply, turning her face away, no longer wanting to look at him, aware of how easily he could read her features.

'"Fine" has never been a benchmark I considered worth aiming for.'

Her stomach squeezed. 'It was better than fine. Is that what you want to hear? Did you come here for praise, Santos? To hear that you were *amazing*?'

Out of her peripheral vision she saw him shake his head and then he was crouching before her, his hand on her knee gentle and so kind that it was somehow all the worse. She resolutely straightened her spine, refusing to show him any more overt sentimentality.

'I came here to apologise.'

It shocked her. She swivelled to face him, biting down on her lower lip. 'I was angry that you would choose me to be your first lover, because of all the things I cannot offer you, but I shouldn't have spoken to you the way I did. I don't want that to be your memory of losing your virginity.'

She nodded a little awkwardly. 'I'm not—I wasn't building it up to be some big, momentous event.' She cleared her throat. 'It's not like I was "saving myself" or anything so quaint.'

He pounced on her denial. 'So how does it happen then that a beautiful woman in her twenties had never had sex?'

'I just hadn't.' She pulled away from him, standing, turning a little to look out of the window. The Aegean glistened beneath her, beautiful and expansive, bright and blue.

'There has to be more to it.'

'Why?' She angled her face to his. 'Why can't it be something I just never got around to?'

'Because you are a sensual woman, and to have not indulged that side of your nature makes no sense.'

She nodded, his confusion easy to understand. 'It's a long story and I'm not sure it really matters.'

'I don't like mysteries.'

Her laugh was involuntary, a small sound of disbelief. 'Is that what I am?'

He didn't answer.

'I'm sorry I didn't tell you,' she said honestly. 'I wondered if I should but then once we were in the pool house I couldn't really think of anything except—'

'Except?' He moved a little closer, his face almost touching hers.

She swallowed. 'What we were doing.' She turned back to the window, needing some mental space from him.

He stood beside her for several beats, and a thousand thoughts and feelings rammed into her brain, asking to be spoken, but she stayed quiet, staring out to sea.

'Please let me know if you need anything,' he said a little formally, taking a step back from her. 'If I did hurt you, and you need—'

She shook her head in frustration. 'I'm not made of glass, Santos.'

'I'm aware of that.'

'Are you?' She regarded him carefully, her stomach in knots. There were many things about her life she might have changed if she could but she'd never wished more keenly to reach back through the fabric of time and alter her social experiences. She was aware how out of kilter she was much of the time—an anomaly—yet she'd learned to cover that, to integrate for the most part. But with Santos she felt like all her usual defences were missing; she was vulnerable and raw.

'I am sorry.'

'Stop saying that.' She brushed his apology aside. 'I get that you wish it hadn't happened, that you wouldn't have slept with me if you'd known I hadn't done that before, but *I knew* and I chose to have sex with you and I'm still happy with that decision.' She realised, as she said it, that it was true. 'I'm glad we had sex. I liked being with you. I'm sorry if that's disrespecting your wishes but I need to say it so you can stop tormenting yourself.'

She didn't let him speak. 'I'm not secretly imagining changing my name to Amelia Anastakos. I'm not fantasising about waking up beside you every morning for the rest of the time I'm on Agrios Nisi. I'm a big girl, Santos. As you keep pointing out, I'm in my twenties, and I understand how men like you operate. Sex is sex, and I'm more than okay with that.'

He stared at her, the words wrapping around him, each of them perfectly chosen to relax him, a balm to his worries. She was letting him off the hook, making him understand that she'd gone into this with her eyes wide open. His only objection, the root of his anger, was his fear that he had unknowingly hurt her—that perhaps he'd led her on in some way, that she'd chosen to give him her virginity because she'd been hoping it might lead to something bigger, but she was telling him clearly that wasn't the case.

She'd wanted to have sex. That was all. It was no big deal. Meaningless, temporary, perfect.

So why didn't he feel better? Why hadn't her words done a bit to relax him? Why were they having almost the opposite effect?

I understand how men like you operate.

Men like him? Men like his father, did she mean? It coated the inside of his mouth with acid. He was nothing like Nico Anastakos. He'd spent a lifetime proving that.

'You should not have let me be your first. I cannot give you—'

'God, Santos!' She laughed, shaking her head. 'I just told you, you don't have to *give* me anything. I don't know what it is with you. I've never met anyone that I looked at and felt…'

Her words tapered off. What had she been about to say? *Felt like I wanted to rip their clothes from their body*?

She closed her eyes on a wave of embarrassment.

'It shouldn't have happened.' When he sighed, his breath fanned her temple, warm and distracting. She angled her face away.

'You don't have to worry. It definitely won't happen again.'

One of his stepmothers had bought him a puppy—a little brown Labrador. Santos had named it Atrómitos—Atró for short. He'd been ten, and it had been very easy to love the dog. Hard to lose it when the inevitable separation occurred and his temporary stepmother decided to take Atró away with her.

During thunderstorms Atró had cried, and the noise Santos heard in the early hours of the morning was so reminiscent of that sound he thought he was slipping back in time. He pushed up in his bed, his heart pounding, disorientation making him frown, and then he moved as the reality of what was happening woke him fully.

'Cameron.' He didn't pause to pull on a shirt. Striding from his bedroom in only a pair of boxers, he moved through his home towards the suite of rooms he'd assigned his son. The cries grew louder as he approached. He pushed open the door and then paused.

His son was crying, but he wasn't alone. Amelia was beside him in the bed, her arms wrapped around him, her hair like burnt caramel in the soft light of his room. He hadn't seen her in days—not since he'd left her room with an uneasiness in his gut that she was casting him in the same light as his father—and for a moment all he could do was stare. Her elegant fingers moved over Cameron's head, brushing the curls away from his temples, her words too soft for Santos to catch. Her pyjamas were hardly intended to seduce—a T-shirt and a loose pair of pants—but, knowing her body as he now did, it didn't matter how she chose to dress herself. His reaction was instant—a stirring in his blood, a question his body wanted answered.

After a slight delay, she appeared to notice him, moving her eyes towards the door, her lips compressing, casting her face in an expression he didn't understood.

He forced himself to look away from Amelia. *Christos*, he found that harder than he cared to admit. His son's little face was streaked with tears, his eyes bloodshot, his small body moving with the violent force of his sobs.

'Can I…?' Frustration bit through him. He wasn't used to this—not knowing what to say, how to act. He'd felt like this ever since he'd found out about Cameron. He hated it.

Amelia almost felt sorry for him. His uncertainty was patently obvious. How could he see his son in such obvious distress and not simply rush into the room and bundle him into a reassuring hug? Perhaps he would have if Amelia hadn't reached him first. Perhaps it was her being here that was confusing him.

She grimaced, turning her attention back to Cameron, very close to wishing that it had all never happened. Even as she thought it, she pushed the very idea away. She'd never regret what they'd shared.

'There, there,' she murmured, stroking the darling boy's hair, brushing her lips over his brow. 'I'm here, darling.'

'I just…' His little voice was so sad, and Amelia's heart ached for him. 'I miss her so much.'

'Of course you do,' she agreed, catching one of his hands and squeezing it.

Without intending it, her eyes moved to the door. Santos was blocking it. The light cast from the lamp was faint and golden, shading his face in a collection of geometric shadows.

'Would you get Cameron a drink of water?' she suggested quietly.

'Water, *nai*.' His voice did funny things to her stomach. He moved quickly, turning and leaving, relieved to have something to do.

Amelia kept talking to Cameron, reminding him of all that she knew about Cynthia and of England; of the first day they'd met—short little anecdotes that seemed to work. When she made intentional little mistakes, Cameron, in that way children had, effortlessly corrected her. 'No, I wasn't wearing a red shirt, because we were dressed in house colours; it must have been blue.'

Santos didn't take long, striding across the room. She looked in his general direction rather than towards the wall of muscles that was right at her side.

'Thank you.' She held the glass out to Cameron. He'd stopped crying now, though his breaths were shallow. He drank half and then Amelia stood, almost bumping into Santos—she would have done so had he not moved quickly, sidestepping her with easy athleticism. She placed the water on the bedside table and rearranged an exhausted Cameron, easing him back against the pillows, his little face dark in contrast to the crisp white pillows, stroking his hair until his eyes grew heavy.

'Amelia?'

His voice was thick with tiredness.

'Yes, dearest?'

'I'm glad you're here.'

Her heart flipped over in her chest. She straightened,

watching as sleep devoured him, turning his breathing rhythmic, relaxing his little face.

Santos moved behind her, surprising her, and she stiffened, bracing her body to ward off its usual, predictable, unwanted response to his proximity, but he was only turning off the lamp. The room plunged into darkness.

Amelia moved towards the door, aware he was right behind her, crossing into the corridor.

'What happened?' he asked, almost unnecessarily.

'He had a dream. About Cynthia.' There was a little light out here, coming from a room down the hallway. A quick glance showed the foot of a bed. Santos's room? Great. That was a detail she'd prefer not to know.

'He was so upset.'

'Well, yes,' Amelia agreed. 'He woke up thinking it had all been a terrible nightmare, that his mother was still here, only to realise he's living that nightmare.'

Santos's jaw clenched tight and Amelia could have kicked herself for being so insensitive.

'I don't mean that knowing you is a nightmare—'

'I know what you meant.' His eyes lingered on her face, so her heart skipped a beat.

'Anyway…' She let the word hang in the air. What was she waiting for? An invitation? How ridiculous.

'You're so comfortable with him.'

That pulled on her focus. She lifted a brow, but before he could say anything else he put a hand in the small of her back, guiding her a little way down the hallway, away from Cameron's bedroom.

'I'm a schoolteacher,' she said quietly. 'I spend my days with six-year-olds, and I've known Cam for years. It's easy for me to be comfortable with him.'

He nodded, but his eyes were still appraising her, distracting her, making it hard to concentrate. *What genius?* she thought with a self-deprecating grimace.

'You just need to spend time with him,' she urged quietly. 'Getting to know him will make you feel more comfortable.' She tilted her head to the side. 'You work such long hours. It's no wonder you don't feel comfortable with him yet. Why don't you take some time off? Or even truncate your work day a little so that you can have breakfast with him, or dinner? It takes time, Santos,' she pressed when he didn't say anything. 'There's no magic pill, no secret. Time and attention.'

His expression was like stone, reminding her of the first night here.

Do not expect miracles while you are here. Your concern is my son's happiness, not his relationship with me.

'Anyway,' she said again, on a small sigh. 'He's asleep now.'

'Nai.'

Neither of them moved. The air around them seemed to thicken, making breathing almost impossible. God, he must work out a lot to have a physique like this. Her eyes followed the ridges of his chest, chasing each undulation until her breath was burning inside her lungs and her fingertips were tingling with a desire to follow the course of her eyes.

She had to break free of him now or it would be too late. She stifled a groan but before she could turn and move away he lifted a hand and curved it over her cheek.

Neither of them spoke, but she felt a thousand and one things deep in her soul. 'I am very grateful you came here, Amelia.'

For Cameron, she mentally added. Of course, for Cameron.

She nodded, dislodging his hand, and took a step back while she still could. 'So am I.' Silence wrapped around them once more.

He broke it. '*Kalinychta*, Miss Ashford.'

'Goodnight, Santos.'

* * *

He couldn't say why but after Amelia had left him, disappearing into her own room, he didn't return to his own. He couldn't. Not while his son's cries were still at the uppermost of his mind. He had no idea what he could do to ease the young boy's suffering if he awoke again but he wanted to be there if grief tore through his sleep once more.

It was a long night but Santos didn't sleep. Instead, he sat beyond his son's door, crouched in the corridor, his head bent, his breathing deep, perched ready to react if Cameron needed him. He couldn't explain why, but in that moment, for that night, Santos obeyed one of his instincts—that to comfort his son.

The other instinct—to be wrapped up in Amelia Ashford and how he'd like them to spend their night—he ignored resolutely.

It's no wonder you don't feel comfortable with him yet. Why don't you take some time off? Or even truncate your work day a little so that you can have breakfast with him, or dinner? It takes time, Santos.

She was right. Of course she was right. He couldn't avoid the fact he was a father. He might not have any idea how to *be* a father but that didn't change the fact. And since when had Santos Anastakos been a man to run from the unfamiliar? Never. Whatever he'd faced in his business life, he had conquered, even when that meant scaling an almost impossible mountain.

This would be no different.

A week after Cameron's broken sleep, after he'd spent the night in a silent vigil outside his son's room, Santos surprised them all at dinner—Talia, Cameron and Amelia—even more so when he took a seat at the head of the table, accepting a plate of food and a wine glass from one of the helpers Chloe hired through the summer to keep on top of the housework.

He watched Amelia across the table as she spoke to Cameron and Talia, completely calm and reserved, no hint of emotion on her features, no hint of warmth at his presence. What had he expected? A marching band? For her to pause proceedings and congratulate him on doing something so banal as returning home a few hours earlier than normal?

'That can't be true!' Talia laughed but Amelia shook her head so her dark hair shifted around her face, distracting him with its glossy, water-like consistency, reminding him of the way it had tousled around her face when she'd been in the bed in the pool room.

'It absolutely is.'

'How can it be?' Cameron placed his cutlery neatly in the middle of his plate. Santos turned his attention to his son and as always felt the clip of pain—the gaping hole inside him where knowledge and familiarity should have been. Cameron had excellent manners—a credit to his mother, he supposed. He wished he could remember more about Cynthia. The truth was, he'd been twenty-seven and celebrating a huge takeover of a rival shipping company the night they'd met. He'd spent most of their time together either responding to emails or drinking Scotch.

'The warmth in the atmosphere causes a thermal expansion,' Amelia said with a smile. She lifted her knife, holding it in the air. 'When the weather gets warm, the iron that was used to build the Eiffel Tower grows bigger—expands—until it's around four inches taller than in winter.'

'I don't believe it!' Cameron laughed. 'It's a building, they can't change shape.'

'Not shape, necessarily, just size,' she insisted, laying her knife back down. 'When I was studying in Paris, we measured it over the course of the year.'

'You studied in Paris?' Santos's voice came out deep and Amelia's gaze flicked to him, something flashing in her eyes so it was impossible not to feel the snaking heat of response. It had been several days since he'd last seen her and when she looked at him now he wanted to stand up and drag her body to his, to throw her over his shoulder and carry her upstairs. He wanted to spend a long, hot night making love to her, rather than the rushed coming together they'd experienced in the pool house.

'Yes.' She lifted one perfect brow in a silent challenge then turned back to Cameron. It was as if she felt nothing for Santos, no temptation, no curiosity. Frustration shifted inside him—he wanted to kiss her until that ice dropped from her completely, until it melted away in an incontrovertible acknowledgement of desire.

'How did you measure it?'

'With lasers, of course.' She smiled and Santos tried to focus his thoughts; the strength of his erection beneath the table was hardly helpful.

He could see what a good teacher she'd be. She was patient and engaging and seemed genuinely passionate about the subject matter.

'But what—?'

'No more questions for Miss Ashford.' Talia grinned, standing up and resting her hands on the back of the chair. 'It's time for bed.'

'But it's only seven-thirty!'

'Exactly,' Talia said with a crisp nod. 'The perfect time for little boys to have their stories read.'

'I'm not tired.'

Amelia's smile was all indulgence. 'You always say that, right before your head hits the pillow and you're fast asleep within minutes.'

Something inside Santos shifted. Guilt? Jealousy? He had no idea about his son's bedtime rhythms.

Cameron opened his mouth to challenge that statement but then nodded with a glimmer of obedience. 'Okay, then.' He stood up and rounded the table, coming to Amelia's side. She lifted an arm around him, holding him there, burying her face in his hair, and for a minute there was such a look of unguarded sadness and love on her features that his breath snagged in his throat.

'Goodnight, darling.' She kissed his hair, smiling directly into his eyes. Warmth replaced the sadness; she was beautiful.

'Night.' Cameron moved further down the table. It was a new thing for Santos to dine with his son. Even in England, Santos had come home too late for Cameron's mealtime. They therefore didn't have any kind of routine established and the little boy looked unsure as to what to say or do to his father. It clutched something tight in Santos's chest.

He smiled reassuringly, his gut churning for how alike they were—Cameron could have been Santos at the same age. 'You know,' he said thoughtfully, scanning the little boy's face. 'Paris is only a short flight from here. Perhaps we could go there and see the magical, growing Eiffel Tower for ourselves?'

Cameron's eyes turned into little round plates of blue. 'Really?'

'Really.' He shifted his attention to Amelia. 'What do you think, Miss Ashford?'

She sat back in her seat as a young woman cleared the plates. 'I think Cameron would enjoy that,' Amelia said with a small smile, reserved just for the little boy.

'I would.'

Santos laughed. 'Then I'll arrange it.' He didn't expect his son to hug him. It was still new—they were learning. But he reached out and tousled Cameron's hair, then put his hand on his shoulder. *'Kalinychta.'*

Amelia's eyes flew to his, and now heat sparked between them. She wasn't ice. Not at all.

'What does that mean?'

'It means goodnight.'

'Kalinychta,' Cameron repeated, his pronunciation close to perfect.

'Excellent,' Santos praised.

'Kalinychta,' Cameron said again, apparently enjoying the feeling of the word in his mouth. He repeated it to Amelia as he left the room, Talia's arm wrapping around Cameron's shoulder as she shepherded him away for the night.

Leaving Santos alone with Amelia.

'Well.' She moved to stand, as though she couldn't leave quickly enough. He shook his head, the single gesture holding her where she was a moment. Their eyes held, a challenge moving from him to her and being returned with twice the intensity, so his whole body began to ache for her, to want her, to imagine what being with her would be like.

'When were you in Paris?'

She reached forward, toying with the stem of her wine glass. It was filled with a clear liquid—mineral water. 'I went last summer.' She sipped her drink.

'To measure the Eiffel Tower?'

'No, that was when I was a student.'

'A school exchange?'

She hesitated a moment, as if choosing her words with care. 'No. I was enrolled at the Académie for a time.'

He couldn't say why he was surprised. Perhaps it was the idea of a teacher from a down-at-heel comprehensive school having studied at one of the most prestigious institutions of tertiary education in the world.

'What did you study?' He leaned back in his chair, reaching for his own glass—his filled with red wine from grapes that were grown here on the island.

Another hesitation. Was he imagining the blush on her cheeks? For what reason?

'Mathematics.'

He watched her as he took a drink of wine then replaced his glass on the table. 'That's your speciality?'

'I don't really have one speciality,' she said, obfuscating a little, and now she stood, fixing him with a cool gaze. 'I do, however, have work to do.'

'It will wait.'

Her expression clearly showed surprise. 'I beg your pardon?'

'Don't beg my pardon,' he responded, his eyes half-shuttered, his chest expanding with the strength of his need for her. 'Just sit back down and talk to me while I finish my dinner.'

'Mr Anastakos…'

'Amelia.' He laughed then, a thick, gruff sound. 'Do I need to remind you of how well we know one another?'

Her lips parted on a small noise of shock. The ice was gone. He wondered if she'd been like that for Cameron's benefit. Perhaps it was a defensive mechanism, so that no one else realised what had happened between them?

She shook her head a little warily. 'No.'

'So, please, call me Santos. And sit down.'

She stayed right where she was, staring at him, so frustration bubbled through him. He pushed his chair back, standing, moving to the chair at his right and drawing it from the table.

'Sit,' he instructed, his eyes mocking. 'I don't bite.'

He saw the way she swallowed, her hesitation making him want to pull her into the chair—better yet, onto his lap. He didn't. His desire for her was hard enough to control without bringing any physical contact into the equation. But he had to control it. Amelia was off-limits.

'Fine.' He stayed where he was as she sat down, pushing

her chair in a little, resisting an impulse to brush her shoulders with his fingertips. She was wearing a simple dress with spaghetti straps, her bare skin flawless and golden. When they'd made love, his stubble had left red marks there. On her shoulders, above her breasts. How long had they stayed on her skin before fading into nothingness? And why could he think of little other than dragging his mouth over her body now, leaving the same trail of red marks, the same covering of goose bumps, over her skin?

'Cameron was very happy you came home for dinner.' She said the words with a slight hint of reproach and he understood her reasons for it. He wanted to tell her that he was new to all this, and to be patient with him. He wanted to tell her that he didn't know what the hell he was doing with the child, but that he wanted to work it out.

But Santos wasn't a man who generally bared his soul, so he said instead, 'And you, Amelia? Were you happy I came home for dinner?'

CHAPTER EIGHT

'I'M HAPPY YOU spent some time with your son.' She evidently chose the words with care, her manner crisp. He dipped his head forward, concealing a wolfish smile, before changing the subject.

'How long were you in Paris for?' He sat down in his own chair with a lithe athleticism, reminding her of some kind of wild predator, all strength and muscle.

'A little over a year.' Her mouth was dry but her water was finished.

'Would you like some wine?'

She eyed it for a moment before nodding. The moment he'd walked into the room she'd begun to tremble, her insides awash with fierce recognition, as though he were a magnet and she the perfect polar opposite.

When she was thirteen, she'd been badly bullied by a student at college. The girl was seventeen and should have known better but she'd made it her mission to make Amelia's life hell. Amelia had prided herself on not showing the bully how badly it hurt, nor how upset she'd been with the cruel name-calling. She'd perfected a calm exterior that rarely failed, even when her insides were being shredded to pieces. Her heart had been slamming into her ribs and her pulse filling her ears with a tsunami-like power but, outwardly at least, she'd kept calm.

With Santos, that had been almost impossible and tonight, the first time she'd seen him since they'd slept together, the effort had cost her. He'd strolled into the dining room, in the midst of their happy domesticity, and her body had begun to reverberate, as if recognising its master. She'd found it almost impossible not to look at him during dinner but she hadn't been able to look—not without staring. It had been a difficult forty minutes. Wine was welcome.

She watched as he poured the rich burgundy liquid into her glass, half-filling it.

'What is it?' She lifted it to her nose, inhaling its wooded fragrance.

'Xinomavro.' The word had an almost magical-sounding quality. 'A type of grape varietal that grows well on the island.'

'You grow it here?'

He made a noise of agreement. 'It ages well, so each harvest is bottled and stored for at least five years before it's sent to my homes around the world.'

She stared at him for several seconds and then laughed. 'I'm sorry, I know you're probably used to that, with your helicopter and jets and whatever else, but do you have idea how unusual what you just said is?'

His expression showed a hint of amusement. 'I do.'

She took a sip, her eyes roaming his face, the same flicker of need that had been tormenting her all week flaring to violent life. She'd felt it endlessly—need, desire, impatience and hunger. What they'd started had launched a thousand wants within her. At twenty-four she'd had her first sexual awakening and, far from satisfying her curiosity, it had only served to fill her with renewed curiosity.

'I can't imagine growing up with that kind of money,' she said honestly, thinking back to her own childhood, how marred it had been by intense poverty—how incredible the contrast when she'd started travelling and suddenly they'd been able to afford some non-essentials, and eventually even a few luxuries. As a child, she hadn't really connected her activities with an improvement in her family's fortunes; she'd just been grateful things were slightly less strained at home.

'It was normal.' He lifted his shoulders, but there was

something in his eyes that had her waiting for him to elaborate. After a moment, he did. 'I was born into money but my father lost almost all of it.' She leaned forward and beneath the table their knees brushed so she almost jumped out of her seat, jerking them away. His eyes showed a hint of speculation but he reached down and put his hand on her knee, holding them where they were then stroking her flesh so stars began to dance against her eyelids.

'How?' Her question was husky, coated by her unmistakable desire. 'I would have thought that to be impossible, given your wealth.'

'Bad investments. Messy divorces.' Santos grimaced.

'Plural?'

'Plural indeed. He's currently on wife number nine, and that marriage looks like it has just about run its course.'

'Nine?' she repeated, her eyes wide with disbelief. 'How in the world…?'

'He's a hopeless romantic.' Santos said the words lightly enough but she felt the undercurrent of irritation, his strong sense of disapproval. 'Each wife is younger than the last—my current stepmother is my junior by several years.' He shook his head.

'And the divorce settlements are expensive?'

'Were.' His lips were a grim line. 'He signs pre-nuptial agreements now, limiting what his wife is entitled to.'

Was it any wonder Santos had proclaimed a distaste for marriage and commitments?

'But the first few, when I was still a boy and a teenager, were costly. The fortune was divided, and divided again, so it was left to me at eighteen to take over the running of things. My grandfather had taught me from a young age and I enjoyed it—I lived and breathed the business and had a knack for investments. It took me the better part of a decade but I shored up our interests and transferred away from old corporate strategies to more nimble, digitally based options.'

'Impressive.' And she meant it. His business acumen must have been brilliant, given what his father had done to their wealth.

'Not really. It's just where my talents lie. Did you always want to be a teacher?'

The rapid-fire conversation change had her shaking her head before she could stop herself. 'No. I took a pretty circuitous route to this occupation, actually.' The wine was spicy and made her feel warm as she sipped it.

'Via mathematics at the Académie?'

'Right.' She chewed on her lip, wondering at the temptation to speak honestly with him when she made a habit of keeping her background to herself these days. Having been a child prodigy, trotted out for newspapers and television talk shows, had taught her how valuable discretion was. Additionally, most people tended to be intimidated by her, or became too embarrassed to speak honestly, as though she might be critiquing their sentence structure on repeat. Isolation had been part and parcel of her life as a child and teen. For the first time, it played no part in her life; she generally ensured it stayed that way by not mentioning her academic career.

'What were your other specialities?' It was as though he knew how close she was to opening up to him and understood exactly the question to ask.

'Physics.' She looked at her wine as she spoke. 'My first degree was in physics. My postgraduate as well.'

'First degree? How many do you have?'

'Three.'

His surprise was obvious even without looking at him. She felt it in the way he shifted in his chair and in the tone of his voice. 'Three?'

Heat flushed her skin. She ran her fingers along the stem of her wine glass.

'No wonder you never got around to having sex. When in the hell would you have found the time?'

He laughed and she found herself laughing with him, shaking her head a little, but a moment later he was quiet, leaning forward and putting his hand over hers. Sparks flew through her veins, startling her with their intensity.

'You've been teaching for a few years. It doesn't add up.'

'No, probably not,' she drawled, and then words began to drop from her mouth without her conscious decision. 'I graduated my physics degree at eleven. Maths at thirteen. I got my doctorate at fifteen then decided to study education.' She lifted her shoulders. 'I would have gone straight to teaching, but I was too young at sixteen, obviously, so spent a few years working with space agencies and doing some research projects.'

He was silent. When she lifted her eyes towards him he was staring at her as though she'd relayed all of this in an alien language.

'You're some kind of genius.'

'I don't really like the term genius,' she said after a slight hesitation. 'It's often misunderstood, certainly misapplied, and it's incredibly elitist. I have particular aptitudes. Where your strengths lie in business, mine are in mathematics and science. I was born being able to comprehend it and, because that's reasonably unusual, was given unbelievable opportunities to develop that predisposition.'

'Fine, not a genius,' he said with a shake of his head, his beautiful blue eyes roaming her face. 'How old were you when your parents realised you were—gifted?'

She sipped her wine, the myth of her brilliance one she'd heard her parents tell in interviews—interviews they'd been paid for, of course—so many times, she could almost repeat it verbatim. 'I spoke in full sentences at six months of age. That's unusual, but actually in people with extraordinarily high IQs it's common.' She flushed. 'I appreciate how that must sound—'

'It sounds like you have a nose on your face, two eyes in your head and an extraordinarily high IQ,' he interrupted quietly, squeezing her hand. His words, and the simple acceptance of her brain's abilities as merely something she'd been born with, filled something in her she hadn't realised had needed filling. She nodded, just a small, involuntary movement.

'By the time I turned one, I was reading and comprehending full books. At eighteen months, my parents had enrolled me in a monitoring programme that's a global initiative. Children like I was are watched, tested, benchmarked endlessly. Sometimes, though it's rare, a child can exhibit early signs of high IQ and then simply plateau. For those that don't, the programme tracks development and finds placements that will, theoretically, stimulate cognitive skills.'

'What kind of placements?'

'I undertook several subjects at Walsh when I was five.' Amelia named the American Ivy League that had been her first introduction to education. 'From there, I spent two years in Japan, at the Nagomyaki Institute, and so on and so forth.'

'Your family moved around a lot, then?'

'They came with me, at first, but after a year or two they returned to their normal lives and left me at school to study.'

Amelia's eyes met Santos's and saw something in their depths that pulled at the fibres of her being.

'You travelled on your own? To America?' His frown was harsh, his disapproval obvious.

What could she say? She felt the same way, now that she was an adult. 'America, Japan, Sweden. I was very capable,' she offered by way of excusing her parents, even when emotionally she couldn't really justify their actions. 'But it was hard,' she said on a sigh. 'I was still a child and I think there was an expectation that emotionally I was on par with my intellectual abilities. I wasn't. I used to get nightmares, terrible nightmares, and all I wanted was my mum.' She shook her head a little, the maudlin thoughts the last thing she wanted to consider. 'Anyway…' she tapered the word off, lifting her shoulders. 'That's ancient history.'

He took a drink of his wine, then placed his glass between them. 'Where do your parents live now?'

Something sharp jabbed her inside. 'They're in London.' She spoke carefully but the words were still rich with emotion.

'Do you see much of them?'

She swallowed past the lump in her throat. Six years and it was still almost impossible to accept the state of her relationship with her mother and father. 'We're estranged.'

'Because they sent you around the world when you were practically young enough to be in diapers?'

Her expression lifted a little into a tight smile. 'It's at their choosing, not mine.'

He was watching her with obvious surprise. 'Why?' he prompted eventually, when she didn't elaborate.

'Because I opted to become a teacher. And teaching isn't a particularly well-remunerated or regarded profession—at least, not like being a world-renowned astrophysicist.'

His features showed his lack of comprehension. 'And so?'

She took a small sip of the wine then pushed the glass away. As delicious as it was, the fact she didn't drink often meant it was already making her feel a little light-headed and tingly. Or maybe that was Santos's proximity and having the full force of his attention.

'And,' she continued slowly, to give the words less time to hurt. 'We were really poor. My dad was a welder, and didn't have a lot of work; Mum wasn't qualified for anything so took work when she could but, when I came along, they were paid all this money—'

'By whom?' he interrupted, business-like as he honed in on the facts of what she was saying.

'By the programme conducting research, initially—they were paid annually to keep me enrolled. There was a lot of media attention too and they had an agent who found them interviews and the like. Then, colleges were vying for me to attend, and in the end it came down, largely, to how much they were willing to pay. I didn't know any of this.' She shook her head, the words a little scathing even when she'd long ago made her peace with the financial aspects of it. That wasn't what really hurt.

'That's exploitative.'

'They were very poor, Santos.' She gently defended them.

'Perhaps; but, while I don't think that's necessarily any justification, I was referring to the universities.'

'Ah.' She nodded. 'I got a lot out of it, though. I hated leaving my parents, I hated being away from home, but I loved the learning. I was challenged and pushed for the first time in my life.'

He nodded thoughtfully, easing back in his chair. Her hand was cold compared to the warmth of his touch moments ago. 'You were their meal ticket.'

She winced at the phrase, but it was accurate. 'Yes.'

'And they came to consider your income as theirs?'

Her face paled a little. 'They managed my income,' she said softly. 'When I began to consult at space agencies, any payment was being handled by dad. He took a management fee.'

'A considerable one?' Santos's voice was flattened of emotion, but not enough. She heard the disapproval there and ingrained protective instincts that had her lifting her shoulders. 'I'm not really sure.' It wasn't true. After they'd argued, she'd taken the reins of her own career and had realised how much money had been flowing through her bank account—both in and out. The reality of that had almost broken her.

'And so at five years of age you sat through courses designed for—what?—sixteen-year-olds?'

He brought the conversation back to her studies. She lifted her brows in silent agreement.

'You didn't have any friends your own age?'

She pulled a face. 'I didn't have any friends at all,' she said seriously. 'What teenager wants to spend time with a child?'

'But as you got older?'

'I was still young and, by then, pretty socially awkward. What I had in academic ability I absolutely lacked socially. But eventually, yes, I met someone—a friend. He was the first person to introduce me properly to the Classics, and through them I learned so much about emotion and motivation.'

'And you're still friends?'

'Yes. We're close.' She smiled. 'He's very important to me.'

She wondered at the slight shift in Santos's expression to something like speculation. 'And yet you and he never…?'

'Never…?' she prompted, even when she knew what he was asking.

'You weren't intimate?'

'No. Brent's like my only family now—there's no way I'd ever do anything to ruin that.'

'So you might have been interested in him but for the fact you don't want to confuse friendship with sex?'

She ignored the jangling of nerves in the pit of her stomach. 'Until I met you, I'd never known anyone I wanted to have sex with.'

His eyes swept shut for a moment, his expression impossible to read.

'Amelia…' There was a warning tone in his voice. She ignored it.

'I'm only being honest.'

'It shouldn't have happened.'

She made a noise of frustration. 'Yeah, well, it did. Are you going to ignore me for the rest of the time I'm here?'

He angled his face away. 'It's for the best.'

She stared at him, frustration eating her, but whatever doubts she'd had earlier his determination to box away what had happened, as though it was a simple aberration they could both forget, filled her with a sense of absolute determination.

'Are you seriously going to sit there and act as though you can just flick a switch and feel nothing for me?'

He turned to face her, his eyes showing impatience. 'I don't *feel* anything for you.'

'I'm not talking about emotions.' She rolled her eyes. 'I mean chemistry. Desire. Lust.'

He ground his teeth, his jaw tightening with the movement. 'What do you want from me?'

'I want you to look at me. I want you to stop ignoring me and pretending it didn't happen. I want you to acknowledge that you still want me.'

When he turned to face her, his expression was like granite. 'It shouldn't have happened.' He stood, scraping the chair back.

But she wasn't ready for him to simply walk away from her.

'You keep saying it shouldn't have happened, but I wanted it to! And I'd do it all again. I'd do it again right now, if you weren't acting like a coward, too scared to face up to this.'

He made a growling noise. 'You have no idea what you're talking about.'

'Don't I? Or is this what it's like for you? You have sex with a woman and then move on without a backwards glance?'

'Generally, yes.'

She blanched a little, so he felt a wave of remorse.

'But we are living in close quarters for the next few weeks and, believe me, ignoring you is best—for both of us.'

Amelia had waited up on purpose but the sight of Santos striding into his home still hit her with an unexpected wave of sensation. Emotions fired through her, and her body responded in kind, as though recognising its master. How she hated that.

'Amelia?' He stilled, his eyes sweeping over her in that way he had. 'What are you doing awake?'

'I want to talk to you.'

He compressed his lips. 'We've already spoken.'

'It's not about us.' Hurt lanced her, his easy dismissal making her feel like a nuisance. 'It's Cameron.'

Wariness crept across his features. He moved towards her, pausing a few feet away, a safe distance, but none the less her senses went into overdrive.

'Go on.'

'I get that you're ignoring me, but if the by-product of that is you ignoring him, not being home the whole time he's awake, then my being here is completely pointless.'

'I disagree. You being here is meant to help Cameron adjust to life on the island, life in Greece. You're doing that.'

'And what about helping him adjust to you?' she pushed, her eyes loaded with feeling.

'I told you, my relationship with my son is not your concern.'

'That's ridiculous,' she retorted angrily. 'How can you say that?'

'He's *my* son.'

'Not that you'd know it,' she retorted, then wished she hadn't when he took a step backward, as though physically reeling from her comment. She took in a breath, needing to remember how to stay calm when calm was the opposite of how she felt.

'Look, when I'm not here, you're going to need to know how to be some kind of father to him. You've uprooted him, dragged him across to Greece, and for what? So he can be pampered by people he doesn't know?'

'He has you.'

She shook her head. 'I'm not enough. You're his *father*. And if the reason you're staying away all day and into the night is because you don't want to see me then I'll go away again, Santos.'

'Don't threaten me.'

'I'm not threatening you. I will pack my bags and leave tomorrow unless you promise to start spending time with him.'

'It's not that easy!' His voice was raised and there was something in his features, a sense of panic or disbelief; she couldn't say. He controlled his temper, lowering his voice. 'It's not that easy.'

'It's not meant to be easy. He didn't choose to lose his mother, and you didn't choose to discover you're a father to a six-year-old boy, but that's the situation.' She held his gaze. 'If the idea of seeing me is so distasteful to you—like you're worried I'm going to throw myself at your feet or something—then don't. Believe me when I tell you, I'll very happily go to the other side of the island when you're in the house, if that's what it takes.' She glared at him to underscore how serious she was. 'Just spend time with your son, Santos. He needs to know you.'

CHAPTER NINE

Knowing she was right did nothing to mute his irritation. In fact, it only served to increase it. What the hell had he been doing?

He'd brought Cameron to Agrios Nisi and sooner or later he had to find a way to draw him into his life. He had to break through the barriers and forge some kind of connection with his child.

Amelia was completely right. Worse, she was right that he'd let a need to control the desire he felt for her come between spending time with his son. That was unforgivable and yet it was also confirmation.

Confirmation that he was more like his father than he cared to admit. Completely incapable of giving his son what he needed.

But that didn't give him an excuse not to try.

'Cameron?' He found the boy building a spaceship out of plastic bricks in his room, and watched him for several moments before crouching down at his side.

'It's a Jedi cruiser.'

Santos's smile was instinctive. 'You like building star ships?'

'I guess so.' Cameron shrugged and Santos's heart went out to him.

'What else do you like?'

Cameron's eyes were exactly like his own. Santos stared into them as something beat across his heart.

'I don't know.' Another shrug.

'Do you like the beach?'

'I never saw the beach before I came here.'

Anger flashed in his belly; he ignored it. 'I have a yacht, you know.'

Cameron hesitated a moment. 'I like building yachts.'

'Do you?'

'Mmm… Big ones. All white. I make the sails out of paper. Sometimes fabric. Once I cut up a shirt of Mum's and she was very cross.'

The little boy's skin grew pale. He jerked his gaze back to the bricks, fumbling with them a little. His fingers weren't steady and he jabbed his space ship, knocking it so it fell to the floor and broke apart.

They both stared at it for several seconds.

'Let me help you,' Santos offered, wondering how long it had been since he'd played with bricks.

'No.' The word was firm, surprising Santos.

'You want to do it on your own?'

'I want you to go away.' He glared at Santos with a mutinous expression. 'I want to be alone.'

Something flared inside Santos. 'Cameron.' He spoke gently, not exactly sure how to handle the outburst. 'I know you'd worked hard on building that, and you're disappointed it's broken, but there's no need to speak like that. I was only offering to help. If you'd prefer to build it on your own, then I will just sit and watch. Is that okay?'

'I want you to go!' He pressed his palms into his eyes and then made a small sobbing noise, but he swallowed it, fixating on anger instead. 'Go away!'

Santos wasn't used to being told what to do but the boy was clearly distressed. He stood quickly, hovering for a moment, before walking towards the door. He was only two feet down the corridor when the door was unceremoniously slammed shut behind him. He winced, shaking his head, a rush of frustration exploding through him.

* * *

It wasn't Amelia's fault, but that frustration turned towards her, so he found himself walking through the house—at four o'clock on a Tuesday, when he should have still been in his office—in search of the woman who'd guilt-tripped him into doing something that evidently neither Santos nor Cameron wanted.

He found her by the pool, wearing a red one-piece bathing suit. He ignored his body's now predictable response. 'Santos?' She stared at him in obvious surprise, scrambling to her feet. 'What are you doing here?'

'What do you think?' He didn't mean to stand so close, close enough to smell her vanilla and strawberry body wash teasing his nostrils. 'I came home to spend time with my son.'

Her smile was like a ray of sunshine, piercing the fiercest storm cloud. But it didn't pierce his mood. 'I'm so glad, Santos.' She lifted a hand to his arm on autopilot, pressing it to his flesh. He fought an urge to pull away.

'Don't be. He threw me out of his room.'

She stared at him for a second and then laughed, the sweetest sound, something that threatened to unpick his anger. But he wouldn't let it. He *was* angry, and he was lost—completely lost. He'd never wanted to be a father!

'I'm sorry.' She sobered when she realised he was glowering at her. 'It's just the idea of anyone, let alone a sweet six-year-old kid, physically throwing you from anywhere is kind of absurd.'

'He told me to get out, in no uncertain terms.'

Amelia blinked at him, shaking her head. 'That doesn't sound like Cameron.' Her eyes narrowed. 'What did you say to him?'

'Nothing!' Santos growled. 'He was playing with bricks. I complimented him on the ship he'd built. I told him I have a yacht. I was about to suggest we go out on it for the afternoon and then he just lost it.' He expelled an angry breath. 'He broke his construction. I offered to help fix it. He snapped.'

'He's a little boy,' she said quietly. 'With big emotions. You just have to be—'

'Patient, yes, you've said that. Then let me be patient. Let me do this in my own time. You're the one who pressured me to spend time with him but he's not ready.'

'He's not or you're not?'

'Don't psychoanalyse me.'

'Well, then, don't be so childish,' she retorted. 'You know what? He might have thrown you out of his room but he'll calm down, and he'll see that you came to him, that you made the effort. It's not always going to be plain sailing but learning to trust that you'll be there for him is what you need to work on. Let him calm down now, then later go to him again. Let him see that even though he lost his temper you still love him. Trust me, he needs to see that.'

'What do you base this on?'

She spoke without thinking. 'Years of knowing what it feels like to have no one in your corner.' She wished she hadn't been so honest when his features showed obvious curiosity. 'Give him time. And keep doing this. Come home, spend time with him. Be in his life without pressuring him.' She dropped her hand to curve over his, entangling their fingers. 'Okay?'

His fingers gripped hers right back, his features taut, revealing nothing, so she had no way of knowing what he intended until his head had swooped down and his lips claimed hers, his tongue driving into her mouth, his body curving around hers, the kiss filled with passion, anger and annoyance. And she felt those things too, biting through her, so she kissed him back with the same intensity, grinding her hips, frustration exploding in her gut.

'I wanted to ignore you,' he growled, but his hand lifted

to the back of her head, holding her there so his mouth could ravage hers, dominating her in every way.

'You have been.'

'Not well enough. Not really.' And then he was lifting her, pulling her towards the pool house, his body so strong and powerful, hers so full of need that it didn't even enter her head to demur, to put a stop to this.

They'd been fighting over Cameron, but was it possible they'd really been fighting each other, this instinct, looking for another way to satiate the violent needs somersaulting through them?

He kicked the door shut behind them, moving her to the bed, dropping her onto it but staying standing, looking down at her.

'Thée mou, voítha me,' he said intently. 'What am I doing?'

'You're making love to me,' she said simply. 'And it means nothing, except that in this moment I want you and you want me,' she promised, sitting up so she could reach the button on his jeans. 'You don't need to worry about hurting me.'

He chased her to the bed, though, stripping his clothes as he went before turning his attention to her bathers, pulling them from her body as quickly as he could, revealing her nakedness to his hungry gaze.

'This is madness.' He pushed the words into his mouth as his hands ran over her body, worshipping her curves.

'Yes.' She kissed him right back, hard and fast, wrapping her legs around his waist, drawing her towards him. He swore softly, breaking away from her just long enough to pull a condom from his wallet—he'd begun to carry them as a precaution after last time, which should have told him how realistic he found the whole 'ignoring her' approach.

'Amelia?' Sanity was almost gone but there was still a thread—just enough. 'Are you sure?'

She pushed at his chest in response, flipping him to his back. 'I've never been more sure of anything in my life. Make love to me. Now.'

'Christos.' He turned to face her, his eyes showing complete surprise. He wasn't sure he'd ever had such fast sex. What had it been—ten minutes? He felt as though a whirlwind had raced through the pool house. They'd rolled off the bed, onto the floor, knocking over a bedside table and lamp at some stage. Usually, he liked to savour the experience but passion—everything—had overwhelmed him completely.

'Don't freak out.'

It was such a ridiculous thing for Amelia to say—such a mirror of his own sentiments—that he laughed. 'I'm not, believe me.'

'Okay, good. It's just, last time, you totally freaked out.'

He propped up on one elbow, looking down at her. 'I did. A little. I hadn't expected it. Then or now.'

'No,' she agreed, staring up at the ceiling before shifting her gaze to his face. 'I like being with you.'

A warning light flared inside his brain.

Don't freak out.

'I know who you are,' she said quietly. 'And what your limitations are. I'm just saying I like being with you. I don't think you should go back to ignoring me again.'

Mortified, he angled her face towards his. 'I have no intention of it. That was to protect you, not to hurt you. I was trying to simplify everything. It didn't work and I was wrong.'

'Yes, you were.' She smiled, though, reaching up and running a hand through his hair. 'So what do you intend, then?'

His chest tightened.

Don't freak out.

'Because I'm only here for a bit under a month, and neither of us wants to get involved in anything serious. But I do want to do this again. And again. And again.'

He laughed. 'I get the picture.'

'So what if we agree that we just...keep it simple?'

'It's not simple, though, *agapitós*. Cameron adores you. If this ends badly...'

'It won't.'

He shook his head. 'You don't understand. I witnessed enough relationship breakdowns in my childhood. They're difficult to watch from the side-lines. Seeing people you care about hurt each other is not something I want for my son.'

'First of all, this isn't a relationship. Not in that sense. It's just an...arrangement.' She grinned, the sexiest smile he'd ever seen. 'And, besides, we can make sure no one knows about this.' She shrugged. 'Especially Cameron.'

'And can you say with confidence that you will feel that way in five weeks' time, when you leave the island?'

She laughed, shifting a little, bringing their bodies into more intimate contact. 'You think you're so irresistible, don't you?'

His eyes held a warning.

'You think every woman on earth is at risk of falling in love with you.'

'I didn't say that.'

'I'm more worried that *you'll* fall in love with *me*,' she said with an impish lift of her shoulders, drawing his gaze to the dusky pink aureole of her nipple. 'After all, I'm quite unique, you know.' She laughed, to show she was joking, but he didn't.

His expression was deadly serious. 'I don't believe in love—not romantic love, in any event. I don't ask you not to love me because I'm arrogant, so much as because it's utterly futile. I will never return it. This is just sex.'

* * *

A small smile moved across her face as she lifted her head, resting her chin lightly on his bare chest. He slept. Breath moved in and out, rhythmically, reliably; beneath her his heart beat, strong, regular, deep. Day was just preparing to break, whispering its promise beyond the window, urging the night to fade into nothingness, emerging in a blaze of triumphant orange somewhere near the horizon. It had been a warm night and they'd fallen asleep with the windows open. The curtains billowed a little, adding to the magic of that pre-dawn moment.

Do you think I want to wake up beside you every morning I'm here?

She'd thrown those words at him after they'd first slept together, the absurdity of the expectation making them ring with defiance in that moment.

But it was exactly what she'd done several times now in the three weeks since that afternoon in the pool house, when they'd both been so angry and passion, tension and need had spilled over, offering them the best kind of balm.

She woke early—it was part of her make-up, her overactive mind rousing her into the day well before light broke across the sky—and she never stayed in his room once she was awake. But this morning, she was tempted.

New to the ways of intimacy, she hadn't realised that hunger could be impossible to satiate. She couldn't have understood that each time they were together only seemed to increase her dependency on him, not lessen it as she'd anticipated.

Desire hammered through her veins now, thready and demanding, so that she ignored her usual pattern of behaviour—sneaking back to her room before anyone else was awake. Instead, she slowly eased the sheet from his broad, tanned body, exposing him inch by delicious inch, her eyes feasting on a chest that was broadly ridged—so familiar to her now that, despite her lack of artistic talent, she knew she could easily and confidently sculpt it from clay, just from memory alone. When the sheet reached his waist he moved just a little, shifting in his sleep. She stiffened, staying perfectly still, her eyes locked to his face until his breathing had resumed its steady, rhythmic pattern.

She pushed the sheet down his thighs lower still and then let it drop back to the bed with an almost silent swish, pressing against him. She bit down on her lip, her pulse rushing through her at an unbearable speed, and then she moved slowly in the bed, her eyes on his face as she moved.

He worked long hours. Despite the beauty of this island, he left it each morning at seven-thirty, like clockwork, and returned about twelve hours later. He spent around half an hour with Cameron then, and she worked, trying not to think of him when the fact he was in the house made it almost impossible to concentrate.

They only saw each other at night. And every night had made her more aware of her body's needs and likes, of what she was capable of, of what she could feel, of how all-consuming physical desire was, until she found herself wondering how she'd ever existed without something as biologically imperative as sex.

He had driven her wild, showing her how her body liked to be pleasured, using his fingers, himself, his mouth, to drive her to orgasm after orgasm.

With a small smile tingling her lips, she dropped her mouth over his arousal, his guttural noise in response shooting barbs of pleasure through her. She felt him shift, and when she blinked her eyes towards his face saw that he was watching her, his eyes still heavy with sleep, his lips parted in slumberous sensuality.

She'd never done this before—never even imagined doing something so intimate, at first—but as he'd continued to teach her what her body was capable of, she'd begun to harbour fantasies of how she could visit that upon him. She knew her experience might make her less than spectacular, but feminine instincts were driving her, so she moved her mouth up and down his length, letting her tongue brush over his tip before pushing him deep into her mouth once more, so he hitched against her throat. She made a small murmur of appreciation—he was so large, so hard; and, as she continued to take him deep into her warmth, he spoke in Greek, low and husky, the words impossible to comprehend, yet she grasped his meaning.

He was as filled with desire as she had been the night before, when he'd lashed her with his tongue, his strong hands holding her legs apart, permitting him full access to her femininity.

'Amelia, please.' There was a plea in his words but she didn't answer it. She didn't know what he wanted and she wasn't sure she cared. This was perfection. Feeling him like this, inside her, and seeing the answering wavering of his control, was some kind of fantasy come to life.

'You must stop.' His hand pressed at her shoulder. She paused, lifting her gaze to his while her lips stayed pressed to his tip.

'Why must I?'

'Because if you don't…'

'Yes?' She took him deep into her mouth then and he cursed—in Greek, yet his tone made the meaning of his word abundantly clear.

'Amelia.'

She laughed softly, the sound carrying across the room towards the ocean.

'Santos,' she said his name sternly. Then grinned. 'Relax.'

'Not bloody likely.'

She laughed again but, a moment later, neither of them was laughing. She moved faster, completely captivated by the intimacy of this and the ancient, feminine rush of power that trilled in her veins. Driving him beyond wild was possibly the most addictive thing she'd ever done. His fingers dug into her shoulder, and his voice filled the room, but she didn't stop, not until he'd surrendered to her completely, his pleasure exploding through her, his hoarse groan wrapping around her.

Lifting on to her haunches, she then straddled him, smiling, settling herself on his waist and pressing her hands to his chest.

He captured one of her hands as it trailed towards his nipple, lifting it to his lips instead and pressing a kiss against the inside of her wrist. 'Have you tried contacting your parents?'

For a moment, pain lanced her chest. She met his eyes then looked away towards the dawn sky and the shifting ocean beneath it. 'I call them a few times a year. They don't answer, and never return my calls.'

Her pain was obvious; she could feel it spreading through her and she forced a smile to her face. He didn't return it. 'Don't look at me like that, please.'

'How am I looking at you?'

'Like you feel sorry for me. Like you're working out how to fix it.'

His frown was a flash in his face. 'It seems strange that your parents would choose not to have you in their lives. And stranger still that you would accept it.'

'What can I do? You can't force someone to love you, Santos. It's taken me a long time to accept it, but at the end of the day my value to them was always tied up in my academic success, and how that translated financially for them. I—as a person on my own—don't particularly matter.'

'If that's true, then they don't deserve to have you in their lives.'

She couldn't respond to that. She'd come to a similar

conclusion years earlier but that didn't take the sting out of it. She tried another smile and squeezed his hand. 'It's fine.' She wasn't sure if she was saying that to herself or him.

He was quiet for a time, so that only the sound of the ocean rolling towards the island broke the silence. A moment later, she shifted her weight away from him. 'I should get back to my room.'

'Oh, no you don't.' He grabbed her arms and tumbled her to the bed, his body weight on top of hers now.

She laughed, pressing a palm to his chest. 'What are you doing?'

'You can't wake a man up like that without giving him the honour of repaying the favour.'

'I think I'm still well and truly in your debt,' she said, her lips twitching with amusement, her heart hammering with anticipation.

'But who's keeping score?'

She couldn't reply. Not when his mouth wrapped around one of her nipples and his fingers moved between her legs, pushing all thoughts from her mind completely.

'What are you doing tonight?'

He watched as she pulled her clothes on, each movement unknowingly graceful, her body lithe and beautiful.

'I'm going to double-check some equations before I email them off, and then Talia and I had talked about taking Cameron to look for shells.'

He nodded distractedly, the activity perfectly suitable for a day such as this. And he had a mountain of work. But, in the back of his mind, he was conscious of the days racing past. Nights were a sensual blur, nights in which he could indulge his cravings for this woman piece by piece until—momentarily—he was satisfied. But mornings broke faster than he'd have liked, and she was always gone, a phantom of her in the throbbing of his pulse and the hardness of his body. In two weeks, she'd leave the island for good, and he was mostly relieved by that, because already he could see how easily he could become addicted to her. Addicted to her body, he reminded himself forcefully, because that was what he found himself waking up craving.

Sex.

And sex was something he understood. But there was something different with Amelia, the way being with her made him feel. Perhaps it was simply her presence on his island, a haven he generally kept private. Or perhaps her fierce intelligence added another dimension to their dynamic—he certainly found them sparking off each other in a way that was wholly new. Or perhaps it was everything about her.

Whatever the reason for his fascination with her, he'd be glad when she left. It would be liberating not to feel this drugging sense of desire in every waking moment, and once she left the island she'd take with her temptation. He wouldn't think of her again—not often, anyway.

But for now, she was here, and he wasn't foolish enough to look a gift horse in the mouth. 'I have to go to the office this morning, but I thought I could come back earlier. Around lunchtime.'

She slowly turned to face him. 'Oh.'

It wasn't exactly the reaction he'd expected. That dredged a grim smile to his face—since when had Amelia reacted as he'd expected?

'I'm not invited to collect shells?'

'Of course.' She shook her head. 'I could use a full day to work.'

He narrowed his eyes. 'I meant to come with you.'

'I don't think that's a good idea.' She tucked her shirt into her trousers, her narrow waist drawing his attention before he transferred it back to her eyes.

'Why not?'

'Because we agreed Cameron—no one—would find out about us.'

'And you think collecting shells will be some sort of public declaration of intimacy?'

A blush coloured her cheeks. He loved how easily she did that.

'No, of course not.' And then a second later, 'But there's an inherent risk to it. When you and I are together, and no one else is around, there is a zero per cent chance of someone learning about this. Those odds increase exponentially if we throw in an afternoon with Talia and Cameron.'

'Fine, then,' he said, wondering why her response was so frustrating to him. 'Then come to Athens with me today.' Her eyes were huge in her face, and she shook her head numbly.

'If I wouldn't agree to an afternoon here on your private island, why in the world would I agree to go to Athens?'

Exasperation made him expel a harsh sigh. 'Because it's beautiful and you'd love it?'

'I've been to Athens.'

Something like impatience burst through him. 'Not with me.'

'Besides.' She changed tack. 'Cameron is looking forward to looking for shells, and it would mean the world to him if you'd go with him. He's really warming to you.' She hesitated. 'You're making such progress.'

And he was. He'd followed her advice of a few weeks earlier, waiting for Cameron to calm down before approaching him again, keeping a safe distance, simply watching, letting him know he was there. He'd discovered a love for block building and, over time, he and Cameron had begun to work on a project together. As they worked, they talked, so that they were really getting to know one another. She didn't need to push him to spend time with Cameron any more; he did so because he enjoyed it.

'Let's make a deal.'

'I'm listening.'

'I'll spend the afternoon with Cameron.'

Her smile was like a burst of lightning, bright and fascinating, her nod one of obvious approval.

'And you'll have dinner with me.'

Her smile dropped and he tried not to think about how unusual that response was to a dinner invitation. 'Why?'

'Why not?'

'Because that's not… We agreed…'

'We agreed we wouldn't fall in love.' He laughed. 'Do you think you're so irresistible I can't sit across a table from you without formulating marriage plans?'

He intentionally turned her own words back on her, reminding her of how she'd sneered at his arrogance early on in their relationship—or whatever this was.

'Fine, then. You've got yourself a deal. But don't you start getting all starry-eyed at my witty dinner repartee.'

He grinned, feeling a lightness move through him. 'I'll try my hardest.'

'This isn't exactly what I had in mind,' she drawled, staring out at the Acropolis. It was illuminated gently in the evening, golden lights washing over the ancient pillars.

'It's the best food in town.'

'And is it always empty on a Friday night?'

'You were worried about someone finding out about us.'

She shook her head. 'And so what? You booked out the restaurant?'

'Damen has known me a long time. He didn't mind.'

She shook her head, but she smiled—how could she not? 'Just as well I know how you feel about relationships because otherwise this could be construed as incredibly romantic.'

His skin paled so she had to bite back a laugh. 'It's not.'

She rolled her eyes. 'I'm joking.'

He relaxed visibly.

'How was shell hunting?'

His smile was natural and she felt something like relief spread through her. Cameron had been through so much. She wanted, more than anything, for him to connect with his father. It wasn't necessarily easy, given what he'd lost and the age he was at, but they were already making such inroads.

'He was quite excited by several of the "specimens", as he insisted on referring to them. I didn't want to tell him that shells such as these wash up along the shore all summer long.'

'He's a budding scientist,' she said proudly. 'He's got keen observation powers and an unquenchable thirst for knowledge.'

'And you are an excellent teacher to harness that.'

A man appeared, wearing dark trousers and white shirt. 'Here we are,' he said, a broad smile on his face. 'For the lady.' He placed a champagne flute in front of Amelia, and a beer for Santos, who nodded his thanks.

'Damen, this is Amelia Ashford, my son's teacher. Amelia, Damen has been running this restaurant since the dark ages.'

The older man laughed, rocking back on his heels. 'You make me feel old now, eh?' He reached out and, to Amelia's surprise, patted Santos on the head. He lifted a single brow but otherwise didn't respond.

'I've been coming here since I was an infant,' Santos explained when they were alone again.

Amelia couldn't hold back her grin. 'That's pretty sweet.'

'Sweet?' His laugh was gruff. 'I don't think I've been called that before.'

'I was calling Damen sweet,' she corrected with a saccharine tone. She sipped her champagne, then recalled what they'd been discussing before Damen had arrived.

'Where will Cameron go to school?'

Something tightened on Santos's face. A look of alertness. 'I'll meet with some headmasters next week.'

Her stomach rolled. 'Here in Athens?'

'Most likely.'

'So he'd travel over from the island? Or do you have a home nearby?'

He looked towards the window. 'I have a place not far from here. I prefer the island but the city will be more practical during term time.'

'I suppose this will mean a lot of changes to your life.'

He took a drink from his beer, holding her gaze over the rim. 'Yes.'

'So you're usually based on the island?'

'I consider it my home, but I spend a lot of time travelling.'

'Will you be able to curtail that now?'

'As much as possible.' He dipped his head forward. 'At least until he's settled into school and his new life.'

Her heart panged in her chest, his consideration not completely unexpected, yet it did surprise her. He obviously read that on her expression because his smile was almost self-mocking.

'You thought I would just carry on as I had before?'

'I hoped not,' she offered in response, running her fingers down the stem of her glass. 'He's a very special child and, after what he's been through, I'd love to think you could make him happy again.'

'Me too.'

'The thing is.' She shook her head, surprised by the admission she'd been about to make.

'The thing is?' he prompted when she didn't finish her sentence.

She sipped her drink and searched for the right words. 'He can be quite anxious; nervous. I think that's one of the reasons I've always felt protective of him.' She tilted her head to the side thoughtfully. 'As a little boy, when he first came to Elesmore, he and I were in our first year together and I think we had the same first-day nerves.' Her smile was laced with nostalgia.

'Why did you decide to become a teacher?'

She sighed a little. 'Do you think it's strange?'

'Unusual,' he clarified, his grasp on the nuances of English flawless despite the fact it was a second language.

'I suppose it is. I could have done anything, and I did. I loved my work with the space agency, but it's teaching that I enjoy most.' She considered how to best explain that. 'I was given a lot of opportunities because of my IQ, but there's something valuable about helping everyone reach their potential, even kids who have to struggle to learn to read and get their heads around early maths.'

'And this is also why you chose a local comprehensive?'

'Instead of some kind of toffee-nosed public school? Is that the kind of place you went to?' she queried.

He tilted his head in silent confirmation. 'I went to the same school as my father, and his father and his father, went to.'

She smiled. 'Of course you did. Sometimes I forget you're part of some kind of dynasty.'

His smile quirked.

'I was drawn to a comprehensive, yes. I'm not so sure financial status should have any place in education.'

He sipped his beer, his eyes holding hers over the glass.

'Additionally, I felt that a public school would be more interested in promoting me to their parent body—the fact they had someone with my academic background on faculty would have become a selling point. Elesmore knew that anonymity was one of my requirements for accepting the job.'

'So none of the parents know about your previous life?'

'I prefer it that way. It's been my experience that, once people learn about that one fact of who I am, it becomes all they can see in me. I don't particularly like that.'

'You're more than your IQ?' He said it in a way that was teasing, so she smiled—an unusual response when she was discussing the pain and isolation that had resulted from her genius.

'It's just how my brain works.' She shrugged her slender shoulders and his eyes flicked lower, taking in the hint of cleavage exposed by the silk dress she was wearing. He reached across the table, lacing their fingers together in a simple gesture of intimacy.

'I like the way your brain works.'

She smiled, her eyes resting on their hands, hers a light gold and his a deep tan. 'Anyway, I met Cameron, and I've always felt an affinity with him. He's a very bright student, and quite sensitive. He feels things strongly, and that sometimes puts him out of step with his peers. Cynthia's death rocked him to the core.'

'Naturally.'

'I guess, I'm saying that I'm glad he has you—and that you seem to realise the importance of being there for him right now.'

He squeezed her hand. 'I want to be a good father to him but it's not something I ever planned for. I was actually determined that I wouldn't have children.'

'Don't you need to continue the family name or whatever?'

'I have a half-brother for that.'

Surprise was evident on Amelia's face. 'You do?'

'Andreo, yes. He's married, and far more likely—or so I thought until recently—to be the one to provide the Anastakos heirs.'

'How does he feel about Cameron?'

'He's surprised, but looking forward to meeting him.'

'Does he work with you?'

'He runs our Asia Pacific operations.'

'You're close?'

'We're...products of the same upbringing.' He flashed a tight smile and she knew him well enough to know it foretold a subject change. She was getting close to something he didn't want to discuss.

'You had an unhappy childhood?' She squeezed his hand back, drawing his gaze there.

'You know about my childhood.'

'Your father's divorces.'

'Right.'

'And you were unhappy?' she pushed.

'I was ambivalent.'

She tilted her head to one side, analysing his explanation. 'In what way?'

His sigh was a fierce expulsion of air. 'Our home life changed dramatically, year to year. Children cannot help forming attachments to the people they live with. I would come to care for my latest "stepmother" before my father would invariably end the marriage and I'd never see her again.'

Amelia's stomach rolled. 'You don't keep in touch with any of them?'

'Andreo's mother,' he said quietly. 'But not the others.'

'God, it sounds like some kind of club: the Ex Anastakos Wives.'

'With a costly entrance fee.' He shook his head.

'That's why you're so dead set against relationships?'

'Yes.' The directness of his answer surprised her. 'In my experience, nothing good comes from fooling yourself into believing you need another person to "complete" you, or whatever it is that makes people pledge their undying love.' His cynicism was obvious.

Damen appeared then, placing some delicious-looking meals before them—fried cheese, rice wrapped in vine leaves, lamb croquettes and some pitta bread with dips. The smell made Amelia's stomach growl—she hadn't realised how hungry she was.

'I saw these women almost broken by my father—their hurt and pain.' He shook his head in condemnation. 'I have no difficulty understanding his short attention span. I think in this way he and I are similar.' She ignored the sharp barb in her side. 'But he could simply have dated them and moved on when the interest faded. Marriage is so inherently filled with hope and promise—to offer himself to these women, only to bore of them within months.' Santos shook his head again, irritated. 'He is a living example of what I do not want to become.'

'And so you also view women as disposable, but you make sure they know that in advance,' she pointed out archly, only to encounter a heated look from him.

'Disposable is not the right word.' He frowned as he re-evaluated that. 'Or, if I were to describe a woman as disposable, I would expect her to say the same of me. I'm very careful on this score, Amelia. I don't enjoy the idea of hurting anyone.'

'You're *afraid* of hurting someone,' she corrected subtly. 'Your father has made you that way.'

His expression changed to one of shock. 'I don't think I'm afraid of anything.'

She laughed then, a soft sound. 'You're too tough for fear, right?'

He grinned in response, and the seriousness that his confession brought shifted, leaving an air of relaxed intimacy between them. 'Absolutely, *agapitós.*'

CHAPTER TEN

'DID YOU KNOW it took just a little over fifty years to build?' she asked, pointing up to the Acropolis. He resisted an impulse to tell her he knew pretty much everything about the world-famous landmark. Pride in his heritage had made him a scholar of the local history.

'And it is taking almost that long to repair it,' he joked, casually slinging an arm around her shoulders, drawing her closer to his body. It was a balmy summer's night and, though the sun had set, the air was still warm and humid. She was wearing a simple dress, but no less distracting for its simplicity. All night he'd been pulled between two desires—firstly to enjoy her company and conversation, and secondly to push at the flimsy spaghetti straps until the silk dropped low enough to reveal her neat, round breasts.

'I'd love to see what it looked like back then. The damage it's sustained is such a tragedy.'

'It's part of it, though,' he murmured in response, his eyes taking in the pocked pillars, the crumbling ruins that had been central to so many wars since its creation. 'Each mark tells a story and speaks to the building's defensive capabilities. It might look better without the damage but it would have a less rich history; it would have played a less vital part in Athenian society.'

'And that would make it less emblematic,' she agreed, looking up at him, her dark eyes intriguing and speculative.

'You said you've been to Athens. Was it to study?'

'I worked at the observatory for a few months.'

'You enjoy physics?'

'Yes, very much so.' She smiled again.

'You don't regret leaving it to become a teacher?'

'I didn't leave it. I made a conscious decision to continue my work, but I wanted to have another focus. I enjoy the challenge of physics, the possibilities and—it's strange to say it—the cathartic relief that comes from taking vast numerical sequences and wrangling them into some kind of order. It's a truly sublime process—up until a month ago, I would have said better than sex.' She winked at him and he laughed, pulling her closer, her body fitting perfectly against the ridges of his.

'And this wasn't enough for your parents?'

He felt her stiffen a little at his side.

'They didn't let me stick around long enough to explain that I wasn't abandoning my science work altogether.'

'Would it have made a difference?' A motorbike zipped past, loud and distracting. She waited until the sound had ebbed completely.

'I don't know. I think not—my desire for anonymity was at odds with their plans.'

'They enjoyed the fame that came with your success?'

She made a guttural noise of agreement.

'How come I haven't heard of you?'

'Well, outside of England I wasn't exactly famous,' she said with a self-deprecating laugh. 'It's not as though I'm the only person in the world with above-average intelligence.'

'What exactly is your IQ?'

Even in the moonlight he could see the heat that flushed her cheeks. Or perhaps he was simply familiar enough with her to know that she was modest—almost to a fault.

'You don't have to say if you would prefer not to.'

'It's fine.' She expelled an uneven breath. 'Around two hundred.'

He let out a low whistle. 'That's ridiculous.'

'It's just the way I was born.'

He stopped walking, wrapping his arms low around her waist and looking into her eyes. 'It's not a fault, Amelia.'

'I know that.'

'You shouldn't feel embarrassed by it.'

'I'm not. It's isn't the IQ that embarrasses me, it's people's reactions to it. It's being seen to exploit something that I had no hand in acquiring.'

'How is that different to what a supermodel does?'

She lifted her brows. 'You're calling me a brain equivalent to a supermodel?'

He laughed at that. 'Apparently.'

'I suppose everyone has different dispositions. Perhaps if my parents hadn't…'

'Gloried in your brilliance?' He was teasing her but she was frowning, a little divot between her brows that he wanted to wipe away.

'They turned me into someone people knew about. They did interviews and got me in the papers; that was all part of it. For a while, my life felt like a circus. I had no control over where I went and what I did, and while I enjoyed the academic side of my life—I truly love studying and felt most at home when I was absorbing new information—I craved a normal childhood too. Friends, games, fun. Laughter. I don't think I laughed my entire childhood.'

He lifted a hand, cupping her cheeks, looking down into her eyes with genuine sympathy. 'You must have felt disappointed in them.'

'I do. But they're still my parents. I would have forgiven them—I can understand how difficult it would have been to bypass the opportunity to improve our financial standing—but they've cut me out of their life, Santos. I'm *persona non grata* to them and they did it so damned easily.' Tears sparkled on her eyes and something inside him shifted painfully.

'They were so angry with me. At first, I presumed they'd

get over it. But they never did. They stopped returning my calls, changed their numbers, blocked my emails. I tried going to their home to speak to them—they moved house. I have no idea where they are now. I presume in London, because leaving it wouldn't make sense, but I don't know for sure. I bucked their plans and they cut me out of their life as though I meant nothing to them. To my mum and dad, my only point of merit was my intelligence—and what that meant for them. The realisation was one of the hardest I've ever come to.'

Santos was not a violent man. Having a front row seat to his father's life had taught him that all strong emotions had the potential to be disastrous, so he was generally guarded, but in that moment he wanted, more than anything, to shake her parents for what they'd done to her. Not only in shutting her out of their life but in turning her into their prize performer and neglecting to care for her whole self.

'You deserve better than that.'

Her smile was lopsided, a ghost on her face, haunted by grief. 'I felt worthless.' She lifted her shoulders. 'It was hard.'

She spun out of his arms and began to walk once more, her eyes trained on the Acropolis with its golden lighting. 'My friend Brent introduced me to the Classics a long time ago. I loved them for their dynamically drawn emotional peaks and troughs, but it was only once I was living my own Aristotelian tragedy that I could see what they were really about.'

Santos waited for her to continue.

'The purpose of a Greek tragedy is almost to purge you of grief, so, while you may watch the play and feel everything on the spectrum of sadness, there is an inevitable catharsis that comes after that—a relief from the pain that is supposed to result in an emotional lightness.'

He considered that, and in the back of his mind he wondered at her perspective on things, and how much he enjoyed her ability to weigh in on any subject. What did he expect? Intellectually she clearly blew him out of the water, but far from being threatened by that he wanted to absorb what he could from her.

'Did you feel lighter once you'd gone through the tragedy of your argument with them?'

'Eventually.' She said the word with a smile that was more like herself, light and simple, happy. Relief spread through him. 'It took a long time to accept the finality of what they'd done, and also how earnest they were in wanting me out of their lives. It wasn't so much their decision as the way their decision showed me that even my own parents thought of me as unimportant. Unlovable.' She winced a little, and her honesty had him wanting to rush to fill the silence with assurances. But what could he offer?

'None of this was your fault,' he said with firm determination. 'I don't know them but the impression I have is that your parents are absolute fools to have let such a trivial matter come between you.'

'The thing is, it wasn't trivial. Not to me. My vocation is a reflection of who I really am, in here.' She pressed her fingers between her breasts. 'I think teaching is one of the most worthy and important professions. In a thousand lifetimes I would always have chosen to be doing this. I love working with children; I love their optimism and potential and the fact they're little sponges, brains ready to learn and acquire information.'

Her passion throbbed inside his veins, her words carrying a physical weight that ran through him. It would be unfair to compare Amelia to the women he'd dated in the past—she was different from anyone he'd ever known, male or female—but he couldn't help thinking that she was the most captivating woman he'd ever slept with.

'If you became a bit of a minor celebrity in England, how have you been able to avoid recognition now?'

'I'm using my mother's maiden name,' she said simply. 'Grandma Ashford and I were close. When I chose to reinvent myself, it felt appropriate to honour her in that way.'

'So you're not completely alone?'

The light shifted from her eyes. 'She died a few years ago.' Amelia swallowed, her throat shifting. The moon cut through a cloud, bathing the footpath in front of them in silver light.

Amelia reached out a hand, as though she could touch it, then pulled it back almost awkwardly, her eyes jerking up to his.

'What is your actual name?'

She hesitated for only a brief second. 'I was born Amelia Jamieson.'

He hadn't heard of her, but that didn't mean anything. As she said, press coverage had probably been at its strongest in the UK.

'Well, Miss Ashford, I think you are brave and I think you deserve to be happy. I also think your pupils are incredibly lucky to have you.'

'I suppose we should go back to the island soon?' She glanced at her wrist watch, surprised to see it was almost midnight.

They'd walked all over Athens after dinner, with no destination in mind, simply a desire to be together, side by side. At least, she thought they'd had no destination in mind, but here, in an upscale neighbourhood surrounded by modern homes that were four storeys high, he nodded towards one.

'Or we could stay here?'

She wrinkled her nose. 'I'm gathering it's your Athens home and not just some stranger's place you think looks okay for a night's accommodation?'

He grinned and her heart skipped a beat. It had been a pretty perfect night. She felt so comfortable with him, but that didn't change the fact that every now and again he smiled, or looked at her with eyes that were smouldering, and she lost the ability to breathe altogether for how completely, heart-stoppingly handsome he was.

'It's my place.'

She eyed it, hesitating a little.

'It would probably be better for us to go back to the island.'

'Why?'

'Because if we spend the night here there's no way Talia won't put two and two together.'

'And get four. So?'

'I thought we agreed no one would find about this.'

'It's Cameron we care about protecting. Does it matter if Talia works out that we're sleeping together?'

Her heart skipped another beat, this one less pleasurably.

Does it matter if Talia works out that we're sleeping together?

Why did she want to pull at that sentence, to inject something else into it? Because they weren't just sleeping together. She'd felt more connected to him tonight than ever before and that wasn't about sex.

'It's your decision,' he said quietly, his eyes wandering across her face, studying her thoughtfully.

'It would be good to see where Cameron's going to live,' she conceded, after a beat had passed.

His smile dug right inside her. 'Come on.' His hand reached for hers and she put hers in it, smiling for no reason she could think of as they crossed the street together and took the stairs to his front door.

He didn't use a key. There was an electric pad and he swiped his watch across it, so it opened with a soft click. A light automatically came on and Santos stood back, gesturing for Amelia to precede him into the house.

A high-ceilinged corridor gave way to a staircase to the left and a lounge area on the right.

'Would you like a drink?'

'Perhaps a tea?'

He flashed her a grin at that but lifted his shoulders, detouring away from the living space to bring the kettle to life. She watched as he made their drinks—coffee for him, tea for her.

'Won't you be awake all night?'

His grin was laced with seduction. 'I can only hope.'

Her pulse slammed through her like a tidal wave; heat began to build low in her abdomen.

He led her upstairs then, and up again and again, until the steps narrowed, there were fewer and a small door opened onto the roof of the building, giving an uncompromised view of Athens and the Acropolis.

Above them, the stars shone against an inky black sky. She expelled a sigh of contentment, cupping her tea in her hands, watching as Santos pulled a brightly coloured blanket from a basket, spreading it across the roof, over the surface, before returning to the basket to retrieve some cushions. He scattered them over the blanket, then gestured for her to take a seat.

'Nice touch,' she drawled, using humour to defuse the fact that her heart was fluttering wildly inside her. She moved to the blanket, settling herself cross-legged on one side of it. He stretched out on his side, an arm propped beneath him, his body turned towards her. 'Is this a standard seduction routine, then? I imagine it works pretty well.'

She was sure she felt him bristle at that. 'Actually, I don't come up here often. I thought you would like the view.' He lifted his eyes towards the stars so she immediately felt childish for having waved his playboy reputation between them. She winced and turned her attention to the ancient city sprawled before them.

'I do. Thank you.'

'Does it bother you?'

'What?'

'That I date a lot of women.'

'You mean sleep with a lot of women?'

He sipped his coffee and she could feel his eyes heavy on her profile. He didn't answer her question.

'Why would it?' She angled her face to his, her expression carefully blanked of any emotional response.

'I'm so different to you.'

'Actually, you're similar to me in more ways than you're not.' She took a drink of her tea then placed the cup on the ground beside the mat, wriggling down to lie beside him, her body inverse to his, a mirror image of his position. On autopilot his hand curved over her hip and her gut kicked with the anticipation that contact evoked.

'How so?'

'We're both loners, choosing to stay isolated from any depth of human connection rather than be hurt by someone we love. You do that by having meaningless sex with whatever woman takes your fancy. I do it by losing myself in my work and refusing to get involved with anyone.'

She hadn't consciously appreciated it before that moment, but as she spoke the words she realised how true they were.

'In my case, it's more that I don't see the value in that kind of relationship. I appreciate finding your "soul mate"—' he said the word with derision '—and living "happily ever after" might be the aspiration for many people, perhaps even the meaning of life, but for me, it's not. Everything I have seen has led me to believe it's a flawed goal, and that people make themselves unhappy by aspiring to it. I am not a loner. I enjoy the company of others.'

'But on your terms,' she interjected softly.

He appeared to think about that a moment, then nodded unapologetically. 'On terms that are mutually agreed and which leave no room for misunderstanding or hurt feelings.'

'I wonder if that's possible.'

'Why wouldn't it be?'

'Well, I don't know if emotions can necessarily be so neatly corralled into order.'

'Which is why I keep them *out* of my life.'

Her smile was indulgent. '*You* do, but I'm not so sure every single woman you've ever been with could say the same.'

'It's something I make clear before I get involved with a woman.'

She rolled her eyes, laughing a little. 'That's just a way of absolving yourself of guilt. People change. Someone might think one thing and then circumstances conspire to alter their expectations. You don't think it's possible that even one of the women you've been with wanted more from you than you were able to give?'

'If I thought that, I would end it immediately.'

'To save her from being hurt?'

'Exactly.'

'You've got it all worked out.'

'You're mocking me.'

'A little,' she conceded, reaching behind her for her tea and lifting it to her lips, then placing it on the mat between them.

'I think you're wrong.'

'Statistically, that's not likely.'

A grin flashed across his features. 'If you bring statistics into it then you have an unreasonable advantage in this argument.'

'I didn't mean for us to argue.'

'You're challenging my lifestyle.'

'I'm pointing out that it might not be as perfectly neat as you imagine, that's all.'

'And all the evidence tells me it is.' He lifted his broad shoulders and the hand on her hip began to shift, his fingers moving rhythmically over her flesh there, so holding onto her thoughts became difficult.

'Now you're pushing your own advantage.'

'Am I?' he challenged with mock innocence. 'How?'

'By making it impossible to think clearly.'

His grin showed he knew exactly what he was doing. Unapologetically, he dropped his hand to the bottom of her dress, sliding it up her thighs.

'I'm more interested in your dating life than mine, in any event.'

'What dating life?' she said with a small laugh. 'And why?'

'Because what I do is not uncommon. What you do is—'

'I know.' She flinched a little, the fact she had been a virgin until recently something that confused even her.

'You're a beautiful, fascinating woman. I find it impossible to believe you hadn't been asked on dates…'

At that, her feminism bucked hard. 'My not having really gone on dates bears no correlation to whether or not I was asked.'

He laughed softly. 'Naturally. So you just turned down any offers?'

'I accepted some,' she conceded. 'At Brent's urging. Good practice, he'd said, and I guess he'd been sort of right. But, honestly, I was so bored out of my brain I contemplated stabbing myself in the eye with a fork,' she joked.

He lifted his brows. 'So my witty and insightful conversation is how I won you over?'

'Nope, it's all down to sex appeal with you, sorry.'

'I'm flattered.'

'You probably shouldn't be. I'm basically reducing you to an object.'

'I don't think I mind.'

She grinned. 'I'm glad to hear it, because I intend to objectify you a lot for the next little while.'

'Why not start now?'

He thought she was asleep. She'd been quiet a long time, her head pressed to his chest, her hair loose along his arm. He'd been lying there, staring up at the stars overhead, replaying their evening: her rapid-fire conversation, a smile playing about his lips as he recalled the perfection of how it had finished—making love here beneath the ancient night sky.

'I always loved stars.' Her voice was a murmur.

He stroked her back, wondering what time it was. Two? Three?

He heard her yawn then she nuzzled in closer, her body cleaved to his. 'When I was nine, and incredibly homesick, I used to look out at the stars and imagine my mum. Did you know we're all made of stardust?'

'I thought that was just a song.'

'No, it's true.' Another yawn. 'Stars that go supernova create all the elements. We're more than ninety per cent stardust.' Her breathing slowed, and once more he thought she'd fallen asleep. Indeed, when she spoke next, her words were heavy, almost slurred.

'I used to look out at the stars and take comfort from the fact that, through them, my elemental make-up and my mum's, we were connected even though we were far apart. Stars bind us all together, in a way.'

CHAPTER ELEVEN

THE INTERNET WAS littered with articles about her, and photographs too. As Amelia Ashford had said, Amelia Jamieson had been in every broadsheet newspaper several times. But Amelia had also been modest. She'd told him some of her story without revealing many of the things others might have bragged about. Such as the scientific breakthrough she'd made as a ten-year-old that had led to a whole wing of a university in Texas being named after her. Or the research she'd done that had added a new dimension to the way scientists viewed star formation. She hadn't told him about the awards, the accolades, the grant money.

Her life, up until she'd made the decision to branch off from her scientific work and become a teacher named Amelia Ashford, had been completely different.

While he was in awe of her genius, he was even more in awe of her courage. To disregard the accolades and praise that was part and parcel of her success, to disappoint her parents and start a whole new life completely on her own, took guts and bravery. While he'd known she was special, seeing the full picture made him appreciate the full extent of that. Photographs of a young Amelia did something to his heart, layering cracks into it. She looked so young and so intensely vulnerable.

It also made a whole heap of sense when it came to why she'd turned up on his doorstep at Renway Hall like a lioness preparing to defend Cameron. She hadn't had anyone to stand up for her interests as a child, and she hadn't been prepared to let that same thing happen to Cameron.

It was hard not to feel a sense of affection for someone who was prepared to go in to bat for your own flesh and blood—and who'd single-handedly salvaged the relationship. Without Amelia, he didn't want to think about where he and Cameron would be.

'Working?' He propped one shoulder against the door of her office, scanning the whiteboards. Each was covered with incomprehensible mathematics. The first time he'd come in here and seen it he'd felt as though he were landing in a parallel universe. He was by no means intellectually lacking but his skill set was totally different from this. Mathematics was useful to him when it came to bonds, and profit and loss schedules, not these kinds of complex equation.

'Mmm...' She was scanning a piece of paper on her desk. She lifted her eyes to him, then a finger. 'Hang on one second.' Without turning away from him, she spoke again. 'Bishop to E7.'

Santos scanned the desk and saw that there was a tablet propped to her left. A man's face filled the screen. Handsome with blond hair, overly white teeth, a swarthy tan and green eyes. 'You're sure?'

She rolled her eyes but there was a wink in them for Santos. 'Absolutely. I have to go. I'll talk to you tomorrow?'

'No worries. Later, Millie.'

Millie? Heat shifted inside Santos. It wasn't jealousy so much as surprise, he told himself. He wasn't sure what he'd expected her friend Brent to be like—surely that was who she was talking to—but it hadn't been this.

'Playing chess?' He covered his unexpected response conversationally.

'I'm three moves away from check mate. He doesn't realise it.'

'You don't have a board.'

'It's in here.' She tapped her head.

He laughed. 'Of course it is.'

'Did you need something?'

Another burst of flame exploded inside him. It was the middle of the work day; it was unusual for him to be here, in her office. But the sense that he was unwelcome sat ill around his shoulders.

'You're busy?'

'I'm—no. Not really. Just familiarising myself with the class list for this year, starting to plan some lessons.'

This year. Term began soon; she'd be leaving. And, while it was strange to imagine what life on the island would be like without Amelia, he was also glad that their time together was almost drawing to a close. He wasn't foolish enough to pretend their forced proximity hadn't threatened to complicate his usually straightforward approach to relationships.

When Amelia left, he and Cameron would move to Athens and he'd return to a normal sort of life. He'd meet other women, and before long he'd forget about Amelia.

No. He'd never forget about her, and he didn't actually want to, anyway. But, once she left, his life would return to normal; he wouldn't crave her like this. It was simply a question of proximity and habit.

'I'm going to stretch my legs on the beach. Want to join me?'

She blinked, the offer apparently not what she'd expected. 'Where's Cameron?'

'He's napping.'

Amelia's brows shot upwards. 'Napping? Is he ill?'

'He's exhausted,' Santos admitted sheepishly. 'I took him to the fishing village this morning. We hiked, swam, ate. I gather I wore him out.'

Her heart felt as though it were being gently warmed. Santos spending time with Cameron made her feel an intense wave of relief. When she'd first arrived she'd had no idea how Santos would ever fill the father role in Cameron's life but the pieces were falling into place. 'I've been meaning to ask about that—how come there's a village on an otherwise private island?'

'Come for a walk with me and I'll answer.'

She tilted her head a little. 'Bribery?'

'Absolutely.'

'Fine.' She dropped her pen and stood. The sight of her in a pair of linen shorts and a simple T-shirt made him want to forget his suggestion of the beach and instead drag her to his bedroom. He swallowed hard and spun away before he could do just that.

The sand was warm beneath their feet. He took her hand on autopilot as they approached the shoreline, and felt her eyes jerk to his in response, but she looked away again almost immediately.

'So the fishing village?'

'Right. That was my grandfather.'

'He built it?'

'No.' Affection ran through him. 'My grandfather was a great man, Amelia. I wish…'

I wish you could have known him.

He cut himself off from saying the overly sentimental line, wondering where the hell the words had even come from. 'I wish he was still here, but he died when I was in my teens.' He kicked at the water; it splashed ahead of them. 'He was close friends with Daniel Konopolous, who was apparently renowned for his skill as a fisherman. In stormy weather and at any time of the day he could return with full nets. He lived on this island, but the village was losing its numbers, with people moving to the mainland. My grandfather bought the island, including the village, and allowed the fisherman to live and fish rent-free. There's been a fishing community here for a very long time; he didn't want to see that heritage lost.'

'And you still support the village?'

'I like having it here.' He reached down, picking up a

piece of pale blue sea glass and handing it to her. She studied it as though it might have secret properties.

'So you don't charge them anything?'

'Why would I? I don't need the money.'

'I thought you lived and breathed business. Such generosity isn't routed in commercial principles.'

'Perhaps not,' he agreed. 'But it's born of decency. Besides, I have no doubt my grandfather would come back and haunt me for ever if I made the slightest attempt to alter the arrangement.'

She was still looking at the sea glass. After a moment, she lifted it towards his face. 'This is the exact shade of blue as your eyes.'

The observation was simple, and perhaps it came from a scientific perspective, but that did nothing to stop the sharp blade that seemed to be drawing along his sides. And if he'd been wondering if she was reading something into that, or being sentimental in her own way, she lifted her hand and tossed the sea glass out to sea, smiling at him in a way that showed how wrong he was. What had he been afraid of—that she'd treasure the gift of sand-softened glass for ever?

She had done nothing to worry him on that score. Everything was going just as he would have wanted—simple, easy, no emotional demands. It was perfect. As if to cement that, he caught her around her waist and lifted her to his chest, so she tipped her head back on a laugh as he carried her out to sea.

'I'm fully dressed!' she warned and he arched a single brow in response.

'Is that an invitation?'

'Cameron could see.'

'He's fast asleep.'

She searched for something else to say but he didn't give her much opportunity. Striding deeper into the water, once it was halfway up his chest he dropped her into it and she squawked, spinning round and instinctively splashing him. He laughed, dropping into the sea himself, reaching for her, bringing her thrashing body closer and kissing her through the saltiness of the ocean.

She stopped moving and stood still, pressed to him, her body wet, their clothes clinging to them. When they kissed, nothing else seemed to have light or meaning; the world ceased to have a purpose beyond them. He deepened the kiss, his tongue duelling with hers, and she retaliated, using his body to move higher, her mouth pressing to his, her hands driving through his hair, her breasts flat to his chest. He groaned, moving deeper in the water until she was floating and he was keeping them standing, and only here in the safety of that depth did he push her shorts down, so he could cup her naked buttocks and hold her against his hardness.

The sun baked down on them, hot and unrelenting on the back of his head as he kissed her, his erection jerking between them, his body alive with a desperate hunger that only she could meet.

How could it still be like this between them? For weeks he'd been waiting for desire to wane, yet it hadn't. Every night together brought them closer to the end, making him aware of the temporary nature of this. And that served to increase his urgency, to make him yearn for her even at times like this—when they'd been together only the night before.

'You are so perfect.' He spoke the words in Greek, safe in the knowledge she wasn't fluent in the language and wouldn't understand them. 'This is perfect.'

Her response was a soft moan into his mouth and a roll of her hips, a silent invitation that came from her own overwhelming need for him.

'Please…' The word was one she said often when they were making love, begging for him to quench her needs, and he never needed to be asked twice. He had no protection—a foolish oversight, but they had only been coming for a beach walk—he hadn't expected this. Why? Why hadn't he, when their needs were always paramount? And what had he wanted, then—simply to walk hand in hand and talk? Who the hell was he turning into?

In rejection of that, he moved his hand between her legs, his eyes on hers as he found her most sensitive cluster of nerves and strummed it, his fingers knowing exactly what she liked, how to pleasure her, how to drive her wild and then hold back, to extend her fevered need.

'I want you,' she insisted, tilting her head back, her eyes scrunched closed.

'I don't have a condom.'

'I do.' Her cheeks were already pink from the heat of passion but he suspected there was a blush in there too. 'It seemed like a wise precaution to start carrying something,' she explained with a shrug, reaching behind her and pulling a foil square from her back pocket.

'You have no idea how good that looks to me right now.'

'To both of us,' she assured him, using her teeth to open the square. Her hands found the tip of his cock and expertly rolled the protection over his length, if somewhat teasingly, so a hiss burst from between his teeth.

'Christos.'

Her response was to lift up and wrap her legs around his waist, taking him deep inside her, an inaudible curse escaping her lips as she lay back in the ocean. His hands gripped her hips and he moved her, pulling her back and forth at first before his hand shifted to her femininity, strumming it as he moved so she whimpered and pulled to sitting, pressing herself against him and moving up and down his length, using her feet wrapped around his back for purchase.

Her first orgasm almost brought his own from him. He ground his teeth together, refusing to succumb to that temptation, needing more of this before he brought an end to it. Her breathing was frantic and he kissed her, sucking her panic and pleasure into his mouth, holding her against his body as her feminine core spasmed around his length.

Before she could find her equilibrium, he began to move again, pushing into her and pulling out, his hands roaming her body, his mouth devouring hers; or was it the other way around? A fever had gripped them both, making it impossible to tell who was pushing and who was taking; they were a jumble of hands and limbs and frenzied movements.

'God, Santos!' His name was tormented. She cried it out but the ancient ocean swallowed it away, the elements surrounding them making this all the more powerful. When her body was at its breaking point once more, he went with her, releasing himself with a guttural oath, burying his head in her shoulder, breathing her in, feeling every breath of hers in his lungs, his own lungs barely able to inflate his chest sufficiently.

The waves rolled with an audible gush; the ocean breathed alongside them and the sun beat down, the elements fierce and organic, and Santos stood there pressed to Amelia, holding her against his body until the world had tipped neatly back onto its axis.

'Your shorts are floating away.'

He lifted his head from her neck, confused at first before her words made any kind of sense. He angled his head to their left where, sure enough, his clothing was floating on top of the water.

'Mine too, come to think of it.' She laughed a little unsteadily.

'Stay here.' He pulled away from her with genuine regret, free-style swimming to their clothes and catching them in his palm.

'Thanks.' She took them from his outstretched hand

when he returned. He put out an arm of support and she gripped it while she pulled on her shorts, smiling at him as though she was waking up from some kind of dream.

'That's not what I expected when we came out here.'

'Me neither, though I suppose that shows we should always expect it as a possibility.'

'That's true. One week a rooftop in Athens, the next a private beach in the Aegean.' She shook her head, her mouth curved in amusement.

'Tonight, a roof-top garden in Paris?'

'What?'

Her smile dropped, showing surprise. His tone was nonchalant, casual. 'I offered to take Cameron there, to measure the Eiffel Tower. I'm sure he'd enjoy it a lot more if you were there too.'

'Oh.' Uncertainty shifted in her expression. 'Are you sure?'

'Why wouldn't I be?'

'It's just… Paris.'

He waited.

'You know, city of love?'

He burst out laughing. 'And you think this holds some danger for us?'

Heat stole into her cheeks. 'No, that's silly.' She laughed, but it was shaky. 'But I'll have to get back to England soon. Paris might be better kept until after I go.'

'Paris is next door to London. Why not stop in on your way home?'

The finality of his offer filled her head with doubts. It was so casual, so carefree, as though 'the way home' was simple. As though a little detour would mean nothing. And it shouldn't. It wasn't the fact it was Paris, *per se*, but that it was yet another shared experience, something they were doing together. The night they'd spent in Athens had already begun to transform her dreams. Falling asleep in his arms beneath a starlit sky had seemed to weave her past and present together—fears and grief from her childhood, encapsulated by the heavenly spectre of glistening particles in the sky, had acted as some kind of balm. And ever since then she'd found it impossible not to think about that—and about him.

Santos had been clear about his wishes for this from the start, and she wasn't stupid enough to hope for more from him, but nor could she deny that she was starting to *want* more. The idea of returning to England was no longer one she faced with any degree of pleasure. Nor was her teaching job—though that seemed impossible to believe. Her village and school community were the first home she'd ever known but they weren't the only place she felt at home. Now, there was this island and this mansion, and even his place in Athens. It was anywhere Santos was.

A foreshadowing of disaster curdled her blood so that, as the Anastakos jet came down to land over the city, even the sight of beautiful Paris didn't arrest the worry inside her. Perhaps the real Greek tragedy of her life was still ahead of her.

'It's not getting bigger.'

Amelia met Santos's eyes over Cameron's head and smiled. It was a smile that hurt a little—everything hurt at that point. She knew she had to leave but that didn't stop her from feeling every single emotion.

'Not recognisably, no,' she answered, her voice a little raspy. 'It's a very gradual process that takes days of intense heat.' She tousled her fingers through his hair then reached down for his hand. His small one fit inside hers and she squeezed it.

'It's still beautiful.'

She smiled at Cameron again. 'Yes.'

'Mummy used to talk about the Eiffel Tower,' he confided as they began to walk along the Seine. Santos held Cameron's other hand in his and the three of them walked in a line.

'What did she say?' It was Santos who asked the question, his voice gruff.

'That it was one of the most beautiful things she'd ever seen.' His smile was tinged with sadness. 'She told me there's a very fast train that travels here and that we would take it one day.'

Sadness flooded Amelia. She glanced at Santos. His expression was steely. 'I'm sorry she isn't here to see it with us.'

She knew him well enough to know that he genuinely meant that. Her heart trembled a little.

'Me too.'

They walked in silence for a few hundred metres. 'Can I get some ice-cream?'

'No, darling,' Amelia murmured.

At the same time Santos said, 'I don't see why not.'

Cameron looked from one to the other and then leaned closer to Santos. 'Thanks, Dad.'

Santos couldn't help his reaction; his eyes flew to his son's face first and then to Amelia's. Her eyes sparked with his. They'd both heard it; they understood it. Dad.

Such a small word but the meaning… It ricocheted around them, exploding like a pinball inside Santos. Emotions he hadn't known he possessed welled inside him.

Dad.

He was a dad.

He closed his eyes for a moment, and when he opened them Amelia was smiling gently, her gaze warm on Cameron's little face. 'I'm out-voted, then.'

'Definitely.' Cameron licked his lips. 'Can I get two scoops?'

Santos laughed, a laugh that was so full of joy and pride; he was almost euphoric. Something about that moment felt utterly perfect. 'Don't push it.'

Santos's penthouse wasn't far away and, after picking up their ice-cream, they walked towards it, surrounded by the ambient noise of Paris. As they turned into his street, they were confronted by a night market. In the time they'd been out, it had been completely set up from scratch. Tents were side by side, lights had been strung from one side of a narrow walkway to the other and the stalls boasted all sorts of treasures. Jewellery, books, art, more books. She lingered at one for a moment then kept walking, reaching for Cameron's hand.

An artist with an easel stood perched at the end of the street. Amelia smiled—he was so quintessentially what she might have imagined a Parisian street artist to look like. Silver hair at the temples, slender, dressed in corduroy trousers with braces over a loose shirt, and a beret on the top of his head, the angle of it charming and jaunty. A family sat before him, their picture being faithfully and quickly mined from the blank page.

'Amelia, look!' Cameron pointed at the portrait, drawing the attention of the little girl in the picture.

'Don't move, Angela,' her mother instructed in a broad American accent. The girl's eyes remained focussed on Cameron, with that curiosity children instinctively have for other children, before she turned back to the artist.

'Can we do one?' Cameron squeezed Amelia's hand, looking up at her and smiling. 'Please?'

Something stuck hard in Amelia's throat. 'Oh, I don't think so.' She bit down on her lip, because even as she issued the refusal a part of her wanted to agree. 'It's late.'

Santos watched, as surprised by his son's suggestion as Amelia evidently was.

'But please,' Cameron insisted. 'So I have a picture of

you. For when you…go.' The last word was little more than a whisper, but it screamed through Santos. The pleasure of a moment ago disappeared like a popped balloon.

Amelia's eyes lifted to his and Santos held her gaze, his expression impassive even when his mind was firing. The bond between Cameron and Amelia was unmistakable. It was why he'd insisted she come to Agrios Nisi, and he'd seen evidence of that bond again and again. But hearing Cameron ask for a picture because Amelia was leaving made Santos feel two things: irresponsible, for not properly having appreciated that there was risk in this step—risk that Cameron would become too attached to a temporary part of his life; and excluded, because Cameron's love for Amelia was so apparent. Santos didn't know if their connection was something he'd ever have with his son. He wasn't sure he'd ever have it with anyone.

Amelia had been trying to help him—but that wasn't the answer. Santos had told her that repeatedly. *He* needed to focus on his relationship with Cameron. It was no good to feel excluded from their bond—he had to focus on being the father Cameron deserved. Fear had driven him to employ Amelia—fear of being alone with Cameron, of not being what the little boy needed, but that wasn't acceptable. Santos had never run from a challenge and this was the most important of his life. He would conquer it—he had to.

'What do you say, *monsieur*?' the artist called, taking payment from the mother of the family he'd just drawn and giving his full attention to Santos. 'Let me draw your beautiful family. Your wife and child should be captured on paper, no?'

'Yes,' Cameron agreed with a grin.

'Another time,' Amelia demurred gently then, to Cameron as she guided him away, 'We have plenty of photographs together on my phone. I'll send one to your dad to print.'

Cameron, though, was unusually determined. ‘Why can’t we get a picture, though? Like that other family before?’

‘Because we’re not a family.’ Santos’s words cut through them all, like the shockwave from an earthquake. His eyes met Amelia’s and held her startled gaze for a moment before he crouched in front of Cameron. ‘You and I are a family, Cameron.’ His words were throaty and guttural, filled with an emotion that surprised him with its strength. ‘Amelia is just a friend. It’s different.’

No one spoke for the rest of the short walk to his apartment. Even Cameron was quiet.

But Amelia’s mind had been flooded by his words. *Amelia is just a friend. It’s different. We’re not a family.*

The silence filled her with a sense that she was drowning.

She felt as if she was on the outside looking in on something incredibly beautiful and warm but being lashed by snow and ice. She was their ‘friend’, except she wasn’t. Her place in both of their lives was temporary.

They were a family. She didn’t belong.

The next day, she’d leave. Soon Cameron would start a new school, make new friends and have a different teacher; and, while he might—for a time—think of Miss Ashford, before long she’d be a tiny figment of his imagination, slipping through the recesses of his mind until she was gone for ever. As for Santos?

At the door to the building that housed his penthouse, she looked at him without meaning to, only to find his eyes were resting on her face. Her heart stuttered. Would he think of her when she was gone? Would he miss her?

‘Let’s go upstairs.’

She nodded her agreement, but her insides were awash with doubts. She hadn’t been stupid enough to think saying goodbye would be easy but she'd had no concept of just how damned hard it would turn out to be.

He was used to Paris. Used to the Eiffel Tower, used to the city, used to its sounds and smells, but being here with Amelia on their last night together somehow made it different. New all over again, like the first time he'd come here.

'You were annoyed by him?' Her words reached across the room and he fixed his gaze on her face intently, as if committing it to memory. Maybe he should have let the artist draw the damned picture. He didn't have a photo of himself with Amelia. What a childish thing to care about! Since when had he wanted photographs of his lovers? Boxing her neatly into that shelf filled him with satisfaction. Amelia was no different from anyone else he'd been with. Even as he told himself the comforting fact, he acknowledged it for the lie it was.

'Who?'

She sipped her Scotch, her expression morphing into a grimace as the unfamiliar alcohol assaulted her. 'The artist.'

He searched for the right words. He had been annoyed. Jealous? Excluded? Worried? None of those things particularly did him credit. He focussed on the small part of his response he could claim without a sense of shame. 'I was annoyed for Cameron. He doesn't need to hear that kind of thing—that we're a family when it's patently untrue.'

He shifted his gaze across the room, his eyes landing on the door that led to Cameron's room. They'd left Talia on the island—it was just a short trip, and easy enough for Santos to manage Cameron on his own. Truth be told he was, in some ways, looking forward to being alone with the boy. It was a double-edged sword, though, because that would only happen once Amelia had left.

'It was a natural assumption,' Amelia murmured, but

her eyes had fallen away, her expression frustratingly shuttered from his.

'Just as it's natural for Cameron to wish he were part of a family. It's something he's never known—even with his mother. But allowing him to indulge an illusion will only hurt him in the long run. We're not a family and it felt important to explain that to Cameron. Do you disagree?'

It felt good to say the words, as though they were important somehow. Her expression flickered slightly but then she tersely moved her head sideways. Her dark hair was glossy in the evening light. 'No. I…think you were right.' But it was a soft statement, swallowed by swirling emotions. Her concern for Cameron was obvious.

'He'll be fine,' Santos assured her after a quiet moment. 'Don't worry about him.'

'I'll always worry about him,' she said simply, her smile melancholy.

'You don't trust me?'

'I care for him,' she clarified. 'I think loving someone and worrying about them probably go hand in hand.'

He stiffened, her easy use of the word 'love' sparking inside him. She was talking about Cameron, not him, but it nonetheless felt as though danger were surrounding him.

'I was a little…surprised too. I hadn't realised what we would look like, from the outside.' Her smile was awkward. 'It's been a long time since I've had anything even remotely resembling a family.' Her cheeks flushed pink. 'I know we're not. I just meant what people might have thought…'

Her loneliness opened a huge hole in his chest. He tried to cover over it, to ignore it. He'd made a choice to stay single, to avoid emotional commitments, but she hadn't. Not really. Her parents had devastated her, and she'd gone into a mode of self-protection ever since then, but she deserved to be a part of something; she deserved to be loved. The certainty rolled through his gut. She *deserved* to be loved.

The idea of that stirred something uncomfortable within him but also brought him a wave of happiness because, more than anything, he wanted her to be happy.

He couldn't make her happy.

Offering her weekend assignations when it suited him would be a bastard's move and she deserved better. Once she left, he'd never see her again; setting her free was the best thing for her.

He resolutely changed the subject. 'Who won your chess game?'

'I did.' Her features relaxed. 'I almost always do, though.'

Santos narrowed his eyes thoughtfully. He had to set her free—and perhaps she wouldn't even mind that much. 'So why do you suppose he continues to play against you?'

'He's a far better player now than he was when we first started competing,' she said simply, taking another drink. This time, her face didn't contort with the hit of alcohol.

'You don't think there could be another reason?'

'Such as?'

'Such as he's attracted to you?'

'Brent?' She pulled a face. 'No way. He's definitely just a friend.'

But Santos wasn't so sure about that. It seemed unlikely and impossible.

'Honestly, there's nothing between us—and never has been.'

'Maybe you should revisit that.'

'Why?'

'He seems nice. You obviously have a lot in common.'

'You don't mean he "seems nice". You mean he's handsome, and therefore I should feel attracted to him,' she challenged.

'I wouldn't really know what you find handsome,' he responded lightly, drinking his Scotch.

She rolled her eyes. 'I've had very lovely looking men

ask me out in the past, thank you very much. That's not what I'm into.'

'You don't like attractive people?'

Her easy smile morphed into a frown of deep concentration. 'The fact you're attractive isn't why I was attracted to you.'

'So why were you?'

He leaned forward, his need to hear her answer surprising him.

'Why after living as a nun or a social isolationist did you decide you wanted me to be your first?'

She stared at her drink so he wanted to reach across and lift her chin, tilting her face towards his, but he didn't. He waited, impatience making his gut clench.

'I can't really say,' she said a little breathlessly. 'I think my stardust and your stardust just aligned.'

It was such a romantic thing for a scientist to say that her expression was self-conscious, and then she laughed. Only to his ears the sound was slightly brittle.

'Sorry. That's a load of nonsense. I bet you can't wait to see the back of me tomorrow.'

CHAPTER TWELVE

'Do you have to go?' Pain was lashing Amelia from all directions. The sooner she stood up and walked out of this penthouse, the better.

'I'm afraid so. School starts next week and I have to get the classroom all ready for the new students.'

Tears filled Cameron's eyes. 'I want you to stay here with me.'

Her heart squeezed. She wanted that too, more than she could say. She refused to look at Santos.

Everything was different. Even the way they'd made love the night before had been different. Slower, more explorative, as if they'd both been committing every single detail of each other to memory. It had been a goodbye, an act of passion filled with finality. It was the last time they'd be together.

She'd woken early, slipped from his room, showered and dressed, already mentally imagining herself back in England, in her own home, far from Santos Anastakos and his seductive way of life.

'She can't, Cameron. Miss Ashford was good enough to spend her holidays with you but now it's time for her to leave.'

The coldness in his words was for Cameron's benefit but it only added to the excruciating minefield she was navigating.

'Then I want to go with her.' His little face assumed a truculent expression. 'I want to go home.'

Now she did look at Santos and saw a dark emotion in the depths of his eyes. Neither of them had predicted this. 'You have so much to look forward to, darling. You're going to love your new school, and make so many new little friends.'

'I like my old school and my old friends. I like *you.* I want to go home. I want to go home!' He burst into tears, tears that broke Amelia's heart. He hadn't had an outburst like this in weeks. She wrapped her arms around him, drawing him into a bear hug, holding him right where he was. She wanted to give into a similar breakdown, but didn't. For Cameron, she held it together.

'I'm sorry,' was all she could say, and she meant it from the depths of her heart. She was sorry for all that this little boy had lost. The years he'd missed out on having a father in his life because of a decision his mother had made, then the sudden loss of a mother he'd adored and now the terrifying new start that was before him.

'Do you remember what I told you when we first came to Greece?'

He shook his head, his eyes still overflowing with tears.

'I told you that every night, when you look up in the sky, I'll be looking up at it too. And we'll see the same stars, and we can smile and wave at each other, and you'll know that I'm thinking about you and you're thinking about me. Deal?'

But his lips formed a belligerent frown. 'Please don't go.'

A tear slid out of her eye. She wiped it away discreetly as she stood. 'I have to.' That was firmer, her 'strict teacher' voice. She pressed a hand to his shoulder, squeezing it gently. 'You be a good boy for your daddy, okay?'

Cameron's response was muffled.

Santos crouched down, his eyes at Cameron's height. 'Why don't you go get your shoes on and this afternoon we can go to the very top of the Eiffel Tower?'

'Without Amelia?'

Santos's jaw tightened. 'The view is exceptional. Go and get your shoes.'

Cameron hovered for a moment and then turned on his heel, half-running into his room and slamming the door.

Amelia startled. 'He'll be okay.'

Santos's head jerked in silent agreement and his eyes locked to hers for a moment that filled her with a whole new type of pain. He began to walk towards the door, his stride long. Amelia moved more slowly, aware that every step brought her closer to the end of this.

Everything inside her was pulling, tightening, making her ache in her entire body. Her heart was screaming at her to say something, to suggest they have one more night together, but it was too late for that even if she'd wanted to. She and Santos were consenting adults who'd gone into this with their eyes wide open but Cameron didn't deserve to have his little heart broken any more than it already had been.

They'd agreed this would be the end of it; they had to stick to that.

At the door, she lifted the handle of her suitcase, propping it to her side. 'Leo will take you to the airport.'

'I would have been happy to take the train.'

His smile seemed distracted. Was he already wishing she'd leave? Planning how he'd fill his nights when she was no longer around? The idea activated her pride; she wouldn't let him know how hard she was finding this. 'It's a door-to-door service.' He lifted a hand then, cupping her cheek, running his finger over her lips so she closed her eyes and inhaled, breathing him in. Every fibre of her being was shouting at her to say something. But what?

'Thank you.' Her heart exploded. 'For everything.'

He lifted his other hand, cupping her face. 'I am the one who should thank you, Amelia. I won't forget you.' His eyes were earnest, his voice throaty. She believed him. But that didn't change the fact he'd also replace her swiftly, as was his habit, and never contact her again.

Her stomach rolled; her heart splintered. She had to get out of there. 'Take care of him, okay?'

Their eyes clashed and there was so much in that look, so much unspoken and important. 'I will.' A gravelled admission that exploded through her.

She could barely look at him as she walked away, and every step towards the lift was an agony. The doors opened and she stepped inside, only then trusting her gaze to flip back to the door of the penthouse, craving one last look at Santos despite the fact she could see him with her eyes shut.

The door was closed.

He pressed his back against the door, his breathing rough, his body tense. Adrenalin hammered through him.

Go after her.

But what the hell for? Another night? Two? Until he no longer felt this addictive yearning for her?

He had always had the deepest determination not to hurt women—women as an abstract concept. With Amelia, that became very specific.

He wouldn't hurt her. With his life, he pledged that.

Inviting her to stay longer would be a doorway to pain and he couldn't do it. Already he could see her ambivalence and uncertainty. She'd been carefully measured but he knew her better than that now.

He had to let her go. He wasn't his father. He didn't use women for his own selfish purposes, disregarding how that might affect them. Santos was perfectly capable of having a sexual affair without letting his emotions into the equation, but he wasn't so sure about Amelia. The street artist's comment had simply cemented his doubts on that score. She deserved a family—not the illusion of one but the real deal. And, the longer she spent with Cameron and him, the more likely she'd be to imagine… He shook his head against the door, his lungs bursting. It was impossible.

He stayed pressed to the door for several minutes. Long enough for Amelia's lift to have reached the lobby, for Leo to have lifted her suitcase into the boot, for him to have pulled the SUV out from the kerb and begun the drive to Charles de Gaulle.

And so she was gone.

He wasn't a fool. The fact he hadn't been with another woman a month after he'd last seen Amelia was an indication of how much their arrangement had affected him.

He wasn't interested in being with anyone else. Not yet. The idea of having sex with any other woman left him cold.

He told himself it was just as well—Cameron wasn't adjusting well to life in Athens and was taking more of Santos's time and attention than he'd anticipated. But, still, his nights were free. Once the six-year-old was in bed, Santos was able to do as he wanted.

And yet he spent his time alone, in his study, catching up on work or losing himself in board reports. He also cursed the day he'd ever met Amelia Ashford.

Teaching made Amelia happy. Winscott Village made Amelia happy. Playing chess with Brent made her happy. Her work on the Hayashi Analysis made her happy.

But in the four weeks since leaving Paris—since leaving Santos and Cameron—Amelia had felt a heaviness deep inside her that nothing was able to shift. There was no happiness in anything any more.

It was a grief—but different from what she'd gone through when her parents had cut her from their life. Those emotions had made sense.

This didn't.

She and Santos had been clear from the start. She'd known all along that she'd be coming back to Winscott to take up her teaching position. She'd known it would end and she'd simply enjoyed the time they had.

So why did she feel as though she was barely holding it together?

The days were something to be got through. She taught, and she went through the motions of being the teacher her pupils needed her to be, but at the end of the day she locked up her classroom and went home, stripping off her clothes as she walked to her bedroom, where she would curl up in bed, pull the duvet to her neck and simply stare at the wall.

The nights were the worst.

She'd outgrown nightmares as a ten-year-old but they were back now. Awful, terrifying nightmares—Cameron running through fire and her not being able to reach him, Santos following behind, neither of them coming out. It was all so vivid that she'd wake up in a sweat and take several seconds to remind herself that it was just a bad dream—they were fine. So far as she knew, at least.

The nights when she didn't have nightmares were even worse, because then her head was filled with Santos—all the ways he'd made himself some sort of master to her body and its impulses; all the ways he'd made her feel more alive than she'd known possible. Those dreams were a form of torture from which she never wanted to wake.

The loneliness was awful.

Having accepted that she was binary within the universe, for the summer she hadn't felt that. She'd felt like she was part of something.

A sob filled her throat. She swallowed it, staring at the wall, squeezing her eyes shut. It was no good. Tears ran down her cheeks. She dashed at them, her heart unbearably heavy, and pulled her knees more tightly to her chest.

She'd *felt* like she was part of something, but she hadn't been. It had been an illusion and Santos had warned her about that right at the very beginning. She'd told him she was capable of separating a physical relationship from anything more.

And can you say with confidence that you will feel that way in five weeks, when you leave the island?

'Oh, God.' She sat up in her bed, brushing her hair from her brow.

She'd done the exact opposite of what she'd promised him. She'd fallen in love with him. It wasn't just sex. Maybe it had never been. Maybe she hadn't just been being trite when she'd said their stardust had aligned.

Santos had been different.

On the first day they'd met, she'd wanted to kiss him so badly. Why? Because he was different and something about him called to her. Generally, her understanding of the world was informed by science, but in this moment she subscribed to every theory she'd ever heard about soul mates and fate.

'I'm in love with Santos.' She pressed her palms into her eyes, shaking her head from side to side in disbelief. And yet there was also a bubbling euphoria, a feeling that almost bordered on the edge of hysteria. She was in love with Santos. Completely. Completely and utterly in love with him. Pushing off the duvet, she stood, a sense of purpose flooding her body for the first time since leaving Paris. Perhaps even sooner than that, for the last week or so of their time together had been tinged with a sense of powerlessness, as though she'd been on a train and couldn't get off.

She loved him.

She had to tell him. Regardless of what he said, she needed him to know. He was scared of hurting her, but was he just letting that fear stop him from having what he really wanted in life? Did he want her like she wanted him?

It was Thursday. The idea of having to get through a whole day at school before the weekend was a unique form of torture, but that same sense of purpose made it possible.

She loaded up her phone and began the practicalities, booking flights, organising what she could.

She had to tell him. She'd think about what came next afterwards.

She was sure Cameron would be asleep at eight o'clock on a Friday night, and that was important. As much as she was desperate to see the little boy, she understood how confusing it would be to him, and he deserved better than that. So she'd waited outside his Athens home, her nerves doubling by the minute, her doubts plaguing her, uncertainty ripping through her.

But she knew she had to do this. She needed to tell Santos the truth.

Finally, a minute after eight, she walked up the steps, memories of the last time she'd been here and taken these steps flooding her mind and body. That night had been perfect. If she hadn't loved him before then, she'd definitely fallen hard for him on that evening in Athens.

It was cooler now, autumn wrapping its grip around the country, so she wore jeans, a sweater and a scarf at her throat. Her fingers shook as she lifted them to the door, hesitating for a moment before pressing the buzzer there.

A moment later, it pulled inwards and she braced herself, wondering if it would be Chloe or Leo, perhaps Talia.

It was Santos.

Santos Anastakos, looking so familiar and so different, so untouchably handsome and expensive in a bespoke suit that fit his body like a glove.

'Amelia!' Her name was torn from him, shock evident in all his features.

'Hi.' Her voice was barely a whisper. Inwardly she cursed and tried again. 'How are you?'

He frowned, his eyes shifting beyond her, as if he could

somehow understand what she was doing there if he looked hard enough. This wasn't a good start.

Shock though was quickly set aside, his face assuming a distant expression, so he looked at her as though she were a polite stranger. Her stomach dropped to her toes.

'I'm fine. And you?'

As though she meant nothing to him. As though her being here was an inconvenience. Her knees felt weak, like they might not be able to support her for much longer.

She had to do this. She needed to tell him and see where the chips fell.

'Are you going somewhere?'

A frown flashed across his face and he dipped his head forward in silent response. 'Soon.'

Great. A time limit. She toyed with her hands and then stopped, sucking in a deep breath and searching for courage. She loved him and, whatever happened, he deserved to know that. She couldn't live in a world where he *didn't* know how she felt. But the fear of being rejected by him was enormous. She braced for it, straightening her spine, her eyes awash with deep, raw emotions.

'How's Cameron?'

His face tightened, his eyes stormy. 'He's—a work in progress.'

'What does that mean?' For a moment, thoughts of her own misery were driven from her head.

Santos compressed his lips, a muscle throbbing at the base of his jaw. 'Did you come to speak about my son?'

Her heart squeezed. He was being so cold! Her stomach looped in on itself. 'No.' She shook her head, closing her eyes. This was a disaster. But she'd come all this way; she had to do it. Whatever fine beam of hope she'd had when she'd boarded the flight in London was now flickering to darkness inside her.

'But I'd be lying if I said I haven't been thinking about him since I left.' She swallowed. 'And about you.'

The sharp intake of air, signalled by the rising of his chest, was the only indication that her words had any impact on him. His features were blanked of emotion but there was agony in his eyes, a torment that made her heart ache.

'Come in.' It was a command, short and sharp. Hope lifted through her. She looked beyond him but memories flooded her, memories that would eat her alive if she wasn't careful. She shook her head. Whatever he said, being out here felt like a tether to her real world and like a slipstream to escape, if she needed it.

'This won't take long.'

He nodded. Was that relief she saw on his face? Her heart dropped.

'You were so specific, Santos. Right at the start of all this, you were abundantly clear about how you felt and what you wanted. I know that you intended for us—what we were—to be a physical affair that ended when I left.'

His eyes seemed to be tied to hers by some unseen force. He stared at her and she felt as though he were touching her. Butterflies shifted through her belly. Finally, he moved his head, just a tiny mark of agreement. 'We both agreed to that.'

'Yes.' She sighed. 'But it turns out you were right. It's hard to separate emotions from sex. I thought I could do it but, God, Santos…' She shook her head, a dreaded film of tears filling her eyes so she closed them for a second, blinking furiously.

He was tense. She could feel it emanating off him in waves, slamming into her. 'What are you saying?'

'What do you think?' She shook her head and a hysterical laugh bubbled out of her. 'I fell in love with you, just like you said I would.'

His face paled, his jaw tightened. 'Amelia.' He shook

his head and then reached for her, putting a hand around her arm. 'No. You can't have.'

Another laugh, completely humourless. 'Well, I did.' She drew in another breath, waiting for it to fill her with some kind of courage. 'And I don't think I'm the only one.'

If it was possible, his face paled even more. 'I was so honest about this.' He groaned, reaching down and squeezing her hand. He took a step out onto the landing, his body closer to hers, as though he wanted to touch her but also knew it would be too complicated. 'This is the last thing I wanted.'

Her throat felt as though it were lined with blades. 'Are you sure about that?'

He ground his teeth. 'Absolutely.' His eyes shuttered closed for a minute. 'I don't love you, Amelia. I'm sorry if I did anything to confuse you, anything to lead you on. I wanted what we shared but I always knew and accepted that it would end.' The words slashed her insides, tearing her to ribbons.

'I don't believe you.' She held his gaze even when her courage was faltering. 'Tell me you haven't thought about me.'

He hesitated for a moment.

'Tell me you haven't missed me.'

He was completely silent.

'Tell me you don't love me.' Her voice cracked but it was so important to hear him say those words.

'If I say those things, it will hurt you, and that is the last thing I want to do. Let me say this instead: I want now what I wanted then. Our relationship ran its course.'

It was, somehow, worse than if he'd just agreed with her. It was an admission that nothing about what they'd shared had affected or changed him at all. Where her heart had been blown wide open, making her not only open to the possibility of love but accepting of its inevitability, he was the same man he'd been before.

She'd come here because she'd thought it was important for him to know how she felt, but now the futility of what she'd set out to do weighed her down more than anything else.

At least before she'd had hope, and she'd had the happiness of her memories—a happiness that might have returned in time.

Now, there was nothing. How could she look back at any of the times they'd been together and not see that what had been an incredibly special moment for her had meant literally nothing to him?

The sound of a taxi door closing had her turning on autopilot and she used the shift as an opportunity to wipe an errant tear from her cheek.

'Santos, darling, I'm so sorry I'm late.' A woman—not Maria but cast from the exact same mould, all leggy, slim, tanned with long blonde hair—stepped from the car and sashayed towards his home on sky-high heels. Her dress was like a second skin, moss-green with a deep V at the front and a slit to mid-thigh.

Amelia spun round to face him, the situation only just making itself obvious to her. What a fool! Here she was pouring her heart out to him and he was waiting on his date! His lover?

She was going to be sick. Oh, God.

She wanted to say something pithy. Something that would make light of this whole affair. She wanted the ground to swallow her whole. But her heart was breaking and she couldn't hide that from him.

The woman came up to them, smiled with curiosity at Amelia then pressed a kiss to Santos's lips. Bile rose in Amelia's throat.

'I don't think we've met.' The woman extended a manicured hand. Amelia stared at it.

'No.' Her voice sounded hollow. She couldn't look at Santos but politeness had her shaking the other woman's slim hand. 'I'm just someone who used to work for Santos.' She swallowed. Tears were engulfing her. She didn't—couldn't—say goodbye. She turned away, gripping the railing for support as she quickly moved down the steps, beyond grateful for her sensible ballet flats. She would never have been able to make a speedy getaway in heels like the other woman's.

The other woman's.

The way she'd leaned in and kissed him… They weren't strangers and this wasn't a first date. The idea of him being with someone else made her ache all over. The taxi was still there, the driver filling something out in his notebook. Amelia tapped on the window as she pulled the passenger door open. But Santos was right behind her, his hand on the door, his body framing hers as she moved to take a seat.

'Wait.' The word was drawn from deep within him, thick and dark. 'Don't go yet.'

A sob bubbled from her throat. 'Why not?' Her eyes lifted to his house. The front door was closed, his glamorous date no doubt ensconced inside.

'You told me all of this. You said I wouldn't matter. You said you'd never love me. You warned me. You haven't done anything wrong.'

He was so close. She could feel his breath, each one ripped from his body. She had to get out of here. A full-blown breakdown was imminent and she wouldn't subject him to that. She loved him enough not to want him to suffer unnecessary guilt. After all, what had he really done wrong? He'd warned her from the start.

I don't believe in love—not romantic love, in any event.

I don't ask you not to love me because I'm arrogant, so much as because it's utterly futile. I will never return it.

He stared at her and she waited for him to speak, but he didn't, and thc impossibility of all of this just made it worse. She sank into the taxi, her hand on the door. Still he stood there, his frame blocking the door from closing.

'Please just let me go now.'

He continued to stare at her, his expression dark.

Tears filled her eyes; her heart was breaking. 'I need to go.'

The plaintive cry did it. He seemed to rouse from something and step backward. A second later she pulled the taxi door closed and it drove away, taking her from his home, away from a scene that would be etched in the fibres of her being for ever.

CHAPTER THIRTEEN

EVERY MORNING FOR the next week, he woke with a feeling of weight bearing down on him, suffocating him. Every day for the next week, he struggled to so much as breathe.

When he slept, he saw Amelia. Her eyes, her smile, her frown, her pain. The moment Pia had arrived and Amelia had seen her, he'd wanted to throttle something, or to reach out and stop time, to undo what had just happened.

How could she fail to believe he was sleeping with Pia? And then Pia had kissed him and stood at his side, as though they were a duo and Amelia a stranger, and he'd been incapable of doing anything but standing there, so blindsided by what she'd said, by the heart she was offering him, that he'd been temporarily immobilised.

It hadn't been good enough. Amelia had looked at Pia and believed that he was already seeing other women. Hell, hadn't that been his plan? Hadn't he thought that taking Pia to the fundraiser ball—an event for which he was on the board—might lead to him feeling something for her? And he would have been relieved if that had been the case. If finally he could have looked at another woman and felt even the slightest flare of interest.

Amelia couldn't have known that he'd been celibate since Paris. Amelia couldn't have known that the idea of so much as having dinner with another woman disgusted him. How could he sit across the table from someone else and make small talk when anyone else now bored him senseless?

His father's announcement—that he was getting divorced again—only added to the weight pressing on Santos's chest. All these people and their damned belief in 'love'. It destroyed lives. Look at Amelia and how she was feeling! She'd let herself fall in love with him and now she was suffering.

He focussed on two aspects of his life to the exclusion of all else: Cameron and his work.

But, two weeks after Amelia had turned up on his doorstep, Cameron came home from school with a torn shirt pocket.

'What happened?' Santos reached out and ran his finger over it, something in the little boy's demeanour instinctively leading him to understand the seriousness of this.

'Nothing.' Cameron crossed his arms over his chest. 'I don't want to talk about it.'

'Cameron?' Santos's voice was unintentionally sharp. He softened it with effort. 'I cannot help you if I don't know—'

'Just leave me alone.' Cameron burst into tears and stormed down the corridor, slamming his bedroom door shut.

Great.

He listened to the little boy's sobbing and pressed his head against the wall. Everything was falling apart. A year ago his life had been ordered and neat. He'd been absorbed by his work, his commercial success a blinding light, and he'd enjoyed his social life too—sex, friendships; easy. He'd been *happy*.

He pushed up from the wall a little, his chest straining. No, he hadn't been happy. He'd been existing. The only time he'd ever really been happy was on the island, over the summer. That beautiful, enormous mansion that was his connection to his heritage, a place where he was most at home, had suddenly felt like a *real* home. Returning each evening to Amelia and Cameron had become what he'd lived for. Knowing that within minutes of his helicopter touching down he would see Amelia, that he would be able to steal a kiss when Cameron wasn't looking.

His stomach clenched. Her smile had become the most important thing in his life. But she wasn't smiling now. She was miserable, and all because she'd fallen in love with him.

Just like the women who'd loved his father.

Pain was the inevitable cost of love. How could she fail to see that? Why hadn't she protected herself better? Even her own parents had failed her, so why the hell had she put her faith in him? How could she have thought loving him was a smart idea?

Because she couldn't help it; a voice in his head demanded to be heard. *Love isn't like that.*

He listened to Cameron's sobs subsiding a little, and then went into the kitchen, pulling out a box of ice-creams and opening one. Even that filled him with memories.

Maybe if he'd been stricter from the start, enforced tighter caps on what they were, rationed Amelia to being a 'sometimes' lover… Perhaps if he'd come home later, made sure that while they'd been sleeping together they weren't also dining together, working side by side, doing all the things that might in different circumstances have characterised a real family…

He felt like he'd been punched in the chest. He didn't *want* a real family. But he did want Amelia. He wanted her in his life, smiling, happy, pursuing her dreams but at his side.

But then what? another voice niggled at him. What if in a year's time they wound up in this exact same position? What if he was even more like his father than he realised? What if he promised her the world and then changed his mind?

He knocked on Cameron's door.

'Go away.'

'I have ice-cream.'

A pause. A sob. Then the door handle opened to reveal his son's tear-stained face. Santos felt an anguish unlike anything he'd ever known. He wanted Amelia on a lot of levels but there was this, too. With her at his side, everything made sense, and he knew he was a better parent with her support. It was only a small part of why he needed her, but it was the straw that had broken the camel's back.

He wanted her, but this time he'd be more careful. He'd protect her better. What he needed was a contract, a document that spelled everything out in black and white, a way of ensuring she wouldn't get hurt this time around.

This had been a mistake. Amelia was a scientist first and a teacher next. She was, as it turned out, definitely not a cook. She stared at the front of her apron, covered in a pale yellow goo, and turned the tap on with her elbow. Water spurted out too hard, splashing her face. She ground her teeth together and eased the tap off, pushing her hands beneath the stream then adding some soap and lathering them up.

'Make pasta, they said. It will be easy, they said.' She cast an eye over the tragedy of her chopping board. Whatever the heck she'd assembled, it more closely resembled some kind of blobby sea creature than it did anything edible.

When her hands were clean, she moved back to the chopping board—the mess wasn't contained to one patch of timber, though. It had spread over the kitchen bench. Flour, broken eggs, a rolling pin that would probably never look the same. The television chef with his cockney accent and roguish smile had made it look so easy.

He'd lied.

It wasn't easy.

Grimacing, she lifted the chopping board, preparing to throw the evidence of her failure away, when the doorbell sounded. Casting a glance at the clock, she replaced the board and wiped her hands on the sides of the apron, making sure they were dry.

The supplies she'd ordered for her pupils were already two days later than expected. That had to be them. She moved through her home, not stopping to check her appearance in the mirror—she knew she must look a mess, with flour on her cheeks and in her hair, wearing a sloppy jumper and loose-fitting jeans, but what did she care?

She pulled the door inwards, preparing to sign the postal form and take the box of stationery, except it wasn't Russell, the familiar Royal Mail delivery guy.

'Santos?' Everything inside her began to quiver. The cells of her body went into overdrive. With an enormous effort, she assumed a mask of cool civility, but it was almost impossible when she felt as if she were being electrocuted.

'Amelia.' His brow crinkled and his eyes swept over her, the corner of his lips pulling into a small smile. 'What the hell have you been doing?'

Oh, God. She must look…terrible. But so what? She refused to care about that. Tilting her chin, she held his eyes. 'I'm cooking.'

'Really?'

It was a joke. She ignored it. Her body was buzzing and humming and her chest was compressing. 'What are you doing here?'

He sobered, nodding, shoving his hands in his pocket. 'I came to see you.'

She bit down on her lip. 'Is something wrong?'

'No. Yes.' He stared at her, then expelled a breath. 'Can I come in?'

She looked over her shoulder, then turned back to him. 'I…okay. Just for a minute.'

'Thank you.' She stepped back, giving him plenty of space to move by without touching her, but it still wasn't enough. His hand brushed hers and she almost jumped out of her skin. She covered her response by pushing the door shut with a resounding click. From there, she kept her distance, maintaining at least a metre of space between them when they reached the living room.

He looked around, his eyes taking in all the details, so she tried to see it as he must—the homeliness of it, the simplicity and cosiness. It was completely different from his perfectly designed living spaces.

She squared her shoulders, assuming a position of defiance and defensiveness rather than showing how affected she was by his presence.

'Christos.' He shook his head, then dragged a hand through his hair. 'I have no idea what to say to you.'

How could he not hear her heart? It was slamming into her ribs over and over, so loud, so painfully persistent.

'Then why are you here?'

'Let me start with this.' He nodded decisively, moving towards the window and looking out at the empty field that ran beyond her house, all the way to the stream. 'When you came to Athens, I was going to a fundraising event. I'm on the board and obliged to attend. It wasn't a date.'

And, despite the fact he wasn't looking at her, she turned away from him, staring at a photograph on the wall.

'I didn't sleep with her. Or anyone else. I haven't moved on from you, Amelia.'

She kept staring at the photo, his words wrapping around her, making her heart hurt, her breath burn, her body sag.

'I wanted to, though. That night, I thought that if I could just do something I normally would that maybe I would start to *feel* normal again. Maybe if I went out with someone like Pia, laughed with her, flirted with her, you wouldn't take up such a huge part of my mind any more. I needed to perform an exorcism, and I thought that would work.'

Amelia spun round to face him, hurt showing on her features, her eyes huge in her face. 'I don't know if that's more offensive to her or to me. You thought that you could sleep with her and forget about me? You'd actually use another woman like that?'

He blanched. 'I thought I'd feel *something* for her. Desire. Need. Anything. But I haven't felt a damned thing since you left. Why is that?' he asked, crossing his arms over his chest. 'How come you're all I can think about? How come you're the only person I want, the only person I need?'

She clamped her mouth shut, her head issuing a stern warning to her heart. None of this meant anything. He was annoyed by her hold on him, but hadn't that been the case all along? He'd been transfixed by her and waiting for that to wear off. He hadn't wanted to feel that way; he didn't welcome any of this.

He was moving closer to her and, while she braced for his nearness, there was a tiny part of her that wanted to welcome him. That wanted to run towards him and beg him to stay a just bit longer. She hated that part of herself. Speaking of exorcisms…

'How come waking up without you makes me feel like I'm missing a part of myself? How come you're the last person I want to see before I fall asleep at night?' He moved closer, his body almost touching hers now. She made a small noise, a choking sound. Of fear? Or of want?

'How come everything feels dull and pointless without you? How come I look for you all the time? How come I miss you so much I can barely breathe?' Another step and his body pressed to hers, his hand lifting to cup her cheek.

'How come I have told myself all my life that I would never be like my father, that I would never let a woman fall in love with me, and I sure as hell wouldn't ever love a woman, and yet I love you?'

She drew in a deep gulp of air, shaking her head and stepping backwards. 'Don't.' It took all her willpower and strength to separate from him. 'Don't come here now and say this. Don't you dare.'

'I fell in love with you, Amelia. It is the opposite of what I thought I wanted but here I am, a broken man, an incomplete man, without you in my life. Your love has become the sum total of what I want. What choice do I have *but* to come here and say this to you?'

'You hurt me.' He winced as though she'd hit him. 'You did exactly what you've spent your whole life telling yourself you wouldn't, and you hate yourself for that, so you're trying to fix it. You can't just say you love me! That's not the answer to this.'

He shook his head, moving closer again, his body wrapping hers inwards, his arms linking behind her back. 'I'm not just saying this to make myself feel better. Yes, I hurt you.' He dropped his forehead to hers. 'I hurt you and seeing that pain on your face is an image I will never forget. When you looked at Pia, when she kissed me, the look in your eyes…' He shook his head, the sentence unfinished.

Pain was burning her insides anew. 'Please don't.'

'But your hurt was matched by my own. I have been miserable without you, and all I can think about is the rest of my life, spending it like this, and there's just this huge, dark void. Without you, nothing has meaning. You are my everything, Amelia.'

She sobbed, her eyes pleading when they met his. 'Please don't say these things.'

'Do you love me?'

She swept her eyes shut, her lips parted. 'Of course.'

'Then why can't I say this? Why can't I say it back to you?'

She sobbed and shook her head. 'Because I know what you want in life and it's not this. You shouldn't have to change who you are because of me.'

'You changed who I am and what I want. Until I met you, of course I felt that love was a fantasy, a ridiculous construct. Until I met you, I'd never been in love before.

You taught me to love—I love you, I love Cameron; you opened my heart. I'm still terrified of hurting you, or not being the father he needs, but you showed me that loving someone isn't about not feeling afraid, it's just about showing up and doing your best. Being there for the person you love. All I want in this life is you, Amelia.'

He brushed his lips to hers and she felt as though she were being breathed back to life. Her heart began to sing. 'That artist in Paris saw something I was too stupid to recognise. Or maybe I recognised it and was just too stubborn to accept it. We *are* a family—you, me and Cam—and we should be together.'

Her heart was soaring inside her. 'I can't believe this.'

He compressed his lips and nodded, lifting a hand and padding his thumb over her lower lip, his eyes following the movement before he dropped his hand and stepped away. 'I've given it a lot of thought. I hurt you and I would be a fool to expect you to simply forgive and forget. I know I need to prove myself to you again, and I'm prepared to do that. Here's what I want.' And suddenly, he was the self-made billionaire tycoon success story all over again. Powerful, commanding, completely in his element.

'The school year has just started—I know you won't want to leave your students midway through. And Cameron has just started his new school and, while it's not exactly working out as I'd hoped, I don't believe in giving up, so I think it's important he persevere a little longer.'

Her heart skidded to a stop. 'What do you mean, it's not working?'

'It's a long story.'

'Is he not happy?'

'No, he's not happy. And, while I think he's struggling with the school and his peers, and the differences of culture and language, ultimately I think he misses you more than he—at six—can put into words.'

Her heart cracked open. Tears ran down her cheeks. 'I miss him too.'

A muscle jerked in Santos's jaw. 'Give me the rest of the school year.' It was a command but she heard the uncertainty and doubt, as though he was worried she would refuse him. 'You can fly to Athens on weekends and I'll come here as often as I can leave Cameron. You can see for yourself how serious I am before you agree to this.'

'Agree to what?'

He stared at her blankly. 'To marry me, obviously.'

She stared back, just as blankly. 'To marry you? Santos, you don't believe in marriage.'

'I don't believe in my father's marriages, but I believe in anything you and I do together.'

A tremble ran down her spine. He blinked, as if just remembering something, turning towards the sofa and picking up a slim leather document wallet. She hadn't even realised he'd been carrying it when he walked in.

'To that end, I've had this drawn up.' He pulled out some paper and handed it to her. His eyes were boring into her so it was hard to concentrate as she skimmed the words.

'A pre-nuptial agreement?' Her heart sped up. 'You've had a pre-nup drawn up? I haven't even agreed—'

'I wanted you to see it before you did agree,' he said quietly, the words earnest and husky.

'*If* I were to marry you, it wouldn't be for the money. Do you honestly think you need to protect your fortune from me?'

'Read it.'

She glared at him then flicked the front page. Then the next. It was all standard legalese until she reached the division of assets list on page three.

'This says that if we got divorced you'd pay out ninety per cent of your shares in Anastakos Inc. to me.' She kept reading. 'And give me the island?' Her eyes lifted to his, her skin paling.

'Keep reading.'

She swallowed and turned the page. 'You'd give me shared custody of Cameron.'

'If you agree to marry me, you'll be his stepmother. I would never ask you to love my son as your own without affording you genuine parental rights. Including custody. I know you love him, Amelia, and he loves you. We're family.'

'Santos.' She shoved the papers at him as though she'd been burned. 'Stop.'

He shook his head. 'I need you to understand that I've thought all this through. I'm not just offering to marry you on a whim. I'm prepared to go all in with this.'

'I think you're missing the point of a pre-nuptial agreement. They're intended to *protect* your fortune.'

'This one is to protect you.'

She shook her head, none of this making any sense. 'So you end up married to me for a lifetime because you can't afford to divorce me? Santos, no. Marriage shouldn't be about money. It's a leap of faith two people take together. Just loving you is enough for me—that's enough to show me that I can trust our future. A pre-nuptial agreement that prepares for divorce? It makes me think you're still just as afraid as ever.'

'Afraid? I'm terrified. I'm terrified of hurting you, and I'm terrified of failing you, but my God, Amelia, what I am most afraid of is living my life without you. If I walk out of this lovely little cottage without knowing that I have made you understand how much I love you? That scares me more than I can say.'

She lifted her eyes to the ceiling, tears filling her lashes.

'This pre-nuptial agreement is not because I don't trust our future. It's because I do trust it. I want to marry you, and I do not believe, for even one moment, that our marriage will fail. I am willing to bet everything I own, everything I am, on that because, as far as I can tell, there's no way I can lose.'

Her eyes widened and she glanced at him, his words weaving through her, making her smile for the first time since leaving Paris.

'You really love me?'

'Oh, yes, *agape*, with every single fibre of my heart, and I always will.'

It was the longest year of Santos's life, but it was what he'd promised Amelia and he had no intention of breaking that promise. He understood how important it was for her to finish her teaching year, but a few months after they'd agreed to marry all he wanted was to have his family together under one roof. His fiancée, his son, the rest of their lives ahead of them.

It was the right decision to wait, though. Cameron settled into a routine at school and had made some good friends. While Santos hadn't doubted the strength of his love for even a moment, he was glad for Amelia's sake that they'd waited a year because proving himself to her was hugely important.

Their wedding was small, just as they'd both wanted. Just a few friends, including Brent, some teachers from Elesmore, some of his closest friends, his half-brother and father. They'd married at Damen's restaurant, the view of Athens glowing beneath them, and then they'd flown to the island, just the two of them, to start their married life in the very place his life had really started. It was only in meeting Amelia that he'd truly become whole.

On their first night as a married couple, Amelia lay with her head on Santos's arm on a blanket spread across the beach, the sand beneath them, the water lapping close to their toes, looking up at the sky. Stars sparkled and the ancient beauty of the sky seemed to congratulate them. Of all the stardust in all the world, they'd found each other, and their happiness was perfect and for eternity.

* * * * *

MILLS & BOON

Coming next month

ITALY'S MOST SCANDALOUS VIRGIN
Carol Marinelli

Dante's want for her was perpetual, a lit fuse he was constantly stamping out, but it was getting harder and harder to keep it up. His breathing was ragged; there was a shift in the air and he desperately fought to throw petrol on the row, for his resistance was fast fading. 'What did you think, Mia, that we were going to walk into the church together? A family united? Don't make me laugh…'

No one was laughing.

'Take your tea and go to bed.' Dante dismissed her with an angry wave of his hand, but even as he did so he halted, for it was not his place to send her to bed. 'I didn't mean that. Do what you will. I will leave.'

'It's fine. I'm going up.' She retrieved the tray.

'We leave tomorrow at eleven,' he said again as they headed through to the entrance.

'Yes.'

She turned then and gave him a tight smile, and saw his black eyes meet hers, and there was that look again between them, the one they had shared at the dining table. It was a look that she dared not decipher.

His lips, which were usually plump and red, the only splash of colour in his black and white features, were for once pale. There was a muscle leaping in his cheek, and she was almost sure it was pure contempt, except her body was misreading it as something else.

She had always been aware of his potent sexuality, but now Mia was suddenly aware of her own.

Conscious that she was naked beneath the gown, her breasts felt full and heavy, aware of the lust that danced inappropriately in the air between them. The prison gates were parting further and she was terrified to step out. 'Goodnight,' she croaked, and climbed the stairs, almost tipping the tray and only able to breathe when she heard the door slam.

Tea forgotten, she lay on the bed, frantic and unsettled. So much for the Ice Queen! She was burning for him in a way she had never known until she'd met Dante.

Mia had thought for a long time that there was something wrong with her, something missing in her make-up, for she'd had little to no interest in sex. Even back at school she would listen in on her peers, quietly bemused by their obsessive talking about boys and the things they did that to Mia sounded filthy. Her mother's awkward talk about the facts of life had left Mia revolted. The *fact of Mia's life*: it was something she didn't want! There was no reason she could find. There had been no trauma, nothing she could pin it to. Just for her, those feelings simply did not exist. Mia had tried to ignite the absent fire and had been on a couple of dates, but had found she couldn't even tolerate kisses, and tongues positively revolted her. She couldn't bear to consider anything else.

And while this marriage had given her a unique chance to heal from the appalling disaster that had befallen her family, the deeper truth was that it had given her a chance to hide from something she perhaps ought to address.

A no-sex marriage had felt like a blessing when she and Rafael had agreed to it.

Yet the ink had barely dried on the contract when she had found out that though those feelings might be buried deep, they were there after all.

Mia had been just a few days into the pretend position of Rafael's PA, and the carefully engineered rumours had just started to fly, when Dante Romano had walked in. A mere moment with him had helped her understand all she had been missing, for with just a look she found herself reacting in a way she never had before.

His dark eyes had transfixed her, the deep growl of his voice had elicited a shiver low in her stomach, and even his scent, as it reached her, went straight to form a perfect memory. When Dante had asked who she was, his voice and his presence had alerted, startled and awoken her. So much so that she had half expected him to snap his fingers like a genie right before her scalding face.

Three wishes?

You.

You.

You.

LET'S TALK
Romance